Praise for

COSMIC LOVE AT THE MULTIVERSE HAIR SALON

"A funny and romantic romp through time and space, complete with yearning, community, and the idea that love truly wins—everything I love in a queer romance."

—Ashley Herring Blake, *USA Today* bestselling author of *Dream On, Ramona Riley*

"*Cosmic Love at the Multiverse Hair Salon* is a wild ride that will have you laughing, crying, and swooning all at once. What starts as a quirky, multiversal meet-cute quickly builds into a poignant exploration of friendship, love, loss, and grief. There's nothing better than a book that makes you really feel something, and Mare has proven herself a master of crafting a moving narrative."

—Alexandra Kennington, author of *Blood Beneath the Snow*

"*Cosmic Love at the Multiverse Hair Salon* is a heartfelt ode to the queer community, perfectly capturing the comfort and sense of belonging that comes from finding your people. It's also a story about the mysterious wonders of the universe. Tressa Fay and Meryl fight against the complicated web of time and space just to be together, which might make this the most unabashedly romantic sapphic love story of all time. This book is proof that love can absolutely reshape the world."

—Bridget Morrissey, author of *That Summer Feeling*

"A mind-blowing read! *Cosmic Love at the Multiverse Hair Salon* is a whip-smart, ultra-flirty romp through time and space that is not to be missed. With every twist in the time-space continuum, I fell deeper for Tressa Fay, Meryl, and their unforgettable crew of friends. A must-read for romantics who believe in destiny and delight in interdimensional hijinks!"

—Taleen Voskuni, author of *Lavash at First Sight*

"I fell in love with this book at the speed of light! Tressa Fay and Meryl get all twisted up in the fabric of the universe, and it's sheer delight to watch them find themselves, and each other, time after time. Annie Mare infuses their romance with more nerdiness, sexiness, and mystical queer heart than one world can hold. Luckily, there are many!" —Joanna Lowell, author of *A Rare Find*

"The prose is so sparkling and strong. . . . There's a creative sense of rebellion: If you're already in the worst timeline, why not change as many things as you can and see if you end up somewhere better?"

—*The New York Times*

"This gently mind-bending read featuring a touching sapphic romance across time and universes is perfect for fans of Casey McQuiston's *One Last Stop*."

—*Booklist*

"A heartwarming multiverse tale of fated love, family, and memory."

—*Publishers Weekly*

"Mare successfully blends speculative fiction with sapphic romance in this well-written multiverse love story."

—*Library Journal*

"If you're looking for a unique spin on sapphic romance that takes thought experiments about the nature of reality and makes them super queer, this book just might be for you."

—Lesbrary

"A fun sapphic romance about falling in love across timelines."

—Book Riot

"With lol moments and tender moments, this [is] a perfect love story."

—Red Carpet Crash

TITLES BY ANNIE MARE

Cosmic Love at the Multiverse Hair Salon

A Star-Cursed Heart

A STAR-CURSED HEART

ANNIE MARE

ACE
NEW YORK

ACE
Published by Berkley
An imprint of Penguin Random House LLC
1745 Broadway, New York, NY 10019
penguinrandomhouse.com

Book design by Alison Cnockaert

Library of Congress Cataloging-in-Publication Data

Names: Mare, Annie author
Title: A star-cursed heart / Annie Mare.
Description: First edition. | New York : Ace, 2026.
Identifiers: LCCN 2025039431 (print) | LCCN 2025039432 (ebook) |
ISBN 9780593817506 trade paperback | ISBN 9780593817513 ebook
Subjects: LCGFT: Fiction | Romance fiction |
Fantasy fiction | Lesbian fiction | Novels
Classification: LCC PS3613.A7388 S73 2026 (print) | LCC PS3613.A7388 (ebook)
LC record available at https://lccn.loc.gov/2025039431
LC ebook record available at https://lccn.loc.gov/2025039432

First Edition: May 2026

Printed in the United States of America
1st Printing

The authorized representative in the EU for product safety and compliance is Penguin Random House Ireland, Morrison Chambers, 32 Nassau Street, Dublin D02 YH68, Ireland, https://eu-contact.penguin.ie.

For F, B, D, and H. You did what you needed to take care of each other. Thank you. You got me here.

I know not whether these ancestors of mine bethought themselves to repent, and ask pardon of Heaven for their cruelties; or whether they are now groaning under the heavy consequences of them, in another state of being. At all events, I, the present writer, as their representative, hereby take shame upon myself for their sakes, and pray that any curse incurred by them . . . may be now and henceforth removed.

NATHANIEL HAWTHORNE, *THE SCARLET LETTER*

A STAR-CURSED HEART

I.

HECTOR'S TAVERN

> **The chain that bound her here was of iron links, and galling to her inmost soul, but could never be broken.**
>
> NATHANIEL HAWTHORNE, *THE SCARLET LETTER*

THE GRAVEL SURFACE of the parking lot clawed her cheek open on impact, and for a moment all she felt was the sting. Ashes Steadfast pulled her knees into her chest and gave herself one self-pitying second to breathe. Breathing was a good way to figure out if she'd fractured a rib.

Lucy stood six feet away with her short whisper of a dress blowing against her legs in the January wind. She wasn't cold. The devil didn't get cold. Or tired. Lucy Prynne didn't have a soul to vigilantly defend against temptation. When she tilted her head to look at Ash curled up on the ground, her eyes didn't need to be guarded. Lucy's eyes were knowing and kind, understanding and fascinated. Eyes that were easy to surrender to.

Ash had done it before. Once, she'd belonged to Lucy, and Lucy had belonged to her. Back when they were just girls and none of this seemed inevitable. Back when they believed their love could defeat a three-hundred-year-old bargain to balance good and evil.

Ash and Lucy's fights were one part metaphysical fisticuffs, one part ex-girlfriends who knew where the buttons were and how hard to push. The Prynnes, humanity's devils, tempted and reaped. The Steadfasts, dressed in unadorned black (hair shirt optional), tugged innocents back from the brink with a charming side of puritanical idioms too boring even to embroider on a pillow.

Powers may vary. Lucy's sneaky dropkick had sent Ash flying on more than one occasion. In addition to controlling the weather, she had a knack for conjuring seductive backdrops to unburden people of their souls. Ash, like all Steadfasts, had the super strength and the super knack for a guilt trip necessary to fight the devil.

Blood dripped from her chin, soaking the gravel. Her rib seemed okay. She knew her role. She wasn't interested in feeling her *feelings*.

"Lucy," she croaked.

"Ashes." Lucy always called her by her full name. No one else did. Footsteps crunched across the gravel, and then the illusion of her oldest friend filled her field of vision. Light brown hair in teetering stacks of tumbling curls. Those eyes. "You're still breathing."

Ash couldn't tell if this was an expression of disappointment or merely an observation. Instead of wondering, she made herself pay attention to the pinching sensation of drawing cold air into her lungs. She imagined the beat of her heart as slow and strong, easily moving steady pulls through her muscles. The longer it had been since they last met like this, the harder it got to keep her head in the game.

It had been a while. Months.

Focus on the *fight,* she scolded herself. Not the shape of Lucy's body under the thin, creamy silk of her dress. Not the rough fry of her voice that always sounded like she had just awoken to the welcome sight of an indulgent lover.

Lucy held out her hand to help Ash up. The pulse in her wrist was visible beneath a thin gold bracelet. Temptation. Evergreen.

There had been a time when Ash looked a lot more like the fallen than the savior. She wore colors, for example. Kissed girls (one girl). Felt the sweat bead at the back of her neck and gleam over her bare shoulders while she held an instrument under bright lights in front of dancing people hazed with smoke. Back then, she was unscarred and unbothered. She was in love. She had dreams. She had a future. She had Lucy.

Lucy. Not this apparition who didn't even feel the cold that seeped into Ash's bones.

Focus.

She grabbed Lucy's wrist, not her hand, never her hand, and forced the muscles in her hips and thighs to lurch her body upright. She kept her knees bent, her grip tight, until she had enough leverage to bring the other woman's forearm forcibly across her chest, turning her into a tidy missile that Ash grasped by the hips and tossed.

An enormous charge of golden light detonated from Lucy's body. It raced across the ground, illuminating the night, sparking the bulbs in the parking lot and drawing shadows from the dozen or so silent figures in black who stood in a solemn circle surrounding them. These were her Puritan ancestors, Ash had to assume, spectating on these fights to remind her of her duty.

It was a never-ending tug-of-war. If she let go of her end of the rope, the territory these forebears had paid for in violence would be forfeit. Her absence from the battle would feed a swell of lost, entitled souls. The balance that kept people safe would tip, knocking over the world.

Surrender was the only way to end it. If she died fighting, or Lucy did, the next paired set of Prynne and Steadfast descendants would just be tapped to take their places. The curse reset its players like bowling pins, frame after frame, forever.

She and Lucy had tried to break the pact with love. Total bust.

Ash had even tried to end it on her own, by running away to New York, but Lucy found her.

When she'd limped home last year from that failed escape attempt, she'd wondered if their fathers had the right idea. Don't fight. Instead, nurture a cold war of stasis. Circle each other with fingers on the trigger but the safety engaged. Never let the other out of your sight. Exchange defanged diplomacy and ignore the sweetness of blood at the back of the throat. But even this noble experiment had failed. Ash's father died, if only briefly, and the curse passed itself along.

Ash had come to the weary conclusion that the only choices this bargain offered were to fight or to give up and let the world go to ruin.

She wasn't ready to give up. Numb as she'd become, she still felt obligated to the innocent. The biggest dream Ash allowed herself these days was *don't die*. Not today. Not dying was no way to live, but she hadn't come up with anything better. If she survived tonight, she could look forward to waking up tomorrow and not dying. But if she gave herself an opportunity to feel her *feelings*, she might feel something dangerous, like hope.

She unzipped her black motorcycle jacket. The cold stung, though her underarms and the skin beneath her breasts were slick with sweat. "What's brought you here tonight, Luce?"

Panting, Lucy wrapped her arms around her middle and heaved herself to her side. "Such an incredibly existential question."

It wasn't. It was a practical question, one Ash needed the answer to in order to hold these meetups at bay. She hadn't been thinking of her lost love. She hadn't been thumbing through old photos or strolling over memories of the good years. She knew better than to indulge nostalgia. Any strong emotion called the devil to her door, which was why Ash kept her life as straight as a ruler.

She'd even told herself it wasn't *Lucy* when she'd felt the compulsion to come to Hector's Tavern tonight—that her body's insistence was only about how long it had been since she'd seen Hector and how much she'd been missing him lately. But she'd arrived to find the parking lot dark, the lights out except for a perfect golden circle. Inside it, a couple leaned against the front bumper of a cherry-red pickup truck. Drifting, swirling sparkles filled the air around them. As she strode closer, she could make out a handsome young man talking with both hands, his face lit up with more than the preternatural light around him, his words tumbling over themselves in his mesmerized excitement.

It wasn't exactly true that people were talked out of their souls. Once a person believed they could have anything they wanted, they would gladly talk the devil into taking it.

Free will was tricky as hell.

Ash had stood in the shadows, camouflaged by her black

jacket, boots, and jeans (though the near-white blond braid that snaked over her shoulder was a dead giveaway). She listened to the man, Nathan, who turned out to be a regular at Hector's and an employee of the factory across the street. He wanted to be a country music star. He was sketching out his dream of touring the Southeast when Ash crashed the party.

Now Nathan leaned against the tailgate of a truck, frozen in a sphere of gentle snow, perpetually waiting for Lucy to finish what she'd started or for Ash to stop her.

"Allow me to clarify. Why are you at Hector's?" They'd never fought on the property of their mutual friend before.

Lucy lifted herself up on an elbow, merciless gravel rolling under her bare arm. She paused at every new position of her body to hiss through her teeth. She was vulnerable, on the ground, within reach of Ash's heavy black boots. Ash could finish her.

The thought made her stomach twist, sick.

Lucy got her feet beneath her. She brushed gravel dust from her bare arms. "You're here. That's why I am."

It was what she always said.

Ash rushed her, coming in with her shoulder low. She anticipated the crunch of Lucy's ribs against her collarbone and the knob of her shoulder. She was an instrument. She was a knife. She was sorrow stopping the source of tears.

She was flying.

This time, she managed to skid on the seat of her jeans and keep her breath in her lungs, but she'd never get used to the force Lucy commanded in her own defense.

"Will you give us a freaking *minute*?" Lucy shouted.

Ash brought her feet flat to the ground, ignoring how the

ass-first landing had made her lower back feel like it was on fire. "Us? You mean you and that guy?" She glanced at Nathan in his supernatural bubble.

"I do not mean me and that guy." Lucy's brown eyes had lost their softness. "I mean *us.* I mean that I want a minute, *one* minute, to talk to you."

That got Ash's attention.

She could not trust, at all, that the devil had put Nathan inside a hell-made light-up mirrorball after his factory shift as a way to bait Ash into coming and *talking* to her.

Ash had a routine, a rhythm. She worked wherever the temp office sent her to file or enter data or answer the phone. She took her dad to his appointments and did the chores he couldn't do for himself anymore. When the weather started to get cold and the nights came early, it was easier. If the dull ache in her chest got sharp, she could go to bed at six o'clock.

But even her most rigid devotion to the modern equivalent of nothing but chopping wood, carrying water, and walking the earth could not prevent a confrontation with Lucy forever, any more than it could kill the part of her that howled in protest against her ascetic life. *That* part of her wanted a triple espresso with extra cold foam. A septum piercing. To crack open the case that entombed her double bass and play until her forearm muscles seized up. It wanted sweaty dancing and stupid, sloppy sex. That part of Ash sometimes made decisions that ended in knifing abdominal pain and throwing up blood, or migraines like glass breaking inside her skull. Other times, Lucy herself extracted the price of sin from Ash's body.

They didn't *talk.*

"Let him go first." This seemed like a safe move. After all, she had already made this demand. It was what she'd done right before Lucy picked her up and slid her face across the parking lot like an air hockey puck.

With a toss of her hair, Lucy strode over and through the perimeter of the bubble of light to Nathan. "You can leave," she said.

The young man's expression was that of a Labrador retriever confused by the rain. "But I need to play you the song I'm working on. It's the one I told you will hit." He turned the volume up on a recording of his voice humming over a halting chord progression.

Lucy gave him an indulgent smile that flipped her Cupid's bow into a round upper lip and sunk double dimples into her cheeks. "Seems like he wants to stick around," she told Ash. "Unless you'd like to change his mind?"

Uneasy, she glanced at the man caught between them. The devil could compel a person to bare their soul, but only Ash could feel what would give someone the strength to hold on to it. In the throes of more than one of their fights, she'd wished for a more useful power. Psychic chains. The ability to heave up chunks of asphalt with her mind and remorselessly fling them at people.

The kind of thing that would be helpful for escaping a trap.

She turned her full attention to Lucy's captive. "Nathan. Do you remember what your mother said?"

His brow folded with the discomfort of emerging from a beautiful dream. He frowned, then tapped his phone silent. "She said to remember that Joni Mitchell made her own way. The only path for Joni to do something no one else had done was one she made for herself." As he spoke, the light around him began to gather up and sink into the crown of his head. "No compromises. The audience can tell if you've had it too easy."

He was gazing at Ash now, his expression stuck somewhere between bewildered and sad. No one who was caught up in Lucy's thrall welcomed rescue. Ash murdered their false hope, and they resented her for it. Her duty was the definition of thankless. "That's good advice your mom gave you," she said.

He came the rest of the way back to himself, looking as scared as they all became when they started to realize they didn't remember how they'd gotten to the place where they found themselves alone with two strangers in the dark. Both hands in fists, he gazed toward his pickup. "Hey, could you tell that girl I had to take off?"

"Yeah." The lights over the parking lot came on. "I'll tell her."

She watched him get into the cab of his truck and peel out of the lot. When it was quiet enough to hear the soft drone of twenty-four-hour sports news from inside the tavern, Lucy brushed her hair away from her cheek. The wind was mixing up her curls in every direction. "I guess that's one point for your team," Lucy said. "You must be proud."

Ash had a spider plant hanging in the window of her monkish studio apartment. She watered it. It got sun. She removed its browned leaves and checked it for pests and fed it with dark green liquid fertilizer every so often. But if she let herself feel *pride* in that plant, nearly bursting its pot and overflowing with little hanging clones of itself, then her nose started to bleed. Or a handful of her hair fell out, dropping to the floor in lifeless webs.

The wages of sin were death. She assumed that was why saving souls didn't make her feel good.

Lucy stepped closer. *That* felt good.

Ash rolled her shoulders and imagined herself shucking the pleasure from her skin. She didn't dare look into the darkness beyond the blue-white illumination from the parking lot lights. She didn't need to see the Dead and Righteous Brigade standing in their judgmental circle to remind her she was letting down her team. She'd been waiting ten years for a vibe *other* than judgment from them. For one of them to identify themself, say, or fill Ash in on the lore. Her dad was not a talker. She'd figured out most of what she knew about the curse by herself, through trial and error. She could use a few pointers from folks who'd been in her boots and died wearing them.

Pointers, or a means of escape.

"You're bleeding." Lucy pointed at Ash's cheek. Her voice was warm, with a husk to it. Soothing.

Ash sighed. "I'm sure Hector was thrilled when you lured one of his patrons to the parking lot. Did you even pay Nathan's tab?"

Lucy sucked air in through her nose with the suddenness of someone who had been slapped. Ash, Lucy, and Hector had been friends since kindergarten, when he'd moved to Green Bay from Zapopan, Jalisco, after an incident with a local miraculous shrine. The past was a minefield they both knew how to weaponize.

"Hector's my friend, too." Lucy stalked in a slow, pissed-off circle around her.

"Not really. He's just loyal to the memories. You come around here, and he starts hoping maybe you've finally left enough people soulless in this world to warm the shard of obsidian you call a heart. It's not fair to him."

Lucy's tight jaw reminded Ash of the girl she'd grown up with. Of both of them sitting in the high-up crux of their tree, the bark rough on their backs, their legs woven together, talking in the purple twilight about the future after high school. They'd wanted to conquer the world together, not take up arms in an ancient conflict whose terms were set long before they were born.

She pinched herself, sending the vision away. Another took its place. The ambulance lights on the afternoon her dad collapsed. For long minutes, the living room washed red, then white, as the EMTs pumped their arms and his ribs cracked sickeningly. Rye Steadfast had come back from the dead, but not soon enough. Heartbroken, Ash went looking for Lucy at their tree. She didn't know yet that in the moments when her father was dead, Lucy's dad, Draven, had disappeared, and Lucy Prynne became the devil.

Lucy blamed Rye for Draven's disappearance.

Ash blamed Draven for Rye's heart failure.

Of course they fought, both of them overflowing with denial and anger in the first potent stages of their grief. Ash had wept all the way to her car, her vision grayed out from the blood pouring from the wound at her throat, her chest tight with shock at the new powers that chained them to every generation before theirs.

They were cursed. They'd always been cursed. They always would be.

"Why am I here?" she asked again, her voice tight and flat.

"I want us to talk."

"To *each other*?" Ash sharpened her incredulity into a scoff that made Lucy take a step back. A lock of hair caressed her neck and snaked over her sun-kissed collarbones.

"There was a time we'd talk for hours."

"There was a time you weren't reaping souls for a cheap thrill. We're not friends anymore."

"We weren't *friends.*"

It was never a great idea for Ash to get into the past with Lucy. It felt too much like cliff diving into Lake Michigan at Cave Point, or kissing a girl and feeling her fingers toy at the hem of your shirt. Taunts were safer. "When you found me in New York, I was half-dead already. It must have been so exciting for you, lured by the smell of my soul rotting out of my body, ripe for harvest because I'd deserted my post."

She'd cut the leash and run, fleeing to the biggest city a Wisconsin girl could think of to finally be free, only to break out in pustulant, full-body welts that wept bloody exudate while her eyes streamed with acidic tears. She started waking up screaming, feeling like every bone in her body was breaking at the same time. Her terrified roommates kicked her out and changed the locks. She'd ended up in Central Park, where Lucy found her. From there, things had gone downhill fast.

Focus.

"You could have had this mortal world to yourself," Ash said. "Bad news, though. There's not much left to corrupt. Pretty sure your side's nearly won."

Lucy's cheeks were flushed. "You're always such a sulky, self-righteous pain in my ass."

"Not always."

"Ashes."

Lucy moved closer, making Ash rock back on her heels and swallow over the hard lump in her throat. "Come on, tell me the truth," Ash said. "Is torture really such a good time?"

"I am not here to fight you!" The air seemed to get thicker, as if it were taking in the anger from Lucy's body. Her already dark brown eyes had gone black. Their surroundings receded and muted, leaving only the two of them.

"You're not, huh?" The sarcasm sounded weak. "Because I've been avoiding you for months. I crawled home from our last get-together, happy to never see you again."

Lucy pressed her hand to the exposed skin above her breasts. "You're such a coward." A gentle breeze blew her nothing dress into soft ripples. She smelled like sunscreen and chlorine. The actual temperature hovered around five degrees. "You want to believe I'm evil walking around in your poor lost girlfriend's body. Whatever story lets you sleep at night, I guess."

Ash kept her eyes on the ground under Lucy's feet. It was blacker there, and it had started to spin. The skinny trees rimming the parking lot were bending in an icy wind. "Your dad did the same thing, you know," she countered. "Tried to make my dad feel narrow-minded and foolish. What is it, a kind of reverse-psychology-style temptation?"

Lucy pressed her fingertips to her eyebrows. She used to do that to keep herself from panicking. Her hair, already big and curly, was getting bigger in the gathering whirlpool of wind. "Remember when we could talk without talking? Remember when I didn't have to explain everything six different times, twelve different ways? Let me make it very clear for you. I'm not here for Nathan, and this isn't about Hector or our dads, you *ridiculous* goth."

"So it's about you and me?" Saying the words aloud, even dripping with irony, unbalanced Ash enough that she had to run her hand over her braid.

"She thinks for herself, folks!"

No. Lucy was trying to make her lose control, lose her temper, lose anything at all if it let the devil in. And it worked. It always did. "Tell me what that's supposed to mean!" The wind snatched Ash's voice away. "Girls' night? You want to braid my hair? Or is it time to set some healthy boundaries, maybe gerrymander this town into neighborhoods of good and evil? If you *want* something—" She had to stop, her breath coming up short. The wind whipped strands of hair from her braid and blew them in her eyes. "If you're trying to *get* something from me other than a fight, you're fucking out of luck, because that's not part of the deal. We can want." She caught her breath again, put her hand to her mouth. Her heart was *racing*. "We can want, and we can want, and we can want, but we can't *have* anything from each other. Want is the only free will you and I get." She stared into the other woman's eyes as if she could press her feelings into her with her gaze. How could Lucy stand there, the world spinning above and below her, her eyes fixed on Ash, and not see that she was fucking laid out?

But that was her dance with the devil. Lucy softened, sought her out, pleaded, and Ash turned to stone.

Ash came apart, dropped a piece of her heart, tripped toward her, and Lucy transformed into a stranger.

She forgot to focus. That was her mistake.

It was why she wasn't braced for the next blow, the shock of electric heat and the smell of burning leather as it split from Lucy's spectral whip. She steeled herself against the inevitable disorientation, ignoring the smoking arm of her jacket. The only thing that distracted the enemy enough to give Ash an advantage was holding her attention, so she kept their eyes locked as she dropped her hip close to the spinning ground, reaching her hand behind her to hold up her weight so she could sweep Lucy's legs from under her.

Lucy grunted and fell to her knees. From the ground, Ash could see blood well up in the scrapes. Her own arm felt hot and sticky beneath the leather sleeve of her jacket.

She rose to a crouch. In her periphery, the sky had started to spin in the opposite direction of the ground. It made her middle go light with anticipation.

Lucy's chin lifted. "What do you want, Ashes?"

Shit. She lost her grip on Lucy's gaze, scrambling to hold on to the edges of her satiny-gold soul as it unwound inside her, stirred by the one question she could never answer without handing over the win.

Ash had to bite her tongue, her cheek, choke herself with her own breath, to keep from telling Lucy everything, just the way she had when they were girls. But not since. Not even when Lucy tried to cut the answer from her throat.

She wiped a wet red palm on her thigh and reminded herself how she was destined to die—with nothing, and, if she had done everything right, in pain.

She thought of how her dad had looked in the hospital, his skin gray, hanging on to the life that had been handed back to him with rough compressions that broke his bones.

How she could never fall in love again.

How she would never have a partner, never have a kid, never have a real friend or anything resembling a life, because she was on this earth for one reason only: to kill the feral animal of her own dreams in order to maintain the cosmic balance.

"Go back where you came from." The austerity took hold of

her internal battle. Her words were plain and black and final. "You're not wanted here. I don't want you here."

Lucy's eyes went wide, but before she could speak, the sound of Hector's voice broke into their private world. "Ash! Lucy!"

They turned to see him standing in the parking lot in his heavy down coat. He paused to cinch the hood around his ears, knocking the frame of his glasses askew. "Knock it off! Did you hear me? You can't do this here." He gestured between the three of them. "We're supposed to be friends, but there's a portal to hell opening up in my parking lot."

"Hector," Ash began, rushing to explain.

"No," he interrupted. "I've heard it. It's sixteen eighty whatever-the-fuck, Massachusetts Bay Colony, a dark night of the soul for Faithful Steadfast and a deal with Old Nick, the father of lies himself." Hector shoved his hands into the pockets of his coat. "Have either of you ever stopped to think about how ludicrous that is?"

Ash let herself glance at Lucy, who was sneaking a look at her. They both shrank away from Hector's lecture.

He sighed, a long and tired sound that pressed against every bit of tender guilt in Ash's body. "I have been trying to figure out how to tell you two, given the circumstances. Since you're both here . . ." Hector looked up at the sky as if for strength. "Ovidia's pregnant. We're having a baby. Actually, two babies."

Sudden joy chased the rest of the fight out of Ash, with envy, sharp and sour, rising right up behind it.

"That's wonderful, Hector," Lucy said. "Congratulations."

He gave her a tight smile. "Thank you. Ordinarily, I'd ask you both to be godparents." He shook his head. "I'm a realistic person. That doesn't mean I don't want this to fucking end."

"I can't talk to someone who won't listen." Lucy wrapped her arms around herself.

Hector looked at Ash.

"Progenitor of lies, remember? I listen, she wins, and then it's hell on earth."

"I'm going," Lucy bit off.

"Don't bother." Ash zipped up her jacket, hissing when her sleeve rubbed against the fresh whip wound, and started to walk away.

But before she did, she let herself look at her two oldest friends and remember the three of them sitting in the bed of Hector's old F-150 in parking lots like this one, drinking Jarritos they'd bought from his cousin's mercado and doing nothing until the sun went down and they noticed their shoulders and arms were sunburned.

For less than a second, Ash looked only at Lucy, and for just that brief, fleeting span of time, she looked like the girl Ash had known and loved for as long as she could remember.

Not at all like the devil.

II.

EPHRAIM STEADFAST HAS DOUBTS

> **Under the leaden infliction which it was her doom to endure, she felt, at moments, as if she must needs shriek out with the full power of her lungs, and cast herself from the scaffold down upon the ground, or else go mad at once.**
>
> **NATHANIEL HAWTHORNE, *THE SCARLET LETTER***

ASH GAVE THE door to her father's house two hard raps before she entered and scraped the snow off her boots with the boot brush.

"That you?" Her dad opened the door to the kitchen and leaned on his quad cane.

"None other. Your gout bothering you?" She followed his shuffling gait into the kitchen, where he eased himself down onto a chair at the table. He wrapped his hands around the same mug he'd drank his coffee from for Ash's entire life.

"I made an appointment," he said.

That meant that yes, the gout in his big toe was raging so badly he likely couldn't let the bedsheet rest on his foot. "When's it for?" Ash reached for a piece of whole wheat toast with the cholesterol-free spread he'd started eating in cardiac rehab after his quadruple bypass.

"This afternoon. At two."

"I'll come back at one thirty, then?"

He nodded. He hadn't shaved yet, and the salt-and-pepper scruff of his beard made him seem paler than usual. His hair was still dark, getting a little long. Ash hadn't taken him for a cut soon enough. Guilt made her throat ache, because Ephraim "Rye" Steadfast would never ask. Not for a ride to the doctor or the barber, not for Ash to pick up his weekly groceries. Not even for her company.

She shrugged off her jacket and draped it over the back of a kitchen chair. It was always overwarm in her dad's house. It smelled strongly of coffee and the white Ivory soap he kept a bar of at every sink. The heat pressed the scent into her hair and clothes.

Lucy wants to talk.

Ash watched him sipping his coffee and staring at nothing. She hadn't slept. Eventually, she'd gotten up for the day when it was still full dark, changed the dressing on her arm, and then sat down with heavy black thread and repaired her jacket. The chill in her apartment had done nothing to chase away the obsessive thoughts that had kept her awake.

Why did Lucy want to talk? About what? For the most part, Ash had managed to avoid her since she came back from New York. It had taken weeks for her body to heal. After that, she'd put in for more hours at the temp agency and spent a lot of time here at her dad's, cleaning and weeding and repairing.

Was it *about* New York?

Ash squeezed her eyes shut against the shameful memory of what had happened between them in the middle of Central Park, at a crossroads only the devil could offer. Lucy must know

Ash would never talk about that. She must know that Ash would never, *could never*, talk about them. What they had been to each other. What they were.

Her phone buzzed in her pocket. She ignored how her hand shook when she pulled it out to look at the notification. It was the temp agency, confirming her hours this morning at a law office. After that, she had her dad's appointment to take him to.

Chop wood. Carry water. Walk the earth.

She took a bite of her tasteless toast. It had to be Nathan who'd drawn them out to Hector's last night. His broken-open eagerness to see his dream realized. She'd felt his desire. The intensity was palpable. What his soul wanted had managed to cut through the January bleakness, and so Lucy had been attracted to him, and Ash had been called. Lucy wasn't there because Ash was, as she'd claimed. Ash was there because Nathan's soul needed her to save it.

Lucy's lies were so good, so easy to believe, because they were custom-made. They were lies that made Ash feel seen. Special. That was what the devil did. She lied to whatever it was inside you that was starved. What Ash had to remember was that Lucy couldn't feed her. Not anymore.

That was settled, then. Lucy didn't want to talk. She wanted Ash to give her attention, and to lose focus for long enough that Lucy could finish what she'd started in New York.

That was all.

Rye adjusted his position in his chair, trying and failing to conceal a pained grunt.

"Let me get your medicine." She stood, shaking out her hands. Meds, glass, juice. The row of orange prescription bottles, the oxygen tank by his chair, the gout that left Rye's toe red and disfigured—all of it terrible proof of his humanity.

If she was lucky, she'd end up just like him.

"Here." She put the pills in front of him with the small glass of orange juice he allowed himself, then went to start a new pot of coffee.

"Haven't noticed these have done much good." He tossed the pills back. "Might as well be candy."

"You don't eat candy. But if you think candy would make you feel any better, I'll get you some."

He grunted, this time on purpose.

Was he born joyless, or had the curse made him this way? She knew that she, at least, hadn't come into the world fitting the Steadfast mold. Ash had been a precocious, loud kid. She was put on a series of behavior plans at school, even as teachers described her as one of their favorite students. Music education burred off the edges and helped her find her identity in making as much noise as possible in front of as many people as possible in as little clothing as she could get away with.

Rye would make rules, and Ash would break them. He'd lecture her, and she'd turn his warnings into song lyrics. Sometimes he'd lose his patience, and she would be almost relieved to hear him yell, finally. Like her existence had an impact on him.

His guiding principle was clear, even if how he felt about her wasn't. *The black sheep sees the wolf.* He'd told her a hundred times, starting when she was too young to understand. Was she the black sheep and Lucy the wolf? Who was he in this scenario?

Even now, the phrase meant almost nothing to her.

She was not the most sensitive of girls, as he had pointed out more than once. It took his death for Ash to find out she really did love him. At the same moment, she took up his curse and within hours understood why he had been so taciturn and wounded. It hurt to live. She lost her dad, Lucy, and herself on the same day, and when she raged against that loss, she literally bled. And so she became the person her father wanted her to be. Quiet. Deliberate. A hard worker at tedious things. A young woman who wouldn't lose her whole heart to a girl, who would winnow her life down so much, there was nothing left of it to lose. Her hair, her music, her queerness faded to black. She turned into one more Steadfast in a long line of Steadfasts, watching for the wolf.

"Dad?" Ash brushed toast crumbs off the table.

"What is it?"

"Lucy wants to talk."

She held her breath while her heart sent out pulses of icy slush. She was shocked to hear herself say out loud what she had been obsessing over all night.

Ash didn't tell her dad anything about Lucy for the simple reason that he didn't ask. A decade ago, in the hospital, he'd given one long look at Ash's neck, angry scarlet and still healing from their first fight, and said nothing. As Ash's life became more narrow and ascetic, Rye had kept silent.

It was not a neutral silence.

"Why?" His question had no intonation.

"I don't know. I felt like I had to go to Hector's Tavern. When I arrived, she was taking a man's soul in the parking lot. She tried to tell me she only wanted to talk, but obviously that's a lie." Ash wished she sounded more sure of this. Lucy's exasperation had seemed genuine.

Her dad's hands dropped to his lap. His eyes were on the table. "She didn't say why, though?"

"No. Does it matter?" Ash couldn't read her dad's tone, but the blandness in his expression made her suspicious. He had an opinion about this, or something bothered him, or he knew something, but Ash had a better chance of convincing him to buy a top-of-the-line fully automated luxury massage chair than getting him to share his thoughts.

"If it doesn't matter to you, then it doesn't matter." He took a noisy sip of coffee and waved his hand. "Forget about it." The look he gave her then was long and stern, and her stomach twisted with pain. Not spiritual pain. The ordinary kind inflicted by a father on the daughter who'd never measured up to his standard.

Ash's mother had been a one-night stand before Rye took up the fight. She'd left Ashes by his front door, a note pinned to the shawl wrapped around her body. *I named her Ashes. She's your curse to bear.* It was the only thing she knew about her mother, because it was the only thing her dad would tell her. The fact of her abandonment was the only fact that mattered.

Lucy's story was a variation of the same song. Her mom hadn't wanted any part of what was coming. She'd only stuck around a few years before she bounced.

"Even if we'd managed to start a conversation, we were interrupted by Hector," Ash said.

"And if he hadn't interrupted, you would have talked?"

"No." Her vision tunneled like it used to when she was young and Rye lectured her. She touched her tender arm to bring herself back to the room.

He didn't say anything more for long enough that Ash felt

herself disconnect from any impulse to engage with him on this subject. It hurt too much, and like all hurt connected to her dad, what came next for her was anger. It made her think of the dark figures gathered in a ring around Hector's parking lot. Rye would fit right in with the Dead and Righteous Brigade. He'd probably join them before long.

"Ash."

"No. Don't worry about it." She knew her tone was bitten-off, but Rye didn't account for her angry feelings any more than he accounted for her softer ones. "I should get going."

He put his hands flat on the table and looked at her in a way she couldn't walk away from. "You know I talked to her father every day. All the time we weren't obligated to you girls."

Obligated. There was a word.

"Draven and I let the balance hang on who was convinced of what the other said from moment to moment. Like the last temptation in the desert, but instead of going on for forty days and forty nights, it went on for twenty years. The temptation of Rye and Draven. To make sure he never took a soul."

Her dad had won. She was losing. That was what he meant. Ash shook her head, unsettled and irritated with him for unsettling her. "So you think I should talk to her."

"It didn't make a difference, did it?" His lip line went white. "All that talking."

"But Draven was kept from taking souls. You just said. I fight Lucy, and she's taken plenty. I guess that means you had it right." Ash's jaw muscles locked up. Why did it always make her so furious to know her dad was right? That he always did the right thing? Shouldn't she be proud of him? The Puritan, the Steadfast, who'd never faltered?

His eyes got sharper. "Where does she live?"

There was something irregular about the question. The silence that followed it rang against the minute bones of Ash's inner ear.

Where did she live?

Lucy's bedroom in the house she'd grown up in had purple curtains with coin fringe, a mandala tapestry, and a daybed covered in pillows. But Lucy didn't live there. The house had been sold years ago, been painted a different color, and gotten new windows and a driveway.

Ash didn't know where Lucy lived. She had never asked.

Lucy knew where Ash lived. They'd once had it out on the sidewalk in front of her building.

"Why would I know where she lives?" She took another bite of her toast. Her tongue revolted at the queasy slide of low-cholesterol spread. The corn syrup sweetness of the whole grain bread turned to acid. Something was . . . sideways.

"Because you know everything about her."

"Knew," Ash corrected automatically.

Rye scraped his fingers over his jaw in a way that made her notice the circles under his hollowed eyes. He had a sharp nose and strong, expressive eyebrows that she had inherited. If he wore a collared shirt, he was not infrequently mistaken for a priest.

He hadn't been an attentive father. He wasn't a soft man. She'd spent the last ten years trying to love him because she knew she didn't want to lose him again. She did for him what he let her do. His health was terrible. He spent most of his time uncomfortable. He hardly spoke. But he always answered the phone when she called. He went to the doctor without complaint. There were moments, over the years, when Ash had thought that he *must* understand more than he let on about what her life had become. She believed she'd seen it in his eyes and felt it in the rare occasions when he'd patted her shoulder.

It wasn't good enough, but it was what she had.

"I don't know where Draven lives," he said. "I don't know *if* he lives. I have my doubts about the approach I took, but you always want to rush into everything. Whatever you would talk about with Lucy, you wouldn't know where she took what she learned from your conversations. You wouldn't stop to think what she might do with it."

Prickles bloomed in her veins from her neck to over her scalp and down to her heart. Here she sat in front of him with a face rashed by gravel, a cut on her arm that she'd glued shut, and a feeling of confusion about her duty to save the world that she could use some wisdom about from the *only person alive* who'd been in her place. But he never gave her that. He'd never passed over a guidebook or told her a euphemistic bedtime story to help her understand the rules. There had never been a Rye and Ashes training montage. She just fumbled through this, one fight after another, while he sat in judgment. Her anger fired white-hot, and she spoke without thinking, just like the rebellious teenager he still seemed to think she was. "Did it take you ten years of watching me break my body to come up with that little gem of advice?"

"When would you have listened to me?"

Ash stood up, her knees water, her head static. The only thing she wanted was to get out of the house—a familiar sensation from growing up here. Walk away, run away, bolt from the feeling of always, always being wrong. "I have to go. I'll see you later for the doctor."

She stumbled out the door and over the lawn, punching her boots through fresh snow. She got into her car and peeled out of the driveway. She had to keep moving so she wouldn't scream. Lucy wanted to talk. Hector didn't want Lucy and Ash to fight. Her dad wanted her to remember to hold Lucy at arm's length like he was still afraid Ash would sneak out of the house in the middle of the night to make out with her at the park across the street. And every time she saw Lucy, the sun found her best angle. She was literally magic. Hector had his bar, his wife, two babies on the way. Ash couldn't help but assume that Draven was doing *exactly* what he wanted to do, wherever he'd disappeared to. Her own dad was retired. Dying had set him free, even if what he chose to do was crumble into dust, sanctimonious and dour.

How dare any of them give her a job evaluation? When she wore color, she got *hives*. Music—the only thing she'd ever been good at—made her sick.

Lucy. Lucy. *Lucy.*

She had to go to work. The law office expected her in an hour. She needed breakfast. After work, she would pick up her dad and take him to his appointment. Chop wood. Carry water. Walk the earth.

Ash was halfway to downtown when she saw it.

She pulled over into the parking lot of the radiator repair shop, put her car in park, and looked at the new billboard thrust over the placid traffic of a slushy Green Bay weekday morning.

GO TO THE FOREST

There wasn't any small print crediting the campaign to the Department of Natural Resources or even an RV dealership. No website. There was only a QR code.

Ash narrowed her eyes at the black-and-white box, stark against the edge-to-edge full-color photograph of the deep woods that took up the billboard. She hoped she was wrong, but she knew she wasn't, and sober reality started to rush in, tightening her chest and making her cheeks furiously hot.

GO TO THE FOREST

She held up her phone, captured the code, and watched the screen load.

It was a website, but without a menu, only a single landing page. A map. A deliriously attractive map, as in, a map *made* to induce delirium, thrall, excited heedlessness, by a cartographer able to direct even someone with no sense of direction to precisely where it wanted them to go.

Which was the forest.

It would be the kind of forest no one could resist. A boundary between worlds, one light and one dark. The forest was where the devil and other nasty things lured people to stumble on naked women capering around bonfires, flying into the sky. It was where you were led off the path and promised desire as velvety as the canopied dark. The forest was what the Puritan Steadfasts and Dimmesdales and Chillingworths had built fences to keep out, and the original Prynne? She'd lived right at its edge with her illegitimate child and an apron full of witch's potions, her chest emblazoned with a scarlet letter A for adultery that she reportedly wore with pride—another sin—and decorated with golden embroidery.

Even if Ash didn't know how much of these half-told stories were true, she knew what this billboard was for and who'd put it there. Lucy wasn't done with her. Whether Ash wanted to talk or not, Lucy would call her to battle over and over again.

She swiped the map away and tossed her phone into the passenger seat, then drummed her fingers against the steering wheel. She didn't have time for this, and it would absolutely take time. There was no efficient way around it. There would be no law office, no quiet file room that smelled like dust and had a work desk with a label maker and boxes of stiff file folders where she could get a handle on everything that had happened since last night.

"Very literally goddamnit." Ash grabbed her phone and slammed it into the holder. The map cheerfully relit the screen.

She didn't need the navigation, but she was curious if it would be even a little subtle. As she drove north, she saw that no variety of subterfuge or sophistication had been employed. Instead, the app/website/map/summoning had taken on the husky voice of Ash's first desperate celebrity crush—Mariska Hargitay as Detective Olivia Benson on *Law & Order*—and it gave only cardinal directions, Ash's overwhelming preference. She also noted that she was not using any gas on this journey, which had already gone on for a while. She was pretty sure that if she opened the glove box she would find a pristine pack of American Spirits with a lighter balanced on top, though she hadn't smoked since high school.

The turnoff was well marked, of course. The parking lot

curved along a cedar fence featuring an arched opening into a trail dappled appealingly with sunlight. There was no snow, just trees choked with impossible leaves, fat with midsummer growth. There were several vehicles in the lot from which happy Midwesterners unloaded camping equipment, coolers, and, horrifyingly, children.

She got out of her car, slamming the door so hard that a crow cawed and took flight. "Everybody get the fuck out!" she yelled.

Nothing. Sometimes it was enough to confront people with the unnaturalness of a pale woman dressed entirely in black with a blanket of near-white hair, fresh wounds, and a carmine-red scar bisecting her throat, but today she would have no such luck. People in Wisconsin loved nothing more than a new place to drink.

She scanned the would-be campers, these good folks lured by the billboard to drop everything on a weekday morning. She focused on what they believed in that urged them to make good choices. What stopped them before they took a risk.

Ash closed her eyes, lightheaded with the rush of their worries. Their personal mottos and fear saturated her mind, too loud to ignore, buzzing with anxious energy that made her nauseated. When the cacophony had died down enough to bear, she started walking around, talking to them, feeding what they believed was the best part of their souls back to them. She couldn't know what part of what she said landed—if it was the reminder about work, the warning about an icy walkway that hadn't been shoveled yet, or simply that this forest was too good to be true—but they decamped one by one, with longing stares toward the opening in the fence.

When the last car had exited the gravel lot, Ash grabbed hold of the cattle gate and barred the entrance, looping over a fat chain and closing the padlock that waited obediently for her to trap herself behind it.

The light faded, and the wind started up, accompanied by faint strains of violin music. Classic. She shuddered out a breath, kicking up rocks with her boots as she made her way to the path, which now glowed a deep red.

There had been stretches over the years when Ash saw Lucy every day—fought with her, fought for souls—and those stretches were never good. They were weeks of exhaustion and wrapping ice packs around her shoulders and taping gauze to her face. She cried, curled up in her bed, trying to steal as much sleep as she could before it started again, wondering if she'd have to ask her dad for money because she couldn't work. Worse, she couldn't save them all. It was like trying to keep sand in a sieve.

Ash wasn't sure she would make it through another one of those seasons.

The farther she went, the more the red light receded into the trees like smoke. The path was dark with old needles and leaf mold, bordered with moss so green it seemed nearly to illuminate the ground. She kept her eyes averted from the darkness between the trees. The path grew narrow, partially grown over with soft nettles, low enough in places that for a few feet she would start to lose her way, her heart racing, self-recrimination loud in her head.

This was a bad decision. She should have gone to the law office and made the devil work for it if she wanted another fight. Ash had been thinking about Lucy too much. Letting her feelings in, letting them make her weak.

She wasn't sure how long she'd been walking when the trees started to get smaller, younger, spaced apart, and the path trailed away into grass and ferns that hit at the top of her boots. The ambient light of the deep forest had been replaced by silvery moonlight, though it was much too early for the sun to have set.

Then the woods gave way to a clearing. That was new. Sometimes it was a crossroads. Sometimes there was a table, a chess set, a bottle of spirits. Once, she'd tripped over a dice cup. Another time, there had been a big, soft chair with an enormous pile of novels next to it, all of them with covers that made her want to blush and die reading in equal measure.

But this was just a wide-open space with ill-defined borders, filled with wildflowers clustered around a mirrorlike pond. It felt like a familiar park. Ash could stride through the ferns and grass to the pond or lean against one of the large boulders. She could gather a bouquet or rest under the trees.

Behind her, she could see where her heavy boots had flattened the grass and, beyond that, the moss-lined trail through the trees, still open if she wanted to go back to the parking lot. She felt, deep down, that if she went back the way she came and got into her car and left, what would happen would be nothing. She had a choice.

She never had a choice. She'd anticipated that this demon-fueled illusion would close the way behind her, lock her in, lock her horns to Lucy's. But she could leave. Or she could know more.

Free will. The tricky fine print.

She decided to make her way cautiously to the pond. The plants in the meadow caught in the laces of her boots and tickled the exposed skin in the rips of her jeans. The stalks of the grasses breaking and her breath were the only sounds. No birds, no insects, no hidden crunches and huffs of larger animals.

No people, surrounded by the light of their souls, eager to bare their desires.

The ground grew flat and stony as the edge of the water came into view.

"Hi."

Lucy sat in a folding aluminum outdoor chair. It was the old-fashioned kind with orange-and-yellow nylon webbing, frayed around the edges, used for years and left out in the sun. It was just like the chairs their fathers used to set up in their yards in the summer. Her hair was frizzed into a non-style that made Ash notice her perfect skin, brown Bambi eyes, and feigned expression of innocence.

Ash walked over. A second chair obediently manifested. She sat.

Lucy turned to face her, tucking a leg under her long skirt. Her gaze was as unrelenting and confusing as ever.

"The billboard isn't fair," Ash said. "'Go to the forest,' just at the time of year when everyone is tired of winter."

"I don't know what you mean."

"The QR code on the billboard"—she crossed her arms—"that opened the map to this place had its black pixels arranged like a horned goat."

"It's not like I get to approve a mock-up. It doesn't work like that." Lucy worried the brittle plastic armrest of her chair. "Do you know this place?"

"I don't. I didn't know the woods, either."

"No." Lucy cleared her throat. "I didn't do this. Did you?"

"I go where I'm called," she answered automatically, not even sure what she was protecting.

Lucy's eyes blazed bright with vexation. She didn't like Ash's answer, but she didn't like anything Ash did. It was kind of the point.

Abruptly, Lucy stood. Her chair collapsed with a muted clatter.

Ash tensed, readying herself as a familiar black, hard feeling iced over her heart. She rose slowly, her feet planted apart, her vision narrowing to Lucy. Her arm stung. Her body was sore. When she took a deep breath, it felt like half air, half vacuum. *Don't die.*

Lucy put her hands in her wild hair, and a wind kicked up and snapped her long skirt against her legs. But before Ash could say anything—and what could she say?—Lucy picked up her collapsed chair and threw it into the grass. She strode away across the meadow without a backward glance.

"What the fuck?" Ash managed to ask . . . no one. She glanced over her shoulder at the path she'd taken to get here.

It was still there. It hadn't moved. The moonlight illuminated it like it was bordered with landscaper's lights.

There was no backward glance from Lucy, no thrown-away dry comment, no wink. She genuinely seemed committed to her departure. As Ash thought about it, she realized it had been a lot easier than was typical to convince the people in the parking lot to leave. The ambiance Lucy summoned to trap souls was usually much more captivating than this meadow. Ash hadn't even felt compelled to come here. She'd seen the billboard and *decided* to come.

She could leave. She *could*. It was only the two of them, and if Lucy kept walking away at that clip, soon enough Ash would be alone. If she left now, she might still make it to work on time. She could avoid ending the day with another split lip or a cracked rib.

But she hesitated, thinking of how Rye had filled her with suspicion and not a little anger after she told him Lucy wanted to talk. Even though that was what he and Draven had done.

He had doubts. He doubted her.

Ash knew doubt in her bones. Every time Lucy asked her what she wanted, she doubted, because how could it be true after all the generations of Steadfasts that had come before her that what Ashes Steadfast wanted more than anything was the devil?

She made her choice. Before Lucy could disappear over the false horizon, Ash followed her.

III.

ROGER'S FIELD

> She thought of the dim forest, with its little dell of solitude, and love, and anguish, and the mossy tree-trunk, where, sitting hand in hand, they had mingled their sad and passionate talk with the melancholy murmur of the brook. How deeply had they known each other then!
>
> NATHANIEL HAWTHORNE, *THE SCARLET LETTER*

"LUCY!" SHE SHOUTED.

The other woman stopped and whipped her head around. Her hair billowed out behind her, longer than it usually seemed. The frown between her eyebrows was enough to make Ash regret chasing after her.

"Just . . . stop." She looked up at the sky, now a mirror to the strange landscape below. Her own black-clad form stared back at her. Unbound white hair flying. Scar like a judgment at her throat. "I don't keep a journal, so I don't know if I should have expected a tournament between us was coming up, but I'd like to ask if we could set a date this time."

The sarcasm collapsed in the heavy atmosphere between them. Ash felt her ears heat. She'd *pursued* her. Far from being lured, she had chased Lucy into this particular hellscape, not even knowing what it was to her. She turned away from her pale-and-shadows reflection to kick at the dirt. "Listen."

"I'd like to ask *you* to listen, but you wouldn't." Tossing her head, Lucy caught sight of her own reflection in the sky. Ash watched her eyes widen at the size of her hair before she used both hands to smooth it down. The gesture was too Lucy. Her imperfection in this place made her seem human. Even Ash felt more . . . more. Her ancestors weren't here. The atmosphere was flat, muffled, and it hadn't stopped changing.

She could leave.

It forced her to admit she didn't want to.

"I have a question," Lucy said.

"You always do. This is the devil's entire thing. It's not the questions that are tricky, it's what you do with the answers."

"If you can hear me through the fingers in your ears while you sing la-la-la, here it is. Are you different?"

"Am I different from what?"

"From before." Lucy's cheeks were a hectic pink. "I want to know if you're fundamentally made of something you were never made of back then. I need you to tell me if you even remember before, or if when you lie down at night and try to think about it, everything *before* is as blacked out and colorless as your tragic clothes."

It was a light jab, but it hit Ash with a shock of apprehension. She didn't *try* to think about it. She tried *not* to think about it, knowing that if she did try, she would remember everything.

Wouldn't she?

"Of course I'm different," she said. "I had to be. Things got very real, very fast." Her voice snagged, dry and airless, and she made herself stop talking. It was always a bad idea to answer Lucy's questions.

Wasn't it?

Ash put her hand against her throat, where the skin had healed thick and shiny. Her fingertips traced the raised edges of her scar, the border between what she'd been and what she was now.

"*No,* you aren't. You're still in there, Ashes." Lucy swallowed and looked quickly at the ground, as if she were fighting tears, which was impossible. The devil didn't cry. "How you look now, how you act—it's just your reaction to what you think *I* am. But what makes you think I'm not the same as I always was? Or, no, here's a better question. Why can't you tell I *am*?"

"The person I knew wouldn't do what you do." As she spoke, the scene around them shifted. Now there was tall grass, cattle gates hinged to barbed wire, long stands of conifers, maple, and red oak. She almost recognized it.

"You don't *know* what I do. But, for the record, the Ashes I knew wouldn't harrow people with their own oppressive beliefs, much less scare them by wearing black leather and boots." She crossed her arms over her skimpy eyelet top, held together by some kind of ribbon magic. "You hated how you grew up. I watched you hide CDs and makeup in the back of your closet. You got a work permit at fifteen so you could buy yourself pink camis and jeans with crystals on the ass from Hollister."

That was true. Ash had played upright bass in the school orchestra and jazz band, and then with groups around town that got gigs at weddings and parties. She'd taught herself electric bass and, like Nathan, recorded herself humming melodies for songs she wanted to write. Somewhere under her bed was a box with Moleskine notebooks full of lyrics and a now-empty cashbox that she'd put extra money in to save for a drum set.

Lucy loved math. She'd enjoyed subverting the boys' and teachers' expectations of the dreamy girl wearing floor-length hippie skirts by acing every honors and AP exam and then testing right into college-level classes. She'd talked about NASA. What it would be like to be the one who wrote the language that sent people to the stars.

They hadn't had any faith in the inevitability of what their fathers warned them would come. Their own vision of the future *was* the inevitability. Their love. Their first kiss. The kisses that came after. Every single kiss more real than anything their fathers told them.

But they learned quick enough that it wasn't a dusty custom. It was blood sacrifice. It was fire. It was light and dark.

It was the worst breakup of all fucking time.

Ash resented everything skidding so far off script. In this new place, it felt like full summer, the cicadas sawing away, the sun settled back down in the sky in the golden hour of dinnertime, and she was suddenly flooded with anxiety for not having started home yet—a feeling she hadn't had for a lot longer than ten years. Home was at least a twenty-minute walk from Roger's Field.

Roger's Field. That was the familiar landscape this hell had rearranged itself into. Their place.

No, a *facsimile* of their place.

"It's pretty late in the game to try to have this kind of conversation," she said. "Especially when we have hundreds of years' worth of evidence it doesn't work."

"You don't have anything like evidence." Lucy glowered at her. "You have what Rye told you. I have less than that."

"This isn't evidence?" Ash scraped her fingernails over her scarred throat. "Or this?" She shoved the waistband of her jeans down over her hip, showing Lucy the blistered mess that used to be a tattoo. She'd faked an ID to get it when she was sixteen—two pairs of scissors with rainbow handles, open and slid together. The most subversive declaration of what her body was pulsing with that she'd been able to think of. "What about the hives I break out in when I'm touched? Or how sugar makes me vomit? That I can't breathe when I play music? Or that I can't *come*?" She shook her head hard, sending her hair swinging. "You're right. I haven't changed. Everything I've done, I've done because I had a good reason, up to and including locking my life up like a novice nun's."

Lucy searched Ash's face, her expression puzzled, her eyes full of tender empathy.

Ash couldn't bear it. "Tell me what I'm wrong about!"

"You're wrong about what happened to us."

She wasn't. That day at their tree, the day her father died, they'd argued, weeping, yelling, neither of them listening. Ash saw her soul. It snicked from her body like a ribbon yanked from a braid. It was hot and golden, and it wrapped itself around Lucy's silver-gold soul while the wind battered them both.

They'd lost the only parents they had. They'd been given power they had promised each other they would never take up. But when push came to shove, Lucy hadn't hesitated to use it, drawing the soul right out of Ash's body. And when Lucy got a second chance in New York last year, she'd fucking *tried it again*.

Ash didn't want to lose her soul. But here she was, not leaving, setting caution aside exactly the way her dad tried to warn her not to, simply because she was *curious*. She wanted to know what Lucy wanted to talk about. She wanted to know what more was possible. If anything more was possible. Because if what Ash had right now was what would always be, then maybe she *wasn't* as good as her dad.

Maybe it was only a matter of time before Lucy inevitably won.

"I know what happened under that tree," she said. "You're *not* the same. You're *not* the Lucy I knew. That night and this scar are all the evidence I need of that, however much you—" Her throat closed, and she clenched her teeth to keep from betraying her weakened conviction. "However much you look like her. Sound like her. Seem like her. Sometimes."

Lucy took a step closer. "The Ashes I knew cut off cargo pants at the knees and used paint pens to draw wildstyle graffiti on them. She wore them so low, you could see the waistband of her Under Armour boxer briefs. She undercut her hair until it was a floppy mohawk and turned thrifted Hawaiian shirts into crop tops. The Ashes *I* knew kickflipped her skateboard and kissed me with a lip ring that gave me goose bumps when I felt it on my neck."

Shit, shit, shit. Ash had let her get too close. She couldn't move when Lucy leaned forward and wound a lock of white-blond hair around her finger. The sensation sluiced over her like warm honey, flipping and cramping her stomach low down. "This." Lucy pulled the lock. "And this." She let it go to pinch the leather of Ash's jacket. "It's a mask you hide behind. And I didn't bait you into going to Hector's. I wouldn't have tried to talk to you if I didn't think I had to. I don't want to talk to this." Lucy drew a circle in the air around Ash's body. "You lie to yourself that I'm as happy as you are righteous, and you're the perfect picture of righteousness when we're fighting, aren't you? Just like I'm the perfect picture of soul-drunk and sin-high. But tell me that's how you feel when you're talking to Hector in his bar. Tell me you don't long for a real purpose. An actual life."

Ash ignored the way the corners of her eyes had started to burn. She'd listened to Lucy for too long. "So your laughter, the dancing, playing the devil's chess with avaricious men—that's not what you want, Luce? Because, let me tell you, it *looks* like more fun than crying tears of blood every time you stare too long at a pretty girl in the grocery line."

Lucy blinked. "No wonder you're always so grumpy."

"I'm a Steadfast. There's been a Steadfast on this watch for three centuries and change. It gave us something to do after a long day of trying witches—"

"Trying women," Lucy interrupted. "Drowning them. Hanging them. Casting them out. Your Steadfast had a choice not to make that bargain with my ancestor, who was also a woman, a regular human woman who *he* turned into a demon."

Ash scoured her mind for a counterargument, but her grasp on the history was weak and her faith in this fight a tattered burden. "Just tell me what we're doing here."

"I don't know what we're doing here." Another breeze started up, and the way it rustled through the pasture and the trees sounded real and alive. "I didn't know what we were doing at Hector's last night."

"We were fighting."

"Sure. And after it was over, you went home to your empty cell, because you get to do that. You can go see Hector and

Ovidia anytime you want, even though you hardly ever do. You can walk under your own power to Kettle's and talk to the barista who's worked there since we were in high school. You have a phone and a car. I understand that you can't have any kind of life you would have chosen for yourself, but you have a life."

Ash made herself meet Lucy's eyes, even as her stomach swooped, remembering her dad's question. *Where does she live?* "You don't, you're saying. You don't have a life." She tried to infuse the statement with sarcastic doubt, but she was reeling.

"What's your definition? I'm genuinely curious."

"I don't want to talk in circles. Just . . . what you said. I have an apartment. I have a job and chauffeur my dad. I have that much of a life. What do you have?"

"This." Lucy stretched out her arms. "I have this place for this moment. I have what we did in Hector's parking lot last night. Our fights. But there isn't any part of my life I live without you, not since the moment your dad's heart stopped."

That couldn't be right. That was—

No. It had been ten years. Ash had lived through a full decade of quotidian Midwestern grinding along, grim holidays with her dad, changing seasons, car registration stickers and grocery runs and training and fighting until her knuckles were a white-to-pink-to-maroon gradient of fresh wounds over scar tissue. All that time, Lucy was . . . outside of time?

"But you bleed." She was looking at every part of Lucy, really looking at her, something she never allowed herself to do. Lucy was *real,* wasn't she? The scenes Lucy conjured made her feel disoriented and sick, but *Lucy* didn't. Even though Ash always told herself the person she fought wasn't Lucy anymore, when they touched, when they stood close, she couldn't pretend it didn't feel the same.

Lucy yanked up her skirt and showed Ash the rough, angry state of her knees. "It only hurts or heals when I see you. I'm only alive when I see you, and I don't mean in a Taylor Swift love song kind of way." She let go of her skirt. "My dad was *always* there, so I have no idea why it's like this for me. He never told me about anything like this. He never told me anything except that it was important to learn, to read, to exercise my brain so I could debate with you someday, or maybe figure out how to stop it. He was glad I loved math because I think he hoped we could math our way out of it. I don't know. Maybe I could, if I had time. But the only time I have is with you."

Ash's heart had started to beat fast enough to make her dizzy.

"It's felt urgent since New York, Ashes, and I know you don't want to talk about what happened there, but I think it got us close to . . . breaking through. Ending this. But I don't know how, and I feel like you know things that I don't, and I know things you won't hear."

She couldn't think about that. "*Where* do you go?"

"Nowhere." The other woman looked at her with sad eyes that were the same as Lucy's eyes in every way. "I'm nowhere, Ashes. Maybe I'm no one. With you, I bleed and hurt. Eat. Breathe. Hear. Move. Think. I *live* when I'm with you. I *am* when I'm with you. And the whole time, you're trying to kill me."

Ash wasn't trying to kill Lucy. Her body wouldn't let her. Whatever magical strength she had, she kept a leash on it. It was why she assumed the Dead and Righteous Brigade had to watch her so closely—because she wasn't getting the job done. "So that means that all this time I've been trying to stay away from the fights, stay away from you . . . ?"

Lucy rubbed her hands over her face. "I didn't want anything when I found myself at Hector's but to talk to you. I knew it had been a long time, because the last time, it was warm, but there were autumn leaves falling, and now it's winter."

"Not here, it isn't."

Lucy looked around the summertime of Roger's Field. Their place. "No. But this is new. I don't know why this happened. Maybe I did it? When you left Hector's, all I wanted was to have a chance to be somewhere you would talk to me."

"Why did you come last night, then? For Nathan?"

Lucy looked blank. "You mean the musician?"

"How do you find your quarry, the people to make the deals, if you can't be anywhere but where I am? *I* don't know Nathan. I wasn't at Hector's. I'm called to *you*, and I always find you hip-deep in someone's soul when I get there." Ash made sure to infuse the observation with skepticism. She was running out of weapons.

"I don't *find* them. There's nothing, and then there's someone telling me everything—telling me about the interior of their heart and their dreams, what's written on their soul. And at first, it's wonderful."

"Until I get there, you mean."

"No, I mean that it's wonderful because I'm with someone, and it's uncomplicated. I'm so glad to occupy the same bit of time and space with this person. To talk to someone and take in as much as I can about the world and how it's changing and what's happening. But then I feel it."

"What? You feel what? Go on. Tell me." Her leeriness was a

parody now, the boastful confidence of a cartoon villain, but she wasn't ready to put it aside. Ash wasn't meant to know the things Lucy was telling her. She wasn't supposed to try to empathize with this perspective. She wasn't allowed to feel curiosity about what this was, or what Lucy did, or how. This knowledge was forbidden, plainly, because if it weren't, her skin wouldn't be tight with goose bumps, and she wouldn't feel the impulse to whisper.

Lucy gathered her hair in her hands and wound it into a curly rope that she draped over her shoulder. Ash noticed her slim wrists and the soft, unmarked skin of her hands. "I feel whatever they want," she said, "that they think they don't deserve. Who it would hurt. How it would go wrong. What would make it dirty in the end. But I also feel what would make it wonderful. You have to understand, they make the bad part of the bargain themselves." Lucy's rough voice brushed over Ash's skin, sinking inside her. "I try to remind them of what's truly motivating their dream, but they push it away for a cheap copy and pay for it with their souls, where their real dreams are written." She ran her fingers through her curls, freeing them and shaking them behind her shoulders. "You, on the other hand. You think you're saving them."

"I *am* saving them. I save them with the best part of their souls."

"No, Ashes. You stop them from ever asking for what they want again. You stop them from listening to the real dreams of their real soul. Nathan wants to make beautiful music so the world can feel something. Now that you've stepped in, he'll never sing anywhere but the shower."

Ash couldn't believe this.

She did believe it, but she *couldn't.*

The wind gusted, and Lucy wrapped her arms around her middle. Her shirt didn't cover her belly. She was cold. Freezing her ass off.

That wasn't right.

Lucy always dressed for beauty, to charm, as a lure. The weather didn't matter.

Ash looked around. They were still in Roger's Field—but now it was the *real* Roger's Field, as far as she could tell. "What are you doing?" Ash stepped toward her, then second-guessed herself. "You need a coat. Or just . . . you know, magic your own weather like you always do."

"Can't." Lucy's breath made alarming white clouds. "I'm stuck or something." Her teeth chattered, and her fingers were leaving blue-white impressions on the skin of her upper arms.

Ash's phone buzzed in her back pocket. She reflexively reached for it, then stopped. Her phone didn't work when she was with Lucy. It was always a moment out of time.

She hadn't known that Lucy never walked out of those moments.

She pulled her phone from her jeans. There were multiple messages previewed on the screen from both the law office and the temp agency. She had been out here for what seemed like forever, but only twenty minutes had passed. That was how long it had taken to drive from where she saw the billboard to the forest turnoff.

"Something is fucked up." This place was *definitely* Roger's Field. It was definitely nine fifty in the morning. This was the same weather she'd woken up to.

"No shit." Lucy's teeth and chin were trembling so much, it

was alarming. Before Ash could think about it too hard, she pulled off her heavy leather jacket and held it out.

Lucy looked at it with longing. "You'll get cold."

"I'm wearing a wool sweater, and I have long sleeves underneath. Take it." She shook it at Lucy.

Lucy accepted the jacket. The pleasure on her face as she slid into the quilted lining, warmed by Ash's body, sluiced down Ash's own spine. "Zip it up and let's go," she said impatiently. "You're sure you can't get out of here?" The path they'd taken had vanished now, of course. No magic forest abutted the *real* Roger's Field. Ash started to walk across the field to the tree line closest to the road. She really fucking hoped her Corolla would be there.

"I told you, it doesn't work like that. I don't open portals. I'm simply wherever I am. With you. From there, everything sort of organically grows. The environment. What I'm doing. What role I'm playing. The weather."

"You're not making choices."

"Not about any of that."

"And you're really nowhere when you're not here?"

Lucy's expression was tense, even suspicious as she buried as much of herself as she could in Ash's jacket and stumbled over the uneven and frozen pasture in her sandals. "That's the only word I have for it. Nowhere. Asleep. But not in a restful way."

They walked toward the oak trees closest to the road. The only sounds were their feet crunching in the field, Lucy's teeth chattering, and the occasional caw of a crow.

Until there was a harsh, squeaking *woof.*

Shit. Ash didn't have to hear the unnerving wooden clonks

of bones hitting against bones to know that Helegar, of all creatures unholy, had arrived. Lucy stopped walking and crouched on the ground to stroke the circling, wiggling, wagging animated skeleton of her frequent companion.

"Thank you, baby," Lucy cooed as the undead miniature dachshund pushed his long, forever-smiling skull against her cheek, deliriously happy in her arms, kicking up the stink of a long-dead mouse stuck in the wall. She kissed him between the hollow sockets of his eyes.

"Ugh."

"He can't help it." Lucy gave her ghastly familiar another kiss. "Helegar, we have company."

He leapt to the ground with more upsetting osseous noises, then shook vigorously like he was shedding water. His bones magically covered themselves in short red fur, thin over leathery skin that didn't quite cover his ears, so that they looked like a bat's. His eyes filled in, cloudy with cataracts, and his tongue unrolled from his pointed face, panting the foulest breath imaginable, indescribable in its moist fug. He sat down, wagging a tail that still had a point of bone sticking out the end of it, looked at Ash, and released a fart.

"That's not better." Ash stepped back as he wiggled forward and attempted to jump up on her, asking for her face to be presented for kissing. "In your dreams, Helegar."

He wagged his tail—a beast with, ironically, nothing at all left of him but his soul.

"He comes to me when I'm unhappy. To make me feel better. He's the good part."

Well. That was fucking awful.

They started walking again, nearly to the trees. Helegar zigzagged ahead of them, lifting his leg at every little hump of snow as if to baptize it with dribbles. They stopped talking, trudging toward the road with no idea why they were there, in a place familiar to them, loved once by both of them, that Ash never visited anymore.

And then they saw it at the same time. Their tree.

Huge in a sea of smaller, middle-aged oaks, it must have been the original oak, spared when a settler first farmed this land, maybe as a marker or land division. It had concentric rings of sturdy branches, the lowest over a stump. It was easy to use the stump as a mounting block and scrabble up, climbing from there to their spot just above the tops of the other trees. In that scoop of wide branches, hidden by leaves, they'd liked to talk. Later, it was where they'd had their first kiss, both of them blushing and laughing and daring each other.

They stopped at the trunk, Helegar sniffing around its roots madly, whining in his chest.

"Why are we here?"

Lucy didn't answer. Her shivering was starting to get concerning.

"Well, we're not going to figure it out like this. We should head for the road. You can't get us back to the forest parking lot, by chance? The one where my car is?"

"And then what, I get in your car and you give me a ride? Where?"

"I don't know where the devil goes when she's lost. I was hoping you could tell me if we got there." Her phone hadn't stopped intermittently buzzing. She hoped the temp agency wasn't going to fire her.

Lucy scooped up the dog, her fingers nearly blue as they stroked Helegar's unnaturally leathery ears. Then she stilled.

"What?"

Lucy walked right up to the tree. Helegar started whining again. "This is strange."

Ash moved next to her.

Scarred deep into the creased texture of the red oak's bark, she saw their carving, dug with a pocketknife that Lucy had won as a prize at Girl Scout camp. It was a heart as big as a dinner plate, with a big LP + AS. The bark had healed along its raw edges, the sappy wood gone dark and smooth with age.

But what Lucy now traced with her fingertips wasn't their old heart. It was the one *linked* to it, carved much neater, the letters stylized with little curves and serifs instead of blocky, childish forms.

HP + AD

"That wasn't there. We didn't hook our heart to another one. Why did they hook it to ours?" Ash had never seen this carving. The oak was in a pasture. The only path of desire was from the direction of the road they would meet up at to come here. Their carving had been the only one when they made it as giggling girls. "It must have been put here after we stopped coming."

"I don't think so."

"That's the only explanation." She reached up to touch the initials, avoiding theirs. This new carving wasn't new. It was at least as old as theirs, the scar it made in the oak tree long since healed over.

"It wasn't here last week," Lucy said.

"We didn't fight here last week."

"No. But once I'm somewhere, like I am now, its history kind of . . . fills in. I remember what should be and what's changed and why." There was something in her expression that punched Ash in the diaphragm—a puzzled, haunted look that was familiar.

She'd last seen that look when they'd met at this tree after Rye had died. Before they'd fought. Before Lucy cut her throat.

Had she ever known what put that look on Lucy's face? Where she'd been before she came to the tree that day? Had Lucy seen her father one last time before he disappeared?

"No, I didn't explain it right." Lucy sounded as if she were emerging from a fog. "I don't exactly *remember* the memories. But it's *like* I remember it the way I would have lived if I had the life I wanted. In that life, last week, I came out here to think about us, and this wasn't here."

Ash couldn't let herself really consider that.

"Look." Lucy blew out a breath. "You can either help me figure out what the fuck is going on—"

"Tell me the alternative," she interrupted.

"The alternative is that every time something like this happens, we keep on ignoring something that *may* be what we need to get out of this. And we carry on doing that until one of us is killed and some other poor relative is called up."

"And that's what you want, to get out of this? To be free?"

"You genuinely never listen to me."

"What I mean is, it's not just you being you, tempting me with what I want in a brand-new, extra byzantine way, to check and mate with the prize of my immortal soul."

Lucy let out a frustrated growl, and Helegar barked, snarling at Ash. "Agree to disagree!" she shouted, stomping her sandal into a root. "Fuck! Fuck! That hurt!" She pointed at Ash with the hand that wasn't holding Helegar. "Look at me! I'm freezing to death. I don't know where to go, and I *hate* that my best option is to follow you and depend on you. I'm sick to death of you, Ashes! Leave me out here to freeze. I don't care."

Helegar yipped and wiggled up to lick Lucy's neck and face.

Ash closed her eyes against an intrusive thought—the same intrusive thought she'd had a thousand times before. *Why not sell your soul to hell once and for all? Sell it to have Lucy.*

"What do you want me to do?" she asked. The wind was picking up.

"Something's changed. I don't know what, but this is a clue. We can try to figure it out. Maybe you can ask your dad." As she spoke, Helegar had started sniffing the air and madly struggling. Lucy put him down. As soon as she did, he took off.

"Helegar!" Lucy shouted. "Come here!"

He barked, following his nose, running hell-bent for leather. Ash watched him get smaller as he gained ground. "Does he do this a lot?"

"No. He stays with me."

"Then he's tracking something. And that's new. Another new thing."

Ash tested her mental grip on the slippery ledge she'd been straining to hang on to, and then, all at once, she thought, *Fuck it.*

She let go.

"Ashes!" Lucy shouted.

But she was already running after Helegar, trying not to trip over ice clods and tree roots. Helegar was barking like he had definitely sighted something. He stopped, howling, a front paw in the air until he lay down on the ground. When Ash caught up with him, he wagged the end of his tail at her. His fur melted into dust around him, and she was confronted with his bony self. The empty sockets of his eyes beseeched her. The white-and-black-and-gray world of Roger's Field started to spin, going deep green and, with an abrupt stop, warm and sunny.

Ash stood in the parking lot of the forest. Helegar was gone. She spun to look at the path, but there was a boulder in front of it. The cattle gate stood open, unlocked.

Confused, she rubbed her hands down her arms.

Her jacket was gone.

"Lucy!" she yelled. The warm air and trees hushed her voice like a heavy blanket. Her shouting didn't even disturb any birds. Her heart hadn't stopped racing. She'd have to ditch work and her dad's appointment and drive to Roger's Field to extract Lucy. Whatever was happening, Lucy was out in the weather without any protection, and at least in this realm, she was going to lose toes if Ash didn't act fast.

She jogged in a trance toward her car and yanked the door open. On the passenger's seat was her jacket. Her phone buzzed in her back pocket. It was nine twenty. There was only *one* text from the temp agency, wanting confirmation she'd be at the lawyer's office at nine thirty.

She looked everywhere, all over the lot, worried about Lucy in the cold. But when she reached down and felt her boots, they were dry, not wet with melted snow. She checked the time again. The time that hadn't apparently passed at all.

Finally, she slumped into the driver's seat and texted that she'd be ten minutes late.

Her strongest impulse was to summon Lucy, but she didn't have the faintest idea how to do that.

She started her car and turned onto the highway, the mirage of the summer forest fading behind her and the trees—the real trees on the other side of highway—bare and snow-covered.

When she looked one last time at the lot in her rearview, she saw a woman standing at the edge of the lot.

Ash jerked the car into park in the middle of the road. She unbuckled her seat belt and turned around in her seat, forcing herself to look.

The stranger wore long black skirts, with a rough brown apron over her black blouse. Her shiny-dark hair fell nearly to her waist. She was young, but she was obviously from a long time ago. Beautiful. Staring. *Angry.*

Ash's hand trembled where it rested on the door. She'd never clearly seen a lone entity from the Dead and Righteous Brigade, only their shadowy forms in a group. This woman's hair responded to the wind. The sunlight was on her face. Ash could make out the weave in the fabric of her apron.

They were after her now. She and Lucy had done something wrong, and they'd sent this woman in retribution, this woman who looked almost familiar.

The shape of the woman's mouth. The speaking eyes.

Lucy? Someone connected, *related* to her?

Ash squinted, wondering if she was seeing things that weren't there after the intensity of the morning. She'd always assumed the Dead and Righteous were Steadfasts, like her. What role would a Prynne have in the game of darkly cheering Ash on?

And where *was* Draven Prynne? Was Lucy's dad in a different nothingness state, not really asleep or awake? Was that because her dad wasn't fighting him? Was Rye *supposed* to be fighting him?

Did he know something about this, and that's why he'd asked her where Lucy lived?

The woman shook her head at Ash, then turned around and walked into the woods, the lush branches closing around her.

But it followed Ash all the way back to town as she fought with her questions, trying to answer them—the woman's anger.

IV.

CALLIOPE'S SAGACITY

> The angel and apostle of the coming revelation must be a woman, indeed, but lofty, pure, and beautiful; and wise, moreover, not through dusky grief, but the ethereal medium of joy.
>
> NATHANIEL HAWTHORNE, *THE SCARLET LETTER*

ASH WATCHED HER friend Calliope lean in to put her elbows on the table. When she ran a hand over her glossy beard, the swoopy, shiny waves of her faded-rainbow hair swung forward to reveal the partially grown-out undercut over her ear and neck. "If you ask me—"

"Which I did not." Ash wrapped her hands around her mug of black coffee. The afternoon was bitterly cold, the light bright through the windows of the coffee shop where she'd arranged to meet with Cal.

Cal, the little bit of life in her life. Hector was Ash's friend, but Cal was a friend Ash had made *after.* Just for her. In the wake of her encounter with Lucy—both encounters—she had been contemplating calling Cal when she finished up at the law office, but before she could convince herself to do it, Cal had called Ash.

It wasn't the first time Cal's instincts were right.

"*Didn't* you ask me, though? Could've been a dream I had, but that's not a distinction. For me." Cal smiled. "So, *if you ask me*, you and one Lucy Prynne had a fight. But I have a feeling it's more complicated than that. Don't bother to deny it. You have all the luster of the beige vinyl siding on my mom's duplex. Do you want some blusher? Or, wait—I have half a sample size of highlighter that's a little too gold for me." She dug into her enormous bag.

"No, I'm good."

Cal put her bag aside and leaned forward again. "But you did fight. I'm right about that. I'm a *diviner* of these kinds of things. A person's love life is to my gift as a microscope is to a tiny protozoa. There is clarity. There is detail. There is exposure, no matter what is invisible at first glance." Her hands gently wrapped around Ash's wrists. "Looks like it was a bad one."

"We fought," she confirmed. "Then Hector stepped in." The half-truth made her tongue feel like she'd licked a battery.

Cal's eyes widened. "You guys were hanging out with Hector? Did he pull a *Parent Trap* and get you together under false pretenses in the hope you would work things out? Not his style at all, drama respects him, but hmm. I might like it. I might feel that he could really work that."

"No." Ash shook her head to clear it. She never lied to Cal—she couldn't lie to anyone without suffering mystical castigation—but she also didn't tell Cal everything. Particularly the preternatural parts.

The closest she had come was the night they met. She'd fought with Lucy over the soul of a gig worker who delivered food and drove fares for the apps. It had been more brutal than usual, and in the bitter aftermath she'd found herself standing in the middle of a busy downtown street, a honking sedan swerving around her. Lucy had trebucheted her into traffic miles away from her car.

Ash was walking back past Foxy's, Green Bay's small but fierce queer club, when she heard singing.

It had been worth it—the dizzy headache that came with being so moved by music, dancing along even though she was pretty bruised up from the fight, with a cut lip that she hadn't noticed until Calliope left the stage after her set, spotted Ash, and came over with a damp rag.

Tell me all about it, she'd crooned, and Ash nearly had. She'd almost surrendered to the indulgent impulse to spill the entire sordid story. But she'd stopped herself, wanting to protect this princess-like being, so pretty in her sparkling makeup and heels.

Meeting Cal had reminded her what it felt like to yearn, to crush on pretty girls. A romance wasn't what Cal was to Ash, or ever would be—Ash couldn't, and Cal was already in love with her man. But sometimes the point of a crush was just to tell you who to pay attention to. Caring for Cal was Ash's only real defiance.

She had thought.

In the quiet of the law office this afternoon, it had occurred to Ash that she wasn't as resigned to the curse as she might have been. She'd tried to grow around it as much as she could, like a tree growing up and through a barbed-wire fence. Instead of testing the otherworldly strength the curse gave her, she'd tested what she could get away with. She had tested it and tested it until she'd gone to New York in a blaze of disobedience.

The impulse to push back against what oppressed her had never left Ash in ten years. Maybe that meant something.

"Lucy and I both ended up at his bar," she said, careful with her words.

"That's fantastically hard to believe, but I'll allow it because the celestial mechanics have been churning out serendipity lately. I can't walk down the street without getting hit by one amusing convergence after another." This was how Cal talked. In addition to singing and dancing at the queer club where Ash had met her, on weekdays she had a business that offered what she called "holistic psychic services" in a tiny office next to the tattoo place on Broadway. "Why did you end up arguing?"

"Would you accept that it's complicated?"

Cal leaned back and tossed her hair, drawing attention to the multiple gleaming earrings she wore in each ear. "I would accept it, but I would be disappointed, and not because you're once again leaving my curiosity unsated." Cal captured Ash's gaze with her own. The dark ring around her irises made a mandala that held Ash's attention. "How long have we known each other?"

"Years. Five? Six?"

"That's right. And in all that time, have I ever pushed?"

Her stomach dipped at Cal's entirely fair question. She didn't mean that she hadn't pushed against Ash's obviously dammed-up feelings or flinty exterior. She wasn't chiding Ash for never putting on a costume and turning up at one of her infamous Halloween parties, for turning down invitations to girls' nights out, bowling outings, camping. No, she meant she hadn't pushed about the things that didn't make sense. Five years' worth of excuses Ash gave her for her strange hours or her lack of ambition. Her ongoing entanglement with an ex whom Cal had never met. "You've never pushed me." Ash closed her eyes. She could smell Cal's perfume, Arquiste Peau, salty and powdery and as soft as her skin looked. Everything about Cal was soft. Her expectations especially. "I'm sorry."

"You've been hurt. Our bodies can't tell time, which means that if you're hurt and don't find a way to process it, your body is going to keep reacting as if the hurt just happened. I suspect you're burdened with generations of hurt, and there's a strict script you've been led to follow that you believe makes you safe. I understand that and know how to be patient with it. I'm not going anywhere."

Something tight unknotted in Ash's chest. She felt strange. The mandala in Cal's eyes—was it real or a figment of her imagination? She couldn't be sure. But Cal's acceptance was real. She trusted it.

Ash avoided Lucy's eyes. She found it difficult to convince herself they were a trick. Or a lie.

Lucy had said she was sick to death of her. Sick to death of seeing her, even though she only lived when she was with Ash. Sick to death of fighting. She found Ash tedious, and this was someone who'd admitted the best thing in her life was a foul-breathed animated dog corpse. Reasonable, then, that she wanted a way out.

Ash didn't know how to give her one, but Calliope might. A woman who lived by no one's script but her own, who sang like heaven was opening above, and who glittered with every color on earth.

"I'm going to tell you something," she said. Her heartbeat was a muffled pulse in her ears. "It's heavy, and I won't blame you if you decide after I tell you that you need to call someone to get me evaluated. I've been there before. I've checked myself into inpatient care a couple times, just in case, but they never find anything worth keeping me for."

Cal interlaced her fingers and resettled herself at the table. "Okay, lovie. Whenever you're ready."

She drew in a steadying breath. "Over three hundred years ago, back when there was a Puritan colony in Massachusetts, one of my ancestors, Faithful Steadfast, made a deal with the devil."

She glanced at Cal, but the only reaction was the predictable explosion of hot shame inside her own body. She waited for the inevitable spiritual castigation, tasting gall at the back of her throat. It didn't come. Cal didn't so much as raise her eyebrows. Her full upper lip was shiny with bright pink lipstick under her perfect mustache, which framed a tender smile.

Ash palmed the back of her neck. "It was a bargain, I guess, although sometimes we call it a curse. Lucy and I do. It was meant to confine the fight between good and evil—or part of it, at any rate—to their line of mortal descendants. One person in each generation of Steadfasts and Prynnes picks up where the previous generation leaves off. The direct descendant, usually, although there's some wiggle room since not every generation has kids, either on purpose to try to stop the curse or because they die too soon." She plowed on without a glance at Cal. "I'm the current Steadfast, and Lucy's the devil I fight. We knew this from when we were little. She and I were friends, next-door neighbors. Girlfriends, later. We wanted to break the cycle, but when my dad died on the table, even though modern medicine brought him back, the deal was done between us."

Ash took a deep breath against the tight feeling in her throat. "Also, I should say, Hector knows. And he can perform miracles. He doesn't talk much about leaving Jalisco with his parents, but it's not a secret. His parents were important members of their community and church. One day, when he was a tiny kid, he touched the face of a weeping Mary at a shrine. His mom grabbed his hand away, but then her psoriasis that had plagued her for years disappeared before her eyes."

"Not surprised at all that Hector's waters run deep." Cal smiled wider.

Ash blinked. *Cal believed her.* She had never been able to count on being believed by anyone outside the circle of the Steadfasts and Prynnes. The Midwest believed in cordless trimmers and well-maintained snowblowers, not the mundane magic that made curses, prophecies, and miracles.

"People lined up," she said with caution. "He healed them. Then a priest who said he'd been sent by the Vatican visited the family, gave them a suitcase full of money and papers, and told them to get out of town."

"I bet. Hard for the church to consolidate power when a kid is healing his neighbors."

"Yeah, so they left. It's been tough for his parents, but they never discouraged him. He takes away pain. One of my teammates on my high school soccer team twisted her knee, and he fixed it. Once, he touched my infected eyebrow piercing and the hoop fell right out. The skin was perfect. Not even pierced. But it's just pain that he can heal. He can't take away who people really are. Like his wife's sister—he once healed a deep cut she got from a broken glass at his tavern, but she's still deaf. She's still *her*."

"I understand."

"But their family had to run. Anyway"—Ash made herself breathe—"Lucy and I, we came up with all kinds of ideas as kids. When we got older, we fell in love." Her nose and eyes burned. "We were teenagers, but we knew it was real. Other than Hector, everyone else had their doubts. Who trusts two teenage girls to know how they feel?"

Only a faint line between Cal's eyebrows disturbed her placid expression. "Me. I do. That's why you're telling me."

Ash pinched her nose hard against a sincere swell of gratitude that brought tears to her eyes. She sniffed, mortified, and waited for her punishment to come. Welts on her shoulders. A stinging rash on her neck and chest where the feeling was most intense.

Nothing happened.

"We were certain our love would end it," she said.

"Are you certain now that it didn't?" Cal reached into her bag and extracted a folded handkerchief with rainbow lace around the edge, which she handed across the table.

Ash breathed in the clean smell of the handkerchief. She pulled down the neckline of her shirt, showing Cal the scar at her throat. "This is from our first fight. I don't even know how we ended up at our tree—we had a special tree. We were both so angry."

She stopped herself, listening to a discordant sound inside her. *Had* they been angry? They'd screamed at each other. They were both crying. She remembered that Lucy had looked as fragile as glass. But everything about the encounter, when she tried to bring it into focus, remained a blur.

At the time, she couldn't believe it *was* happening. Neither

Lucy nor Ash had ever seen the curse in action. Their fathers had only talked—their endless debates through the summer nights, sitting in their webbed nylon lawn chairs, conjuring philosophy and theology, Helegar in Draven's lap. It wasn't exciting. There wasn't violence, or glamours, or magic.

It meant that under the tree with Lucy, Ash had been having a crisis of faith in the midst of her grief. The only person she had known to bring anything that big to was her best friend, her girlfriend, but Lucy was in a bad way. Her father had disappeared. She'd lost even the grounding of a linear existence. When she had demanded to know what Ash wanted—

Was that what Lucy had asked her?

Ash ran her finger along her scar. She *didn't* remember the injury. That was the truth. She didn't know quite how it had happened. If it was a knife, if it was the first manifestation of Lucy's powers, if Lucy or her grief had sent a tree branch flying at Ash.

In her heart, Ash had never believed Lucy hurt her on purpose. She had thought, rather, that it was inevitable. A call to take up arms in the war that was their destiny. They were girls. Eighteen, but girls, still, with no experiences other than the experiences of children. What happened that day at their tree was a black tantrum of loss, not a fight. But how could they have known the difference?

"I'm sure that I'm cursed," she said. "I definitely didn't sign up to wait out the rest of the days in front of me, fighting when I'm called, wearing a rotation of black T-shirts, renting a studio apartment with less than five pieces of furniture and driving a gray 2003 Toyota Corolla. I rejected this duty. I pushed it away so hard that I pushed away my dad, but it came for me anyway."

Her knee had begun to bounce. Ash set her foot flat on the floor to stop it. "My entire life consists of avoiding pain. That's it. That's everything. But you can see how well it's working out for me." She gestured at the cut on her face, swollen and scabbed. "I like my coffee light and sweet, but I can never have it that way. Is the world worth saving without good coffee, Cal? Or music? Or a pretty woman in my arms, grinding against my thigh?" The words rushed out of her now. She didn't try to stop them. She was past embarrassment. "If what I'm supposed to do is crush myself to keep the world from ending, isn't it understandable that sometimes I'd rather see the world end?"

The view through the big front windows of the coffee shop was discouraging. The snow had been pushed by the city plows into tall, dirty piles that matched how Ash felt inside—everything actually good about her scraped up and rearranged into a meaningless gravel-pocked landscape with no beauty. Just her duty and what she'd done to fulfill it.

Right at the edge of what she could see out the windows, there was a row of dark figures, dead and righteous as ever. So much easier to be righteous when you were dead.

But Calliope was the most alive person Ash knew. Her blouse was acid green, her makeup vivid, her eyelashes too long to be real. She was as beautiful as a soul, shining and captivating. She had a boyfriend who was tall and sharp-jawed, with a tattoo of garden flowers that grew from his collarbones to one wrist. He gazed at Cal like she was sacred and kissed her like he was starving.

"Help me," Ash said. "Please. If you can. I mean, I don't know how you could. Sparkly highlighter is not going to do it, I don't think, but I guess anything's worth a try."

"Oh, honey. I thought you'd never ask." Calliope pulled her huge, soft leather bag into her lap and held up a finger for Ash to wait while she dug through it with her other hand. She pulled out a white day planner with a crystal clasp. From it, she extracted a card with a gold foil design on its back. She put the card face up on the table.

"The Devil." She placed one shiny acrylic on the card's face and tapped it.

Ash peered at the oversize card. It was illustrated with a beautiful naked figure, smooth curves of muscle, top-surgery scars depicted as crescent moons on their chest, and curly rose-gold hair to the waist and between their legs. The figure held a long-stemmed flower against their smiling mouth. More flowers wrapped around ram's horns that spiraled from each side of their head. Their feet were cloven, though the hooves were shaped like platform heels. Sharp stiletto nails tipped their fingers, one nail pierced with a hoop that matched the ring through the devil's septum.

The illustration made Ash smile. This devil wasn't scary. It wasn't evil, even as it referenced horns and hooves. In that way, it was familiar.

"You know I read cards," Cal said.

"Of course. You've never given me a reading, but I haven't asked." She drew the card closer and put her hand over it, warm against her palm.

"I've kept that card with me since I met you. The night before, I'd had a dream. You were in it. Head-to-toe black, bruised, scarred, locked down."

Ash's mouth went dry. "Cal."

"Let me finish. In my dream, I asked you who you were. You

told me your name was Faithful. But then your true, magnificent self showed up—sides shaved, lip ring, ripped clothes." Cal touched Ash's temples, mouth, and shoulders in turn. "There was underboob, there were sequins, and there was still attitude, but phew!" She fanned her face. "A *different* attitude. The kind that's juicy bait."

Ash's cheeks went hot, her heart racing at the mention of Faithful. She'd just told Cal about Faithful, of course, and so Cal could have filled in the name after the fact, but Ash didn't believe that. Not in the least. No one with Cal's light could fail to be connected to a whole universe that other people couldn't see.

"Then, in this dream, you transformed again," Cal said. "This time, you were the devil."

"I was?"

She pointed to the card. "Not this legend here, but the one the preachers invite to look into our windows and crouch in the corners of our bedrooms. Blistered skin, bloody teeth, a smile that means the person you're after perceives only what they want to until their soul is ripped from their body in ragged pieces."

Ash could almost see it. She could feel how the bones, muscles, and skin of her body would break as her form changed.

"When I woke up, I pulled my cards, and this was the one on top. *This* devil, though, means change. I'd always understood this card to be neutral. Everything changes. But I didn't put this card back in the deck. First, because change meant something different after my dream. In it, you changed. You literally transformed. Second, because when I woke up, I came to know everything you just told me. That you are a Steadfast from a long line of Steadfasts. That you believe Lucy is the devil. That your fight is mortal. That Hector is a healer. All of it, as soon as I woke. I thought about it for some time. Once I decided to love you, I had a visitor."

"Who?"

Cal grinned. "Such a stinky boy, but ever so charming. He couldn't get enough of a lemon roasted chicken I'd made."

"*Helegar,*" she whispered, as goose bumps raced down her spine. Cal was smiling, almost laughing. "Wow. A truly revolting portent."

"Pure love comes in many forms." Cal reached out and cupped Ash's jaw for a moment. Her hand was warm. "It's a testament to your ancestors you've held the line for this long, but you must have known it would have to end. The good news is that now you're not in it alone. You found me. You asked for my help. Ash, my love, I'm not invited on transcendental travels without excellent reasons. Also, it seems you have your old friend Hector on your team. Very handsome, but more importantly, I think he might be willing to apply more than the parlor-trick version of his gifts if he knew the result would be the end of this spiritual baggage between you and Lucy."

Her hands were shaking. "You mean . . . ?"

"I mean that if at one time you and Lucy believed love was enough to break this cycle, you were onto something. I'm not saying this is a true-love's-kiss situation. Those are easy, and a dime a dozen, honestly. The universe loves love. This requires what the card says." Cal tapped it with her nail again. "Change. Not the easy kind."

"Change." She didn't know why the word made her feel such dread.

"You must believe things you've never believed before. Do

things you think you can't do. Resist experience. Resist safety. Get in trouble. And all the while, there are forces that simply do not want you to try. Forces in you. Forces outside of you. You *can't* do this alone, in fact."

Ash's heart felt like it was filling with blood from a thousand tiny wounds. It was tight and struggling to beat, excited and inhibited at the same time. She thought about Rye and Draven and their endless debating. They'd believed they were changing the script Cal was talking about, but it didn't work. They had spared her and Lucy nothing. "Why now?"

For the first time, Cal frowned, and something dark gathered in her eyes. "I shouldn't have to tell you." She lifted an eyebrow.

A freezing wind cut across Ash's nape. She looked away from Cal and watched the walls and windows of the coffee shop collapse in the snow.

They were in Roger's Field.

But it wasn't Calliope who'd brought them here. *Ash* had done this. She didn't know how she knew that, but she had no doubt. This was *her* place. Hers and Lucy's.

The cold pressed through her clothes, against her skin. It felt like death. It dulled Ash's thoughts and slowed down time. She couldn't think of anything but sleep.

She closed her eyes. Cal put her arm around her shoulder and squeezed.

"Stay awake," she said gently. "Look."

Ash squinted across the field. The oak tree loomed huge against the gray sky.

There was a body beneath it.

"Lucy!" She trampled over the snow toward her. Lucy wore

the leather jacket, but beneath it she had only scraps of silk, her feet in sandals. She lay curled on her side beside the tree with Helegar barking and running in circles around her.

Ash felt as though she were running through water, cold and deep, and she couldn't stay on her feet. She finally reached Lucy, whose hair blew loose around her head. Ash pushed it away, her hand shaking with cold. Lucy's eyes, staring back, were no longer brown, but iced-over white. Her brows and eyelashes were frozen. Her skin blue. Her lips nearly black.

She wasn't breathing.

Ash ran her hands over Lucy's face. She didn't get a response. She pressed a cheek to her cold mouth, to her chest, but there was nothing. Her own limbs were too slow and clumsy. It took forever to turn Lucy's stiff body so she was flat on the ground, to unzip the jacket and stack her hands over the unbeating heart.

The first compression was useless violence, jerking Lucy's head. Ash's tears fell over her hands. She was trying to scream Lucy's name, but she couldn't get anything past the block in her throat. She pushed into another compression.

Lucy shattered.

Ash collapsed, weeping on the navy crystals, which were all that was left of Lucy, trying to gather them in her useless hands. The wind froze the tears on her face. Helegar tried to clean them off her cheeks, his tongue warm, his throat whining in distress. She needed help. She wanted someone here to help her put Lucy back together. Cal was still where Ash had left her, across the field, her colorful hair a startling flag in a place so washed out.

But the woman was here. The woman Ash had seen at the edge of the forest.

Her expression wasn't angry anymore—only kind, only understanding—but Ash couldn't speak. She took in a breath, and it nearly gagged her, it was so warm. When she tried to yell again, she gasped instead, and the sounds of the coffee shop's whistling kettle gasped with her.

"Calliope," she whispered. The coffee shop's walls unfolded from the snow, enclosing the space bustling with people. The tea kettle was loud. Ash and Cal were once more sitting across from each other at the table.

"Do you understand?" Cal's mouth was firm, her eyes pitying.

Ash could still feel the frozen shards of Lucy's body in her hands. "Lucy. She's—"

"She's okay, my darling. For now."

"But we're not going to survive this. That's what it means. If this goes on much longer, it's going to kill her."

"You brought us to your worst fear." Cal's eyes swirled with silver light. "What you're afraid of isn't a fortune. It's not your future. What you're afraid of was shaped by the experiences in your past, and by the experiences of your ancestors, but you're here now, with the entirety of a life, with all your gifts, and you can decide to change. You can change so much that you take another path entirely. You can change so much you become the *first* ancestor of everyone who comes after you. That's why I dreamed you were Faithful. Because you have the chance, right now, to be the first in a long line of Steadfasts who use their strength and their magic in the service of love. You have a guide, you know. She hasn't rested. She's anchored to the earth by centuries of this battle. I wouldn't ignore her. She's scary as fuck."

The woman. The angry Prynne in a dark skirt. Ash's mind

filled with the vision she'd seen of her, furious and staring from the border of the woods. Her guide?

Go to the forest, the billboard had said, and Lucy had made it clear she wasn't responsible for the message.

It was Ash who'd made the woman angry. Or Ash and Lucy together.

"My strength," she said. "My gifts. Like being able to take us to Roger's Field just now?"

"Yes. Every Steadfast before you has always had something inside them they might have practiced, might have celebrated in order to change the pattern. Most have been too afraid of that gift to use it, or they've never found a line in the script that gave them permission. But it's there. You can try things you haven't tried before. Big things."

The sun passed from behind a cloud, and light poured into the coffee shop. Cal's expression warmed. She yanked up her bag to retrieve a bright pink glass tube with a golden top, which she unscrewed to reveal a small wand. "May I?"

Ash nodded, speechless.

Cal cradled Ash's face in one hand and began dotting the cosmetic over her cheeks. "You have the bones of an Anglo-Saxon warrior." She applied blusher with the soft applicator while Ash's heart kicked back into rhythm. "Now don't worry about this being too much. Anything Selena Gomez makes with her blessed hands is classy, as a rule." Cal smoothed and tapped her fingers over Ash's face. "Look!" She held up a little blue pocket mirror, and Ash took it to study her reflection, rosy with blush, but with dark circles under her eyes and skin as pale as her hair.

She glanced at the card on the table. The enigmatic smile of the devil in the illustration. The makeup made her cheeks burn threateningly, but she never wanted to wash it off.

"What do I do?" she asked.

"Every journey begins with a single step." Cal repacked her bag with a private smile. "Not the kind of advice I charge people for, but it's a classic for a reason. If you're asking, it seems obvious you might want to track down Lucy. Have a conversation. The kind where no one yells."

Ash tried to imagine how she would find her.

"Or don't." Cal stood up. "You can't know what will happen either way. Humans never stop getting surprised by the outcome of even millennium-length cycles. It's part of your charm."

Calliope waved as she walked away. The bell over the door rang longer than should have been possible after she left.

V.

WISCONSIN STATE HIGHWAY 57 TO THE HOLLAND TUNNEL

> Thus they went onward, not boldly, but step by step, into the themes that were brooding deepest in their hearts. So long estranged by fate and circumstances, they needed something slight and casual to run before, and throw open the doors of intercourse, so that their real thoughts might be led across the threshold.
>
> NATHANIEL HAWTHORNE, *THE SCARLET LETTER*

ASH PULLED HER sunglasses from the visor and slid them on to fight the glare bouncing off the icy snow along the shoulder of Highway 57.

She was thinking about Lucy.

Specifically, she was thinking about the fact that Lucy had aged. Her body had gotten fuller. Her bones had settled in her face. There were faint expression lines at the corners of her eyes and new freckles on her skin.

She'd changed.

The idea that Lucy's body was changing but somehow leaving her soul behind in a liminal place was repellent. It couldn't be right—*right* in the fundamental sense. She hated to think about Lucy living that way. She tried to imagine what it would be like to know herself and her body only within a disconnected biography made up mainly of fighting, arguing, and what people wanted from her.

Oh, wait. That was her life, too.

She squeezed the steering wheel, the road suddenly blurry.

A milk tanker with a blindingly shiny silver tank leaned on the horn in the lane next to her, making her jump. Her thoughts had traveled a long way from the road. She slowed and cracked her window, welcoming the rush of cold air.

Lucy *had* wanted to talk to her. She hadn't wanted to reap Nathan's soul. Her desire to see Ash had delivered them both to Hector's. The Devil card suggested that it was time to do something different. To change. Maybe Hector could help. Maybe both Lucy and Ash had intuited this.

It seemed like the woman—the one Ash guessed was a Prynne ancestor—might be the person who'd conjured the forest and drawn them into it. The woman was angry, but the place she had sent them to was one that Ash could have left. It wasn't compulsory. Then she'd taken them to their tree, which had a new heart carved into it. What were they supposed to get from that?

Or from Cal's vision. A dream. A long time ago, when she first met Ash. A vision with a message that Ash could be the first ancestor.

Apparently, there was more to being Ashes Steadfast than she had ever looked into. She had a power she hadn't known about that she didn't have the faintest idea how to use. It was how she and Cal had ended up back in Roger's Field, where the woman showed Ash what would happen if she *didn't* try something new.

She touched the blusher, still on her cheek. It had been there half an hour, and there were no blisters. No punishment for the risk she'd taken with the makeup *or* for the risk of telling Cal the truth about herself.

Ash wanted to try another test. She wanted there to be more to her life than chopping wood, carrying water, and walking the earth. A way back to really living. Maybe a way back to Lucy.

Although Lucy definitely wasn't looking for a way back to her.

She passed the sign for Door County.

The day she bought this car, she and Lucy and Hector were in the bed of his pickup truck in the hot sun. Hector had suggested driving to Door County. They could go to Cave Point and put their feet in the water. In response, Ash and Lucy hatched an outrageous plan to take an impromptu road trip to New York City for the weekend. *We have been to Cave Point ten million times,* Ash had told Hector, her hand on Lucy's knee. *But we've never been to New York.*

She heard a clunk and a loud pop that startled the word "Fuck!" out of her. Ash tapped the brakes to disengage the cruise control and glanced at the rearview to see if she'd left any parts of her car on the road, but it was only a chunk of ice that had fallen from her wheel well, spraying apart on the pavement. When she looked forward again, she gasped and hit the brakes.

"What the *hell?*"

She gripped the wheel in both hands, braking as hard as she could to avoid colliding with the car that had suddenly appeared in front of her. A loud blast of a horn from behind forced a wordless scream from her throat, and she hit the gas, resuming her speed to match the cars crowding both sides, in front, and behind.

The road had narrowed. The sky was gone, replaced by a ceiling lit by a racing fluorescent strip. When Ash ripped off her sunglasses to orient herself, the white curbs of snow on either side of the road had morphed into an endless tunnel of glossy white ceramic tiles.

She blinked hard. Her body had dropped away from her awareness, but her mind was running in overdrive. She knew this place. She knew the sound of the traffic roar bouncing off the cave of tile. She knew the worn letters on the road, **STAY IN LANE.**

This was the Holland Tunnel, under the Hudson River. Between New Jersey and New York City.

"It's not real," she said aloud. The car behind her blared another echoing honk as her speed slowed again. "I'm under a lot of stress. Too much stress." But she didn't believe it.

"Ashes."

Husky, low. Right next to her on the passenger side of the car.

Now that her new gift—her new ability?—had announced itself in the coffee shop with Cal, ferrying them to a nightmare scenario in Roger's Field, it had apparently decided the second act was a bespoke paranormal road trip to New York with her ex-girlfriend.

"Ashes."

"Begone, demon." Ash concentrated on safely making it through the tunnel. She was not quite ready for Lucy Prynne. The last time they'd been in New York, it had not ended well. She needed a moment to adjust.

A foul smell filled the car, and she heard an earsplitting bark.

"For fuck's sake!" Ash made herself look at the passenger seat then, her lip curling from the unignorable dead-mouse-plus-dog-breath smell of Helegar, who sat in Lucy's lap wagging his bone-tipped tail and looking at Ash with his pleading, milky gaze.

"Hey." Lucy's smile was tight. She wore rusty orange corduroys and a dark wool coat, a long scarf tucked under its collar that had been crocheted in at least a dozen colors. Helegar wiggled and snapped up the fringe of the scarf in his white-muzzled jaw, shaking it hard enough that his fur slipped and revealed the calcified ends of his bare ribs.

Ash snapped her attention back to the narrow roadway. Her hands were sweaty on the wheel. "Yeah, sure. 'Hey.' And I tip my hat to you, too. Because it is completely and absolutely regular to portfenestrate from Wisconsin to the floor of the Hudson River and have your cosmic nemesis appear in the passenger seat with her miniature hellhound."

"Portfenestrate?"

"A portmanteau, Lucy. 'Defenestrate' plus 'portal' equals portfenestrate."

"Oh." Lucy chuckled. "That's clever. Do you happen to know where we are?" Helegar was play-growling in Lucy's lap. "You said the Hudson. Is this New York?"

"It depends what direction we're going. This is the Holland Tunnel, so it could be New Jersey. There's a blue tile mosaic that tells you when you cross over the border, but—"

"We're heading toward New York," Lucy interrupted. "The woman driving the car behind us in the other lane is rehearsing for a Broadway audition in her head, hoping they won't stop her solo until after she starts the second verse. That's when she does a key change and really kills it."

Ash checked her side mirror. She spotted the woman, her

glittery white-gold soul slinked around her shoulders like a blanket. "You shouldn't do that."

"Do what?" Lucy ran her finger down the knobs of Helegar's spine under his fur glamour while he grunt-moaned.

"Coax a soul away from a person just to get directions."

"I didn't!" Her dark brows knit together. "I don't charm people's souls out of their bodies like pulling a snake out of a basket."

Ash tapped the steering wheel. "Do you really think I'm self-righteous?"

"Maybe? I mean, I always *hoped* you were holding your nose every time you stepped in between me and some other person in the middle of telling me about what they wanted. You know, doing your duty, as distasteful as it may be. I didn't like to believe you would crush someone's spirit because you *wanted* to."

"I don't crush their spirits." Ash caught the blue state line in her periphery. They were in New York. The soul of the woman on her way to the Broadway audition glowed brighter. "I stop them from selling their souls to you. I thought."

"Wait. You asked my opinion! You asked if I *think* you're self-righteous—if you've changed. Assuming you weren't self-righteous before, which I have not conceded. Do you want to hear my actual thoughts?"

Every journey began with a single step. Surely, this counted as a foot over the threshold. "I do. Tell me what you think."

Lucy was quiet for so long that Ash nearly told her to forget it. But then she sighed in a whoosh of spent tension. "The short answer is, I don't know. That's why I tried to tell you that I was still me. It doesn't mean I'm the *same*. It means that, given the circumstances, I can still recognize myself. I can tell you that I haven't been taken over bodily by a soul-reaping entity determined to win a fight between good and evil."

"You sure about that?"

Ash wasn't sure about it. She believed Lucy and she didn't, mostly because the consequences of believing her were daunting. If Lucy was the devil and Ash let herself be tricked, it would bring on the apocalypse. Maybe. But if Lucy *wasn't* the devil—if Lucy had never been the devil and was only ever Lucy—what then?

"Of course *you're* different," Lucy said, brushing Ash's question aside. "Sometimes it takes more than a minute when I see you to recognize it *is* you. I don't know how far that goes inside you. I mean, if you had been taken over by a righteous Puritan from the sixteen hundreds, would you even be able to tell? You're a Steadfast. Even before, you did everything your own way without inviting comments, concerns, or feedback."

"Hilarious." *The black sheep sees the wolf.* Maybe Ash had always been more like her father than she thought. She adjusted in her seat, uncomfortable in her skin. She was hot. She still wore her motorcycle jacket. A sweater underneath. The car heater was blasting, sending Helegar-stink into her pores. "Sorry you're stuck spending the only time you get with someone you're sick to death of."

Helegar whined, and Lucy rubbed his gristly ear. "I shouldn't have said that." Lucy's low, rumbling voice soothed Ash's wounded pride. "I was willing to fight you all these years, but you've never seemed to get that I would have been willing to spend *any* kind of time with you."

The flattery made her stomach flip. She pushed it away. "I'm thinking of the time an otherworldly wind swept me off the second-story balcony we were fighting on and I broke three of my ribs. Quite the warm and fuzzy memory."

"Well, *you* try listening to the most tender desires of every person you meet and tell me you wouldn't get a little irritable, wanting some part of a life for yourself."

Not knowing what to make of that, Ash focused on the road. When she saw the first glimmer of light from the tunnel's exit, it occurred to her that she was afraid of a lot more than disappointing humanity as much as she disappointed her father. Friend or enemy, she didn't want to lose Lucy. She had never been willing to take any of their fights to that point. She didn't like to think that she'd made choices to draw out this curse because it was the only way she could see her ex-girlfriend, but the truth didn't care whether she liked to think about it. It sat there in the awkward silence between them.

I would have been willing to spend any kind of time with you.

"What is this, by the way?" Lucy spared Ash from having to dig into that feeling any deeper. "Why are we going to New York?"

"I may have more powers than doctorate-level dourness and super strength. Who knew?"

Lucy cracked her own window, and a whistle of cold tunnel air and traffic noise seeped in, lightening up the Helegar miasma. "Surely *you* should have known. Have you been so incurious? I've done a ton of experimentation."

"On other people, you mean."

"With what I'm capable of. Because having no idea what I

could do, what I was made for, would have put other people in more danger than ignoring the reality of my situation."

Touché. "I'm not sure what kind of day trip my power is sending us on," Ash said. "As far as I know, I've only done this once before, and that time it operated more as an object lesson."

"I guess we'll see what we learn."

The traffic slowed with the approach of the tunnel exit. She tapped the brakes and asked, "Do you know where your dad is?"

Lucy looked out the window. "I dream about him. Sometimes, for a moment, I know where he is, and then I immediately forget."

"That's . . ."

"It pisses me off." She put the window down a few more inches, fully letting in the sounds of traffic and seagulls along with a cool breeze untainted by exhaust. "I think he has a choice. I think *your* dad has a choice. They're free, and what are they doing with it? Is Draven Prynne really going to sulk in the ether forevermore? Is Rye Steadfast going to drag himself from one doctor's appointment to the next until he dies a second time?" She let out a forceful sigh. "Sorry."

"It's not—"

"Actually, no," Lucy interrupted again. "I'm not sorry. Why should I be? Neither of us planned to be here, but at least you got to make a series of decisions that put you in your car. I'm just here. In clothes I didn't pick out. With you, who doesn't want to know me anymore."

"I didn't say I didn't want to know you anymore." Mortified by this stiff, helpless confession, Ash craned her neck to make sure she was crawling toward the right lane to exit onto Hudson Street. She hadn't spent a lot of time in Lower Manhattan, but she'd done this drive and knew it got hairy fast. Since the traffic was the only thing keeping her emotions in check, she welcomed it getting even worse.

Once she'd made it to the correct lane, she pulled her shoulders out of her ears. The day was overcast. It felt warmer here than in Green Bay. The smell of the river was oppressively mineral and fishy, with a note of diesel from the traffic. "You decide where we're going next."

"You're gonna let the devil tell you where to go. Nice." Lucy had the window down far enough that Helegar could stick his muzzle out of it while wiggling with joy.

"Does he need to . . . pee? *Does* he pee? I know he lifts his leg on everything, but I've never been clear on if there are guts in there or what."

Lucy scratched the dog's neck fondly. "He doesn't have to pee, but he likes to go through the motions. Routine is important to immortality."

Ash realized she actually had a lot of questions about Helegar. It would be ironic if an immortal dachshund turned out to be the key to understanding the struggle between good and evil. "Then we should find a park for him."

"I only know one park in New York," Lucy said. "We didn't exactly christen it with pleasant memories."

"Central Park it is." Ash changed lanes again.

"Slow down a second."

When she did, Lucy sent her window the rest of the way down, and before Ash could ask what she was doing, she'd leaned out of the opening. "Hey! Break a leg! You're gonna be amazing! Murder that second verse!"

The woman she was shouting encouragement to grinned and waved back, her soul reaching for Lucy like a silken rope.

Whatever else the devil was, she was *Lucy* through and through.

VI.

THE NORTH WOODS

> The future is yet full of trial and success. There is happiness to be enjoyed! There is good to be done! Exchange this false life of thine for a true one.
>
> NATHANIEL HAWTHORNE, *THE SCARLET LETTER*

"ONION SAUCE?" THE woman hovered the paper boat that held Lucy's hot dog over the condiment tray.

"Absolutely. And the sauerkraut."

"Mustard?"

"Yes! And a hot pepper. *Two* hot peppers."

The vendor piled the traditional toppings onto a hot dog, then tucked a folded napkin into the bottom of the boat with practiced ease. Lucy bounced on the balls of her feet, her navy coat unbuttoned and her scarf hanging longer on one side than the other. She'd located a leather tote in the back seat of Ash's car that produced fingerless gloves and a knitted beanie. The tote was the perfect size for carrying Helegar, who panted hopefully in the hot dog vendor's direction, his eyes on the paper boat.

"And one hot dog for my son, no bun, no toppings." Lucy smiled at the vendor, who had black hair and a square jaw and well-muscled forearms, and who winked back as she pulled a steaming frank out of the chafing dish. Lucy pinched it, offering it to Helegar. He took it down in three rough bites, then burped a cloud of sulfur-scented meat vapor.

Ash shuddered.

"Anything for your friend?" The vendor didn't bother to look at Ash when she asked this. She'd already put the heavy stainless lid over the hot dogs and the plastic cover over the condiments, and she was taking a twenty that Lucy had magically produced, winking again when Lucy waved away the change.

"A pretzel." Ash shoved her hands into the pockets of her jacket, stomping her feet on the pavement. She'd worried a bit that they'd draw attention with Helegar in tow, but Central Park was quiet on a cold weekday afternoon. She'd even found street parking.

When they'd gotten out of the car, Lucy had told her she was hungry in a tone of voice Ash didn't understand. It took her a minute to figure out that Lucy was *excited* to be hungry. She rarely ate, it turned out.

The hot dog wasn't just a hot dog.

The vendor handed Ash her pretzel, salt ticking over the paper and falling to the ground, then accepted the crumpled bills that Ash found in her wallet. It was the last of her cash—no magic tote bag money for her.

"You have a good one." The vendor smiled at Lucy. The muscles in the woman's forearms couldn't have come from selling hot dogs. They were a little showy, honestly.

"See you around." Lucy held eye contact with the vendor while biting into her hot dog. A smooth wave of emerald-gold poured from the vendor's heart to brush past Lucy's cheeks.

"All right. Enough of that." Ash took her companion by the elbow and turned her away from the cart. It sat just off Central Park North. They chose the path that went deeper into the park and turned onto one of the few trails that cut through the North Woods.

Lucy ate her hot dog in big bites as they walked, and Helegar snored from inside her bag. On the surface, all of it was a version of one of the many plans they'd had as girls. Ash would move to New York, and Lucy would take the train in from Cambridge, where she attended MIT to study math. They'd spend the weekend walking around. Lucy would come to Ash's shows at night, and they'd snatch a few hours' sleep before nursing their hangovers at Ess-a-Bagel with hot six a.m. bagels piled with an inch of cream cheese. They'd get to-go coffees to fuel them on their stroll west across the park for the first show at Hayden Planetarium.

They were the intricately embroidered fantasies of two Midwest girls who believed they could make anything happen if they talked about it all the time, daydreamed together, and didn't listen to anyone who said otherwise.

Lucy kicked a clod of ice. "How's your pretzel?"

"Salty." She tore the last piece in two. "Did you want to try it?"

"Ooh, now we're breaking bread." Lucy raised her eyebrows.

Ash stuffed both pieces in her mouth, feeling ridiculous. "How do we do this?" she asked after choking the pretzel down. "Because I'm going to bail if everything we do has to be laced with meaning."

"How should I know? It was your idea." Lucy crossed her arms, slowing her pace. If there had been wind, it would be freezing, but the overcast day was holding, keeping the weather just this side of tolerable as long as they didn't stop moving. "Tell me why you came here, I guess. Not now. Last time."

"It was impulsive." The lie made her nostrils burn, her eyes sting, and her ears ring. She blinked away the tears, hoping Lucy wouldn't notice.

Impulsive was what she had told her dad. Calliope. Hector. The manager at the temp place. The truth was that escaping to New York had centered itself as her primary fantasy within hours of her first fight with Lucy. She never talked about it. She never wrote anything down or looked anything up on the internet. She hid New York from everyone—hid it as much as she could from herself—afraid that if she made real plans, she would burn to literal ashes. When she did pack a bag and buy a plane ticket, telling no one, it was only because burning no longer scared her. She had felt ashamed for so long that shame had become her most familiar companion.

God, the *hope*, though. Ash hadn't been able to eat or drink on the plane to LaGuardia, her stomach was churning so much. She'd tried to sleep, only to be jabbed awake by the Technicolor flashes of that hope—just for small things, like getting another tattoo or going dancing where she couldn't hear anything but the beat. Nothing more ambitious than that.

"I don't believe you," Lucy said with a shake of her head. "I can't pretend to know what you felt, but I know I didn't want to fight you anymore. I didn't want to feel any of the ways that I had been feeling. I didn't want my free will to be tied to destroying you." She stopped walking, her eyes on the path ahead. "You couldn't stay, though, could you?"

"I almost didn't make it home."

"Choosing a life for yourself nearly killed you."

Ash shoved her hands in her pockets, worrying the silky lining where it was coming away from the leather. She knew what Lucy wanted her to hear—that it wasn't *her* who was responsible for what happened to Ash in New York. She had wanted to stay away. She'd been called unwilling to Central Park, where she was confronted with Ash's broken body. Broken by the *curse,* not by Lucy.

But how could Lucy explain what she did next? If what she had done to Ash among the trees wasn't *her,* and it wasn't the devil, then who or what was it? Because *that* was the part Ash tried never to think about.

Lucy crouched down, opening her tote. Helegar leapt out of it onto the path. His bones clattered like dominoes in a line, flicked by a finger. He stretched, his forelegs low and his pelvis high, his sightless skull yawning so big that a tooth rattled from its socket and dropped into the dirt.

Lucy arched an eyebrow at Ash's obvious distaste. "There isn't anyone around. It makes him tired to disguise himself to look like a regular dog."

"His disguise does not in any way make him look like a regular dog." She watched him run in circles down the path, his muzzle to the ground as though he could really smell everything through his hollow skull.

"Do you believe me that I didn't want to fight you?" Lucy sounded uncertain as she picked up and threw a stick for Helegar. "That I tried to leave you be?"

Ash got to the stick just as Helegar did. He looked at her hopefully, but her expression must have told him what he needed to know, because he picked it up and carried it to Lucy. "I think so."

"I hated that I'd been pulled along. Then I saw the condition you were in, and I hated it even more. I never *didn't* hate it, but that was a turning point where I started to *care* about hating this curse again. Hating everyone who came before us. Hating the original Steadfast and Prynne who made it, sang it, wrote it on a piece of parchment with blood—however it got into us."

"Yeah." Ash thought she should probably say something more than *yeah*, but she couldn't get past what Lucy had just made her realize. When she dragged herself home from New York last year, she was angry, too. Not resigned. Not recommitted to the cause. Not dogged or steadfast. *Angry* that she couldn't escape. Angry at everything the curse had taken from her. Angry at whatever god had made this futile, preposterous world.

Lucy took the stick that Helegar had buoyantly brought back with one end threaded through an empty eye socket in his skull. She turned to face Ash. They were both breathing hard from trudging up and down the hills of the path in the cold. The overcast weather had settled into a fog full of frost, making the trees indistinct. "You said in the Holland Tunnel that you didn't know you could do this." Lucy gestured around the woods. "Portfenestrate. You didn't know that I don't exist without you, either. What do we know, Ashes? Not what our dads told us, not what we assumed or guessed or were afraid of. What we *know*."

Ash tried to think about what she'd learned as a kid and experienced a sensation like trying to find her footing on the surface of the moon. She shoved her hands deeper into her pockets. "I know what I've seen you do." Her steps hit a rhythm like marching that her heart beat in time to.

"Which is what?"

"I've seen you play chess at a crossroads with a man who wanted a particular piece of property. I've seen you tempt women—like that hot dog vendor, for example—and pocket their souls like a tip."

"*Tempting?* That's what you thought was going on with the hot dog lady?" Lucy twisted to look behind them as though the woman might still be visible. "I was just being friendly!"

"You've never stopped asking me what I want, especially when I'm exhausted from a fight, even more especially when I won't talk to you and have been working hard to avoid you. I've seen tricks, Luce." This was easier to talk about. "The mirages. Your glamours. How you can appear next to someone on a barstool just as they've started to give up. Or join a party and make people believe they can have love, and they'll get their happily ever after. The kind of thing that could be called witchcraft. Devious stuff."

Lucy looked like she was hanging on to her patience with both hands. It wasn't dissimilar from the expression she'd had right before she trebucheted Ash through Green Bay. "You still don't believe I'm real." Her voice was a snappish scrape over sandpaper. "But do you *know* I'm not?"

Helegar stopped running in circles around them. He turned his head to look at her with a soft whine of protest. "I can't know. No one lives their lives like we do. I know I'm a Steadfast. My job is to fight the devil. The Prynne. If I don't, I suffer. You're telling me not to believe what I've seen, that what you do isn't what it looks like, but you haven't offered me any other explanation."

Lucy opened her mouth to protest, but then she stopped. "Look where we are."

Their ambling walk had taken them to the woods where Ash's brief dream of New York came to an end.

By the time she'd come here, the sores had spread from her skin to the membranes inside her ears and nose and mouth, in her armpits, between her legs. She'd been certain the curse would kill her if she stayed. The Brigade was drawing closer, stalking at her heels as she walked down the sidewalk, and she'd started to believe she would welcome whatever nightmarish thing was destined to happen when they caught her.

But first she'd wanted to see Lucy.

Ash had been sure she would find her here. She'd trudged along, distracting herself from the tender pain of her crusted and seeping feet by thinking of the shape of Lucy's widow's peak and the fine, short hairs that curled into circlets between her ears and temples.

"Ashes."

Only one person said her name that way. Ash had lifted her eyes from the path to a vision of Lucy.

Not the devil. Her Lucy, with roses in her cheeks, wearing an oversize cabled sweater, leggings, and boots, and holding a steaming mug of hot chocolate. Ash had been so overwhelmed with relief, she'd bitten the inside of her cheek hard enough to taste pennies.

This was what she knew. One thing she knew.

She remembered that Lucy's scratchy voice was an oasis in the desert that her own ruined body had become.

She remembered that Lucy didn't try to tempt her or take what was left of her when she was down.

She remembered saying a giant mental *fuck you* to the universe, to three-hundred-plus years of Steadfasts, and beginning to imagine how fucking incredible it would feel to kiss Lucy after days and days of feeling bad. When she'd reached her on the path, she had taken Lucy's hand. It had been a long time since she'd held it, but it felt entirely the same.

Ash opened and closed her hand inside her jacket pocket now, remembering the pleasure.

Then she had been on the ground next to Lucy, face-to-face, soft grass underneath them.

"You told me about a job," Ash said.

"That wasn't—"

"I'm not saying you tempted me. I'm telling you I remember. You told me about a job I could have if I wanted."

"Yes. I did."

Her sandpaper voice had described a sweet full-time gig doing reception alongside sessions work for an indie label. Even better, she'd heard about a spot in an up-and-coming ensemble that needed a bass player. "You can have it all," Lucy had said. "A job that pays enough for a studio apartment with a manageable commute. Health insurance. Friends, music, opportunities. I checked everything. It's taken care of."

The pain in her body had begun pushing toward her fingers and toes, then leaving. It was such a relief that it made her feel high. She'd gazed at Lucy's overgrown hair, as long and tempestuous as she'd ever seen it, and wanted to put her face in it. She'd lost her grip, or let it go—she wasn't sure which.

"Everything you've ever wanted can be yours," Lucy had said. "You deserve that, Ashes. You've worked so hard. You've earned it, and these folks you'll be playing with are so excited to meet you. You'll heal up once I'm gone. Give it a week or so. The rest of your life can begin."

She remembered how Lucy's sweater smelled, how the prickly wool felt against her cheek, what it had been like to finally be in her arms. She'd never wanted to leave. "But will you stay with me?" she'd asked the rise and fall of Lucy's chest. "What will you do?"

Ash let herself return to the moment now, permitting her blood to beat in syrupy pulses at her elbows, behind her knees, between her legs. Lying together, she and Lucy had lingered at the delicious pause at the cusp of a safe sleep, like the purring of a cat nestled in the crook of an arm, or the long beat of certainty before the torrent of an orgasm.

And then Ash remembered, with a dip in her middle, that in the space between their hearts, their souls plaited together, gold and rose, and formed a braid as intricate as the cables of Lucy's sweater.

"Wait," she'd said. "Lucy. Where will *you* go?"

Ash had caught the tail of her own soul in her fist. It was slippery, hot, alive. It wanted Lucy.

"Don't worry about that part," Lucy had said, reaching for her. "Don't worry, baby."

Now, Ash put her hands to her temples and surfaced from her memories like rising from a warm bath to stand naked in a freezing-cold room.

Her hand had gripped her own soul as it tried to swamp

Lucy's, to take it over, take it into itself—and Ash knew that she'd seen this happen because Lucy was trying to make space in the world for her by *taking her own soul out of it.*

A soul that Ash hadn't known Lucy still possessed.

She'd torn herself away and wrenched her body from the ground. The pain dumped over her like embers from a metal pail. She'd stumbled away from Lucy, then ran. Her soul lagged behind as the blood blisters burst on her tender feet.

Lucy hadn't chased her.

She hadn't asked for Ash's soul that day in these woods. She had been willing to give up her own.

That was what Ash knew.

That was what Ash tried never to think about, and for good reason. Her fucking *feelings.* Being here, remembering, her heart felt like it had been pierced through a year ago, the cold steel of this memory lodged inside it ever since. She wiped her face dry with the backs of her hands and looked at Lucy in her bright rainbow scarf, holding Helegar in her arms. "I think," she said, choosing her words carefully, "maybe the roles we're playing are bigger than us. We're something's puppets. Whatever that something is, we're meant to fight until it kills us both."

Lucy's grimace as she set Helegar down was expected, but it still twisted Ash's stomach in a knot. "If we're going to die fighting, wouldn't you rather be fighting against the curse than for it? I've given up on convincing you I'm not the devil, not in the way you think, so I don't expect you to—"

"Stop. Hang on." Ash put her hand up, her head suddenly full of the image of the Devil from Calliope's tarot card and the incredible fact that her friend had been visited by Helegar and seen visions of Ash and Lucy. Cal had seen Ash turn into the devil. She'd strongly suggested that Ash didn't have the whole picture. So had Lucy. So had Hector. "Don't tell me what you think *I* think. Tell me what you mean."

"This is new, Ashes!" Lucy flung her arms wide. "We went to Roger's Field, and we found that carving in the tree together. Then I'm zwooped to the passenger seat of your Corolla—which, teenage you would die, by the way, if she found out you still drove that car—and now we're here in the place you went when you were ready to try something *different*. Here, where I almost talked you into letting me go so that at least *one* of us could get what we wanted."

"But why sacrifice yourself for me? I don't understand."

Lucy shook her head once, hard. "Not getting into that."

Now that Ash had stepped over the threshold of the things she had been most unwilling to contemplate, to talk about, it was hard to pull back. "Okay, but I think it's important. So far, when we put together what we know, we know the basic lore of the curse. Your witchy ancestor and my general of the Dead and Righteous Brigade made a pact, right? Or a deal. They composed a curse that meant their fight would continue in each generation."

"Why, though? Was the idea that one of their descendants would eventually win? What would that look like?"

"Hell on earth, I thought. If I gave up. Surrendered. Like, if you took my soul, it would fuck up the cosmic balance." Ash blew out a breath, trying to remember where she'd gotten that idea from, but the result was the same stumbling sensation inside her head that she'd felt earlier. Something wrong. She put a pin in it. "Truth be told, I don't know if Rye told me that or I made it up. We do know that we're given the strength to fight, that you commune with souls—"

"Thank you for leaving it at that."

"You're welcome." Another mental pin went into the question of what Lucy was doing with the souls *exactly*, if she didn't turn them over to a red man in a flaming chamber of the underworld. "We know you're only here when I am. That I can't experience pleasure or sin without physical consequences."

"We should talk at some point about how genuinely disturbing that is."

Ash rolled her eyes. "We know our fathers held off the violence of the curse by filibustering it, but my dad died anyway, and then your dad disappeared."

"Does Rye have any powers left that you know of? Or do you know what they were before?"

"Not a clue. What about Draven?"

Lucy shrugged.

"Okay. We know that the former Steadfasts have been following me around, menacing me to do better. That's gotten a ton more intense since I came back from New York. Given everything else, it makes me think that they might feel like the curse is threatened. Which is probably good?"

"Who has been what now?" Lucy threw the stick for Helegar again, her expression horrified.

"You don't see them? The shadow people. Figures. They circle around us when we fight. Sometimes follow me. There's a heavy vibe of judgment, which is why I always assumed they were my family."

"Jesus, Ashes. Do you hear yourself right now?"

"And yesterday, right after I left you in Roger's Field, I saw a woman who I think is some ancient relative of yours. She's pissed at me."

"For fuck's sake." Lucy pushed her fingers over her eyes. "All right. Well, I've started dreaming."

"I thought you didn't sleep."

"I don't, not in the regular sense. I want to. It sounds good. Even after we've had it out, I always try to hang on to the world for as long as I can. I want to *stay.* Like, maybe I could go to my dad's old haunts and find him, spend more time with Helegar, make a friend, and, yes, rest. Sleep. I'm not tired, but I remember tired, and my feelings are tired. You can't even understand how amazing that hot dog tasted and how good it feels to wear seasonally appropriate clothes and smell exhaust and urine and trees and twenty other notes that make up New York. But, yeah, I'm having dreams."

"What does the devil dream about?"

"What do *you* dream about?"

"Bad things," she admitted. "A woman screaming in labor. Claws sinking into my chest. Rotten vegetables and manure thrown in my face while I kneel in the mud, my head and arms locked into stocks. Creatures following me, or crouching into corners." Ash met Lucy's huge, dark eyes. "I dream about you splitting my throat open."

The color drained from Lucy's face. "*Me,* cutting your throat."

"Yes. That was bad."

"If that's what you remember happening"—Lucy didn't move her eyes away from Ash's—"I guess I can understand why it would be a nightmare."

Her steady gaze rattled what was left of Ash's composure. She blurted a question to make it go away. "What dreams are you having, then?"

"A woman." Lucy tried to smile. "She's beautiful. Tall. Dresses like a model or a performer. She has mile-long eyelashes and colorful makeup. Long hair with a perfect blowout and a soft, shiny beard."

Every muscle in her body went stiff with shock. "What's her name? The woman."

"Calliope. I can tell it's a dream because even though it's vivid, she knows things only I know about myself and my history."

She would. Ash had told her things.

But nothing she had told Calliope could explain this.

"She's the one who reminded me how I felt the last time I was here," Lucy said. "That I hated it because I was hurting you, making you sick. And that all I wanted to do was figure out how to leave, and to leave you here to have something of what you wanted so one of us could."

Ash hoped she wasn't shaking in disbelief. Cal had been reaching out to Lucy in dreams. She'd been engaging Lucy with memories that suggested the North Woods hadn't been the site of a battle between Ash and Lucy, but something else.

Or all of this was a lie, and Ash had been driven deeper into delusion by the devil than ever before, with Calliope holding the reins.

She dismissed the thought. "Who do you think this woman in your dreams is?"

"Well, she says she's an angel."

"Fuck me." Ash put her hand over her mouth, trying to hold

in what shock she could, and of course that was when Helegar started barking, loud and deep, and ran ahead on the path until he disappeared from view.

"What the hell!" Lucy took off after Helegar, with Ash close behind.

They ran uphill. Helegar was already on the other side. Less sun hit this part of the trail, and Ash's boots kept finding ice patches until it was all she could do to keep from falling.

"Helegar, for fuck's sake!" Lucy was out of breath. There was a high yip, and then the dog stopped barking. "Helegar!"

"Wait!" Ash yelled after her. Lucy had surely forgotten that no real harm could come to an immortal dachshund who had the run of multiple dimensions, which meant that it was actually she who was in danger from whatever Helegar was activated about. Ash got to the top of the hill and ran down toward Lucy's brightly covered scarf. When she got to her—standing in a wide clearing in the middle of the path, with Helegar wiggling in her arms—she stopped and bent over, hands on her knees, panting.

"Ashes." There was something unidentifiable in Lucy's voice that made the little hairs on the back of Ash's neck stand up. "Look."

At first, she thought Lucy was pointing at the tree. It was so massive that it had to be an original tree to Central Park. An oak, its trunk was palpably heavy, as big as a small house, and its first ring of branches could have supported the Brooklyn Bridge.

Even more unbelievable than its size was that it was in full leaf, thick with deep green, scalloped leaves rattling in a breeze that Ash hadn't felt kicking up.

The air was warm. The fog had lifted.

But Lucy wasn't pointing at the tree. She was pointing at the woman.

Her dark hair fell to her waist. Her dress met the ground, unrelenting black. Her arms were crossed.

"Ashes Steadfast." The woman's voice was loud and deeply irritated. "High time, wouldn't you say?"

"Ashes, do you *know* this person?"

"And Lucy," the woman said. "Good afternoon."

She looked back at Ash and furrowed her brows with something that moved her irritation into the category of anger. "I'm Hester Prynne."

VII.

HP + AD

Here was the iron link of mutual crime, which neither he nor she could break. Like all other ties, it brought along with it its obligations.

NATHANIEL HAWTHORNE, *THE SCARLET LETTER*

Massachusetts Bay Colony, the Beginning and the End

HESTER LISTENED TO the pair of snowy owls that had nested in an oak tree outside the cabin. Their low hoots to each other as they hunted broke through the sound of wind in the forest. A comfort.

She'd been afraid when Roger announced he was leaving her at this colony while he traveled to England on business. She'd married him with security on her mind, a pragmatism that didn't match her youth. Her friends were appalled. Roger was in many ways appalling. He was older than her own father, but all those years had seemed to teach him nothing but self-interest and how to count money.

Of course, those two attributes were what Hester was capitalizing on. She wanted security, and she wanted to be left alone. And in the darkest part of the night, dark like it was now, she could be honest and admit that his age was an attribute in another way. When she had asked her father to negotiate the marriage to ensure a handsome settlement came to her upon Roger's death, it had been the first time her father realized that Roger wasn't using his power as a rich man to overpower his family and claim Hester.

Hester was using Roger's pridefulness against him to take care of herself.

She was certain her father didn't know whether to admire her or be chilled by her mercenary scheming, which told her that even he had never been convinced of what Hester believed—that her body and her life belonged utterly to her.

While she was aware of Roger's interests in the Massachusetts Bay Colony, as well as his religious affiliations, she hadn't known enough to take either seriously. She was more than willing to travel to the colony as long as he didn't exercise his right to the marital bed. She had no interest in pregnancy on the journey, or in being forced to stay in Massachusetts in confinement, with a babe, and then to weaning.

He agreed to her condition. The ease of his agreement should have been a warning for Hester to heed, but she let herself enjoy the journey. She let herself revel in the power and comfort she had on Roger's arm in the colony, unpacking crates of beautiful English goods in his two-story, square-cornered house, so new the wood smelled fresh and the fireplace bricks glowed bright.

He came into her room early one morning when it was pitch-dark. He told her he would be traveling back to England on a ship that launched at dawn, and before Hester could integrate her confusion at this announcement, her night rail was over her head and his forearm braced across her chest. He didn't seem so old in his determination to anchor his child inside her, to leave its chain around her ankle in this place.

She had never been so glad to get her courses, and never so angry to be stashed securely away like a chest of expensive goods. He had checked her very neatly.

Six months later, he wrote from England to tell her on what vessel he would be returning and the date. It was only when she understood he would be in these rooms with her in ten weeks' time that she felt as though she'd squandered her freedom. She had been lucky, but her luck wouldn't hold. She spent the two and a half months learning herbs and medicine from a woman who lived in the margin between town and the forest boundary. She learned to make teas to keep a child from taking root and teas to weed one from her womb. She hoped she could avoid a life of growing, birthing, weaning, washing, and burying in an endless cycle stopped only by irrelevance and a widow's bonnet or death.

Roger was ten weeks overdue when gossip began to spread that he wouldn't return. Soon after, word arrived of the shipwreck. Another vessel spotted identifiable debris. A total loss.

She was writing a letter to Roger's solicitors when Faithful Steadfast called on her.

Until that afternoon, her contact with the powerful farmer had been limited. Though her husband had a few dealings with him, she was not social with the severe and pietistic Steadfasts. But Faithful had not come on a social call. He had come in his position as a church elder, though he was not much older than Hester. He informed her he'd been told she had registered Roger's death at the church.

She had.

He asked her if the body was to be received in England or Massachusetts.

It was a shipwreck, she told him. Roger's body was at sea.

Without a body, he told her, and without a Christian burial, Hester was not a widow. Faithful had reached out to Roger's solicitor to tell him the same, citing Roger's affiliation with the church and sharing his documented wishes in this regard.

Hester had received this declaration as only a first gambit, but it wasn't a year before she was truly alone, still married, and without any funds. They were Roger's, and Roger was to be considered alive until, as far as Hester could ascertain, Faithful Steadfast said he was not.

Which was how she found herself here, in a dead wisewoman's cottage at the edge of the forest, where a pair of owls spoke to each other in the dark while she listened to her lover breathe.

"You're awake." Arthur turned in the narrow bed and reached to thumb the soft lobe of her ear. Hester smiled.

"Did I wake you?"

"No. A dream. It was strange." He wound his free arm around her under the quilt. "It was summer. You were in the woods, bare to the waist. Like holding a mirror to a mirror, there were thousands of iterations of you standing behind you, but as I move closer, I see that they aren't you. They're all different people, and they're looking at me expectantly. You look at me and tell me, 'I won't let you sacrifice them.'" Arthur kissed her forehead. "And then I woke up."

"Odd." Hester kissed Arthur back, but on his neck under his ear, on his throat, then his mouth, where she lingered as the arm around her waist tightened. He moved over her, rubbing his tongue against hers, deepening the kiss until they were sighing into each other's mouths, desperate.

He teased her this time, his fingers soft, without any rhythm, making her helplessly wet and begging. He kissed down her body while she smiled at the rafters of her cottage. He found her with his mouth, and when she gasped, she inhaled the volatile oils from the herbs hung and dried there—wood betony, skullcap, agrimony, pennyroyal.

In that long, hitching moment before he kissed her again and sank inside her, she felt that she belonged to the world as perfectly as those herbs belonged to her garden and to the secret places under the trees.

It wasn't until they were spent and panting, their skin cooling, that she looked over at the chair near her bed. There was the stack of his clothes, neatly folded, and on top the collar he kept clean and snowy to wear under his chin, over his heart, while he spoke the words of a God he believed loved him more than Hester ever could.

He was wrong about that.

He was wrong the way men were always wrong about a woman's capacity to love, to forgive, to accept, and to gild and embroider any love they received from a man until it shone bright enough to seem equal to their love for him.

The secret child in her belly fluttered in the aftermath of

their lovemaking. A child made from nothing but love, and perfect. A child Hester had allowed to happen, following a feeling she sometimes labeled foolishness and sometimes power and sometimes fate.

It wouldn't matter if he wouldn't stand for them. She would. She was already.

HESTER WRAPPED THE hemp twine tightly around the stems of the boneset, the vegetal aroma of the plant on the edge of making her sneeze.

At the hearth, Helegar gnawed a marrow bone, his red coat shining in the firelight. From time to time, he looked up at his mistress with bright brown eyes and a wagging tail.

The end of the summer had caught her by surprise. She'd been spending her days in her cottage, processing plants and herbs heaped in wide seagrass baskets. She should have had more infused oils and salves stocked by now, her medicinal and cooking herbs dried and packed into linen bags and crocks. She'd given over too much time to long walks, stretching out her stiff muscles and warming the tight swelling in her joints that had been bothering her more every year.

She'd spent even more time dreaming, if she were honest (and she always was), sitting in her chair in the front of the cottage with a tisane and her eyes closed, her ears full of birdsong. She wasn't dying, that wasn't it, though she was at peace with the idea of death. She simply felt less and less interested in the occupations she had driven at for years.

But there would be sick people in the winter. There would be babies born and babies failing. There would be young women who needed help getting pregnant, help avoiding another child, help ending their pregnancies, and help tolerating and surviving the burden of pregnancy.

There would be old men with toes bursting with gout, and old women, like Hester, who needed the relief that came from herbs that set a false spring in their step as their bodies fought against never having babies again.

They came. Even though the old ones said she was the devil (and even as those same old ones visited her cottage for their cures and poultices).

She *was* the devil, of course, but that was most true when Faithful came around, enraged that Goody Ashford had brought in an excellent crop of rye when everyone else's fields had failed in the wet weather, or that Mary Billingsley had announced her betrothal to the handsome and prosperous son of the Archers even though she was late into her twenties and had been born with a crooked back.

He blamed these changes in fortune, in predestination, on her. The deal he had made meant, in his view, that Hester was the only dissembler of God's will.

When she reminded him that this was what he'd wanted, he cursed her. When she reminded him that his deal had laid on her head the vision to see his parishioners' souls, he cursed her. When she suggested that he might instead have kept his word and let love take its course and time politely ignore the details, he cursed her, and then he forced them into the theatrics that left them both bloodied and tiresome, she was sure, to the God she prayed to (not Faithful's).

Her biggest problem, however, wasn't that she was behind in her work. It wasn't Faithful, who came around less often as he refused help for what she heard was the very ordinary problem of a slow dribble from his dull and inanimate cock.

It was what would come next, after one or both of them was gone.

Hester was motivated to keep him healthy. First, she had no interest in fighting his pietistic nephew, Avenging Steadfast. Second, her daughter, Pearl, was busy with her own matters, her own children, and after a long, sad three years following the early and sudden death of her husband, she had recently installed Constance, the wife of her heart, into her household.

Hester hung the boneset up in front of the window where there was a breeze and grabbed liniment to rub into her hands when there was a pounding on her door.

"Devil Prynne!"

She sighed as Helegar growled and then gave a warning bark. Faithful. She had no hope he had come to see her for his own good.

She opened the door just as his fist was pulled back for another pounding. "Reverend Steadfast. I would invite you in, but I've just lit brimstone in the hearth, and the sound of the vanquished souls burning is a bit loud."

He stepped away from the threshold and stomped to the middle of the yard, making a rough beckoning motion with his hand.

"Yes, thank you. Let's converse outside." Hester looked briefly upward and prayed for the patience she had never once had, then put a hand up to keep Helegar from following as she shut the door. "Shh, my sweet hound. I need you most for comfort. Don't involve yourself with the complaints of men."

Faithful spun on the heel of his shining box-leather boot

(not what Hester would consider sartorial humility) to point at her. "You have gone too far. You have betrayed the terms of the deal."

"Have a seat?" Hester gestured at the chairs in her yard.

Faithful reached behind him and pulled out a knife. "I'm done. I'll burn in hell for making a deal with the devil, but I won't take another breath or see you breathe while my nephew suffers from your evil."

"You've come here to kill me?" Hester adjusted her position so that no simple move on his part could result in his knife stuck between her ribs. She took a breath and pulled the elements closer to herself, feeling the temperature drop and the air dampen in such a way that it might affect his aching joints. "What's wrong with Avenging?"

Faithful took a step closer. "You choose to die with feigned innocence on your lips?"

"Save your dramatics. Why are you here?"

"You knew I would come. You knew I wouldn't let Avenging go—"

"Unavenged? Tell me, what am I accused of this time?"

"Your spell work has done its worst. Even now, he's been reduced to dunking his body in the icy water of Gilbert's Pond to alleviate the irritation of the pestilent welts you've set on him." Faithful coughed. His lips were dusky, and not from pursing too tightly in disgust. His collar was soaked with sweat. He wasn't slurring his speech, but his words came even more slowly than usual, and a glance at the hilt of the knife revealed the skin on the backs of his hands mottled and his nail beds white.

"Faithful." Hester made her voice loud and firm. "You're ill. Sit down."

He took a step toward her. "What I am is dying. I won't last the night. But I won't be dragged into Hell until I take you with me—or Avenging is restored."

She hadn't seen Avenging for at least a fortnight. When she had, he was healthy, or as healthy as a young man could be who wore a vest of woven horsehair under his clothes in full August. His wife had recently borne his eighth son, though the oldest wasn't twelve.

Hester wasn't cognizant of the precise workings of the deal Faithful had forced on them both during the terrible time when Pearl was young and Arthur recently lost to her. She did know that this ridiculous fight was doomed to go on until, she assumed, the Steadfasts came to their senses. That is, if her own descendants were sensible, which they very well might not be. Pearl was a good mother, but the community might tempt Pearl's children, or their children, into abusing the power bestowed by the deal.

What she didn't know was whether, once Faithful died, she would face Avenging or her beloved Pearl would.

Both were terrible options. If Avenging were afflicted with what was killing Faithful, then what? She could only guess at the ways an oath made in bad faith, from belief in the evil inherent in another person's dreams and desires, might make their descendants suffer.

The pact sacrificed their children. And if there was a Hell (which Hester did not believe there was), it was Faithful's willing sacrifice of innocent children that would send him to the flames.

Hester had learned the secular pleasure of hearing the desires of others' souls. She couldn't disparage it or how it secured her power to live as she wished. But she would trade it for her previous exile if her descendants could in return be unbothered.

"Right now, you need to tell me if Avenging is taken with what is killing you." Hester centered the late-afternoon's sun on the crown of her head and drew wind around her. She needed to scare the truth from this weak man.

He squinted, unable to make her out in the light. She could see that he trembled.

"Faithful. Listen. I asked you to let me be a long time ago, and in response you trapped us both. Free me now. Free yourself. Let Avenging and his children go."

Hester was surprised her voice shook so much, but she was crying. Near weeping. She had summoned every last grain and dust mote of love and dignity from this community, from her place in this world, and it had rewarded her with her own ability to love, to have had love, to see Pearl prosper, and to leave her independent. But there had always been a shadow. Even as Arthur claimed Pearl as his daughter, he died, and she was left alone. Even as she returned here and served as a healer and confidante to desires, there was this darkness, poised to cut the throats of those who came after her.

This wasn't God or goodness. She'd known what God was the moment she fell in love with Arthur, when she brought their child into the world, when she sat with him as he transitioned from life to death. The peace that came from love was a gift.

A gift Faithful had spent on righteousness.

Faithful spat on the ground, his saliva thick. He was dying before her eyes, but he held up his knife. "I'll soon give way to the rot of my wretched body, as I should. Avenging is afflicted.

He went from health to sores from the pulpit itself, as he's taken over my collar."

Fuck. Hester sighed, though her heart raced with pain and fear. Faithful wasn't even dead, and it was already beginning. She put her hand on her chest to feel the weight of the wool she embroidered and pinned to her bodice.

"He is afflicting himself," Hester said gently. "Go to him. Put this down. Let him live loving his family. Let him die old and surrounded by all who love him. Not like this. Not like you."

Faithful took a long, shuddering breath, and for a moment, Hester believed he would put an end to it. She would welcome the removal of her worldly powers and the rest of old age without them. Pearl and her beloveds would be free. She could go to Arthur untroubled when she died instead of lingering on, a spirit obsessed with the trials of the living.

"Please." Hester had not once, not ever, begged. But here, now, it was the time to find Faithful's mercy.

He looked at her. His eyes should have been rheumy and far away, fixed on his transition. His body should be wrapped in blankets by a small fire with the sound of the sea on the wind. She had done that for Arthur and many others in their last hours, surrounding them with comfort so they could move in love to the next stage, whatever it might be. Faithful had made her his enemy, but she loved him enough that she would give him that grace. There was no creature alive she wouldn't give it to.

But his eyes were angry. They were focused on Hester with hate. He lifted his knife and stepped right to her, holding the blade level with her throat. "You took everything from me."

She could smell his fear over the rank blight of his corporeal self. She folded her fingers to her palm, catching hold of the glimmer-thin golden thread of his desire—the part of him that believed her and wanted to be changed.

Wanted to be loved.

The thread fattened and yearned toward her, and she reached for it, reached for the salvation of accepting him fully and of him accepting her.

And then he swiped the knife across his own neck and folded to the earth in a pool of blood, choking out his final words. "The devil lies."

She was pulled away into the timeless source of the elements, a place that gave her nothing but a window to generations of needless pain and the duty to try to stop it.

Hester Prynne *would* stop it.

She believed, after all, in love.

VIII.

THE FIRST TESTAMENT OF HESTER PRYNNE

Shame, Despair, Solitude! These had been her teachers,— stern and wild ones,—and they had made her strong, but taught her much amiss.

NATHANIEL HAWTHORNE, *THE SCARLET LETTER*

"YOU HAVE THE Prynne mouth." The woman who called herself Hester sank to the ground, briskly arranging her black skirts around her as Helegar raced to leap into her lap. His tattered elderly fur and flesh grew over his bones, and then he was licking Hester's face, whining in his throat. "My sweet hound," Hester said with a laugh.

"*Your* hound?" Lucy asked.

"What are you doing here?" What Ash actually meant by her question was, *Why are you fully manifested and talking to us now, of all possible times?*

Hester stroked the dachshund as he made circles in her skirts, preparing to nap. "You stopped ignoring me."

It was warm under the tree. Birds began to gather in its branches and sing. Ash was horribly conscious that she was out of practice with feeling. Everything Lucy had said was clanging around in her head, colliding with her own new doubts and questions, ringing against the Devil's card of change that Cal had shown her.

Calliope. Who was an *angel*.

Of course she was. So much about Cal was magical. She was beautiful, love shone from her eyes, her singing voice made audience members cry with wonder. She was a literal diviner, and her fortunes made people see possibilities in their future they strove to realize. There had been moments over the years when Ash felt certain that some kind of enchantment surrounded her, and why shouldn't that be true? Ash herself was subjugated to the will of her ancestors. Anyone who could ease souls back into mortal bodies couldn't truly be surprised to learn that angels were real, or that she knew one. Calliope was the *only* friend she had made since the curse.

"Why are we here?" It was the only question Ash could think of to orient herself on this ever-expanding celestial map of souls, devils, immortality, ghosts, miracle workers, and portal conjuring.

"In New York?" Hester asked. "Or do you mean more in the existential sense?"

Lucy laughed. For Ash, the sound was like taking a particularly fast-acting and highly addictive drug that hit the system like chemical thunder. Unhelpful under the circumstances.

Hester leaned back against the tree. "Did you imagine I brought you here? It seems to me I came to you because you asked, after you'd traveled on your own to where you wanted or needed to be. I would have expected a better question. Something like why I had inserted myself into your business here." The dachshund huffed and opened his rheumy eyes. "Helegar is tired as well. He's been trying so hard to share lessons of his own, showering the Prynnes with his unwavering faith, but alas."

Ash took off her jacket and sat down on it, stretching her legs out in front of her. She knew what to say, but she didn't want to say it aloud. *This is where I found her when I didn't think I could go on. This is where she told me to sacrifice her for my dreams. But that was never the choice—Lucy or my dreams.*

"We fought here" was what she said. "Almost a year ago."

"That's not a question." Hester frowned. "Are you so incurious?"

"All my curiosity has been focused on how many hours I need to work to pay rent and keep myself in black Levi's."

Lucy snorted but pressed her lips together when both Hester and Ash glared at her.

"Tell me about the places you've fought." Hester's demand had a snap to it.

"I don't keep a little map in my diary." Ash knew there was too much mulish sarcasm in her affect, but she had not planned on porting a thousand miles from home only to be taken to school by an otherworldly cosplayer.

"Make a rough list."

Ash sighed. "There was a time at Bay Beach. It's an amusement park in Green Bay."

"We fought there twice," Lucy said. "Once by the water, the second time near and then on the Ferris wheel."

"Where else?"

"The trestles near Luxemburg. The middle of the west side of downtown. There was that business on the athletic field of our old high school. I don't know—honestly, except for the times right here in New York, we've been all over Green Bay, most recently Hector's Tavern. Then we showed up at Roger's Field—"

"Because that's where we had our first fight," Lucy interrupted. "And now we're here. Having a truce."

Ash didn't correct Lucy's terminology. She wouldn't know what else to call it.

Hester folded her hands over Helegar's small form. "Why were those the places where you found yourself with Lucy?"

"I assume because that's where she found people with souls to take."

"But *I'm* the one who would find myself somewhere, with no idea why except I knew I had to wait around for you to show up," Lucy said. "It wouldn't be a tough claim to make that *you* were the one dumping the human soul equivalent of deer apples around town, just so you could catch me in the act."

Ash turned to Hester. "You'll need to get to your point, clearly, or I am going to fight *someone*."

Hester tipped her head, making Ash notice her dark hair, long enough to sweep the grass she sat in. What Ash had taken for a dress at first glance was actually a skirt, shirt, and some kind of bodice with a square neck that buttoned up the front. Her shirtsleeves gathered just above the wrist, rucked together into heavy folds. All the parts of her outfit were black, but they were made of different materials and had slightly different hues. Not cosplay.

She didn't think Hester Prynne was a person, but she had a sense she was not-a-person in a different way than Ash and Lucy were.

"Do you know, Ashes, what the Steadfasts get plenty of but never seem to take advantage of? Second chances."

Something inside her chest came awake. It kicked, a thrashing whiplash of understanding. *Second chances.*

Her first eighteen years had been a study in second chances. Second chances at school, at behaving better for her dad, at getting a song just right, at an audition, achieving the perfect blue for her hair. She'd believed in them. Then pain taught her to believe in whatever delivered her to the next day unscathed and without yearning. Ash would have said she didn't believe in second chances anymore, except she'd brought herself and Lucy back to Central Park, and what was that if not a second chance?

If that was her power—if she *was* the one who drew Lucy out—it meant that some hidden part of her had *chosen* to fight Lucy in the places most important to them. To the two of them. Places that made her chest tight and her eyes sting. And what part of her could that be, if not her soul?

If her soul still had a say in what it wanted. If it couldn't be suppressed by routine or avoidance or pain. If her soul reached out for Lucy and traveled to the places they had been happy or harbored hopes. If her soul was *taking* second chances, bringing her to where she might try.

If all those things were true, then her soul was a tree growing up through a barbed-wire fence. It was hope. Real hope.

Lucy could commune with souls. To her, they were some kind of beautiful truth. No wonder she had been so exasperated with Ash. She really *had* been Lucy all along. Sometimes incandescent with rage, sometimes facetious and petty, sometimes deliberately provocative, but those were moods she might have been in any version of her life. They were human.

Ash didn't blink in and out of existence, and even so, she had been objectively less human than Lucy.

You ridiculous goth.

"But we didn't fight, not this last time in Roger's Field," she said, scrambling to understand. "Or here."

"No. You didn't. I'd say nature was healing, but merely avoiding a fight isn't the same as getting to someplace different." Hester had calloused hands and red knuckles, with round, neat fingernails the same shape as Lucy's. Her mouth was the same shape as Lucy's, too, like she'd said. The Prynne mouth.

Ash resented the implied accusation that she wasn't trying hard enough. She hadn't spent this much time with Lucy in ten years. She hadn't shared a meal with her. She hadn't watched the way her expressions hid and revealed small freckles around her eyes and upper lip. She hadn't been jealous of hot dog cart operators with biceps or let herself remember what it felt like to feel Lucy's scratchy, husky voice against her neck, in the dark.

Even this uneasy truce was enough to remind Ash that she couldn't remember a time when she didn't find Lucy beautiful, even before she fell in love with her. It was enough to convince Ash that her guileless, star-cursed heart had never fallen out of love with Lucy.

But the reason Ash had tried so hard not to think about loving Lucy, wanting her, feeling heartbroken for her, was to avoid what she was feeling right now. Which was terrified.

She was terrified of the stakes that came alongside hope. Terrified that even if heaven and hell and everything in between left the Steadfasts and Prynnes in peace, she and Lucy would still part ways, and if she ever sang a song again—ever held the neck of her bass under colored lights on a stage—it would be to perform songs about losing the woman she loved.

She *was* a ridiculous goth.

She made herself drop her shoulders and take a breath of the overwarm air. "How do we get someplace different?" she asked. "If you're tired and fed up and angry, and no Steadfast has listened to you, and Helegar's messages haven't been picked up by generations of Prynnes, then what are you going to do to help?"

"I'm here of my own free will," Hester said. "I've decided to intervene in Faithful's bargain instead of keeping my place as a guide. I'm ready to rest and be with the people I loved."

Lucy narrowed her eyes at Hester. "If you're done with this, tell us how to undo it, and you can go. You're not the only one who's ready to get on to what's next."

Hester shook out her skirts, making Helegar jump down from her lap to nose around in the grass. "It's not often that a Prynne and a Steadfast know each other well before the oath takes hold. I've watched Prynnes abuse their position. I've watched them run. I've watched Steadfast descendants cut off their noses to spite their faces, and I've watched them suffer. No one can suffer like a Steadfast."

Lucy laughed again, but it was a sad sound.

"Our fathers knew each other before," Ash ventured.

"Not like the two of you. Can't you see?" Hester asked. "They fought until they faded, and then they became shadows with no will or love for anything."

An impulse to defend her father reared up inside Ash, then just as quickly lost its energy.

"I don't care that you've watched generation after generation fuck it up," Lucy said. "You made it so I have to watch, too. I've watched Ashes go numb. It's torture. The thing I seem to be for is feeling people's feelings and desires, but she hasn't got any. I've been asking her for years, 'What do you want?' She thinks I'm trying to weaken her resolve. She can't imagine anything else. And here you are, just *watching*." Lucy crossed her arms, her chin high, her angry dimple sunk into her cheek. "Fuck you for watching. Creeping around when I'm trying to explain, trying to get Ashes to feel, trying to be seen, trying to believe that the way we felt before the curse made any kind of foundation, any kind of anything real, to help us at our worst."

God. Ash willed the film of tears away, swallowing them down until the leaves came into focus. Their deep green color washed to the lobed edges as the middles went deep red and brown. Hester rose to her feet as smoothly as if she'd levitated. The temperature dropped, and the angle of the light changed, revealing the deep gray scuffs in her black leather boots.

"You both think you're different," she spat, in a temper now. "As if life isn't brief, even briefer when you love? Your fathers wasted their love. They might have shown you reasons to adore the world. They might have made you fearless. They might have rejected an inheritance that didn't serve them. How does it feel to keep trying to polish the sharp edges of the rock they put in your shoes instead of taking it out? How does it feel to be here, to have so much space between you, when the people who were supposed to love you best, the parents who witnessed your love for each other, abandoned you to this fight?"

The leaves started to fall, maroon and red and deep brown,

so many that the dry husks brushing against each other in the wind sounded like surf. Ash held a hand out to feel the fall against her palm.

Most of the time, she thought of the person she'd been before as a completely different girl, but wasn't Lucy right? Wasn't she Ash, still? When had she shoved more than her bass into the back of a closet?

And why had only Lucy said anything? Was what she'd become truly what her dad had *wanted* her to be?

Lucy's cheeks and nose were bright red, painful-looking. A vortex of leaves had begun to whirl around her feet.

The leaves came apart, spinning into millions of white crystals of snow, first filling the crooks of the tree's bare branches, then freezing into ice that shrank the tree into one exactly like the others along the path.

Hester was gone.

Helegar began to howl. Lucy picked him up. "Shh. Don't. Don't."

The ordinary sounds of the park filtered in. Faraway car horns, a truck's air brakes, kids at the playground south of the North Woods shouting at each other and their grown-ups, muted by the fog. For Ash, it was always like this—a fantastical otherworldly confrontation followed by insignificant, prosaic life.

She walked over to Lucy, who had her face pressed against Helegar's moth-eaten fur. "You're never around for this part, huh?"

"What part?" Her voice was scratched, broken.

"The part after the big show. When everything is the way it

is for everyone else. That's usually when you've exited stage left."

Lucy met her eyes. "All I want is what's for everyone else. Why don't you?"

"Believe me, Luce, I'm starting to wonder." Ash ignored the way her heart was somersaulting with every beat, making her woozy. She guessed she wasn't dying. She was probably just feeling, finally. "I don't want to be what we've been to each other anymore. I don't want to use what we were against each other. But maybe we can both be the one who gives the other a chance."

Lucy raised her eyebrows.

Ash couldn't smile, not yet, but she did prevent herself from scowling. "I mean in a punk-like way. What if we assume we can destroy it? What if we *know* we can?"

"Like punks." Lucy did smile.

"Yes. Like the big queer punks I always claimed to be and you probably always were, even if it looked more like being a nerd. And then we shake hands, say a pleasant fare-thee-well, and I figure out how to enjoy something or get a hobby. You try to lease an apartment that will let you have a dog so ugly, Instagram would ban his account. Or make him famous. It's hard to call."

"You're terrible at making a pre-quest rousing speech." Lucy kissed the top of Helegar's head and put him on the ground to sniff.

"I'm good at almost nothing." Ash shrugged back into her jacket. "I barely graduated high school, and I've spent the last ten years fighting the devil and making one friend who I haven't given so much as a birthday card. I don't know when her birthday is. I guess she maybe doesn't have a birthday."

"Because you made friends with an angel." Lucy started to walk back the way they had come.

"According to your dreams."

"According to my dreams, yes, which is a new state of consciousness for me and happens to intersect with Calliope the *angel* revealing her powers to you *and* with the last stand of Hester Prynne that we've enjoyed front-row seats to this afternoon. After traveling through a portal."

"Oh, I don't think that's her last stand. She hasn't been shadowing us for a decade just to give us a no-cover floor show and bounce. Roaming ancestors have agendas, I'm pretty sure."

"Why have we been plagued by *my* ancestor, though?" They got to the top of the hill, where Lucy unwound her scarf and unbuttoned her coat. "I'm really feeling a Steadfast is more likely to haunt. They seem more into the menacing. Like, you're brushing your teeth, and boo! There's one looking over your shoulder in the mirror, absolutely disgusted you're not going to floss."

"They do that already, remember? I told you. The figures in black that watch us fight. In my head, I call them the Dead and Righteous Brigade."

"Ashes, that's grim." Lucy dug through her tote and then pulled out a tissue for her cold-induced runny nose.

"It's definitely something. Every time I second-guess myself, they get closer. They're the living embodiment of any kind of imposter syndrome I could have about being a Puritan."

"I hate this for you."

Ash watched Lucy tuck the tissue away and worry her chapped bottom lip.

"Have you noticed anything about your corporeal condition the past few hours?"

"What are you talking about?"

"Panting. Runny nose. Flushed complexion. Hunger. A sudden need for skin care and a brush."

Lucy sent both hands into her tangled hair, haloed by thick frizz around the crown from the multiple magical weathers. "I hadn't. Whoa. Come to think of it, I do feel more like I'm fighting gravity. Like I've just gotten out of the pool. I have a hangnail." Lucy held it up for Ash to see. "Also, I need to pee, but I want to do that somewhere we can also get a snack."

"What do you think it means?"

"Couldn't say, but I don't feel like I'm going to . . . go." She fluttered her hands toward the sky.

"Back to where you do your demonic hibernation, you mean."

Lucy rolled her eyes and immediately tripped on a branch. "Ha! Tell me about your apartment, Ashes. I want to hear about your cool stereo set and the pretty lavender color you picked out for the kitchen. All the art you hung up. Are you doing bamboo sheets? Maybe cotton ones with a kicky print? Or maybe you've gone for a sexier feel, something to take all the women back to so you can have precisely zero Puritan orgasms?"

"You went past touché a couple of digs ago."

"Is it really true?" Lucy stage-whispered, her eyes sparkling. "You can't, you know, get there? What about by yourself? There are a lot of devices on the market that—"

"I take it back." They made it to the paved part of the path. "Our truce is canceled. More to the point, do you have a set of keys in that bag? Something along the lines of money, an ID, or a change of clothes?"

Lucy opened the tote under her arm and peered in. "Oh!" She dove her hand into the bottom. "Yes! Chapstick!" She rubbed it on and recapped it. "That's the good news. Chapstick, tissue, three more twenties, dog treats, a pen, gum, and a lighter. The bad news is there is nothing else along the lines you mentioned."

"Still, if you're, like, *completely* here, then maybe we've already done it. We can drive back to Green Bay—I'm hoping via magic shortcut—and then part ways. I can give you the number of the temp place I work for." Ash tried to keep her voice casual even as her suddenly scratching, complaining, wildcat soul did not feel casual in the least.

"Maybe I can. Ashes, what do you want?"

She started to say something flippant about getting back to her car before she ended up with a ticket, but then the question sank inside her through the top of her head, dropping slowly along every part of her, brushing against dormant desire. The warm flush of her restless soul rose from her sternum and reached toward Lucy. "Fuck."

She had to stop walking, close her eyes, and remind herself that a truce didn't mean sinking her soul into Lucy's . . . anything. The parts of her that had unwound snapped together roughly, making the base of her skull hurt, and then she felt the hot burn of hives everywhere that her clothes touched her skin.

Lucy smiled sadly. "It looks like we're stuck looking for the key to these metaphysical handcuffs linking us together."

Ash tried to laugh at the joke, but she couldn't. It was impossible, after all this time, to watch her soul reach for Lucy, and it was impossible to keep fighting her.

It was impossible to have what she wanted.

Calliope had pulled the Devil's card for her, telling Ash that this time, the devil wasn't who she'd always thought it was.

Lucy was right. They had to find the key that unlocked the bond between them. Lucy deserved freedom.

Ash deserved more than the devil she thought she knew.

IX.

HECTOR TORRES WOULD LIKE A WORD

It is to the credit of human nature, that, except where its selfishness is brought into play, it loves more readily than it hates. Hatred, by a gradual and quiet process, will even be transformed to love.

NATHANIEL HAWTHORNE, *THE SCARLET LETTER*

"OH MY GOD." Lucy shoved a fry into her mouth, dripping chamoy onto her MIT sweatshirt. "You said there were chicken burritos?"

Hector wiped the counter around her. He wrinkled his nose at the wad of used napkins at her elbow before whisking them away. In motion, he was handsome, sharply barbered, with the throwback figure and grace of a dancing musical star like Gene Kelly. "Later. Ovidia made them for our dinner. She'll warm one up for you. We only serve appetizers in the bar."

Lucy nodded, her mouth full. "Cool. And you're sure it's okay for me to stay over? I promise Helegar will behave. It's not like he can ruin the carpet."

Hector and Ash both looked at the dog. Sans fur-trappings, he'd draped his skeleton over a barstool next to Lucy. The tavern was closed for its hour-long break before the second shift got off work. It was dim and quiet with the televisions turned off, every surface still damp from the thorough cleaning Hector had done.

Ash had always liked this tiny ten-table bar. The scent of purple Fabuloso competed with the smell of beer, and Hector and Ovidia brought chamoy to pour over their piping hot fries. Even though Ash couldn't drink, she appreciated a place where a woman in a leather motorcycle jacket with a red-hot scar across her throat could sit alone and not be subject to harassment or questions.

"It's fine for you to stay," he said to Lucy. "It's weird, but it's fine. Ovidia wanted me to tell you she put the clothes she told you about on the bed in the guest room."

"Amazing." Lucy grinned at him. "Thank you."

Hector trained his gaze on Ash, folding his bar towel and lifting an eyebrow. "You said you would explain everything?"

"I did say that." She finished her club soda with lime, moodily pulverizing ice with her back molars until he made a clipped get-on-with-it gesture with his hand. "Let me begin by telling you it's been a *day*."

Ash tried her best to lay out what had happened since the confrontation in his parking lot. She powered through his expressions of incredulity and Lucy's interjections of details that Ash didn't think were necessary to give him the general shape of the situation without completely freaking him out.

After their confrontation with Hester, Ash and Lucy had made it back to the car, blessedly ticket-free. On the way to get bagels, she'd turned down a side street off Central Park North and ended up on Mason Street in Green Bay—a disorienting experience, given it was near-dark and Green Bay didn't have nearly as much urban street lighting as Manhattan did.

"So we came here," she finished, "since, as I mentioned before, Calliope had already told me that you should be a part of this."

"And because Ash doesn't want me to stay at her apartment." Lucy contributed this remark while feeding a fry to her lapdog, making Hector's jaw clench when the chewed-up appetizer fell through Helegar's skull onto his clean floor.

"Pick that up. And you're telling me Cal is an *angel?*" He pulled off his glasses to rub between his eyebrows.

"Sure." Lucy's tone was serenely unaffected by his annoyance. "That's what she said in my dream."

"Cal does have gifts." Ash held up a finger to keep Lucy from adding anything. Hector was about to dial up to a higher level of exasperation, and she didn't want to be on the receiving end. "Clairvoyant gifts that gave her insight into this situation."

"The situation being that one of the parties to the original curse, who has been haunting you, manifested herself in the middle of Central Park on a weekday afternoon to give a stage play of the four elements while telling the both of you she wants you to . . . what?"

"She didn't really say." Ash bit her lip. "It was more of a lecture about how we're fucking up. And how every generation before us has fucked up, maybe especially our dads. But it *feels* like what she wants us to do is something more in the neighborhood of . . . epiphany? Let's say it's getting to the bottom of the entire narrative and questioning everything, just to keep it simple."

"That does keep it simple." Hector's tone wasn't friendly. It was maybe even sarcastic. "And why should we trust this—"

"Ancestor of mine," Lucy supplied.

At the same time, unfortunately, Ash said, "Apparition."

She could tell this characterization did not satisfy Hector's take on the whole situation. Ash wouldn't say she was satisfied, either. The longer she sat on his barstool, the more she felt like something had gotten away from her. Being in close proximity to Lucy while she demolished a large order of fries and a pint of hard cider made the feeling worse.

It was too normal. The three of them. Food. It made *her* feel normal, which made her yearn, because the three of them were not normal. They would never be normal again. She and Lucy were preparing to fight for something that didn't have a clear trophy at the end.

"You think we should be skeptical because she's a Prynne?" Lucy asked. "Because all the Prynnes are devils who harvest souls for the infernal fire?"

"Because she is a fully embodied ancient white colonizer who controls the weather!" Hector barked. "Forgive me for thinking she might have an overarching agenda that she isn't sharing with the class." He slid his glasses back on.

"Which is exactly why, circling back, it's good that Cal thinks you could help us." Ash was well out of practice soothing Hector, but she'd talked him out of an uptight fit enough times to remember the ropes. "Not only do you bring a healthy perspective, but you made it clear the other night that you want this to end. What if you could help bring that about?"

She could tell he was tempted, though she hadn't won over

his caution yet. Ash turned her barstool away from Lucy so she didn't have to look at her while she said what she needed to. "Listen. I need your help, Hector. I've been playing the wrong game on hard mode for a long time, and I don't have any perspective. I might know myself somewhat less well than I thought I did. I have massive trust issues. And I'm possibly a little sad."

That was the ticket. Hector liked to rescue people. He pursed his lips and shook his head, which was what concession looked like on him. "Obviously, I was always going to help you. You two are my best friends. I've missed you. I've never felt right about this thing between you. However." He pushed both hands through his tidy hair, leaving it in disarray. "I have no fucking idea what you expect me to do. I enjoy Cal, but she likes to have fun more than she likes to get to the point."

"We should all get together," Lucy said. How she wasn't glassy-eyed and fully tipsy after a pint of cider following a decade of assumed abstinence was beyond comprehension. "The four of us. Maybe Hester will show, maybe not, but we might be able to get a handle on how to break down our goal of destroying this curse into smaller, more manageable tasks."

"Give me an idea of what the first small, manageable task could be," Hector said skeptically. "As a for instance."

"I know you two think I wave my cloven hooves around singing 'Revolution 9' backward and then another soul gets its horns," Lucy said, "but in fact I consider myself more of a 'heart's fondest desire' guidance counselor. I think I have enough practice to do it for myself."

She hiccupped, and one of her thighs slid on the stool, just a little. Maybe she was less sober than Ash thought.

Hector came around the bar. "All right, time to sleep off the sauce." He took Lucy by the elbow while she hopped down, steadying her as she scooped up Helegar and settled him into her tote. "Remember, top of the stairs, turn left, second door."

"Sleep! I'm so excited. I haven't been horizontal with my eyes closed in a dark room for so long."

She had her foot on the bottom stair when she looked back at the two of them and smiled.

Ash remembered that smile. It was the one that revealed Lucy's slight overbite and her crooked first molar. The one that sank a dimple in the middle of her cheekbone, right under her big brown eyes.

There was a time when Ash's entire occupation had been getting that smile to point in her direction.

This time, the smile wasn't for Ash—it was a gift bestowed on an ephemeral moment—but it didn't matter. Her chest went tight anyway, filling with a humming, low-down buzz. It turned out she still wanted Lucy to have *anything* in her life that made her smile like that.

"Good night." Hector gave Lucy a wave, and she smiled bigger and left.

After an indistinct conversation between Ovidia and Lucy, the door at the top of the stairs closed. The bar fell completely quiet. It seemed like it had gotten darker, as well.

"Ashes Lorelai Steadfast."

She jumped. She had still been looking at the entrance to the stairs. She hadn't said anything to Hector for she didn't know how long, but he'd used her whole name, so it had been longer than an amount of time that would have prevented her broadcasting to him that she was Having a Feeling.

"Hector Juan Garcia Villanueva Torres." She turned her head. He looked worried. Guilt gripped her by the scruff and shook her a little. "You're going to be a good dad," she said. "Twins, though! Wasn't your mom a twin? Do they run in the family?"

He leaned on the bar. "What are you doing?"

"What you've said you wanted more than once. Breaking this curse, releasing generations from a bad bargain, resigning from duty, et cetera. Enough has happened to make this feel like a ripe moment. Lucy and I agree. Imagine that!" She clapped her hands together, a too-loud sound. "It should be worth trying. Maybe we'll unwittingly get ourselves tossed into a fresh hell no one saw coming, but there's not a whole lot to be done about the vagaries of supernatural will and predestination."

He did not smile at this overbright speech. "I meant what are you doing with Lucy?"

A lashing of welts laddered up her back from the waistband of her jeans, hot and stinging—a response to the pleasure she felt at Hector's question.

Fuck. She was fucked.

"What I am *not* doing with Lucy is rolling away from her distance attack of pitching ball lightning at my head while hooking her ankle with the toe of my boot to compromise her balance." The welts felt like they had thorns embedded in them. Even sarcasm was pleasurable.

"*Ash.*"

"Or arguing with her while a kindergarten teacher with his soul half in and half out is frozen in preternatural limbo." The welts raced up the back of her neck.

"I saw." Hector put his hands flat on the bar. "I *saw* how you looked at her. How you have been looking at her."

"We had a strange, very long day, so you shouldn't—"

"Not just today! Not only last night! Always, Ash. How you've always looked at her, even when, or especially when, you couldn't even look at yourself in the mirror."

Every rib she'd ever cracked ached like she'd just broken it. Her back was on fire.

"I've let it go," he said, "because of this fucking torturous circumstance, but I don't see how these new circumstances mixing with old feelings and a lot of shared and painful encounters is going to end without annihilating one or both of you."

Ash looked down at the threads in the rips of her jeans and the knot she'd repaired one of her bootlaces with. Her skin was still prickling, burning, but she tried to let herself feel it. Maybe she was *supposed* to feel it—not as physical pain that deferred or displaced it, but as a feeling. In her chest. In her heart.

"I know that," she said quietly.

Ash felt Hector's hands on her shoulders. On her next exhale, the pain lifted from her scalp, her neck and back, like a ghost floating away.

"This hasn't been fair to you or Lucy," her friend said. "Worse than unfair. It's okay to be angry about it. It's okay to cry about it. You don't have to bear up under it like your dad. But it's not just souls that deserve to be protected. *You* deserve protection. You have no defenses against Lucy Prynne."

She opened her mouth to protest, and he pointed toward the stairs. "Against *that* Lucy Prynne," he clarified. "Why would you? You really loved each other. I know, because I was there, and even though I was a stupid kid, I preferred to be around both of you most of all. It feels good to be around love."

Hector eased his hands from her shoulders. She tried again to take a breath, but it snagged hard in her throat. "I'll be okay."

"You're already not okay." Hector's smile was as sad as his eyes. "You haven't been okay for a long time. You know what I thought when Nathan went out to the parking lot the other night and the outside lights shut themselves off and wouldn't come back on? I thought, 'If Ash still played her music, I'd want *her* to play here.' I'd turn off all one hundred thirty sports channels I pay for in the deluxe sportball package from the cable company and make everyone listen to those beautiful songs you used to sing with your upright bass."

Shit. Shit, shit. Ash hadn't been prepared for a blow so well aimed. "Shut up," she said, without even a hint of the edge or irony she needed.

"This curse bullshit has stolen so much. I'm overjoyed to have Lucy back, but I'm hoping some part of you comes back, too."

Ash pushed a tear off her face with her hand. "I hate when you're sensitive and insightful."

"*That's* what's gonna make me a good papa." Hector pushed his glasses up to the bridge of his nose. "Now. Calliope. She thinks I've got some part in this mission."

"She implied you're not using your powers in full, ultimate super mode."

"The last time I did, the priest in black exiled me and my family to the frozen north. I was five. I spent the next thirteen years living with my parents while they held me back for the sake of safety. I'm out of practice."

"So start practicing."

"I have, actually. Mostly getting into meditation and talking to other miracle workers online."

"Miracle workers are online?"

Hector wrinkled his nose. "Eh, that's strong, maybe. But there's a Discord called the Everyday Thaumaturge, and then a less great subreddit with a lot of drama but a few solid folks."

"Thaumaturge?" Ash's brain was spinning like a nicked quarter. She needed three days of absolutely nothing happening, no new knowledge, and a quiet temp job in some boring business's file room.

"The less mawkish name for a miracle worker." Hector started to speak, then stopped himself. "Um, listen. Don't freak out, but I should probably tell you that earlier this week I was at Costco getting napkins for the bar and a nun approached me out of nowhere. Completely unknown nun."

"Do you know a lot of—"

"Let me finish. She grabbed my arm and addressed me by name. Hector Torres. She told me that parishioners were reporting that their Marys—*their* Marys, like, the ones in their yard shrines or their grottoes—are starting to cry tears of blood. The nun also told me the priest at Our Sacred Family was called to a house by the bishop to investigate a possible possession."

"She told you this at *Costco*?"

"Don't miss the part where I said I do not know this nun and she is stopping me out of nowhere to report on spiritual activity right here in town of the sort that gets reported to the Vatican."

"Why do you think it's happening?"

"Not my point. I'm telling you this stuff so you'll understand why I'm leery of your Hester Prynne. I'm all for ending this, but on our own terms, not getting bossed by ghost people with hidden agendas who like to appear and disappear on their own schedules."

"Do you trust Lucy?" Ash wasn't sure how she would answer the question herself.

"On a mystic ballot? No. As a flawed human who loves who she loves? I do."

"Do you trust me?"

She wanted Hector to say yes. If he trusted her, it would mean there was at least one person in this world who had faith in her judgment—because Ash wasn't sure *she* did.

"You've been here all along in a way that Lucy hasn't. Which is why there are a lot of ways I trust you less." He reached over and squeezed her upper arm. "You're a mess. Your internal moral compass has been hijacked by an ancient patriarchal program. You've done nothing as yourself for years—and don't forget that I was there to witness your dad and Draven becoming increasingly miserable while they ignored you and Lucy as teenagers."

Rye and Draven were getting a surprising number of mentions in this new era. On the other hand, Hector's dad was a house painter who earned six figures and sang along to the radio as he worked. He adored his family. He'd made the best of a situation he in no way blamed his son for or expected him to answer to.

Obviously, ordinary love and attention had a way of getting a person ahead. "Are we assembling a Justice League?"

Hector grinned. "You've got me. I've been spending *my* time growing and learning as both a human and a thaumaturge."

"I love that for you."

"You should. Now go away. The whistle across the street's gonna blow in seven and a half minutes, and the regulars already feel weird that there was a white woman in the bar last night who wasn't named Joyce or Linda. I don't want them to think I've gone all downtown and might add chicken fingers and frozen drinks to the menu."

"I'm leaving." Ash stood and put on her jacket, zipping it up to prepare to jog through the cold to her car. "Listen—"

"I'll tell her you said bye." Hector pulled out a basket of remotes from below the bar. "As long as she isn't passed out face-first in a chicken burrito."

"Sure."

Ash left. Outside the bar, it was full dark, but the lights from the factory parking lot and Hector's lot joined together to hang a canopy of pale yellow over the street.

When she buckled into her car, her phone buzzed.

> Where are you in relation to the devil and the deep blue sea?

Ash couldn't help but smile. It was Cal.

> We're both on the beach and the tide's coming in. Listen, I heard a rumor you might be adding a golden harp to your Foxy's performances?

More like wings . . . and nothing else. I'm flattered Lucy told you about our conversation.

The one in her dreams, you mean?

Nathaniel Hawthorne wrote, in a very famous book relevant to your predicament, "We dream in our waking moments, and walk in our sleep."

Ash rolled her eyes, but she was still smiling.

So it's going to be like that, Calliope?

As it has always been, and don't forget that your bravery brought you to my protection, and my love, and it will again and again. Xoxo

Driving home, Ash might have expected to think about her day. Hester and Lucy, the Costco nun, her dad, her newly insistent feelings. But she didn't.

She thought about her bass, propped up in her closet, and what it would be like to play it in Hector's Tavern.

In her daydream, she didn't wear black.

X.

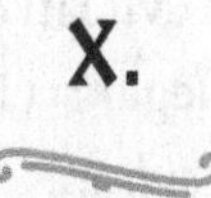

ASHES STEADFAST FREAKS OUT

> **Love, whether newly born, or aroused from a death-like slumber, must always create a sunshine, filling the heart so full of radiance, that it overflows upon the outward world.**
>
> NATHANIEL HAWTHORNE, *THE SCARLET LETTER*

"BLOODY TEARS, HUH?" Lucy played with the ends of her hair. She was back in the passenger seat of Ash's car, this time in baggy jeans and a Green Bay Packers sweatshirt. She'd done her hair in the double French braids she used to wear years ago whenever her curls had gotten too big and frizzy to manage.

"Bloody tears is what Hector said the Costco nun told him. Multiple Marys. Also something about a possession."

"Can we stop at Kettle's for coffee?" There was distance in Lucy's voice. When Ash looked over, she was in three-quarters profile, wrinkling her nose out the window at the gray-beige-white landscape of Green Bay in the winter.

"Are you okay?"

Lucy shrugged. "I'm okay and I'm amazing and I'm freaked. It's a state-of-being garbage pizza."

"Freaked?"

"Don't act so surprised. You've been telling me for years about the consequences of the evil I'm doing."

Ash accidentally met Helegar's cloudy eyeballs, and he seemed to shrug. *I have no idea, either.*

"Did you *do* something?" she asked.

"I was so sure I'd fall right to sleep, but of course I tossed and turned with everything looping and looping in my brain." Lucy made a big, frantic gesture with her hands. Her cheeks were starting to look hot. "I kept seeing faces. All the people. Everything they told me. How they sounded. Sometimes they cry, Ashes."

"Wait. You told us you were more of a guidance counselor for souls. And you definitely said you and I were doing a truce."

Lucy slumped in her seat. "With bloody tears and possession happening, I'm allowed to have doubts, okay? Surely, you've had them, too."

Shame flooded through her. More than once, Lucy had accused her of suppressing people's dreams. She hadn't given it a moment's thought. It had always seemed to her that a person's soul should remain snugly concealed inside them. If it was free—if Lucy could draw it out—didn't that mean her goal was to take it?

But Ash had never really given any thought where Lucy would take a soul *to*. If she cast it to hell, if she turned off its light, if she released it to wander, if she used it to keep her hair shiny?

And as far as that went, had *Ash* done anything to make sure the people she "saved" kept their souls intact, or had *she* been the one to cast them down? Did the people she believed she was saving get rewarded for her sacrifices and their own? Did Cal, an angel, someday collect these souls to be . . . what?

What?

"What happened last night?" The question came out more severe than she intended. "You left in a good mood, you were tipsy, you were looking forward to your chicken burrito."

Helegar's tote slipped at Lucy's side, and he grunted in annoyance. Ash pulled into a spot in front of Kettle's, the coffee shop near her apartment where she, Lucy, and Hector used to hang out for hours in high school, spending less than five dollars between them to sit in a corner between the stacks of used books and play games of chess with half their attention. Kettle's smelled like burned coffee and Pine-Sol, but the big wraparound windows at the front of the shop let in lots of light, and no one ever bothered them there.

She turned off the car. As the heater ticked down, she unbuckled her seat belt and turned to face Lucy. "Come on. Tell me what happened."

Lucy sighed. "The cider hit me a little harder than I thought it would, but after the fries and Ovidia's big dinner, I was more clearheaded. You know that I've never gotten to know Ovidia. Hector wasn't even dating her yet when . . . it all happened, and the few times I'd seen her were because you and I were in the same place at the same time and Hector was there. We hadn't really talked."

"Okay."

"I like her. She and I started talking about the babies. She told me about going to the anatomical ultrasound. It's the one where the babies are big enough to see how they're growing and find out what kind of twins they are. She was nervous. Of course she was. That makes sense. With twins, there are all these special considerations that could make her pregnancy dangerous for her or the babies."

"Is Ovidia okay? Are the babies okay?"

Lucy nodded vigorously, pink from her throat to the tops of her ears. "Yes. The ultrasound went really well. Everyone was healthy. And she told me that the night of the ultrasound they were especially active, and she felt like they were telling her that they were good, and she would be fine." Lucy turned to Ash, her eyes deep and dark and serious. "But then something happened that has never happened before, and I need to be able to talk to you about it. You used to help me put things into perspective. Little things like school tests, and big things like our future."

"I can try, but I can't guarantee I won't resort to our habits and kick you and your extremely smelly dog out of my car if you don't tell me everything *right now*."

"I can't yet. First, we need to talk about more of what we know."

"What *exactly*?"

"Souls."

Ash had an eerie feeling that the devil had entered this conversation for the first time—not the soulless trickster lying in wait in the deepest part of a dark forest, but the figure on Calliope's tarot card. Change. "All right. What about souls?"

"Just . . . bear with me. Way back, after our first fight, I went to wherever I go. When I came back, I was sitting on the bench where we used to sneak smokes near the East High parking lot. I was wearing—"

"Sequins. A sequined minidress I had never seen before. I

hadn't seen you for over two weeks. I didn't know if you were dead or alive, and then, seeing you sitting there, I still didn't know."

"I wasn't sure myself. Not until Mary Beth came."

"The older woman with a cat stroller."

"She got there before you did and sat next to me. She had been crying. I asked her what was wrong. She told me she had taken a job in an office. She had told herself that if her income from making her pottery dropped below a certain number, then that was what she had to do. She was so sad about it that I started to cry, too, and when I held her hand, I was overwhelmed by the pure liquid silver of her soul and how it could change into so many different shapes and figures. It was beautiful. I hated it and I loved it, because it made my own soul want to be heard, but it was as if Mary Beth's soul took mine over. Anything I needed or wanted was so quiet. Silent."

"And then I came along." Ash remembered how the woman's soul had been the same silver as Lucy's sequins. She hadn't known it could look like that. She was barely healed and suddenly in charge of taking care of her dad, who'd been moved to the rehab hospital. In between talking to social workers and nursing staff she had done nothing but cry, ignoring Hector's calls and visits to her house, his pleas for her to tell him what was going on. Her dad scared her. He told her nothing. She was eighteen years old. Lucy was gone. Draven was gone.

Then she discovered what she could do.

"I didn't stop to think," Ash said. "I was only going to take the woman's hand and pull her away from you, but before I knew it, she and I were both on the ground. I didn't know I was that strong. I told her not to end up like her grandmother."

"And her soul went dull and fell back into her body like it had been dropped from a height."

"I was surprised." She had been horrified. Not at Lucy. At herself.

"I ran away, but as soon as I couldn't see you anymore, I was gone again," Lucy said. "I can't even remember how many times that happened before I understood the conditions of my life. Of the curse. And every time I saw you was worse."

"So tell me about the souls," Ash said. "What did you figure out?"

"They *are* the person. They're not for me. I let them see the truth of their own soul and what it wants and what it needs. The only thing I take away from them is doubt. But Ashes, people *compromise* in those moments. They make deals and bargains with their own souls. They decide that they can have what they want, but only as long as they punish themselves in some other part of their lives. They show me what they think are their sins, but it's just what they're ashamed of, what they've never forgiven themselves for or refused to learn. It's relentless, trying to be with someone, trying to love them, while they're punishing themself for no reason."

Lucy had tears in her eyes, but when Ash gripped the steering wheel, it was because she was angry. Hives knobbed over her stomach and made her angrier. Left to figure it out herself, she'd gotten so many things wrong. Not just the fighting, but the reason for it. Her purpose. "That's what you've *been* saying, Luce. It sounds like it's what you would've told me at any point if I'd bothered to ask. What happened last night that made you doubt yourself?"

Lucy picked at her hangnail. "Ovidia's soul spoke to me. We

both watched it come out of her. She seemed in awe of it. She didn't ask me for anything. She took her soul into her arms, and it went back to her, through the bump of the twins, up through her body, where it shone in her eyes with this deep bronze glitter."

Ashes shook her head. Hector would have a fucking stroke if he found out. "And that was different how?"

"Because she didn't want anything. All the other ones have. What does that mean? Doesn't it mean that I *have* been disturbing souls, compelling them in some way, like you say, because maybe all those people were supposed to simply realize their souls belonged to them? So that's been an intense spiral in my head. When I finally fell asleep and then woke up, all I could think was that if I *was* using all those beautiful souls to feel better in the small spaces of time I had, that's *not okay*."

With her thoughts scattered, Ash listened to the wheezing sound of Helegar breathing.

She didn't know what to say to make Lucy feel better, or even if making Lucy feel better was something she was supposed to want. She didn't know how to do this. She wasn't equipped. All those dead Steadfasts who followed her around had been given plenty of chances to tell her what to do. Her father even more. And they hadn't. This curse had taken so much from her that she'd been too tired to ask the kind of questions Lucy was asking. If souls gave Lucy warmth and energy, a sense of belonging and awe for a few short moments between mindless fighting and nothingness? *Good.*

The Brigade, the curse, was going to have to be a hell of a lot more explicit if it wanted to conscript Ashes Steadfast into another fight.

Lucy put her arms over her eyes. "I envy you. You're so sure of your place in this mess. You're sure that you're good and blameless. There's a cause for your suffering and a cause to suffer for."

"Yeah, no," Ash said. "I held on to that before I ran off to New York, but ever since, it's just been something I tell myself so I get out of bed in the morning."

"What's been different since New York?"

"Nothing. That's my point. It's the same grind. I told myself I was doing right by my dad and protecting whoever's next in line from a life of self-sacrificing misery, but now I'm asking myself why my cause has never been to stop this curse once and for all? That's what we said we'd do. If anyone should be spiraling, it's me."

Ash couldn't hold much more feeling inside her. She was angry, yeah, and she was finally sad, and Hector had a point. She was mooning over Lucy. She wanted Lucy, and it seemed impossible. The only way she'd ever figured out to avoid running up against this wall was to cut herself off from feeling. She didn't want to do that. She couldn't stand to hear more puritanical scripts come out of her own mouth. The hives were pissing her off.

If self-doubt had been evading her before, it wasn't now. Chalk it up to two days of unprecedented events. Or to Hector mentioning her music. Or Lucy's hangnail and frizzy hair making her more beautiful than she had any right to be. Or even to Ash beginning to warm to the love that shone out of Helegar's bony eye sockets.

"You know what, Luce? Fuck it."

"Fuck it?"

"Either you're darkness itself and this is your best con yet, or your overlords are using you as a pawn—"

"I haven't met any overlords." There was welcome laughter in Lucy's voice.

"Or, yeah, we've both been sucked into the kind of bullshit trauma that gets coded on a person's genes, and then their kids end up with the same eyes as a murdered relative and remember their life wholesale, freaking out the entire preschool with their stories about when they used to carry a briefcase and work at the insurance agency before they died in a fire."

Lucy's brows knit completely together. "Okay?"

"My point is, *we* keep doing what we've never done before. We figure it out and break this curse."

"We keep talking."

"Yes."

"And we ask people for help."

"That, too."

"And we tell each other what we know so the curse doesn't hide itself in secrets."

"That's right." Pretty soon, Ash was going to pull the pin out of the mental note she'd made to figure out why they knew so miserably little, and why she felt like she'd tripped over a missing stair inside her head whenever she tried to remember what Rye had told her.

"I don't want to stay at Hector and Ovidia's."

"What?" Ash put her hand on the parking brake to set it, then realized it was already set. She pulled her hand away when Helegar started kissing her knuckles with his slimy tongue.

"This is their time. They don't need a houseguest. We have to work on this together anyway. I was thinking that—"

"No."

"No, I shouldn't stay with them?"

"No, we're not going to solve that problem right this minute. But you're not staying in my apartment."

"I didn't ask if I could stay in your apartment."

"Good. Keep not asking." Ash opened the car door. She needed coffee. She wanted to try out eating sugar, too. It wouldn't be fair if Lucy could assume mortal form but Ash still couldn't have a cookie without getting mouth sores.

Lucy hiked Helegar in his tote onto her shoulder and followed her toward Kettle's. "Fine. We will continue to enable your unreasonableness. I'm very used to it."

They both got to the entrance at the same time. "After you." Ash stepped back.

As the heavy door closed behind them and blocked off the cold, swaddling them in the warm damp of Kettle's, Ash reflexively moved to let Lucy walk to the counter first. The hot-and-cold mix of air cycloned around them both, gusting through Lucy's hair so that the next breath Ash took was of soap and fabric softener and Lucy's skin—a smell Ash hadn't had the words for until the first time she stepped into the intense heat of a dry, wood-paneled sauna at a hotel for a high school away game.

Wood. Mineral heat. Ozone.

She came apart like a pile of leaves.

Lucy was real. Real, real.

They were on the same side.

She'd leashed the violence and grown thorns, both to protect *Lucy.* She'd committed to giving her dad what he needed so that she could remind herself why she couldn't love *Lucy.* It had only taken two days of this truce—of what was really the real Ash and the real Lucy—for her soul to feel like it was bursting out of her skin to remind her of what she wanted.

Which was Lucy.

She'd said Lucy couldn't stay at her apartment reflexively, not because they were enemies engaged in a fragile peace, but because now that Ash had some hope, she didn't want to put herself in a position that would be more torture than she could tolerate.

And she didn't want Lucy, who had nothing and no one, to choose her because she was the only choice on offer.

"Ashes?" Lucy looked back, confused as to why she was still standing by the door.

"Go ahead and order. I forgot to call in to work." Ash walked past her, past the rows of aging paperback books to a table where she collapsed into a chair without pulling it out all the way.

She got out her phone, hardly breathing, and tapped a contact.

"Ash? What is it?"

She'd woken Hector up, she could tell. But she was supposed to ask for help now, so he would just have to put up with her. "I don't know how to do it."

"How to do what?" His voice was suddenly more awake. "Tell me what's going on. I can't remember the last time you called me on the phone."

"That's part of what's going on." Ash could hear Lucy talking to the barista. She only had as much time to freak out as it took to place an order. "I don't call you. When I do see you, I have almost nothing to say, and I . . ."

"Glower."

"Yes, I glower. I make you sad. Also, I think I make my dad sad. So I'm sarcastic. I take him to his appointments and go to the durable medical equipment store and Woodman's for him, but I act like he's a tolerable ghost who haunts me by sometimes turning on the radio or filling the room with the smell of coffee."

"You had me, but now you've lost me."

"What I mean is I treat you like a shade from my past. Like something I used to know. I've been here, but I haven't *been* here. I've been behaving like I'm on some kind of permanent deployment to the underworld, or one of those guys who gets sent to land on the asteroid hurtling toward earth."

"Ash, for fuck's sake."

"Sorry. I literally have no idea what I'm feeling right now."

Hector sighed. "Where are you?"

"Kettle's."

"With *Lucy*? For the love of— Ash, this breakdown was coming for you, but I didn't think you'd light the fuse with a nice hot flame of pure nostalgia. Was Firetta's closed?"

"She needed coffee. We were nearby." Ash sank down in her chair, turning her back to the counter so she could desperately whisper into the phone. "Tell me what to do, man. I don't even know why I'm freaking out so bad that I called you. Me and Lucy had this whole conversation—"

"Oh, Lord."

"Yeah. Yeah. And that meant I did not, Hector, I did *not* have my gloomy bulwark in place when I smelled her."

"Smelled her? Jesus Christ."

"That's right. How could I have prepared myself for that? I loved her. You're right. I loved her with my entire obnoxious, wallet-chained, shaved-head, mother-abandoned, wanna-be-alternative-school self, and then I styled myself as her mortal enemy while the emergency room put sixty stitches in my neck. The plan was to let the rest of my life spool out from there, punctuated by occasional sacerdotal cage matches until I disappeared into the east."

"Ash, I love you, God help me, but that was never your plan! Your plan was to audition musicians for your Chicago prog-blues ensemble—"

"Chicago post-blues."

"—and write and rehearse for a demo and regional tour until everyone was set to move to New York, while meanwhile continuously showing your most far-gone, worshipful, tender-butch belly to Lucy until she looked up from her computer screen long enough to agree to be your wife so you could split your time between the Johnson Space Center and the tour bus. *That*, Ashes Steadfast, was your plan, and if you think you've turned your heart to coal hard enough to crush that dream, then none of those mandated troubled youth counseling sessions did you one speck of good."

Hector sounded like his mom, and also like he might break into Spanish at any moment. That was how she knew he was serious.

And he was right. That had been her plan.

That had been her whole entire plan, which she'd archived

in a dark prison inside her where Lucy couldn't reach it and Ash didn't have to look at it.

Once, when she'd been helping her dad organize the storage tubs and boxes in his basement, she'd come across one of those flat-rate white Priority Mail boxes stuffed full of notes and papers. She'd dumped it out onto her thighs to get a handle on what kind of papers they were so she could file them. Searing pain had raced up from her kneecaps to her hips at the same instant she recognized Lucy's handwriting.

They were Ash and Lucy's notes back and forth from high school. Their birthday cards, mementos, keepsakes. They'd disappeared from Ash's desk in her room sometime in the hazy days after her first fight with Lucy—she'd assumed by supernatural mechanism, but it turned out because Rye had boxed them up.

She'd shoved everything back into the box, heat blistering her palms, and thrown it away.

"Can you blame me for putting up a few defenses?" Ash dropped her volume when she realized that she had gotten loud enough to create a pause in Lucy and the barista's cheerful conversation.

"You live in an emotional bunker."

"Not anymore!" she complained. "I have been operating on a cautious watch-and-wait basis with this change in the rules, but caution doesn't work when your impulse is to destroy the terms of the truce with *boning*." Her whisper was a sharp hiss. Ash could feel blisters rising across the skin of her chest. "I don't mean that. It just came out. I'm sorry."

"I'll tell you what you need to do." Hector's voice was crystalline.

"Please. Tell me what I need to do."

"Stop thinking about Lucy and start getting to know yourself."

Well, that sounded impossible.

"Whatever happens, you're never going to be ready for what's next until you know who *you* are," he said. "Until you know what *you* want. Until you can explain *yourself*."

"But—"

"Not explain the curse, or what you think Lucy's doing or thinking, or if your dad cares about you. Your biggest, spikiest defenses are against *yourself* and always have been. Win or lose against the devil, Ash—it doesn't matter which if you pull a Rye Steadfast and turn into a ghost in the end."

Shit. That sounded correct. Her knees felt like Jell-O. Her skin was so tender, she could feel every separate thread of her clothing. "Okay," she told him. It was the only thing she *could* tell him. She'd listened to enough folks bargaining with Lucy to know that uncertain and terrified agreement was all anyone could bargain with at a crossroads.

Hector cleared his throat. "None of that means, by the way, that Lucy can stay at our place long term. It's not that I don't love her, but the room she's in is the nursery, and I have work to do in there. Lucy talks a lot."

Ash closed her eyes. "Not so many places to put up a grown woman with no ID and an undead dog whose farts can clear a room."

"Good luck with that. I'll see the both of you and Cal later. But no earlier than two thirty, because that's when Ovidia's going over to her mom's. She's taking a break from all this."

"Understood." Ash stared at a knot of wood on the surface

of the table and unclenched her jaw. "Thank you, Hector. You're a good friend."

"Sorry, what? Did our connection get weird? Are you still there?"

"Come on. You did the mean part already."

"I love you. I'll see you later."

Ash ended the call and put her phone on the table. "I love you, too," she said.

It didn't hurt.

"Hey!" Lucy came around a freestanding shelf of books. "There you are!" She carried a plastic tray with two mugs and small plates. "I talked Andrea into a tray, because what I remember most about Kettle's is how long you have to wait for your order. I figured if I insisted on carrying everything to my table myself, it would be faster, but then Andrea pointed out I couldn't carry it all myself, and so there began a negotiation for the use of one of her serving trays, which she is very protective of."

Lucy shifted the tray to balance on one forearm while she slid the tote with Helegar off her shoulder and onto the ground.

"Okay, so. Black coffee for you, and from there it's a number of things. I don't know what Puritans eat. You had a pretzel in New York but didn't eat at Hector's. From that, I extrapolated this." She set down a saucer-sized plate with a baseball-sized lump on it.

"Which is . . . ?"

"She called it a 'health cookie.' I think there's oats? It smells . . . fine."

"What did you get?"

Lucy started filling the table with the rest of her order. "I got a Black Forest smoothie, a cheese and summer sausage kabob, a mint brownie, and this stack of chocolate chip cookies wrapped in Saran Wrap." She put the now-empty tray on the neighboring table and sat down opposite Ash.

"What temperature are the cookies?"

"So hot that the butter is leaking out of the Saran Wrap." Lucy picked them up and held Ash's eyes while she licked butter off her thumb.

"I want those." Ash reached out her hand. Was it shaking? Maybe.

Lucy put the cookies in Ash's hand, biting her lower lip.

She was flirting. She'd flirted with Ash in recent memory, in the lead-up to a fight, but this was *Lucy* flirting, which, first of all, Ash had no defenses. She had written at least six songs with Lucy's name in the title. And, second, the way Lucy flirted was simultaneously dorky and bossy—the siren call of butches everywhere.

She cleared her throat. "Can you grab me some cream and sugar?"

"I thought you drank it black. Like your wardrobe." Lucy giggled.

"I do, but I don't *like* black coffee."

"What about the health cookie?" Lucy picked it up and inspected it.

"Give it to Helegar. If anyone needs to heal, it's that dog. I think his fur is getting a hole on the left side."

Ash made eye contact with the dog, who was sitting up in the bag, panting and wagging his tail. His eyes were filmy, but it wasn't hard to see that he was onto her. He could sense that maybe things *could* be different.

She nodded at him, and he wagged his tail.

He loved her.

He loved everybody.

What was that like?

XI.

THE CONTEMPLATION OF DRAVEN PRYNNE

> It is the unspeakable misery of a life so false as his, that it steals the pith and substance out of whatever realities there are around us.
>
> NATHANIEL HAWTHORNE, *THE SCARLET LETTER*

"ARE YOU SURE you want to go in?" Ash stared at the house she'd grown up in.

"No. I understand the logic of talking to your dad. *Academically,* I grasp the importance, but I liked it more as a logical, academic plan than the reality of knocking on that door."

Ash leaned back in the driver's seat. "We don't have to."

"I think we do have to. He's part of this, and that means he should help us stop it. Or stop me. Or end the world, since humanity has so completely fucked everything up."

"If you're hoping to beat your devil rep, maybe don't talk about ending the world." Ash pressed her hand to her stomach, unsure if it had unsettled at the prospect of talking to her dad or if its queasiness was the inevitable outcome of the sugar in her coffee and cookies.

They hadn't given her immediate hives. Or a migraine. She'd eaten them while sitting in a pool of gentle sunlight filtered through the tall-ceilinged space of Kettle's, listening to Lucy tell her side of the story of the time they'd fought for the soul of their third-grade teacher. Nothing bad had happened from the cookies or the conversation, even though Ash had enjoyed every minute of them.

"Ashes?" Lucy touched her arm.

Even two days ago, when Lucy touched her, she would flinch. It was her holy mission to fight the devil at every provocation. If she didn't, she was selfish. But her father sat inside that house with a gray complexion, low-sodium food, and an array of durable medical equipment that didn't do a lot to improve the tan-on-sad decor. There would be no reward in death. He'd already died. It hadn't cheered him up any.

There was nothing in this curse for her.

She looked at Lucy's hand and found the freckle on her pointer finger's knuckle. Even through the leather of Ash's jacket and the cotton shirt she wore beneath it, Lucy's hand on her arm radiated a pleasant warmth. Her light grip, her concern, her sympathetic eyes made Ash want to shift in her seat, turn to look at her face, rest her head against Lucy's shoulder, press her mouth to her skin. It wasn't a new feeling.

"This is confusing," Ash said.

"What's the most confusing for you?"

"Tell me yours first."

Lucy looked down, playing with the zipper tab on the jacket's cuffs. "You know how I told you about the memories I have that sort of backfill in whenever I return from the nothing-place where I go?"

Ash nodded.

"Well, in that life that I haven't lived, you and me are still . . . *you and me*. As if that's the default setting. You're not avoiding me, you're not goading me into a fight, you don't look like you're going to scream or cry. I don't feel desperate, like I have to try to reach you somehow. It's not real. I know that, but I wish I could trust that we'll stay like this. That I'll stay here where it *is* real. The part with you and me."

Ash relaxed first her shoulders, then her grip on the steering wheel. It meant she could feel more of Lucy, more of the weight of her hand. "I don't know what I'll do if what we're trying now doesn't work," she confessed. "I don't want to die. I don't want you to sacrifice yourself. I don't want to fight you. I want . . ."

She didn't know how to finish the sentence.

I want our freedom.

I want my life back.

I want you, Lucy Prynne.

Those were prayers, not plans, and Lucy wasn't someone Ash prayed to.

So she didn't finish the sentence. She let the words be their own sentence. "I want." She looked at Lucy without bracing herself first. Without lifting up a shield to protect her heart. Lucy squeezed her arm, hard, and something collapsed between them, the pieces so small and fragile that it would be impossible to construct it again. It was a small wall between them that Ash felt break, but maybe for now they only needed this single barrier to fall.

Only this one.

"I'm terrified it won't work," she confessed. "I feel like something could break in any direction and then we would be right back in Hector's parking lot."

She watched Lucy's gaze move to the horizon, a few laugh lines crinkling as she thought. "Whatever I've learned about life since I lost you has been from other people." Her voice was quiet in the hushed car. "There was a long while that I resented it so much, I welcomed our fights. I wanted to call down the elements just to feel something I thought was me, *just* me. But then something happened."

"What was it?"

Lucy shifted, tucking her foot beneath her and kicking Ash's heart into a higher gear. She smelled like a lumberyard. Like rain. "I decided I would be curious. I decided that whenever I talked to someone, I would be as much myself as I could figure out how to be with that person. Because we are who we are in relation to others, right? Nobody I talk to *only* tells me about themself. They talk about their moms and their girlfriends, their kids, their best friend. My hope was that if I really listened to these people, I could start to feel who *I* was."

"Did it work?"

"It was astonishing how well it worked. I started to figure out so much, so fast, that I figured out I didn't want to fight you anymore."

"But you never stopped fighting me until the other day."

"I didn't want the *oblivion* of fighting you anymore. The bad-decision high. I wanted to see you, and fighting was the only way I could see you. It was the only way I could try to figure out what you had learned about yourself. About life."

"Nothing, obviously." Ash rolled her shoulders. "I iced Hector out. My dad and I are running on loyalty fumes."

"You two were always rocky." Lucy slid her hand away from Ash's arm, turning in her seat to look at the house as Helegar adjusted his body with a chalky scrape of bone on bone. "It's possible what we think we have to offer has more to do with what we think of ourselves than with who we really are."

"Is that the silver tongue of the devil?" Her voice didn't have any heat. What Lucy said had made her feel a little bit hopeful. Not about her circumstances, but about herself.

"Yes." Lucy smiled a little. "Is that bad?"

"Right now, I accept any and all wisdom, from whoever offers it to me."

Lucy leaned over the gearshift. Ash's belly dipped, and blood raced to her pulse points as Lucy's face came alongside her cheek. "Here's some wisdom." Her lips pressed against Ash's temple, soft, so soft that Ash's eyelids got heavy, and her breathing tightened in her throat. Lucy held the kiss until Ash could map the shape of her lips by the heat they pressed in her skin, and then she pulled slowly away.

"Ashes," she whispered, every one of her freckles ringed with blush.

Ash could only nod. *Yes*. Just *yes*. The Devil card had been drawn for her, and whatever it meant—yes.

They understood each other.

"I think we're ready," Lucy said.

Ash fumbled for the handle and opened her car door. "I'm sure he's been wondering when we'd come inside."

"I know." Lucy smiled as she got out of the car, and Ash led them around the house and inside, where they were met by the familiar smell of coffee and Ivory soap.

"In here," her father called from the front room. He'd probably been listening to news radio before seeing them pull up.

"I'm with Lucy." She held her breath. She hadn't warned him in advance.

"Saw her." Her dad turned in his recliner as they entered the room. "Lucy."

"Hello, Rye." She sounded more like a polite and grown woman than Ash ever was with her dad. "How are you?"

"I'm well." The three of them unwittingly looked at Rye's foot, propped up high on the footrest of the recliner. His big toe was deep red, the size of a Ping-Pong ball. The toenail was long gone, its nail bed bloody and stretched from the swelling. The toe had accumulated so much crystalline waste from gout that it looked like the pointy uric acid crystals would push through the tender skin.

"Good to hear," Lucy said.

"There's coffee, and I just opened a package of Hydrox cookies. Help yourself."

Ash knew that this was her dad's way of asking if she would get him a cup of coffee and a plate of cookies. "I'll freshen your mug and bring you a few."

He grunted, then remembered he had a guest. "Thanks."

"Lucy?" she asked.

"I'll take a few Hydrox." Lucy made her way to the spot on

the love seat where she and Ash had always sat if they were at Ash's house and not in her bedroom, though they only sat there because it made it easier to watch for Hector's truck to pull up and take them somewhere else.

Helegar leapt out of Lucy's tote and raced across the room, jumping into Rye's lap with a clatter of bones. By the time he reached up to lick Rye's face, his fur had managed to slide over his form.

"Helegar." Rye gently rubbed around the dog's shoulders and neck until he wiggled happily into his lap. "You don't seem to be holding up, old man. Then again, I'm not, either." To Ash's shock, her dad gave Helegar a fond, genuine smile.

Ash took a deep breath before heading into the kitchen to pour coffee and grab the cookies. She could hear Lucy asking Rye about his gout while she retrieved mugs from the cabinet.

When she returned, she handed Lucy a dish and set down her father's coffee and cookies on his table. Rye took a bite of one cookie and fed the rest to Helegar. "Decided to get it cut off," he told Lucy. "Who needs a toe?"

"Dad." Ash's protest sounded weak. His doctor had given him this option, and if she were ever going to cut anything off her body, for sure it would be something that looked like her dad's toe. "Your gait would be altered. You'd likely need physical therapy." These were things the doctor had said.

Rye gestured roughly at the cane next to his recliner. "It is already. Can't be worse." His shoulders were rounded. He was in pain.

He was always in pain. He never complained.

She wanted to believe he was like this because of the curse.

The curse was why he'd told her Lucy would someday become her enemy, but was it why he'd called Ash selfish whenever she wasn't stoic? Was it why he'd left her alone to raise herself except when she misstepped and he cracked down without mercy?

"You two aren't here for coffee." Rye didn't sound surprised. Maybe he'd been visited by his own version of nuns at Costco, warning him of what was to come.

Lucy shook her head. "No."

"What was your dad like?" Ash heard herself asking.

"And my grandma, while you're at it." Lucy leaned forward, hands clasped in her lap. "Maura Prynne."

Rye's complexion seemed to take on an even more indistinct shade of gray. "Maura Prynne is more of a mystery to me," he said contemplatively.

Ash sat down next to Lucy. They faced Rye together. "Are you saying your own dad is also a mystery to you?"

"Aren't I a mystery to you?" He didn't deliver the question like a gentle self-own. He looked sad. His hand rested on top of Helegar's head. For comfort, she thought. "Gabriel Steadfast. That was my dad's name," he said after a moment. "I get the sense he tried to outrun the inevitable when he was young. You reminded me of him in that way."

Ash's jaw locked tight. This was an old, tender place—Rye's assumption that she'd been rebellious in order to avoid what was coming for her, when the truth was that Ash had used color and music and rage to dare the curse to take even one thing away. It had hurt so much when her dad told her, weeks after he came home from cardiac rehab, that he was glad to see she'd *matured*. She'd had five dozen stitches in her neck, for fuck's sake, and he knew how she got them.

Rye paid no mind to her anger. "Gabriel's mom had died when he was twenty—"

"Fighting Maura's dad," Lucy cut in. "My great-grandfather. That was here in town. They drowned in the bay."

"Yes. Go on. Tell me the part you know."

Lucy pursed her lips. "My grandmother, Maura, was living in Boston. The curse passed to her when she was in medical school. She'd been raised by her mom, who wasn't a Prynne, so she didn't know what was coming. She collapsed at the hospital and ended up admitted to the psych ward with what they called catatonia. That's all my dad told me."

"When the curse passed to my father, he drove to Boston. Gabriel kidnapped Maura from the psych hospital. She woke up bound and gagged in the back of his van somewhere in the middle of Kansas. That night, they nearly killed each other." Rye adjusted his elevated foot with a wince. "It was a different time. Those years were violent."

"*Those* years," Ash said bitterly. "*Those* were the years that were violent."

"People always say it was a different time when they talk about history," Lucy said. "It's like every generation wants their kids to start from scratch. And daughters are still left confused and parentless."

"Draven wasn't a bad father," Rye said to Lucy. "The two of you were so young. We thought we could talk instead of fight. I wore my heart out trying to talk our way out of it."

Helegar whined in his throat.

"I had *no idea* what I was walking into," Ash complained. "You never told me what the alternative was to those debates, what you were heading off. You never told me about Gabriel and Maura."

"I knew almost nothing," he replied. "Don't you think I wanted to know where I came from? My mom would never say who my dad was, other than his name was Gabriel and she met him after a concert where he played the drums. That he was rebellious. Hardheaded."

You know almost nothing, and yet I remind you of your father. Ash ground her back teeth together to keep from saying it. Rye had always *claimed* he only knew Ash's mother long enough to make a daughter, but if that were true, how had her mom found him again later?

I named her Ashes. She's your curse to bear.

Ash found it hard to pretend that her mother *hadn't* sacrificed her to something she wanted no part of. But what did her mother know? What would Rye have told her?

If her mother had abandoned her to the curse, Rye had abandoned her again. It was almost as if there were some force that needed these babies to be born to do its work. And not just born—left in ignorance, without guidance, alone in the fight. It made Ash think the shadowy mournfulness of the Dead and Righteous Brigade might be fully justified.

"I guess when your dad met your mom, he didn't tell her he was a kidnapper with an occult connection to a clinically insane female med student?"

"I guess he didn't," Rye said with a ghost of a smile. "If he mentioned it, she didn't tell me. I hired a lawyer behind my mom's back to find Gabriel. I told myself that if knowing him didn't answer the questions I had about what was happening to me, then I would ask my mom to get me help, because I'd lost my grip."

"What do you mean? What was happening to you?"

"I could go where I wanted to." Her dad rubbed Helegar's belly. "I could be wherever I wanted to be. I could be *when*ever I wanted to be, except the future. As soon as I felt the desire or the curiosity, I found myself there. I became certain this had something to do with my father. Or I wasn't well. It had to be one or the other."

Lucy's knee pressed into her thigh. Ash knew why. The Holland Tunnel. Second chances. It sounded like Rye had a gift that wasn't dissimilar to what Ash could do.

"Were you able to take anyone with you when you, I guess, time traveled?" Lucy asked.

"No. Just me."

"What did you find out from your dad?" Ash's ears were hot.

"He told me that what I could do would be useful when the time came for me to fight Maura's son."

"Jesus," Lucy breathed. "And just like that, you were drafted to fight in the war. Gabriel and Maura, then you and Draven."

"I was relieved I wouldn't have to turn myself over to a locked ward. Gabriel was paranoid, secretive, covered in scars. But I wanted to get to know this man. I was curious about what he had to tell me about my fate. It's a difficult age for many young men."

"It's a difficult age for young *people*." Lucy's voice was low and soft, though Ash could hear the anger in it. "I imagine Maura also found it *difficult* to be kidnapped from an asylum and bundled into the back of a van. She wanted to be a doctor. And even after she met Gabriel, there were things she wanted. My dad told me his parents loved each other."

"They did. Maura fell in love with your grandfather. When Draven was born, she tried to separate from the battle. It made her sick. She went with her husband and son to California to take advantage of access to any alternative kinds of healing she could find. Then I happened along." Rye was pale from pain, or from their questions. "Without meaning to or knowing. I liked to go to the beach. Other places. Other times. One place I liked to go was another boy's house. He had a big jungle gym and was fun to play with. When we were twelve, playing together, his mother came out to the yard."

"Maura," Lucy said. "Oh, god."

"Draven and I had climbed a tree. We were sitting on one of its branches. He called out to her. She came under the tree and looked at me like I was a ghost. I looked so much like Gabriel, understand. She asked me what my name was. I told her. The next time I went to California, they weren't there. I saw a 'for sale' sign in the yard. Much later, I learned she'd come here in a rage, straight to Gabriel."

Ash felt deflated. The circumstances didn't seem to matter. He had been raised knowing nothing about the curse. So had Draven. Gabriel and Maura had tried to secret their sons away from it, and then the power Rye manifested arrowed him and Draven straight back into the middle of the mess.

Where was the exit?

"By the time I met my father, he wasn't surprised to see me," Rye said. "Maura had been out for blood, fighting to finish him off, and he was ready for backup. I'd only just begun to know him when he and Maura fought their last battle. Then it was Draven and me, and we were grieving, and we'd had enough."

Rye glanced at Lucy with a sigh. "Your father wanted to harvest souls. He told me that. He believed it was important for people to exercise their free will over the fate of their soul. We agreed that he would direct the power of his longing for souls into our arguments. To save humanity, I had to win or keep him at a stalemate. If I conceded, I would have to turn my back on his reaping. If he conceded, he would take himself away. We agreed not to have children."

"But you did have children," Lucy said bitterly. "Both of you. Despite the existence of many reliable methods of birth control."

"And you did die," Ash said. "Because that's the other way it would end, at least for the two of you. Maura's dad and Gabriel's mom died fighting each other. Then Maura and Gabriel. You and Draven. People try to get around it, but nothing works. We're toy soldiers."

"We hoped that a generation without violence would end it. We fought hard, too hard, without recognizing that the physical body is connected to everything else." Rye wasn't looking at her and Lucy now. Ash felt a sensation deep in her mind like dry skin catching on silk thread.

Something wasn't right. It felt like Rye was sketching a picture without shading in the important details.

"Has anyone come close to ending it?" she asked.

"I spent time trying to figure that out. I couldn't track it all the way back. There have been too many short, brutal lives. As far as I know, no one came close." He cleared his throat. "Maybe Draven and I came the closest."

Helegar growled. Ash looked at him in surprise as her father's hand came away from rubbing the dog's neck.

"Where's my dad, Rye?" Lucy's voice had gone from soft to hoarse.

He turned his coffee mug in his hands, staring into it for what felt like an eternity. "He's alive. I don't know what kind of alive. If he's alive like you." He'd been looking at Lucy. Now he looked at Ash. "Or maybe alive like you've been. After he lost his mother, he always wanted to learn everything he could. Not only about the Steadfasts or the Prynnes, but about *everything.* Every religion. Every practice. All the ways that humans have understood the spiritual. He told me that nearly every type of sacred practice gives an important role to contemplation."

"Prayer," Ash said.

"Meditation, walking a labyrinth, sacred dance. Sometimes ingestion of mind-altering substances. He understood contemplation as taking yourself away to get perspective and clarity. After my heart attack, I assumed that's what he went to do."

Helegar lifted his head. His ears went forward, and he stood up, leapt from the recliner, and ran to the love seat, shedding his dilapidated glamour as he went. He jumped into Lucy's arms, and she pressed her face against his skull, her color hectic and awful.

If Rye was right, she had been kept apart from her only remaining family by her father's *decision* to apply himself to contemplation while she lived in a timeless void. Ten years was a lot of fucking contemplation. Had Draven not identified any clarity yet?

Ash rose to her feet.

The history of all of this, what was possible to know, was grim. There had been no happy endings in any era for anyone. So many people were born and then tossed into this muck, and, at least according to Rye, it was all shit.

The point was, there was a lot to think about here before Ash decided exactly what to be most angry with her father about. She had a rich panoply of options, and *her* dad hadn't disappeared for a decade's worth of prayerful alone time.

But maybe there was no clarity to be found. It sounded like this curse wanted to keep the people it controlled in the dark as it drove them to destruction. And after Maura and Gabriel died in a final, angry, finishing fight, Rye and Draven just . . . shook hands and made a new bargain? But if talking had really worked as well as they claimed, why *hadn't* they vowed to share everything they knew with their own daughters?

Lucy used her power for good. She tried to give people comfort, encouragement, self-confidence, healing. Maura had wanted to be a doctor, a wife, and a mother. If the Steadfasts were such paragons, they should have been helping in those kinds of efforts all along. They hadn't. Why, because they were threatened? By what? Care? Love? Sparkly souls making glitter clouds above smiling people? Hester Prynne and Faithful Steadfast had lived in the *same community*.

Had Hester truly been bewitching this community of people, or was Faithful a ridiculous goth?

Lucy met Ash's eyes.

"If my dad is lost in contemplation," she said, "I think I know where he is."

XII.

THE SCARLET LETTER

The letter was the symbol of her calling. Such helpfulness was found in her,—so much power to do, and power to sympathize,—that many people refused to interpret the scarlet A by its original signification. They said that it meant Able; so strong was Hester Prynne, with a woman's strength.

NATHANIEL HAWTHORNE, *THE SCARLET LETTER*

MASSACHUSETTS BAY COLONY, THE COMMUNITY

"THIS IS THE wool we dyed with madder root." Pearl held up the skein and rubbed the wool on her upper lip before placing it on Hester's lap. "And this one was bloodroot." She lined it up next to the other skein, her dark hair falling forward across her cheek like silk.

"What's your favorite?" Hester used her thumbnail to secure another French knot.

"Sumac, because I like sumac tea with honey, but for color I like the wool you sent for from England best." Pearl grinned, pleased she had teased her mother.

"Oh ho, so the goods in the shops are far superior to what your poor wortcunner mother makes with her own hands." Hester formed another knot.

"Of course they are," Pearl said. "Why would I want my mother to work when she could play with me?"

Hester laughed. "Why, indeed?"

Pearl stood up and leaned against Hester's thigh, pulling down the frame she was embroidering so she could see it better. "I know what the *A* stands for."

Hester ignored the way her blood suddenly felt like it would send needles to her heart. She was determined to feel only what she could use now. She could not use fear. She could not use shame. "What do you think it stands for?"

Pearl met her eyes, outsize in her face, especially compared to the double French knots of her upper lip and pointed chin. "Not angels, who the Holy Father sends to sing."

"No," Hester replied.

"Not apples, sweet without bitter sting."

Hester kept sewing, proud of Pearl's obsession with her primer and her terrifyingly clever little mind, but also apprehensive. Pearl was perceptive. Knowing.

"And not awe, which we lay at Our Father's feet. Not apron, which keeps me nice and neat." Pearl touched her mother's face, her hand cool against her mother's hot cheek.

Hester should have anticipated that Pearl would worry this over in her mind. That she would observe everyone in town with deeper scrutiny. Hester had been watching her daughter as she played at the edge of the forest, talking seriously to the birds and voles, which meant she was strengthening an idea to bring directly to her mother.

"Definitely not acorn, from which a mighty oak grows, and not God's animals, who give us meat, and milk, and warmth." Pearl smiled, waiting to be praised before she dealt her blow.

"Your reading is remarkable for a girl of so few years." Hester had told Pearl this before, but her daughter liked hearing it. "Soon you will not need your mother at all."

"I will always need you, because I will never sew or mend, and I will never make bread or soup, and I will never dress myself alone because it will take too long to fasten on all my jewels. So you have to stay. But I do know what this *A* is for." Pearl dropped her hand to settle a finger on the field of ruby-red French knots carpeting the letter. "This *A* is for adultery, which is a sin."

Hester caught her gasp in her throat and let it out in a slow exhale. "Is it?"

"It is. You are an adulterer."

"What do you think that means?"

"I know what Faithful Steadfast thinks it means. I know what the doctor thinks it means. I know it's what Papa punishes himself for. I know you have been given grace, but you have not employed this grace in confession and humble penance, and there is no choice but a trial by your fellow man and God." Pearl had to stop to take a breath. She stood with her shoulders back, proud of the knowledge she'd gathered. "I know it's when you embrace without vows, like Mary and Micah who Papa married at the end of his very longest sermon that made you cry. But you and Papa are not married, so it's also when you embrace and . . . kiss." Pearl looked up under her eyelashes at this word to see if Hester would scold her. "It's when you do that, but the woman is married to someone else. Is it if the man is married to someone else, too?"

Hester welcomed the flash of anger that swamped her rising, frightened incredulity at her small child's revelations, because of course, of fucking course it was when the man was married to someone else, too, even when that "someone else" was the church, and no, no, women did not lure otherwise innocent men to their beds. Adulterous men came willingly and, in her case, in love, with love that she was glad to receive. It wasn't Hester and Arthur's embrace that made the sin. It was the church and its minions who stood smugly by while a loving man flogged himself.

"It is," Hester said. "There are many different versions of the church's sin of adultery."

Pearl raised both her eyebrows. "The church's sin?"

Hester couldn't help it. She laughed. There was nothing Pearl missed. Nothing. It was why everyone in town was helplessly charmed by her and convinced she wasn't altogether human. Pearl should have been the manifestation of sin, but instead she reminded everyone who saw her of who it was they loved, had loved, hoped to love. She was an argument that sin didn't exist. That love existed apart from didactic harrowing.

"Yes," Hester confirmed. "The church's sin. Tell me, my beautiful Pearl, what do you think?"

"I think our cottage is too small and that Papa should tell us to come live with him in the rectory. Or in an even bigger house in town. But I would miss my tree in the forest. Maybe you could live in the cottage, and Papa could live in a big house in town, and I could go back and forth as I please."

"As you please?" Hester smiled. Her Pearl was making her heart ache, not with sadness, but with the simple gorgeousness of her matter-of-fact faith. She would never do anything that discouraged her daughter from asking for what she wanted.

"Yes." Pearl touched the scarlet letter. "I like this color. Make me a red dress."

Hester jabbed her finger with the needle, and a round drop of blood welled up instantly. "Fuck." She put her finger in her mouth and let that be the reason her eyes burned with tears.

Pearl pulled her hand down and kissed her finger. "You got a little bit of blood on the A, but that's okay, because blood is red." Pearl pointed to the drop, already soaking into the wool. Then she smiled at Hester and leaned down and kissed the letter. "It's a good thing you have me to take care of you." Pearl pulled away and ran to the cupboard on her small, sturdy legs. "I will make you a bit of bread and jam to build up your strength, and a plate for me as well, because you are so hard to take care of."

Hester laughed, swiping away the leftover tears.

Pearl cut the loaf in pieces too big and rough and spooned out three meals' worth of jam on her plate. "You know, when you pin the letter onto your dress, everyone will see it and whisper to each other. Like they look at me and whisper."

"Oh, Pearl."

"I don't care." Pearl licked the jam spoon. "They mostly look at me and whisper because I am prettier than all the other children."

Hester started to . . . protest? Redirect? But then she thought that Pearl was very likely right. Humans weren't as pious or prudish or dour as they might be to protect themselves or spoon a mound of power onto their plate like Pearl's jam. There were good hearts in this town. Good minds, too.

Hester looked around at her shelves of salves, tinctures, and oils. She had teas and pots of poultice. Women came to her to ask for them. They told her their maladies. A few times, she had been called to help other attendants at a childbirth. These were women who knew as well as everyone else who Hester was, who Pearl was, and who the Reverend Arthur Dimmesdale was and why he made the walk off the road to Hester's, but they came to her anyway. Perhaps discreetly, but they came.

It was through one of these women that she'd learned of Faithful Steadfast's intention to call her up at church to be branded by the elders with a scarlet letter on her breast. That he believed a hearing well overdue.

She could not fathom what Faithful's great hate for her was or how it was that she'd hurt him. He spent a considerable part of his time finding out how Hester spent hers. She would feel entirely singled out, except that he also engaged himself in the business of everyone else in the community.

He took the sensibilities of the faith into his bones and patrolled the boundaries of the village for witches' marks and evidence of deviltry, sometimes stomping into town with something as innocuous as a snake's shed, claiming that he'd found it in an auspicious place in the shape of an evil sigil.

These dramatics did what she suspected Faithful wanted them to do, which was to scare people. It surprised Hester how much control he had managed to assume with these methods. To Hester, Faithful's approach was laughably maladroit and genuinely graceless. He represented a God that she couldn't convince herself anyone in this community believed existed. He seemed even to have imprisoned Arthur in a version of good that left red, raised welts on Arthur's back. Faithful's influence was strongest with men whom Hester would have ignored otherwise—men who depended on their wives and mothers for everything, unable to even put on their own boots, and yet kept their households under their thumbs and called it protection.

It was dangerous, this shadow church taking hold in the community.

It was why Hester took the woman's message seriously and had decided to reclaim her autonomy from Faithful's plan to destroy it in a sham hearing during tomorrow's service. She would walk into church and sit at her pew with the letter already on her breast—a letter three times as big as was strictly required and not Puritan plain, but festooned with curlicue stitches, ruddy flowers, deep amber birds and beasts, and blown roses in the deepest red.

She would wear it with Pearl at her side, her dark curls brushed out into deep shine, her comportment perfect.

Let everyone yearn for what Faithful wanted to accuse her of. Let Arthur see his daughter and the woman he loved smiling from their pew. Let Faithful fester on the dais, his hearing struck off his agenda in favor of the powerful disposition of the churchgoers to hurry home after the sermon and tend to their needs.

If Faithful could appoint himself an illusory office in this town, so could Hester. More than a few women needed the services of a wortcunner and midwife than were currently available. There were only a few older women who were willing to attend births along with the awful doctor, Roger Chillingworth, who, unsurprisingly, boarded with Faithful.

In addition to serving a need, it would be useful to hear first-hand what the people wanted here, which would help to keep her and her precocious daughter safe.

Hester traced the *A* with her finger.

Checkmate.

XIII.

ICE DEVIL

> He kept vigils, likewise, night after night, sometimes in utter darkness; sometimes with a glimmering lamp; and sometimes, viewing his own face in a looking-glass, by the most powerful light which he could throw upon it. He thus typified the constant introspection wherewith he tortured, but could not purify, himself.
>
> NATHANIEL HAWTHORNE, *THE SCARLET LETTER*

LUCY HADN'T SAID much since they left Rye's.

Ash let her be. She got the strong sense that her oldest friend was working through a wide range of emotions, and when Lucy was agitated, she tended to weaponize things like wind and lightning.

She did ask Ash to drive her to Walmart, and Ash waited in the car with a snoring Helegar until she came out in a new puffy coat zipped to the chin, a beanie, and snow boots.

Then, without consultation, Ash took them to Firetta's, an area fast-food chain with a handful of locations. She tried not to think too hard about Hector's instruction to learn more about herself before laying her whole heart at Lucy's feet. He *had* mentioned Firetta's, but that didn't mean Ash was ignoring his advice by taking Lucy there. Firetta's was Lucy's favorite—so much so that it was where she had celebrated most of her birthdays and a good number of life events in general.

Ash was taking care of Lucy, that was all. It felt good. It felt like something *she* wanted to do, herself, Ashes Steadfast.

"How's your Leapin' Lizard?" Lucy wiped her mouth to ask, then took a long sip of her vanilla malt.

Ash examined what was left of the soft steamed pita folded over cream cheese, spicy chicken, and sweet chili sauce. The honest answer would be that it was fucking delicious, that she hadn't eaten anything like this in ages, that its appeals hadn't diminished in any way, and that every creamy, spicy bite was an exercise in longing, satisfaction, more longing, and presumptive sadness that at some point her sandwich would be eaten.

An even more honest answer would include the disconcerting but agreeable fact that she hadn't received any spiritual comeuppance for consuming this delicious food or otherwise enjoying herself in Lucy's presence—a state of affairs she could not explain or account for but entirely approved of.

"They're still good," she said.

Lucy smiled at her, a smile that came on slow with lots of eye contact, like she could hear Ash's carnal thoughts instead of her thoughts about cream cheese, and she also knew that Ash was remembering how they used to sit on the same side of the booth, feeding each other bites of what they were eating and hooking their legs over the other's legs. "Good."

"Yours?" Ash liked Lucy's face even better with its tiny lines and extra freckles. She liked the way her brows had gotten darker, matching the dark facets of her eyes. Lucy had ordered a sandwich called the Peacenik. It had brown bread and grilled and chopped vegetables held together with preserved lemon hummus and slices of hot Halloumi cheese. It fascinated Ash, this sophisticated order of Lucy's. The Peacenik hadn't been on the menu a decade ago. Lucy had resisted that old version of herself, and it meant Ash was forced to see her a different way *again,* even if it was only as a woman who would order a sandwich with vegetables and moan as she ate it.

"God, it's good. But everything is good. Everything I put in my mouth is a revelation." Lucy ran her index finger along the edge of the sandwich, gathering hummus on her finger.

Egads. "I meant to ask you, *haven't* you eaten? Like, haven't I seen you eat? With people you were . . . talking to. When we were both at the grand opening of Hector's Tavern, for example."

Lucy laughed. "Yes. It tasted muted, though, like airplane food. Or sometimes a little bit disgusting. It's been the same with everything to do with my body. I go to the bathroom, but it's like when you get up to go in the middle of the night, half-asleep, and it happens, but it's forgotten, all the urgency and pain and disgust and relief around it gone. Maybe that's a completely gross thing to talk about." Lucy smiled around her straw.

"But it's interesting. I guess you don't get sick?"

"Not even a sniffle."

"Tired?"

"Not really, except when I know I'm getting close to being . . . to going back. Where I go. But that's more like a headache."

Ash looked down at the last bite of her sandwich. "Why do you think that it's this way for you, and it wasn't for your dad?"

Lucy's sigh called up an answering hitch somewhere in Ash's middle. "I don't know. But I think what broke me out of it was your power of second chances. If what I figured out was that I could understand people and myself in deep and important ways by touching their souls, then I think *you've* been trying to figure your own thing out by taking us to the places where we came of age together. The places where we became ourselves and became us." She leaned forward. "Even the fact that we had our first fight in Roger's Field. That was where we talked about if you wanted to kiss me or I wanted to kiss you, or if this was what having a best friend was like or if it was something else. It was where we were safe, so safe, Ashes. We could change the subject anytime or leave or admit or deny whatever we wanted to. That was *us*, and some part of you has always believed in us. I think you knew that our love could break the curse. I think you've been trying this whole time."

Lucy's throat hollowed out with a breath, and she suddenly broke eye contact.

Ash's chest felt warm. That was more good than she had thought of herself for so long, if ever. She was a wobbly kaleidoscope of feelings and impressions, wind rustling through the leaves of their tree, the sticky press of Lucy's bare leg against hers, and the way her thigh had trembled to hold perfectly still as long as she could, as long as forever.

"I didn't stop trying." She let whatever Lucy could see in her face be seen, even as her cheeks burned with the revelation that she had never been a woman in black with a broken, useless heart.

"No one's soul stops trying." Lucy's voice was velvet. "Nothing that anyone *wants* stops trying to be heard and understood. When we were together in those places where you took us, *my* soul believed that what we were really doing was fighting for each other."

"You did?"

"We might have gotten here sooner if we'd tried hate sex."

Ash sucked in a breath and choked on it.

"You should see your expression." Lucy folded her sandwich wrapper into a neat square. "It could be a meme."

She didn't doubt it, any more than her brain didn't hesitate to imagine at least a dozen different alternative scenarios, right down to Lucy holding Ash against one of the light posts in Hector's parking lot while Ash fisted that tiny little dress.

"I've been thinking." Lucy's voice interrupted this fantasy in a tone distant and preoccupied, the way it used to get when she was deep in trying to explain some math concept that Ash pretended to have a hope of understanding.

"What about?"

"Being gay."

"Obviously, obviously." Ash softened her reflexive sarcasm with a small smile, which Lucy answered with a big, genuine smile of amusement that proved she saw through her defenses.

"An obvious thought given our current pickle. Why do we challenge queerness? As soon as we know it, the first thing we do is question it. They even call it 'questioning,' as if queerness has to be tested. It isn't something that can be simply known, even if you simply know it."

"I worked with someone in a law office who told me that her mom thought being queer was a diagnosis of exclusion. Like a rare disease or illness no one really believes they'll encounter in practice."

Lucy laughed. "Here's the thing, though. When you step into that rainbow, queerness is a beautiful antidote to self-doubt. Especially as time goes on and you realize just how much of the world is queer, and how much of the world's beautiful and impossible things were made by queer people. The government tries to erase us, school boards tell us we're dangerous, parents tell us we're faking it, churches tell us we're going to hell, but it's still so *heady* to simply know, no matter what anyone thinks or does or legislates, that You. Are. Queer."

"Is it how you knew you weren't an instrument of evil?"

"It is."

"It's why I made friends with Cal."

"Absolutely."

"It's why I went to New York."

"Yes."

"And it's why we're going to break the curse." Ash said it out loud to test her faith.

"It's why we're already breaking it." Lucy reached up to touch Ash's jaw with the tips of her fingers, briefly.

Ash hoped it wouldn't be long before she was brave enough to touch her back. She smoothed her hair away from her face. "Where did Draven go?"

Lucy slumped. Earlier, she'd shucked her new puffy coat off and shoved it behind her on the back of the booth, and now she looked like she was emerging from a lumpy shell. "I would have thought he was dead this whole time, except sometimes when Helegar comes to me, he smells like my dad's cigarettes." She pushed herself up to sit straight. "But your dad's theory made me remember where Draven used to head off to in the winter. It was his place where he could hear what he believed were answers."

"How do we get there?"

"We'll need to drive to the boat docks on the west shore of the bay."

Ash ate the last bite of her sandwich, cleared the table, and they made their way into the weather. The silence drifted back between them. She navigated carefully through blowing snow and slush-covered roads. The trees closed in as they approached their destination.

Go to the forest.

As they neared Lake Michigan, she started to notice the slush giving way to a sharpening contrast between the yellow-orange road paint and the deep black asphalt, now lined with perfectly plowed snow. Every road marker was straight and clean. It looked like a movie set, or like they were driving in a snow village miniature on someone's mantel.

"This feels weird." Ash followed the turn-by-turn signs. "Doesn't it?"

"It feels familiar, in the sense that I can tell it's both real and not real." Lucy rolled down her window and stuck her hand out. "It's warmer than it should be."

"Because of your dad, you think?"

Lucy nodded. Her mouth was tight.

Ash followed a sign that opened into a wide, empty parking lot. She slowed to a stop in the middle of the lot but left the engine running, awaiting further instruction.

"Go ahead and park. We can walk from here."

Ash pulled close to one of the drives to the launch, and they got out of the car. She zipped her coat up and put on the fingerless gloves from her pockets before flipping up the collar of her leather jacket. Lucy bundled herself up in her new gear and hiked up her tote until it was snug against her shoulder.

Helegar had his skull head out and was looking eagerly around as they walked downhill toward the ramp. As soon as they cleared the trees and brush, the bay opened up in front of them, blindingly white and frozen solid. Ash counted ice fishing huts until she lost track. There were more than three dozen, fanned out over a few hundred yards of picture-perfect shoreline.

It was all wrong.

The air was more still than in the parking lot. Too warm. More uncanny, the huts were grayed out, monotone, as if they were in a black-and-white movie, and they were as empty as the parking lot. Except one.

That hut was in full color, with a thin wisp of smoke coming from its chimney.

This was a place Draven had made. If it had been real, there would have been other men here, banging truck doors closed, gutting fish, chucking their empty beer cans and whiskey bottles into the dumpster at the far end of the boat launch. But it wasn't real.

It was a foxhole.

Lucy stared out at the shack where her father was. Bright red with a black roof. It seemed to glow.

The ice between the shack and where they stood wasn't anything like the smooth, clean ice of a rink. It heaved at the shoreline in uneven, sharp teeth. It was lumpy with snow, shoved into rough paths that revealed the gray and black inclusions in the unbroken field of white.

The bay was loud. A subsonic bass note rang out and traveled to the horizon, but she couldn't identify it as wind or weather or water. Ash imagined the fathoms beneath, a leviathan moving slowly through the thick, cold water. "I hate this." She wrapped her arms around herself, though she wasn't cold. "People sit out here voluntarily?"

"My dad loved ice fishing. He said he could hear himself think, and it was the farthest from humanity he could take himself and still be in Rye's orbit."

"Do you think he had to stay away from people because they tempted him?"

Lucy looked over her shoulder at Ash. "I'm not sure that's a helpful way to think about it. For sure, he would have wanted to talk to people, and your dad said the terms the two of them set up didn't let that happen."

"I guess my dad probably wouldn't have stuck to their bargain if he went looking for Draven and found him communing with someone's soul."

"Probably not." Lucy stepped down from the concrete launch onto the ice. "Let's get this over with."

Ash followed her, taking careful steps as her heart pounded. The snow squeaked in a way that made shivers race up her spine, and when they passed the first grayed-out hut, she silent-screamed at the sound of lake water sloshing up through what had to be its fishing hole, concealed from view inside the structure. Compulsively, she imagined what would happen if she slipped. Her body would hit the ice and break through it. The strong Lake Michigan current would pull her under the surface, drag her far from any escape, her breath stopped in her lungs, her boots heavy and dragging her into the dark.

She watched it happen on a loop inside her head, again and again.

"Ashes?"

She toed a chunk of snow with the tip of her boot, certain it was a broken shard of ice in disguise, concealing a massive crack. She couldn't identify the next safe step to take. Experimentally, she took a step back, then stopped, stomach sick, pulse pounding at every joint and crease of her body because it occurred to her she might step backward into a bowl of soft ice, secretly melting, invisible unless she checked every placement of her feet.

She wanted to get on her hands and knees, on her belly, to spread out her weight. Wasn't that what you were supposed to do if you were trapped on the ice?

"Ashes, baby, look at me."

Slowly, with excruciating care, she moved into a crouch, then stopped, trembling. She set down her knees on the ice before she met Lucy's eyes.

"Baby girl." Ash could see the place on Lucy's left eye where she had twice as many lower lashes as anywhere else along the lash line. She remembered touching that tiny paintbrush of lashes with the tip of her finger as a prelude to kissing Lucy the way she liked best, with her mouth just a little open and soft, pressing against Lucy's mouth, feeling the erotic plushness of that motionless kiss for long moments before one of them made a horny noise and things got serious. "Look at me."

Ash was looking, remembering the slick texture of Lucy's teeth against her tongue. The way she arched her body up to meet Ash's exploring palms and said her name on an exhale like a plea.

Things she never let herself remember.

Things she'd never been able to forget.

There was a difference between forgetting and what Ash had done a decade ago on the stumbling walk across Roger's Field to her Corolla with her throat's blood tacky in the webs of her fingers. She'd felt the percussive beat of her pulse like the ticking of a stopwatch counting out the steps to her car, to the road. More than she wanted to live, she'd wanted none of it to have happened.

You'll die alone. That was what she'd told herself. She'd said it aloud so she would have to stop crying. Her voice emerged from her broken throat in an unrecognizable, caterwauling croak. *You're supposed to die alone, with nothing and no one.* The earth heaved up to meet her or she tripped, she didn't know. She stumbled and half fell, cold with the dismaying certainty she was about to drop into hell and burn. She caught herself against a bush that raked welts into her skin. *Your name is Ashes. You're a Steadfast. This is what you're for.*

She hadn't forgotten anything.

She'd just done what she'd had to do to survive.

Now, Lucy's hands were strong and warm around her wrists. Ash rested her fingertips on the bare skin between Lucy's gloves and the nylon cuffs of her coat. She had the softest skin. Ash's favorite was the skin under her breasts, so soft it was like it had no substance at all, and a little duskier, rosier, than the pearly skin of her breasts.

"Can you stand up?" Lucy's voice should have disappeared in the low, grinding moans of the ice, but it didn't. It was so clear. She shifted her hands to Ash's forearms and lifted, and Ash followed her to standing, looking at the curls flattened against her forehead by the beanie.

"I'm scared of this ice," she said. "It doesn't feel safe. I think I'm having a panic attack."

Lucy slipped her hands from her forearms to Ash's elbows, then under her armpits to hold her in a full embrace. The muscles in Ash's legs and hips and inner thighs let go with a rush of warmth. She'd been keeping herself together with tension alone.

She put her arms around Lucy. The leather of her jacket made a high-pitched *snick* over the nylon of Lucy's coat, grounding the hug and making it real.

Lucy's arms were tight around her. Ash's face was buried in Lucy's neck, her head cradled in Lucy's palm. "I'll make it safe for you."

After a moment, a hush replaced the low-frequency hum of the lake. Ash wasn't sure how long she stood there, held in the circle of Lucy's arms while the world stilled. She didn't ease away until Helegar nosed up her pants cuffs and pressed against the side of her leg above her boot. His body must have filled back in over his bones, because the nose was soft and wet.

It had begun to snow again in big, fluffy flakes. That was why everything had gone quiet. The weather dropped the sky, making the horizon indistinct and the area of the lake with the fishing huts smaller. Human-scaled.

Lucy watched with approval as the snow lightly blanketed the ice, obscuring the hint of the black lake beneath it at the same time it provided traction.

"You did this." *For me.*

"A Prynne can call down the elements for better reasons than a fight." Lucy slid her arms away, kicking Ash's heart back into panic until she felt a warm hand come around hers. "One step in front of the other. It's not far."

It wasn't. The snow had begun mounding on the ice in such a way that it seemed to outline a white, straight path for them to follow. When Ash took a step on it, it gave in a soft squeak against the soles of her boots. It was the precise kind of snow that someone from Green Bay looked for in order to keep from slipping when they walked their dog on the sidewalks in winter.

Helegar waited in front of them, his tail wagging madly, and then took off down the path, zigzagging and smelling everything more than an inch high. The little dog enjoying himself made the lake ice feel even more manageable. If a dog found joy in it, there was joy.

This was okay. Ash was safe. She took another step, and it was fine.

"I only came out here with my dad once," Lucy said. "I was around twelve. I was excited. I loved the idea of a house on the ice with a tiny stove inside to keep it warm. I brought decorations with me because my dad said there weren't any."

"How'd that go for you?"

"At first, it was good. I did love sitting on the canvas chair bundled up by the stove, with hot tea from Dad's thermos and a candy bar. The decorations were locker decorations, because I knew the framing inside the hut was metal, and I thought it would be cool to get those big puffy flowers for lockers. Remember those?"

"With the magnets on the back. Smart idea."

"I thought so. It was obvious right away there weren't enough of them to make an impact, but I pretended to like them."

"Did you have fun?" Ash focused on one step after the next. On Lucy's hand in hers.

"No!" Lucy laughed. "It was boring. The fishing hole was scary, and every time he brought up a fish—he was catching whitefish to fry—he'd hold it by the tail and slap its head against the rim of the hole, then thread a wire through its gills next to the others that were lying dead on the ice."

"Whoa."

"Yep. Frozen blood built up on the rim of the hole, and the fish smelled bad until he took them outside the hut. By then, there were other men. Everyone was smoking and drinking or telling disgusting jokes about their wives and girlfriends. I was cold. My butt hurt. I could very much sense that Dad didn't want me to complain, so I was suppressing my complaints, which made me antsy. I had to go to the bathroom. I was hungry but had eaten too much sugar in the tea and candy bars, so it was sick hunger. I couldn't guess when he would be finished."

They were only twenty feet from the hut now. "That sounds highly unpleasant."

"Even though I never said anything, he could tell I was done, and I could tell he was annoyed but pretending not to be. Once we made it home, he told me I was old enough to be fine on my own overnight. He left me watching TV and didn't come back before I had to take the bus to school the next day."

The story worked to bring Ash's brain back online. It sounded so bad, but that was how their lives had been. She and Lucy ran back and forth to each other's houses, invented variations on boxed mac and cheese for their dinners, and pooled cash their dads had left for them on dining room tables and kitchen counters, spending it on getting their ears pierced, video games, and faddish jeans. They'd been happy, and the basics were taken care of, but neither one of their dads was providing what she'd consider adequate parental supervision.

She tried to think about Draven back then—what he'd been like, or her own father—but she couldn't. She rubbed her chest. Her heart hurt. "I don't understand why they couldn't carry on with their theological exchange of views while also making sure that ninety percent of our diet wasn't Gushers and Pop-Tarts." Ash stopped in front of the hut, her stomach heavy with nerves, fear, leftover ice adrenaline, and Lucy feelings.

"I kind of want to see him, but I don't know," Lucy whispered. "I'll just have to go through it all again when he inevitably leaves."

"You know what, though?" Ash turned to face her, still holding her hand. "You're the only one of us who fought for the right thing. We're here because of you. The so-called devil." Something about the hush of the snow and Lucy's hand in hers made it easy to say this.

"So-called?"

"Fate dealt you a bad hand, but against the odds and all probability, I'm standing here with you on the ice of Lake Michigan, holding your hand, because you believed in yourself. You found ways to keep faith. So you don't owe him your loyalty. You don't owe him anything. It's okay if you're here for yourself. If all you need from him is his story, you can take that and go."

A few of Lucy's curls blew across her face. Snow had collected on her coat collar and made her skin unevenly rosy. As she looked at Ash, the snow changed. The flakes became slower but bigger, spinning in the weak light. You could see their individual filigreed patterns as they fell.

"Where have you *been*, Ashes? I've missed you so, so much." Her smile was the same indulgent one she'd given Nathan in Hector's parking lot—the one that flipped her Cupid's bow into a round upper lip and sank double dimples in her cheeks. Then, with a confident toss of her head, Lucy stepped up to the door of the fishing hut and knocked, loud. "Dad! It's me."

It seemed like a long wait before the door opened outward with a loud squeal and Draven Prynne stepped out of the ice house, alive. He wore his wavy dark hair in a ponytail. He'd kept his beard neat. He dropped a cigarette in the snow, where it snuffed out with a hiss.

"Lucy." He coughed. His voice was coarse, like he never used it. "Ash. Do the two of you want to come in? It's a tight fit, but you'll be warmer."

"Sure, Dad, we'll join you in your out-of-time fishing hut. Nice to see you, too." Helegar writhed madly at their feet.

Draven moved to the side, and Lucy walked past him. Ashes went in behind her.

The inside was just as Lucy had described it, down to the fading flowers attached to the thin metal supports. The heater was warm, but there wasn't a hole in the ice for fishing. Instead, a rubber mat covered the floor. An outdoor canvas chair, the kind that clicked into a reclined position, occupied one wall. It had an old quilt draped on the back of it. A metal bucket that looked like it was being used as an ashtray hung from the arm.

Helegar trotted to a weathered dog bed set up by the stove. He turned around three times and settled in with a sigh.

"This is how you've been living?" Ash didn't mean to break the silence like that, but the situation was genuinely bleak.

Draven shoved his hands into the pockets of his Carhartt coat. "What can I do for you girls?"

"You know, after we talked to Rye, I thought I was prepared." Lucy tossed her hair, frowning spectacularly. "I wasn't. Why should I be? Why should I be okay with my father avoiding me for years? You abandoned me. You left me alone to live with a bad bargain you knew I hated!"

Draven rubbed his palms together with a mournful expression. "That was it, hon. I knew you hated it, but I couldn't stop it. I hoped you and Ash would build on what we'd tried to do to weaken the deal, but for me, there was nothing left to do but take myself off."

"Except be a dad."

Ash knew that tone of voice. Draven would do well to tread lightly.

"You were grown," he said. "You didn't need a father."

"Oh, come on!" Lucy threw her hands in the air. "An eighteen-year-old girl doesn't need a father, but a three-hundred-year-old miniature dachshund needs his own fucking bed?"

Helegar whined and pressed his head between his paws. Draven looked at the ground. "I killed Rye."

"For five minutes, yeah! But I'm going to have to guess the strain of the curse was only one factor balanced against all the smoking you two were doing, not to mention subsisting on a diet of Culver's ButterBurgers while you did nothing but sit around talking in circles at the backyard picnic table in a cloud of Deet!"

Draven winced with his entire body.

"You left without even waiting to see what was going to happen with your time-lord bestie!" Lucy pointed at his surprised expression. "Yeah, I know about that, mister, and your leaving without even saying 'see ya' meant I thought *Rye* had killed you, and Ash thought you killed Rye, which meant that you two's big hope for us to learn from your example of nonviolence blew up in a column of smoke, because the *very first thing we did* was try to kill each other."

He glanced at Ash's scar. She dragged her finger across it, deadpan. Lucy deserved the backup.

"All that *communication*," Lucy said with disdain, "and it never occurred to either one of you to talk to us. You know what Hester said?"

"Hester's in the mix?" Draven ran a hand down his face. "Fuck."

"Yeah. Met her. Didn't love her, but she's growing on me. She has a way of getting to the point. Hester wondered if we'd ever asked ourselves *why* our dads left us out of these big conversations of theirs. I'm starting to wonder if Hester's approach might've been more effective than what two twentysomething white guys came up with at the tail end of many, many generations of similarly fucked twentysomething white guys!"

Draven let out a long sigh of protest. "This, here, is why I didn't want to—"

Lucy held up her palm. "Absolutely not. Don't turn what your daughter needs to say to you into an excuse for your mistakes. We learned a lot from Rye. He told us what he knows about *his* deadbeat dad and how he kidnapped Grandma Maura out of the sanatorium."

"Amazing," Ash chimed in. "Loved that for us."

"We learned about how Rye can bop around through time. We learned that he blames himself for Ash's being yoked to this curse, but also, like you, he isn't much interested in taking accountability when it comes to *parenthood*—"

"The annoying ghost that haunts this entire drama," Ash added.

"We learned about how you liked to take yourself off for your contemplation and meditation and scholarly pursuits, and then I remembered this place and knew that in actual fact, *nothing* was keeping you from seeing me. You didn't even leave town!"

"Why doesn't Lucy *live* when she's not with me?" Ash burst in, apparently roused by Lucy's lecture in precise proportion to its power to make Draven resemble a collapsed star. "That's fucked-up!"

"Are you able to travel like Rye can?" Draven asked her.

"No, but I think I can portal to places where it's possible to have a second chance."

"There's your answer." He opened the front of his coat and felt around until he pulled out a pack of cigarettes. Before Ash could protest, he lit one. The smoke zipped backward over his head in an obedient contrail that left the hut through the crack at the top of the door.

Ash glanced at Lucy for clarification. "Am I missing something? I thought your dad was a talker. The whole time he's been gone without anybody knowing where he is, he's been here in his man hut with his bone dog. Do I have that right?"

"Not exactly." Draven took a long drag of his cigarette. Very long. The hut was starting to feel too small to hold both Lucy's and Ash's impatience.

She silently counted to ten before she let herself speak. "I'd love to hear a comment, concern, or idea here, Draven."

He reached for his cigarettes, then seemed to notice he already had a lit one in his hand. "I could always take myself back in time, then run time forward again. Not long. A day, maybe. But I can repeat it as much as I want. Rewind. Go forward through the same hours. Rewind again. I use it to think, regroup. When I want, I start back at any time I like. I lose nothing."

Ash would've gasped if she'd had breath left. "Is that what this is?" Ash looked around at the hut. "You've been living in the same handful of hours in this hut, smoking and fishing, for *years?*"

It was gruesome to contemplate. The same weak light. The same weather. The same pack of cigarettes. The same amount of hunger, or fatigue, over and over, forever. Purgatory. A hell of his own making.

Lucy let out a shuddering breath. "Did you ever ask yourself if there might be any consequences of this cowardice for your daughter? Beyond the abandonment. That I might have, say, fallen into a hellish time hole due to your incessant rewinding? That maybe that nothing place where you sent me was where I had to be whenever I wasn't fighting the only person who'd ever loved me?"

Ash felt a hard press against her ankle. It was Helegar again. She looked down into his sockets, and inside the emptiness, she saw a deep, soft love. He'd come to her. He'd come to her because of her horror at what Lucy was putting together.

She picked up his surprisingly warm and solid bones and held him to her chest and focused on his love, given without condition to everyone, regardless of what they were fucking up.

Draven blew smoke out through his nose. "Nothing's worked

like this before. Both Rye and I should be dead, but we're not. The curse isn't working the same for the two of you."

"You could say that." Lucy's voice was rough. "A life without continuity of existence certainly hasn't been working for me."

Draven inhaled more smoke and started to cough. It took him a minute to recover. "Hester said—"

"Hester!" Lucy pressed her fingertips to her forehead. "When?"

"Years ago now. She stopped coming around when I said I wasn't looking to her for answers anymore. No point in her wasting her time on me and Rye. We didn't get her what she wanted."

"To end it?" Ash was surprised she'd managed to speak, she was so blown apart. He made it sound like this curse belonged to Hester, Lucy, and Ash, but not to him. He'd had his try. He'd done his best. Now he was having his ice fishing shack time, alone with his thoughts.

If the Devil meant change, Draven was *not it*.

"She was the first devil Prynne," he said. "She defeated the first Steadfast, Faithful. At least I think she did. She's not the most forthcoming. The problem is, if Hester was going to stop it, she would have by now." Draven glanced at Lucy from under the unkempt shelf of his eyebrows. "I'm sorry. I didn't know how it's been for you. I only guessed a little from Helegar's behavior. I've been rooting for you to figure it out. I don't have the right to say it, but I've missed you."

It was the last straw for Lucy. "I think I have to go," she spat. "We're meeting people."

"Did you find out what you wanted to know?"

The question woke up a thought in Ash's mind that shoved

her anger at Draven aside. "The tree." She nudged Lucy's arm. "The tree."

"What tree?"

"Hester's tree! There's always a tree." Growth and rebirth, maybe. The forest was more than dancing naked in the firelight. She couldn't understand why it was important, but she listened to the voice inside her anyway. "In the North Woods, the big oak, and when I saw her the first time, it was at the edge of a forest. I thought that was because of the devil's association with the woods, but then there's *our* tree in Roger's Field, and how there's the new carving linked to ours. HP plus AD. Hester Prynne plus . . ." Ash looked at Draven.

He shrugged.

". . . plus someone whose initials are AD. I think the tree is important. What if my getting us both to the tree in Roger's Field, and to the tree in the North Woods, is also important, except that the only second chance in both of those places is—"

"The fight," Lucy said.

"The fight, yes, but also, in New York, wasn't that more about you trying to sacrifice your soul so that I could have what I wanted?" Ash spoke with more confidence. She was getting closer.

"I wanted you to have what you *should* have, especially because I got stuck in nothingness thanks to him." She jerked her thumb at her dad without looking in his direction.

"You told me that all the consequences anyone ever had when they gave their soul for a dream was the fine print they wrote themselves," Ash said. "It was their self-doubt, or what they thought they should have to give up, or how they thought they should pay to get what they wanted." Ash took a step toward her and grabbed her hand. "Lucy, if you can't pay with your soul for your dreams, or even bargain with it, then you also can't give it up for someone else. That doesn't work. It was never going to get me what I wanted."

"No?"

"Of course not. We'd already shared our hopes with each other. You knew what I wanted." She could never have made herself take Lucy's soul in exchange for just *part* of her dream. The part without Lucy. That was a bad deal.

Lucy rubbed a tear off her cheek. "So the tree?"

"Yes. The tree. Hester and her person. You and me. Second chances. There's something there, I don't know what, and I've used my brain juice up, but we have to go talk to Hector and Cal. That's who we need now. We have to do *everything* different, and talking to our dads isn't that."

Lucy opened her tote for Helegar. He whined and looked over at Draven, then wrapped his tail vertebrae around himself.

"Okay." Lucy rubbed her hand down the dog's back. Ash put Helegar down. "You stay with him and keep him company, and I'll see you later."

Helegar wagged the very tip of his tail and then trotted to his dog bed, curled up, and seemed to settle into sleep. Lucy pulled Ash toward the door. "We're going. Dad?"

"Yep."

"I love you. I'm angry and disappointed in you, but I love you. I feel like you need to ease up on the contemplation and maybe *do* something?" Lucy looked around at the shack. "You're keeping everything the same. You're keeping me stuck. But I'm not the same, Dad. I'm not you, and all I want is the freedom to be me. Live your life. Whatever it is. Let me live mine. I think that's going to answer more questions for you than contemplating the same fucking day all by yourself."

The small, regretful smile he gave Lucy pinched a tender place in Ash's heart. There was hope there, still. She hoped that Lucy could get what she wanted.

And she hoped that there might be a way, too, for Ashes Steadfast to find a real second chance to make her life her own.

Maybe.

Maybe was more—more of everything—than Ash had felt in a long time.

XIV.

AN ANGEL, A HEALER, A PURITAN, AND THE DEVIL WALK INTO A BAR

> Let them scorn me as they will, strong traits of their nature have intertwined themselves with mine.
>
> NATHANIEL HAWTHORNE, *THE SCARLET LETTER*

ASH PULLED INTO the parking lot of Hector's Tavern. Calliope's rose-gold crossover was already there, but the lot was otherwise empty. They'd agreed to meet up during the break before the factory shift ended.

She shut down the car. They sat looking at the bar.

"At *any point*"—Lucy unfastened her seat belt before settling back against her seat—"my dad could have come to me, knowing what I was going through from firsthand experience, and he could have helped me."

Ash listened to the car's heater tick down. "That is true. He could have. But he did not."

She found it easy to condemn Draven. Her third-party perspective made it simple. He'd failed his daughter. He'd been weak and self-centered and stolen Lucy's life from her.

Now the tip of Lucy's nose was red. She had dark circles

under her eyes. "When the curse passed to me, I didn't know what was happening."

"No?" Ash had known instantly. As she'd followed the EMTs who were keeping her dad alive, loading him into the ambulance, she'd looked across the street and seen a crowd of people dressed in black. Eyes hollow, mouths slack. They met her gaze as one body. Her clothes had started to burn like they were soaked in drain opener, and a drop of blood ran from her lip ring and over her chin.

"No. I was suddenly nowhere. With no one."

Ash tried to imagine it. She felt sick.

"After our terrible fight," Lucy said, "the next thing I knew, I was at the high school."

"Right. The bench. Mary Beth. I'd never seen you so—"

"Glowy? Scantily dressed?"

"I was going to say elegant."

Lucy grinned. "Elegant, huh?"

"Intimidating."

"Go on." But Lucy laughed.

"It was scary. I thought, 'That's it. Lucy is taking the soul of that woman with the cat stroller. Just like my dad said she would.'"

"But Ashes, *what* did he say?"

Right. Right, right. Another question that kept returning. She closed her eyes and tried to focus. She found a memory of his voice and Draven's, drifting through her bedroom window from the picnic table in the backyard. What had they been talking about? Something about god. Punishment. Occasional laughter. The pop of a soda can top.

They could've been talking about anything.

"I don't know. He said enough to make me afraid."

Lucy clasped Ash's hand in hers. "I don't want to feel suspicious about our dads, but I don't think they're leveling with us."

"I don't, either." Ash rubbed her thumb along the side of Lucy's hand. "You know, when it comes to Rye, sometimes I felt like he was teaching me to swim by pushing me off the end of the dock. Sometimes I felt like he didn't believe I was good enough to bother with. Sometimes I spent weeks trying to figure out who my mother was. Sometimes he came into my room when I was crying with a plate of Hydrox. Did he really not understand that if he just went to my orchestra concerts and first gigs and put a rainbow flag on his truck, I would've followed him anywhere and never complained?"

"Draven used to tell me that people like us don't do things like study math at MIT and work for NASA."

Ash met Lucy's eyes in surprise. "Your grandmother Maura was studying to be a doctor in Boston. I'm pretty sure there are only fancy places to study medicine in Boston. Did he mean people like *him*?"

Lucy shrugged.

"You know what I'm realizing, Lucy Prynne? *You* went to all my concerts and motivated me to keep my grades up enough to stay in music. I went to your Mathlete competitions and quizzed you on math, which I comprehended even less than I comprehend how Hester could possibly have had a miniature dachshund in seventeenth-century New England. I sold my guitar so I could buy you the scientific calculator you wanted, and you went to the pawn shop and traded your phone to get it back."

"I told Draven I lost my phone." Lucy smiled. "He was pissed, but he had to get me another one because he was never around. Very strategic move on my part."

"And both of us came up with the dream of New York. The train to Cambridge. It was a dream that *was* for people like us. We took care of each other."

Ash held her eye contact with Lucy. They looked at each other until Ash couldn't breathe. She needed to share Lucy's breath, and so she got closer.

She felt Lucy's breath over her upper lip, remembered the feel of Lucy's mouth, and unwittingly moved even closer. Lucy pulled her hand from Ash's and raked her fingers up her thigh, making Ash shiver with pleasure.

They were in the dark car, the only sound their breathing, their heartbeats. All she could think about was sinking into this rich blackness with Lucy and getting to her skin.

"Ashes," Lucy said, almost against her mouth.

"Yeah." She could feel Lucy's lip against hers now.

"It's dark," Lucy whispered, her upper lip dragging against Ash's with the *k*. "It's dark outside."

Ash shook her head, brushing her mouth across Lucy's. *No.*

Lucy eased away, turned her body, looked around.

"What?" Ash sucked in a breath to try to distract her body from killing her in horny protest as it clenched and hitched and fought for air.

"When did it get so dark?" Lucy asked. "Did a storm roll in? Have we been in your car that long?" She reflexively reached for Helegar in her bag, but Helegar had stayed with Draven. "Oh, god."

Ash reluctantly followed Lucy's gaze. "What the fuck?"

They'd parked right in front of Hector's. Now, where she should have seen a long, brightly lit covered entry with a deep green metal roof over a tidy brick exterior, she instead saw a building stripped of any interest, stained with dirt around its foundation. The brick was covered in graffiti. Hector's meticulously groomed gravel lot had turned into an expanse of old gravel and mud surrounded by a leaning chain-link fence choked with weeds.

Green weeds. In winter.

Ash opened the door to the car. Warm air and the summer night hum of insects rushed in.

Lucy stripped off her coat, and Ash followed her lead. "It's later than it was. Look where the moon is."

High in the night sky. The lights of the factory spilled over the fence.

"Portfenestrated," Ash said. "But why here?"

"Second chance. Must be. Does a particular moment at Hector's come to mind?" Lucy met her at the trunk of the car, where they had a panorama of the deserted lot. There were reverberating metallic bangs coming from the factory and the occasional laugh or shout from a worker on a smoke break in the loading docks.

"Just recently. With Nathan."

"But it didn't look like this then."

"So what's the second chance here?" She gestured at the dark parking lot.

Ash brushed a mosquito away from her cheek. "I don't know. It's Hector who has an attachment to this place. He found it like this and saw the potential."

"He'd talked about running his own place forever."

"A 'real Green Bay place.' He wanted to make a local legacy. You did that for him, remember? When he wasn't sure what he wanted to do with his life after a bad meeting with his high school guidance counselor, you told him you thought he was someone who would want to be a part of the community. This bar wouldn't exist if you hadn't encouraged him to follow his heart. You were a good friend. You are still."

Lucy's brown eyes glistened. "I hurt you."

"You fought for me. You never let go of Hector. You even made friends with Cal. You're *good*, Lucy. You never stopped taking care of me, not even when I gave up."

Lucy pinched the bridge of her nose to keep from crying. "You're here. That's why I am."

It was the same thing she always said, and finally, finally, Ash could admit that she was delighted to hear it. As hard as she'd tried to change her feelings for Lucy, they hadn't changed. Lucy had never stopped talking to what was starved inside Ash. Making her feel special. Seeing her for exactly who she was and feeding those parts of her.

"I'm glad I was wrong about you," Ash told her.

The sawing noise of the insects was loud when Lucy stepped closer and hooked a finger into one of the belt loops of Ash's jeans. Without the slightest hesitation to consider what she was doing, Ash fisted her hand in the sweatshirt at Lucy's waist. Heat sluiced down her back. Good heat. Hot heat. Skin heat. "Sorry," she breathed, and started to let go.

"No." Lucy grabbed her wrist and brought Ash's hand to her waist. "Do that."

"Do what?" She gripped the soft fabric again.

"Whatever you want." Lucy pressed her cheek to Ash's. Its

softness made her eyes close. Her skin was scalding. "Baby girl, do whatever you want to me."

"Luce." Ash pushed her face against Lucy's neck and breathed her in, trying to keep her mouth closed and resist scraping her teeth against her skin or softening her lips into a kiss, trying to force her thoughts away from the rocket ship of eroticism sending them to the ether.

"If you do what you want, I'll slide my hand under your shirt." Lucy's voice slipped between the beats of the rolling drone of summer insects. "I'll touch you. But you have to do one thing *you* want first."

The smiling apple of Lucy's cheek was hard against Ash's jaw. She imagined open-mouthed kisses across Lucy's face, and her knees almost buckled. "Are you trying to tempt me?"

"Only you. You're the only one." Lucy dropped her head to give Ash more access to her neck, to the top of her shoulder where the neckline of the sweatshirt was slack. "Do something you want to do, Ashes. Whatever it is, I promise it will make me go up in flames."

She kissed Lucy's neck, tasting her skin with her tongue, and Lucy shuddered but did what she'd promised and sent her hand under Ash's shirt, dragging her nails up the skin of her waist to her armpit, over her shoulder blade. It made her lose her grip on Lucy's shirt and roughly palm her hip to yank her close. Lucy retaliated with an explicit jerk of her hips that sent Ash's hand lower.

"Maybe . . ." She tried to catch her breath as Lucy's lower lip hovered millimeters from hers. "Maybe this is because we've both been . . . deprived. We shouldn't complicate—"

"What? Shouldn't complicate what?" Lucy pressed a tiny

kiss above the bow of her lip, and familiar tingles that precipitated hives broke like a starburst from that spot. But then the sensation got hotter than tingles, more liquid, a drug that kept the hives away. "Who says I've been deprived? Who says I ever thought this was complicated?"

She couldn't help but smile. Lucy's temptation was unchecked, white-hot sweetness masquerading as wickedness. "How many girls has the devil had, then?"

Lucy pressed another tiny kiss to the bottom edge of her lower lip, with predictable results. "One girl, hundreds of fantasies. One girl, countless orgasms."

"How did you find the time? Or the place?"

"When you were right there, but before we got into it. The times when there were still people around so you couldn't do anything, and I could excuse myself to a private spot close by for a few moments. Do you know how often you've fought me after I'd already come hard thinking about you?"

"Lucy *Prynne*." She pulled Lucy's upper lip into her mouth. Both of Lucy's hands were under her shirt now, moving over her painfully sensitive skin, making her throb everywhere and pulse hard between her legs.

Lucy's nails over the skin of her waist was why she didn't notice the ground vibrating under the soles of her boots. How could she, when Lucy's thigh had notched itself against the seam of her jeans? Lucy's mouth, teasing, then kissing her deep for one eager moment, was the reason she couldn't tell the difference between the loud, tearing sound of splitting earth and vegetation and the ringing bangs from the factory. The air had become heavy with the smell of turned-up dirt, but in her head it was only Lucy, Lucy, Lucy.

Her eyes were closed. Lucy breathed a whisper against her cheek. "It's dark."

"It's night." She kissed Lucy's dimpled cheekbone, then down to her jaw.

"No. Remember? *Too* dark. Now it's even darker."

It made no difference to open her eyes. The moon was gone, the lights from the factory snuffed like candles. The insect song dropped away. In its place, a new sound.

Leaves rustling.

Ash opened her eyes wider and tried to gather up as much light as she could to see, and there it was. The massive black bulk of a tree's trunk. A silhouette of leaves and branches high in the sky. The ground was broken at its roots, which stretched almost to the crumbling building's boarded-up door.

"She's here," Lucy whispered.

"I can hear you." A pool of blue light spread from the roots of the tree up the trunk and lit the bark and lower branches. Hester dropped from where she sat on a wide lower branch, her dark skirts billowing as she fell.

"Stalker," Ash said with a shiver.

"Who's stalking who?" The cool light that emanated from Hester spilled to encircle them, and they stepped apart from each other, in silent agreement that what was between them was none of Hester Prynne's business.

"We're supposed to meet up with our friends in a different timeline, so maybe get on with it." Lucy's mouth was puffy from their kiss. Ash involuntarily touched her own mouth, certain it would be hot with some injury in consequence of the nearly agonizing pleasure she'd felt, but she only found her lips. Unchanged.

But *she* was changed. Her whole self, lit up with pleasure and not an ounce of spiritual castigation, smiling like the Devil on Cal's card.

"You won't be late," Hester said. "But since you're finally starting to pay attention, it's time for you to see this."

The ground rotated under their feet as if the lot were a giant turntable. The tree was now backed by the fence that faced the street and the factory across from it. Their view centered on an alley that didn't exist anymore. Hector had expanded the paved parking lot over it, permitting better street access. But whatever time this was that Hester had put them in, the alley was hemmed on one side by the smaller gravel lot and on the other by a garage that Ash didn't remember ever having seen before.

Then there were headlights.

The truck bounced along the ruts of the gravel alley, turned into the lot, and shut off. It was a big olive green truck. Her dad's.

The truck itself, Ash only barely remembered, but its cab had smelled like wintergreen and smokes and the garage where her dad repaired small engines. There was an open patch of rust in the truck bed that collected water and mud and made a good burgundy paint for little fingers.

The headlights snapped off. Her dad jumped out of the cab and came around the front of the truck, taking no notice of Hester's tree or any of them.

This was a memory. A memory that Ash didn't have, replaying in three dimensions right in front of her.

"Draven!" Her dad's shout made her jump. It had been so long since he'd had posture that straight, since he'd moved so fast or been strong. His hair was thick, and the cigarette he flicked into the night made a long arc to the middle of the lot. He looked around, raked his hands through his hair. He was *young.*

"Ashes," Lucy whispered. "Inside the truck." She pointed. Ash followed her shaking finger, and then her stomach dropped away.

It was her. *Herself*, staring back at her. Four years old? Five? Her hair was to her shoulders, tangled up on one side as though she'd been sleeping, and she wore a nightgown. Barney.

Ash squeezed forward as the memory snicked back into place from wherever it had been concealed all this time.

She had been sleeping. Daddy took her out of her bed and put her in the truck.

Daddy never smoked in the truck and never forgot her seat belt, but both things had happened tonight. She bounced in the seat, watching the smoke stream from the orange-red end of his cigarette out the truck's windows.

Maybe he was taking her to Mai's house. She was too big to stay all day at her babysitter's now, making a fort with the other kids and the walking babies under Mai's big kitchen table and eating mov nyuv—sticky rice sausage—with plastic squeeze bottles of juice. She was in kindergarten, and she hated it. Ash begged to go back to Mai's every day. Maybe Daddy had listened and woke her up early to go.

But when he stopped the truck, it wasn't at Mai's red house across from the park with a pool. It was somewhere dark. She was scared. Her daddy was angry. At her? In this place, there was an enormous tree and a lady in a long dress under it who looked at Ash and shook her head back and forth like Mrs. Woods did when Ash wasn't listening with her eyes. The lady scared her.

Then she saw two more ladies standing in the dark, in the shadows. One of them had long, long white hair like her Tea Time Barbie. That one stared back at Ash. Stared and stared.

Ash slid down to the space for feet and curled into a ball and closed her eyes.

"She's hiding," Lucy said, her voice a raspy whisper. "Did you see her? Did you see—"

"Yes." Ash closed her eyes, her body trembling from the inside out as the memory burned hot in her brain. "Something's going to happen. I can't . . . I don't quite remember what."

"Rye."

Both Ash and Lucy startled as Draven came into view from the other end of the alley, his voice low and menacing.

Another girl held his hand. Lucy. She wore her nightshirt with a pair of jeans pulled on under it, her feet in her fat, fuzzy bear slippers that Ash had coveted and Lucy could barely walk in.

"Put her in the truck." Rye glanced at little Lucy, who didn't look at him or the truck but directly at grown-up Lucy standing next to grown-up Ash, meeting her eyes even as Draven pulled her across the lot to the truck and opened the door and loaded her inside.

"Lucy!" Ash climbed out of the foot well to sit next to her friend, shocked to see her.

"Who is that?" Lucy pointed at the tree and the lady standing under it.

"I think she's a teacher."

"Not Mrs. Van Hueval," Lucy said. "Mrs. Van Heuval is Black."

Ash felt the same pang of disappointment and weird stomach feelings she always did when Lucy talked about her kindergarten. Their dads would not let them be in the same class because they had to be "more social." Mrs. Woods was stricter than Mrs. Van Heuval, and Mrs. Van Heuval did station time where everyone could choose what to do. Mrs. Woods didn't even have stations.

"Who are they?" The other two ladies were looking at them.

"I don't know. Do you want a mini Twizzler?"

Lucy handed Ash a Twizzler a little bit out of its wrapping from the pocket of her jeans. They both pulled their candy out and ate it, watching out the truck window. "What's my dad doing?"

Lucy looked away from the ladies. Ash's dad was standing in the middle, close to the lady by the tree. He had his eyes closed. "It's starting to rain."

Ash crawled toward the truck window that Lucy was looking out of. It was open. The windshield was too rainy to see. "He's getting wet."

That was when Ash noticed Daddy. He was all wet, too, and walking closer to Lucy's dad.

A bright white light flashed, lighting up the sky and showing where her daddy and Lucy's were facing each other, and then there was a sound so loud that she screamed, and Lucy screamed, and Ash grabbed Lucy, holding on to her. Lightning, real lightning, had hit the ground between Daddy and Draven, the weeds burning in a fire that went out as the rain pounded.

"Daddy!" Ash screamed, but their dads didn't look at them. Instead, the sky lit up again, and another lightning hit her daddy's chest, smaller, shaped like a knife, and he fell to the ground.

Crying, Ash tried to open the truck door, but she couldn't do it, she couldn't do it! Her daddy got up and turned his body and kicked Draven—kicked him!—then reached back and made a fist and slammed it against Draven's face, knocking him down.

Then her daddy was on top of Lucy's.

They were both yelling. Yelling and hitting, and Ash couldn't look anymore at them, it was so scary how they rolled on the ground in the rain, both punching and punching each other while all the grown-up ladies stood in a row and stared and did nothing. Her legs were wet. Was it the rain? No. Lucy had thrown up on her slippers. Would she get in trouble?

The truck door opened, but she couldn't scream anymore, even though it was Lucy's dad, covered in blood. Lucy was crying.

"Do it," her daddy said.

Draven touched her head. His hand was warm.

"He took our memories away." Ash watched Draven pick up a sleeping Lucy from the truck, leaving Ash's own sleeping body on the truck seat as her dad, limping and holding his arm, got in it to drive away. "Mother*fucker.* He *took our memories away!*"

Her dad had driven her home. She remembered it. He'd put her into her bed, where she woke up in the morning with no recollection of this event. She remembered that, too.

But she hadn't before.

"Draven rewound us. He rewound us to when they took us sleeping from our beds, so there was no interruption." Lucy put her hands over her face, and the scene dissolved in the rain. The ground rotated. Hester disappeared, her tree vanishing as though it had never been. The earth smoothed itself into the graveled lot, and the parking lot's curbed islands floated up from it, the lights growing up from them, the steel ringing.

The air seemed to become light with sun and freeze at once, returning them to where they had parked. Hector's.

"They lied." Shivering, Ash got into the car for her jacket and Lucy's coat. She handed Lucy her puffer, moving automatically, clumsy with shock. "You know what this means?"

"It wasn't just once," Lucy said.

"No, it fucking wasn't. I knew there was something that didn't make sense! I knew it, but I never would've guessed what it was! How could I have known that your dad and mine didn't engage in a long, philosophical conversation that went back and forth for years like they claimed? They fought, they *cage-matched,* and then cut it out of our fucking heads! My dad, with his bullshit that he's weak from the effort he put into trying to keep us safe, when the truth is he spent his entire adult life catching lightning with his *chest!*"

"All my memories." Lucy dropped her hands from her face.

"I told you about how I would show up to fight you and know I hadn't really been here, living my life, but I had these memories. He was doing that to me, to both of us, even when we were little."

"Filling in the gaps with psychic spray foam." No wonder. No wonder Ashes had felt like something was wrong. No wonder she'd gone to see her dad and felt tipped-over, sideways, *off* in a way she couldn't put her finger on. No wonder she'd tried to remember what he told her about the curse and come up with nothing.

She was too appalled to speak. She turned and looked at Hector's Tavern, just to reassure herself of its tidy, fresh, solid realness.

But little Lucy's limp body in Draven's arms had been just as real.

What could she know about herself—how could she ever possibly have *known* herself—if she hadn't known about nights like that?

"I would have never fought you," she said. Her heart felt like it had been wrenched and twisted in massive hands. A puppet's heart. "I would have never fought you if I had remembered anything like that. *Fuck* that. Fuck that forever. They sent us into a gladiator's ring. Rye knew all along and made me feel the way he did anyway. Like I wasn't good enough and didn't care about anything but myself. I *never* would have fought you if I knew."

"Yeah, and *that's* why they lied, isn't it? If we knew, we wouldn't have fought, and that scared them. That's it. It scared them to think we could do something different, maybe do better than them, so we've been stumbling through this, miserable, and all I've had is a tote bag of bones for comfort, and you get hives if you have a beer or make out with a girl." Lucy stomped her foot, then turned and pointed at Ash. "*Do* you?"

"Do I what?"

"Do you have hives now? Did kissing me give you hives?"

"No. I do not have hives."

"Is your tongue swollen or anything? Are there sores . . . somewhere?" Lucy looked pointedly at Ash's chest.

"No. And you didn't touch—"

"I didn't, but I was on my way to that area." Lucy raised an eyebrow.

Ash looked up at the sky. "What now, Luce? Because as angry as I thought I've been the last several years, I'm figuring out there was an entire other level of angry that was possible. What have we wasted on all of this?"

"To be clear, I have been asking you this question."

Ash's jaw locked, and her back teeth ground together.

"*Please* don't get defensive," Lucy said.

"I'm not. But do we trust that? What we saw?" Ash gestured at the space where the alley had been. "Hester's the original devil. Maybe what she's doing is making sure it *doesn't* end, somehow."

"I hear you. I do." Lucy nodded. "But if I were to bet, I'd say it wasn't Hester who brought us to that horrible night we just saw. I would bet it was *you*."

"I didn't remember it."

"No, but I've been asking you what your dad told you, and you couldn't say, but you always stopped to really think. Like something was there."

"I knew. Somehow, deep inside. That's what you're saying."

Lucy nodded vigorously. "I think you put it together, Ashes, at least subconsciously. You were always so sure this whole thing's fucked whenever we talked about it, even when we were young."

"I'm only sure when I'm with you."

Lucy's eyes widened in surprise, but then she bit her lip. "So maybe it takes both of us. One of us by herself can't do it, but together we can see the truth, remember the truth, get to *all* of the truth."

"Second chances." Ash could still feel that night in her bones. Not what she'd watched along with Lucy and Hester, but what she had witnessed for herself. She had the memory back. Now she wanted to act on it.

"The biggest second chance of all time," Lucy agreed. "The chance to do over whatever the first Prynne and first Steadfast agreed to. After that, if we get there, I'd like a second chance at something that seems a lot more fun."

Now it was Ash's turn to be surprised. The blush on her frozen cheeks felt like it might crack her skin. "Um."

"That's right. Um. You just wait until I have a legal ID and some money and there is no risk of slipping into a metaphysical coma. When we've finished with this curse, it's over for you. I'm going to date you so hard." Lucy smiled, her cheekbone dimple sinking in.

Ash had no defenses. "Should we go inside? Catch everyone up on our quest?"

Lucy hooked her arm through Ash's, and that was the thing—their arms threaded, their bodies pressed together, the human enormity of it—that made Ash swallow back tears.

As they walked up to Hector's Tavern's door, she spotted Cal on a barstool inside, laughing with Hector. "How does the joke start?" Lucy asked as she pulled the door open. "An angel, a healer, a Puritan, and the devil walk into a bar?"

"It's a good one," she said, droll as only a Steadfast could be. "Really takes the audience to church."

Lucy's snorty laugh was entirely *Lucy*.

XV.

SHE HAD NOT KNOWN THE WEIGHT UNTIL SHE FELT THE FREEDOM

> The stigma gone, Hester heaved a long, deep sigh, in which the burden of shame and anguish departed from her spirit. O exquisite relief! She had not known the weight, until she felt the freedom!
>
> NATHANIEL HAWTHORNE, *THE SCARLET LETTER*

"I HAVE SEEN my share of drama." Cal took a sip of her Glenlivet, sending an armful of enameled bracelets to clink together all the way to her elbow. "But there is nothing like the drama of the heavens."

She tipped her glass to Hector, who put another splash of Scotch in it, and then another splash into his own.

Ash cradled her head in her arms on the bar. "You don't have *any* ideas for how we get a second chance at the last three hundred years?"

"And why would I, my love?" Cal was decorated in a tight denim jumpsuit with a hot pink oversize knitted vest, her hair in a high ponytail and her beard styled into curls. "Am I a god?"

"I thought you were supposed to be an angel." Ash met Hector's eyes. He looked away.

Hector had been quiet.

He was never one to waste words, but this quiet felt heavy. Ash couldn't tell if it was only the enormity of what Lucy and Ash had shared or if he was preoccupied with a personal issue.

"'Angel' is a complicated identity." Cal smiled. "Misunderstood. For example, I have much less free will than you might think. I'm guided by a greater mystery, which means I know very little about the intention of my work."

"But you said you *do* know who you're meant to help." Lucy was nursing an enormous Coke and a basket of white cheddar cheese curds that she carefully dipped in ranch in such a way as to not miss a millimeter of the breading while also keeping her fingers clean. It was mesmerizing. "You told me in my dream that I hated hurting Ashes."

"Didn't you know that already?" Ash asked.

"Yes, but Calliope validated my frustration. I had gotten so tired, trying to remember who I was. Who Ash was. How much I wanted all of this to stop. I was sitting on the edge of the abyss and experimenting with letting myself fall. Calliope stopped me."

Ash used her straw to rattle the ice in her empty glass of tonic water. *Starve the devil out.* That was what she'd been trying to do, and her desolate life had driven Lucy right up to the edge. Ash had been so determined not to fight her, she'd almost sent her away forever.

She'd seen what that looked like. Lucy frozen. Lucy shattered. She'd felt what it would do to her.

"That was my fault," she said.

"No, it was because our dads lied and gave us no way to decide if this was a righteous fight or not when . . . oops . . . they were around, still alive, they just didn't want the accountability. Rye went silent. Draven hid inside the same day, holding me hostage. I didn't have much left. It would have been easy to let go completely. But it wasn't *your* fault, and even if it was, I don't care. I don't care about whose fault anything was." Lucy dipped a cheese curd and ate it consideringly, looking from Hector to Ash and then to Cal. "What kept me here," she said, "was only that you noticed me, Calliope. You told me you were meant to help me. You came into my dream and talked to me. You saw me and told me I was worth taking care of simply because I *was*."

Cal reached down the bar for Lucy's hand, and Lucy grabbed onto it and gripped it so hard, her knuckles turned white. "I *am* meant to help," Cal said. "But I can only offer the help a person genuinely needs, and most of the time what a person needs isn't the same as what they want."

"I know that much." Lucy ate another cheese curd.

"Cal, you told me one thing the tarot card meant," Ash said. "That the Devil card means change. What else does it mean?"

Cal eased her hand away from Lucy's, her stiletto nails catching the lights from the bar and reflecting back golden sparkles, like a soul. When she closed her eyes, the quiet bar seemed to pause in anticipation. "Freedom." The word appeared in Ash's mind's eye, decorated in the same glitter as Cal's nails. "The devil wants you to be free, but for that, you have to understand what tethers you."

"But which chains?" Lucy said. "The ones that were locked to us or the ones we locked ourselves into?"

Cal gave her a sympathetic smile. "Almost no one wants to *understand* their shackles and locks. They simply want to be free from them. But if you don't understand them, there will be a moment in the future when you willingly lock yourself up again. Or let yourself be chained. This is why we have the twelve steps, the heroine's quest, the dark night of the soul. Shadow work. You have to look at everything you've refused to look at before you can be free. There's a reason why it's called 'coming out of the closet.' Only what you learn *in* the closet opens the door."

"It's not always rainbows and roses once you come out," Lucy said.

"No." Cal shook her head. "It's something better. A life lived by you. By who you really are."

Ash thought of her bass. The music she'd lost.

She thought of the green truck and her father's cigarette smoke streaming out the window and the way she'd huddled in the foot well with her arms around Lucy's thin body.

Her thigh sticky against Lucy's, their bare feet swinging from a branch in the rustling leaves of their tree.

Her father hooked up to machines at the hospital. Her fear as she stood over his bed.

She thought of New York, her lost mother, the sound of Lucy laughing, the sight of Helegar's bare bones streaking through the grass of Roger's Field.

Her cut throat. Her grayed-out life.

I named her Ashes.

"The devil on the card offers themself," Calliope said. "They hold a flower. They are bare and beautiful in their nakedness. The devil invites you to be likewise naked, to offer your own beauty to the world as a tithe to interdependence instead of the isolation of self-recrimination, shame, and everything else that lives in the dark."

"That *sounds* good," Ash said. "But you're going to have to tell me what it looks like exactly. *Exactly.*"

"You plus me plus Lucy plus Hector plus our families plus our ancestors plus ourselves. None of it can exist without relying on or letting go of the other."

Hector put his glass down on the bar and slid his glasses off, polishing them with the hem of his shirt before putting them back on. "There's something you need to do, Ash. I can help you with it. I was hoping that you two would figure it out yourselves, but I guess I wasn't given the gift I have to help the sort of people who can DIY their own liberation."

"What about the scary nun?" she asked. "The tears of blood?"

"The church likes to issue warnings disguised as an imaginary monster with a lot of fangs," he said with a dismissive wave of his hand. "It worked the first few times, but the truth is I've never believed I was *bad*. I never thought I'd made the lives of the people in my hometown worse by healing them. I don't think my parents' lives were ruined, either, by coming here. On a shitty day, I can convince myself of it, but for the most part I don't have the vanity."

"Wait." Lucy leaned forward. "I haven't been clear on if a scary nun cried tears of blood to warn you not to hang out with us or if a scary nun was making statues bleed."

Hector sighed a sigh only Hector could. "More like the bloody tears of idols *conveniently* started up when I thought about using my gift. That and a few demon possessions. This isn't the first time. Whenever I've wanted to do more than reduce a swollen ankle, someone wearing vestments stops me on the street, and at this point I can't help but think of Faithful."

"Hmm." Cal nodded. "Mm-hmm."

"What do you mean?" Ash asked. "Why is Cal nodding sagely?"

"What did Faithful want, lovie?" Cal took a sip of her whiskey.

What *did* Faithful want?

Ash thought first of her black clothing, her grim apartment, the lack of music, her square-cornered job. She hadn't done anything she'd wanted to do, only what she'd been told was her duty.

Lucy's grandma, Maura, had been told she was mad. Rye wanted a father and got told he was just in time to join the battle. Lucy and Ash had witnessed countless episodes of violence and then had them wiped from their minds so they couldn't remember what they'd seen when they turned to each other for comfort.

The less they'd been told, the less they knew. The less they knew, the fewer choices they could make. Control narrowed a child's world to contain only what the people in charge wanted that child to see. It blighted the future. It left nothing but ashes.

"He wanted control," she said.

"That is what I believe," Cal agreed.

"I don't like to be told what to do," Hector declared.

"The devil wants you to be free." Ash repeated the words Cal had spoken earlier. "Not for themself. For you." She glanced at Lucy. "For us."

"We have to go to Roger's Field tomorrow morning." Hector held out his hand for Cal's glass and picked up the remains of

Lucy's meal from the bar. "But in the meantime, I have about fifteen minutes until I need to open the bar back up."

Lucy started to slide from the barstool, then stopped. "Fuckity. I forgot I'm homeless. Maybe one of you could book a hotel room for me?"

"You're welcome to come stay with Hamish and me." Cal tapped her lip with her nail. "We're having a party for his work at our place tonight, but it shouldn't go later than about two, and the band will be done by eleven. I can figure out where guests can leave their coats other than the guest room. That would be better, in any event, since every year we find a couple or two who've snuck into the guest room to explore their naughty. If anyone barges in, you can tell them to scram and that there's a perfectly functional office down the hall. Unless, of course, you wanted to join them." When Cal smiled, the gem she'd placed on her incisor winked in the light. She caught Ash's eyes with an expression of pure dare.

"Wow. Okay." Ash grabbed her jacket from the chair next to her and pulled it on. "Lucy, you're with me."

"I thought you didn't even want me to ask." But Lucy hopped off the barstool and shoved her arms into her puffer, grabbing her tote. "You said your apartment is too small."

"Both of these things are true. My suggestion is that you ask very, very few questions. I'm still not sure it wouldn't be a better idea to drop you off at the Days Inn along the way, for the sake of us both getting on the other side of this second chance before we, you know, *second chance*."

Cal burst out laughing, and Hector walked away to grab a spray bottle of cleaner from the bar, rather pointedly.

"Come on." Ash shot a glare at Cal, who looked pleased

with herself. "We'll meet the both of you at Roger's Field at nine. Bring coffee. And doughnuts. And bagel breakfast sandwiches."

"Adios." Hector gave them a wave.

Lucy kept up a steady stream of nervous conversation all the way to the quiet street where Ash's apartment building stood, flanked by two streetlights and decorated with a city bus stop. Ash parked in her spot under the leaky metal roof propped up by crumbling concrete support posts that meant she paid twenty-five extra a month for "covered parking."

"Cool." Lucy nodded. Nodded again. "I'll just follow you into Ye Olde Residence."

Ash opened her car door. She thought about saying something in reply, but she had nothing.

She was nervous, too.

She'd spent the drive trying to think about how to deal with this. She had a love seat and one bed. Could she act casual about taking the cushions off the love seat to make herself a floor bed, as if she did this all the time? Did she have enough bedding to change hers and make up this floor bed she had never made up before?

Then there was the fact that her apartment could, in truth, be photographed for *Monk and Cell Weekly*. She didn't even have glassware. She used mugs for everything. Beverages, cereal, soup. She had one chair at a tiny table to eat meals at. Was Lucy going to want anything else to eat? Would one of them sit at the table and the other on the love seat?

It was a studio apartment. She'd be able to hear Lucy sleeping. See her. This gave her goose bumps that didn't feel appropriate.

Going up the stairwell was when she started thinking about their kiss.

About what Lucy had said regarding orgasms.

About the first awkward times they'd been together, the summer after their senior year, delighted with themselves, with the miracle of it, with every single thing they'd figured out.

Her hands shook as she unlocked her door. Her thighs felt heavy. This wasn't then, and their kiss in the parking lot hadn't been that kind of kiss. Ash didn't know for certain that she could survive another kiss from Lucy. No, she hadn't gotten hives, but she'd been ruined to a degree that meant every bone in her body had rearranged itself, her heart beat in a different rhythm, and, worst of all, she *wanted*.

She wanted and wanted and wanted.

She had always accused Lucy of asking what she wanted in order to tempt her into giving up her soul, but that was because she *wanted* to give Lucy her soul. Even imagining it—her soul reaching out to Lucy's, pulled from her body like a silk scarf that touched everything as it slid away—made her shiver. She'd seen it happen, this very thing, in the forest, in New York.

Go to the forest.

"Here we are." Ash opened the door and let Lucy inside. She had to get herself together, but her thoughts were a high-speed slideshow of fantasies that would've given her welts a few days ago. She'd fought so hard for so long to keep this woman out of her head. Now that she'd taken the chain off that door, Ash's thoughts of Lucy had burst through it, leaving splinters in their wake.

Lucy tasted so warm. She felt so soft. Ash hadn't even had a chance to push her fingers into the tangle of Lucy's curls. She couldn't stop thinking about it.

She was oversensitized from long self-denial. That was her problem. Definitely.

Except that none of these thoughts, not one of these feelings, was unfamiliar. She'd felt this way all along, noticing everything Lucy wore, what she said, how she argued, her jokes, her barbs. Ash would unwittingly admire her, be amazed that she kept getting smarter, wiser, more beautiful—and then blame it on the devil, pretending that what she appreciated about Lucy was nothing more than villainy masquerading as glory.

And she hadn't been the only one. It was true that Lucy had sometimes tried to aggravate Ash with flirting, but there had been plenty of times Lucy spoke Ash's name with sweetness, snaring Ash's heart for a moment. When her grin was guileless and sexy.

The truth was that they'd done everything they could to avoid hurting each other. There had been lashing whips, tosses through the air, scrapes and crunches, but with the exception of that first time, when they hadn't known their powers, they'd been sparring.

And pining.

"I guess this is probably what you imagined." Ash hadn't looked at her apartment through anyone else's eyes. She tried not to now. She had no art, even though it was an older building with tall ceilings soaring over the small room, and probably anyone else would have filled the expanse of walls with photos and paintings, even tapestries. The love seat was comfortable but brown and low, and the rug on the wood floors was a study in noncolor.

Her table. Her one chair.

A rolling clothes rack with rows of black.

Her bed.

A bed.

The one bed.

"Of course not." Lucy turned around. "You know that this"—Lucy gestured up and down Ash's body—"is deranged. I focus on you. Not the black leather and the old-fashioned hair. You're supposed to be a thousand different colors, Ashes, no matter what you dress yourself in. I still see the colors."

She turned again and did a slow assessment of the space, then put down her tote and walked directly to the closet door next to the bathroom. She opened it, stepped inside, and grinned.

"See? It's all a disguise. Here you are."

Ash's double bass was in the closet, buckled into its electric blue case covered in stickers and Sharpie drawings. Within the dimness of the small room, it seemed to glow. Her amp's dull gold, glittery housing wasn't even dusty.

Ash walked over and put her hand on the case, so familiar that it made her heart squeeze in pain. "I haven't played."

"You want to." Lucy reached up and touched the humidifier on the closet shelf that Ash dutifully checked to make sure it was keeping the closet safe for the antique instrument.

"So you see all that, even through this"—Ash glanced around the apartment—"and this." She indicated her all-black non-outfit.

"I never stopped seeing you. That was the part that hurt the most, but it only hurt because I had to wait to have you."

"You never believed we wouldn't get here."

"I wouldn't say that. But I had faith. Strong faith comes with doubt."

Ash pressed her hand against the bass's case to keep from touching the scar at her throat.

She could understand what Lucy meant. She could even see her way to someday forgiving her dad and Draven for not doing better.

Not tonight. But someday.

Now, she moved her hand away from her bass and reached to shut the closet door. Lucy put her hand over Ash's. "Leave it open."

The blood rushed into Ash's cheeks so fast, she felt dizzy.

Lucy laughed. "That sounded a lot dirtier than I meant it to."

She tried to smile, but her cheeks were too hot. Her skin was too hot, all over. She shrugged off the heavy leather of her jacket and tossed it to the bed, then shoved up the sleeves of her black waffle-knit. If she had come in alone, like she always did, she would have unlaced her boots and left them by the door. She hadn't, and they felt unbearably tight, her toes pinching, her heels throbbing. She tripped to the end of the bed and pulled at the laces. Her fingers were too big, useless with the double knots.

"Hey." Lucy came over, then knelt down at her feet. She wrapped her hands around one of her ankles. "Look at me."

Ash's skin crawled in protest at the feeling of heavy hair falling into her face, damp against her neck and hot down her back. She was prickly, her clothes unbearable.

It was the first time her body had protested against the Puritan trappings.

One side of Lucy's hair was flat, the other huge and tangled. Her eyes were so dark, her lashes practically as long as Cal's false ones, thicker at the edges.

"Hi there." Lucy squeezed her ankle, then looked at her boot.

She began to pick at the knots with her pink oval nails, her pretty hands. When the knots were untied, she tugged loose the lacing, one level at a time, until the boot was slack around Ash's foot. She pulled it off, then took hold of Ash's instep in its sock and squeezed her way down to her toes.

It should have felt awkward. Too intimate. But it was exactly the right kind of closeness, right now, after everything.

Lucy repeated the ritual on Ash's other boot and foot, and by the time her hand let go of Ash's big toe, every muscle in her shoulders, her middle, her calves, her feet, was loose, but her high inner thighs were tight, tugging at her deep inside with long, thudding, sweet pulses.

Not urgent. Just right. Her body, belonging to her and not the curse, existing alongside Lucy's.

Lucy bent down and made quick work of her own cheap snow boots, grabbing Ash's, too, and taking them and their jacket and coat to the door, where she lined everything up on the boot tray and hooks. She sat next to Ash at the end of the bed. "A little better?"

"I've never had panic attacks before today."

"I think half of the people I talk to have them." Lucy leaned forward and gathered Ash's hair into a bundle, smoothing it over her shoulder and away from her face, which was damp. There was sweat at her hairline, cooling as her heart rate slowed. She had another one of her new kaleidoscope memories of Lucy sitting behind her in an assembly in middle school, playing with her hair. How it felt so good to be touched. Her dad never even hugged her. Lucy's touch had been soft, reverent, unending, and Ash had sunk into it, trusting it, feeling tingles sluice over her scalp and down her neck and arms while her eyes grew heavy in the dark auditorium.

It was a moment that had shifted her love for Lucy in a new direction.

"It's not easy for people to get what they want," Lucy said. "There's something about having what you want that creates fear. Fear of loss. Fear of inadequacy. Fear of being seen. Then there's the self-doubt."

"You said queerness is the antidote to self-doubt." Ash pulled her shoulders away from her ears and let her lower back relax. Lucy responded to this looser posture by bringing her foot from under her thigh to rest against Ash's hip.

"It is. Even if the knowledge is way down in there. It's the best thing about me. It meant I could hold on to me for this long."

"Me, too." Ash touched the sole of Lucy's foot with the tips of her fingers, then pulled away. "I don't think I thought of it like that, but I needed Cal. I wanted her to be my friend. She helped me be less afraid, and now she's helping me get what I want."

Lucy smiled, a flirty, unselfconscious smile. "Which is?"

Ash laughed. "You want me to tell you that it's you?"

"Oh." Lucy laid back on the bed, onto her side, propping her head up with her hand. She drew her legs up. "I always want you to tell me that it's me. The best is if Ashes Steadfast wants you."

Ash took the bait and lay down on her side, facing Lucy. The only light she'd turned on when they entered the apartment was the one above the door. Her blinds were open, so the streetlights in front of the building spilled light over the sill. It meant the high ceiling was all shadow, making the room feel close, the bed an island floating in a sea of dusk.

She didn't know if the Dead and Righteous Brigade was out there, forming a judgmental ring around the apartment complex, but if they were, she didn't care. They couldn't get at her. Not in this bed. Not tonight.

"How are you?" she asked. "How is it being here without interruption, with the free will to go anywhere you like, not just where I am?"

Lucy closed her eyes. "I love it so much. And I hate it, because when I get tired or hungry or cold, I can feel what I missed out on."

"People generally don't like feeling tired, hungry, or cold."

"True, but if I don't feel those things, then I also don't feel greedy for cheese curds or get to sleep and have my own dreams instead of holy visitations. I don't get to know what it is to come into Ashes's apartment from the cold and curl up in her bed and want to kiss her."

Lucy opened her eyes. They were too much, Lucy's eyes—knowing and kind and understanding and fascinated. An irresistible temptation. Ash reached to touch Lucy's face with the back of her hand. Then with her fingertips, gentle. "It's been a lot, the last few days."

"Mmm."

"We've been through a lot, for years and years." Ash let the pads of her fingers trail over Lucy's temple, just to feel how turned on it made her. "There's so much between us."

"True." Lucy ran her index finger down the bridge of Ash's nose. "That's because of how much was going on outside of us."

"Who knew the devil was so wise?" Ash took a deep breath.

"I don't want to make it difficult for you anymore. You deserve to figure out what it is you want without me putting myself in front of you to pick first. We don't know what will happen. What stopping the curse will mean, if we can stop it."

I could do everything right and still lose you. That was what she meant.

"You've had it so easy, then, because you have an address?" Lucy's smile was rueful. "It doesn't seem like you've done much more living than I have, which I might point out is in many ways *more* awful. So what if we both get what we want right now?"

Ash didn't realize she'd slid her foot between Lucy's feet until this question rang a bell through her whole body, and her foot between both of Lucy's felt like sex already. "What if we do?"

"We could lose everything."

"That happened already, and we ended up back here." Ash felt her capitulation like knots in boot laces coming undone, opening her up, making her buzz with pleasure.

Lucy drew closer and rubbed the tip of her nose against Ash's. "Let's go all in. We're both inoculated against the worst. What do you want, baby girl?"

"I want you. That was always my answer."

"I know." Lucy smiled against Ash's lips. "That's why I kept asking, in case you finally told me and I could feel the rush."

Ash smiled back, but then Lucy pulled her bottom lip into her mouth, and the world narrowed to what Lucy tasted like, what she was going to do next, and what their kissing sounded like in the quiet room.

They kissed each other slow.

Slower.

Lucy ran her tongue over Ash's teeth. Ash sucked on Lucy's

Cupid's bow before slanting into a deep, sighing kiss that made her hips lift.

What had she been afraid of? Every possible inhibition melted in the breath between them, coming faster as their bodies became restless.

Ash hooked her leg over both of Lucy's, pressing their hips tight, and they rubbed together in reckless, hitching movements, not able to get enough but still able to get distracted by the other's mouth, tongue, or bite until Lucy moved on top of Ash's body and straddled her thigh.

Ash pushed it up between Lucy's legs, and Lucy brushed a hand over her shoulder, her arm, her wrist, until she did what Lucy was asking and lifted her hands over her head, breaking the kiss for a moment to pant against Lucy's mouth when she banded her forearm over Ash's wrists.

"Is this okay?" Lucy breathed the question into her neck, making her arch her back, press her thigh harder against Lucy, begging her to ride it.

"Don't stop forever." She felt every inch of her naked body under her clothes. Her skin was humming, she was wet, the pain from her nipples was perfect, terrible, throbbing. Her belt bit into her waist. "Luce."

Lucy's name was the only word she could think of to beg with. *Please* was trapped behind the sensations shutting down her thoughts and language.

Lucy pressed and circled herself against Ash's thigh and moaned against her neck. Did it again. And again, just this side of finding a rhythm. "What do you want?"

She arched and turned her head to rub and kiss her mouth along Lucy's jaw, mouth, any part of her. In response, Lucy's forearm pressed harder across her wrists. She attempted to free her arms, but only to feel the way it made her throb and go wetter.

Lucy smiled. "I see what you're doing."

Ash pressed her thigh up just as Lucy ground down.

"Fuck." Lucy gently bit Ash's lower lip, then carefully sat up on her knees, leaving Ash without the press of her body anywhere and therefore suddenly, completely aware of what a mess she was. "What do you want?"

It would be easy to explain how she felt as the result of years' worth of deprivation, but she couldn't. She and Lucy, when they were young women, had experienced sweetness, excitement, but it wasn't this welcome destruction of everything she knew about want and desperation.

They were different. They had survived, and all their growth had been rooted in survival, and so there wasn't a single cell of them that wasn't willing to take in every second of pleasure and amplify it until it reset everything.

Until it reset the world.

"I don't want clothes." She was surprised she was able to say it. She had left her hands over her head because she liked the invisible bonds and the idea of surrendering to Lucy until she died of it.

Lucy ran her hand down Ash's shin, slid her finger under the cuff of her sock, and pulled it off. Ash jumped when she scraped her nails down the arch of Ash's foot. "That's one."

She took off the other sock, rubbing her fingertip between Ash's big and second toe so suggestively that it should have made Ash laugh, but it couldn't, not in the state she was in. This acutely aroused, Lucy could have made her come like that.

Lucy bent over Ash's body, and Ash watched her use the heels of her hands to push the hem of her waffle-knit up and up until it was just under her breasts. Then Lucy picked up the hem with her fingers and brought it up a little more, arranging it to rest just under Ash's nipples. When it was just so, Lucy met her eyes and slid two fingers into her own mouth, as if it was all too much to bear.

"This belt," Lucy said with a genuinely amused smile, "is the belt of all belts." She slid the strap out from the belt loops, then under the metal of one side of the buckle. "Two rows of silver riveted notches in shiny black leather, pierced with double prongs." She yanked the strap back and then over the prongs, and the belt gave way. "It's black, but baby girl, this isn't *plain*."

"I have another one with studs."

Lucy grinned. "You're trying to make me happy."

"Yes."

Lucy leaned forward and gave her an open-mouthed kiss on her belly, dragging her tongue up her middle, over the bottom of the almost imperceptible swell of her breast, stopping just short of the nipple under her shirt, which was *not* imperceptible, even through waffle-knit. "You still use rosemary soap."

Lucy didn't linger any more. She slid the top button of her own jeans free and yanked down the zipper, then pulled Ash's jeans down and over her hips and off, pushing them from the bed. She smoothed her hands over Ash's bare legs, all the way to the leg elastic of her panties. "They *are* black."

"Makes laundry easier."

Lucy laughed as she grabbed the hem of her sweatshirt. She pulled it over her head and her wild curls, revealing a lacy pink bra hardly holding her full breasts up.

Ash closed her eyes, still arching her back and restless. This was how she was going to die. Her body couldn't take this. It looked like one of Lucy's breasts would fall from the lacy cup if she leaned over, and probably the strap would slide from her shoulder then, and there would be so much of Lucy's hot skin and soft breasts in and out of a too-small bra to not touch, if she freed her hands from their invisible cuffs over her head.

"Ashes."

"Hmm."

"Open your eyes, you ridiculous goth."

Ash opened them to see Lucy pushing down her borrowed jeans. "You're not wearing panties."

Lucy stopped, the waistband just north of everything. "Ovidia didn't have any undies she hadn't worn before, and neither one of us wanted to feel weird. Do you want me to keep my jeans on?"

"No." Ash didn't know what to look at first. There was so much of Lucy's skin, of her own skin. She was down to her panties and her top, hardly her top, and Lucy was teasing her and would tease her forever, and Ash would like it and also never live to come.

Lucy pushed the jeans the rest of the way down her legs and reached around her back to unfasten the bra, and then she moved over Ash again, straddled her thigh, this time bare skin against bare skin, and Lucy was wet, pressing herself and her arm against Ash's wrists, kissing her again but this time sloppy, this time down her neck, this time under her breasts and then, with an impatient shove, her tongue on Ash's stiff nipple.

"There," Lucy breathed, and Ash realized she meant where her thigh was, that she wasn't supposed to move it anymore so that Lucy could finish herself at the angle she'd found in rough, downward jerks with her hand on Ash's sensitized breast and both of them lost in a mindless kiss filled with moans until Lucy pressed hard, so hard, and shouted against her neck while Ash reached her hips toward a friction that wasn't there, throbbing everywhere, as close to coming without touching herself as she'd ever been in a lifetime's worth of frustrated, not-quite-there attempts to orgasm.

"Ashes." Her name was a sigh. Lucy's thighs relaxed around hers, and she let Ash's wrists go. Ash brought her hands to Lucy's face to kiss her, breathing hard. "Here." Lucy pulled off Ash's shirt, skimming her hands over her breasts and waist, and then hooked her thumbs into the sides of Ash's panties and slid them off.

Ash's chest, throat, and face went hot. She could feel how wet she was, how it was everywhere, on her thighs, and she and Lucy hadn't been like *this* before. They'd made love like women new to it, going under clothes and testing limits in slow intervals, stopping to laugh and take it in. It made her realize it wasn't experience that made this good and hot and erotically ripe, but all the layers of living with herself, of struggling, of coming to genuinely understand how rare yearning and desire and huge feelings were.

"Please let me taste you," Lucy whispered. She had round blooms of scalded skin over her chest and on her cheeks, as affected as Ash was. "Please."

Ash reached up with her free hands and raked them through Lucy's hair, forcing a noise from her throat. She used her grip to pull Lucy's face down between her legs. Lucy spread her hands over both of Ash's upper thighs and brought her ass to the air on her knees, and Ash had to close her eyes to cope.

Lucy's mouth was so soft and so hot. Ash wanted to catalog everything, this first time she'd had this, experienced this, felt Lucy have her, but the slick touch of her tongue, her fingers digging in to her skin, and the echoes of Lucy's orgasm in her head crowded out her sense of this as a watershed moment, and instead she pressed up for more, then more, and Lucy moaned.

When Lucy's tongue found the side of her clit and pressed and moved in just the right rhythm, the choked sob Ash made was as much about how good it felt as it was about remembering that she had once showed Lucy how she touched herself, a little shy, and Lucy had *remembered* what Ash liked and brought it here to this moment, so that she would buck and buck against Lucy's mouth, not shy at all, her orgasm tightening her muscles from her knees to her chest, sending electricity down her spine as Lucy drew her into her mouth through the very worst of it, the first release Ash had felt in years, then kissed her down, both of them shiny with sweat.

Ash didn't realize she'd fallen asleep until Lucy rose from where she'd dozed between her thighs, her head on Ash's belly. Then she reached down blindly to pull Lucy into her arms as she drew the duvet over them both. They shared the same pillow. Ash braided their limbs together, the weight of their bodies balanced between them.

She couldn't believe she had been afraid of Lucy taking her soul when what she had always wanted was to hand it to her.

Maybe she would lose everything she loved, but she would never give it up willingly again.

XVI.

THE DECLARATION OF ARTHUR DIMMESDALE

Strengthened by years of hard and solemn trial, she felt herself no longer so inadequate to cope with Roger Chillingworth.

NATHANIEL HAWTHORNE, *THE SCARLET LETTER*

MASSACHUSETTS BAY COLONY, THE CONFESSION AND THE CLAIMING

HESTER POURED THE boiling water over the muslin bag filled with wood mint and yarrow, watching the plant pigments swirl away from the cream-colored fabric and into the bowl of water like smoke.

She set the bowl aside and folded strips of muslin she'd taken in from where they were drying outside, preparing them to soak to make the compress. She had broth on the fire that she hoped was palatable, and she'd sent Pearl to pick up Arthur's washing so there would be fresh gowns and shirts to change him into.

Helegar gave a low growl from under her skirts.

Dr. Chillingworth.

"I thought you'd gone, Mistress Prynne." He set the latch behind him, annoying Hester. She'd left the latch undone so Pearl could come in even if Hester was occupied.

"No." Hester focused on folding muslin, making compresses of different sizes, with one ear toward the bedchamber listening for any change in Arthur's breathing.

Dr. Chillingworth chuckled. "I assure you, as a man of medicine I am more than capable of seeing after Reverend Dimmesdale."

"And I assure you he's been bled enough." Hester swirled the herb-infused water and started stacking her compresses in their basin to soak.

Dr. Chillingworth sat down heavily on a wide, finely turned chair. Arthur's chair. "Do you truly believe that the wort of the fields and woods that our livestock eat, that chickens scratch at, can cure a man? If that were the case, a goat would fill his belly with cress when he had a purulent hoof."

"White hellebore root, not cress, and indeed, the goat will kick at the ground to unearth it to cure himself. All of this is in Culpepper's, which I'm certain you are familiar with as a man of medicine." Hester pressed her foot against Helegar's side under her skirts to stop his growling. She didn't need him adding kindling to this particular fire.

The doctor glanced down at her hems, his color reddening under his heavy dark beard and mustache. He had made more than one comment in the past about dogs being permitted indoors. "Reading."

"Yes?" Hester could feel her back teeth grinding themselves smooth.

"When women read, the devil translates the words into her ear. Her mind cannot stay clear, congested as it is by menses and old blood. She can only manage a bad translation at best, instructions from hell itself at worst."

"Instructions for what?" Hester sat down herself and leaned forward as if they were in fact engaging in a theological discussion.

Chillingworth's complexion started to drift to purple, though he kept his expression mild. "Witchcraft. Many witches have been burned who started their practice with a primer."

"Women have been burned, that is true. Likely some of them were literate. I believe the last woman our colony executed, while not a reader, was brought to trial because she trained a hawk to hunt. Useful bit of witchcraft that would be. The foxes are always stealing rabbits from my snares." Hester pressed the last of the folded muslin into the basin, taking a deep breath of the mint to stave off her black rage and panic.

The love of her life and her daughter's father was dying in the next room, and she'd been dogged by Chillingworth and his shadow, Faithful Steadfast, from the moment Arthur came down with fever. Officially, Arthur did not belong to her. Officially, she had never stopped belonging to Roger, a man who had long ago settled to the dark bottom of the sea.

Officially.

But there was something about a pretty, clever child and a helpful, kind woman that meant that daily life, real life, was what became official, or nearly. Children played with other children, often without regard to the history of their parents. There were always sermons, but it was the bread and tea and company afterward that drew people to the pews, and so the fear of recrimination faded. Life and its love of company; attention to the birthing, sick, and elderly; interest in rearing children and laughing with them; listening to the sea on a quiet winter night with a hot fire in the hearth—all of it had proved more sturdy than any decree from the pulpit.

It was life that had protected Hester and Pearl, and Hester knew she had protection when she noticed women admiring the *A* on her chest and how it brightened the bodice of her dress. What it stood for had no more meaning than a posy of flowers tied with ribbon.

The men of this settlement—namely, Faithful and his most loveless allies—had held in reserve the Lazurus-like return of her husband as inevitable. They had done this in order to strip her of his protection, home, and money. They had done this in an attempt to prevent her from a life that contained friendship, pleasure, family, and industry. When she dared to protect herself and secure her own home and funds, making herself useful with vocations that interested and paid her, and when she found friends, love, and pleasure, when she had a child of her very own despite them, they sought to condemn her again, but she muffled their gavel by celebrating what they called her.

Adulterer. Literate. Wisewoman. Wortcunner. Termagant. Witch.

No one had yet dared to call her Pearl a bastard, but Hester knew that the moment the label passed their lips, it wouldn't be long before Pearl was an orphan. It was one reason she was here, at the hearth and sickbed of the one man who could take that power away from them and so leave her life in peace.

It was also why Chillingworth was here. Whoever bore witness to what Arthur might say through the agonal rattle of his death would be the person who held Hester and Pearl's fate in their hands.

But that didn't mean she had to be polite. It only meant she had to refuse to leave.

"You are impertinent." Chillingworth's voice had iced over. "It's not decent for you to attend to a man in his chamber in any event. It has been tolerated, but it should not be. It destabilizes our community, living under God's eye, for a respectable man such as myself to keep silent when you impose yourself in this way."

"I am a married woman." Hester's fingertips were burning against the basin as she pressed them hard against it to keep herself steady. To keep herself from tossing the boiling water in Chillingworth's face, hot oils of wood mint searing his eyes.

"You are the worst kind of sinner curled into the dirty costume of a married woman. You use the sacred as a shield. I have told Arthur, and I have told Faithful. I have told the men of the church. It's only Arthur who protects you now, and he is choking on the fluid in his lungs, no doubt rotted from the inside with shame."

"Fuck you," Hester said, much more calmly than Chillingworth deserved.

"Woman!" He stood up so fast, the beautiful chair came crashing down. One of its inlays dislodged itself and clattered across the floor. He stepped to her and grabbed her arm, jerking her forward, his fingers like claws in the muscles of her arms.

Helegar ran from her skirts and began barking like mad, lunging at Chillingworth's legs and biting him hard enough that he screamed. He lifted his leg to kick Helegar from his boot. The little dog yelped and went silent, dropping to the ground.

Hesitating not a moment, she turned, picked up the basin, and shoved it through the air toward Chillingworth's face. The mint and yarrow tisane hit him like a rogue wave, and the sopping muslin held the heat and volatile herbs to his face, neck, and chest so that his torment lasted for longer than a moment. She knelt to Helegar, who was still breathing and looked at her blearily. For now, she wouldn't have to pull the foraging knife from her apron and stab Chillingworth through the heart with it.

"You will be hanged," he seethed, slapping the muslin to the ground, his face welted and dripping with a strange black fluid. "You are nothing but the devil's cunt, and I should have known when I paid your father to take you off his hands."

It took an interval, her mind recoiling and then reshaping itself around new and old memories, but when the man opposite ripped off his coat, Hester knew for sure. His coat was padded, and its removal revealed a slighter man beneath. A man who, without a char-blackened, heavy beard and broad shoulders, became someone she recognized.

Roger Prynne. Her husband.

He started laughing, pointing at her as the soot dripped from his hair and beard, the gray surfacing before her eyes as his face blistered from her attack. He was still laughing when a heavy key caught against the latch and the door hit the wall.

Faithful Steadfast had come.

She looked from one man to the other, the world around her slowing as if nature itself were giving her time to think.

She would have thought harder, been more clever, had Helegar not barked again and stumbled upright, then run toward the open door, between Faithful's feet, and into Pearl's waiting arms.

"Mama!" Pearl tripped past Chillingworth, the washing she'd fetched dropped in the doorway. Her warm head was under Hester's hand when Faithful reached out and snatched her back by the arm.

Hester didn't need to think. The way Pearl's small body jackknifed when Faithful grabbed it was enough. The bone handle of her foraging knife held secure in her hand when she pressed its curved blade against Faithful's throat—a blade she kept so honed that even the warning pressure against his skin welled up blood. "Get your hands off my daughter."

He let go. Pearl fell to her knees on the floor. Helegar's barking was murderous.

"Are you harmed, Pearl?"

"No, Mama!" Pearl jumped to her feet in Hester's periphery. Her eyes were on Faithful.

Hester pushed the knife harder, and Faithful's blood ran over her knuckles. He closed his eyes with a shudder. "The one attribute I have assigned to you, Faithful Steadfast, is intelligence. I was wrong about that. If you ever look in my daughter's direction again, I will end you, and I won't cease until I've wiped you and your line from the earth."

"Forceful words. I'll remember them when I am deposed at your hearing."

Her duplicitous husband moved to press himself against Hester's side. She felt the damp of his soaked shirt through her sleeve. He took hold of her wrist, pulling, trying to break her hold on the knife, but her body was strong from taking care of her own cottage, chopping wood, carrying water, walking in the woods. Her hands lifted heavy pots and basins, brought forth stubborn babies, picked up children. She imagined roots growing from the soles of her feet, through the planks of the floor, into the earth, and her arms covered over in bark, bulking with immovable power.

"Let go of me," she said. "Step back, Prynne." Her voice sounded like that of a monster who beckoned travelers off the road.

Faithful's eyes went wide. "Prynne?"

Hester pushed the knife a little more, and Roger brought his other hand to the back of her neck, scruffing the skin there in a clawed grip that made her vision go briefly white.

She snuffed the pain out with a quick, deep inhale through her nose. "Don't tell me you didn't know my husband has been infesting our community in a false disguise, influencing you with his vendetta, tending to the sick and doctoring women without the training that would make his ministrations proper. What sort of shepherd are you, Faithful? He lodged with you!"

"A husband has a right to his wife in whatever manner he considers best to deal with her." Roger started wrenching back Hester's neck. "She needed testing. Her family is common, and her father was too eager to be done with her. She made demands of me as if she were a woman who received payment. So I tested her. I came here. Bedded her so that she would swell with my child. Then I watched."

"You went to sea." Faithful's whisper was rough, quiet, but even the small movement of his throat meant the knife sank deeper.

"A man went to sea with the papers of a Roger Prynne, indeed. But I made my watchtower in the woods. I saw what she did when she was brought low, denied the widow's bonnet and tossed from my house."

"*You* did that for him," Hester said to Faithful. "You could have chosen differently."

Faithful closed his eyes again.

"It was repellent to see her sell and barter her services," Roger said, "but I suppose she had to survive. When she started fucking Dimmesdale, I decided to take a more active role. I am, of course, a learned man, and women had been left with tending the ill in this place in a base and wild manner, encouraging witchcraft and pride. This gave me a natural place here. You gave me a natural place, Faithful."

Hester stepped a foot back, slowly so Roger wouldn't notice. He was not as tall as she, and he was elderly and did not work. She needed a weapon to hold Faithful to heel, but she could countervail Roger with the brute force of her body if she had the advantage of surprise.

Helegar's growling stopped. Pearl had been breathing hard, sniffling, but she also went quiet. They knew what she was planning. She tossed her thoughts to Pearl, imagining them landing on her head and sinking into her skull. *Run when Mama starts to fight. Run far away.*

"You did everything he told you to do, Faithful. A liar who sought to make a fool out of us all."

Roger jerked her neck again. "You are an adulterer. A witch. Your child is a bastard. You will burn together, and Faithful will watch from the stocks for his weakness. Arthur is near dead already, and in the maw left behind, Dr. Roger Chillingworth will preside. The Reverend Roger Chillingworth. What was neglected by mannish women and childlike men will be made right, made to prosper, each reclaiming the position given to them by God, so as never to be restless or unsatisfied again." Roger laughed. "They will thank me for ruling them."

Hester wanted to roll her eyes in disgust, but she was losing her grip on the knife, slippery with Faithful's blood, and her shoulders and arms deadened as Roger's grip on her neck compressed vital structures.

She had to make her move.

If only Faithful hadn't been watching her for so many years. If only she weren't so inextricably connected to him, despite her unwillingness to be. If she had treated him with false deference and gone through the motions of placating his desire to control his community, if she'd silenced his angst and disquiet by complying with his ridiculous edicts, perhaps they would not have grown so close.

But like the ivy climbs the stone that both feeds it and crumbles around its roots, she and Faithful had bound their fates together in an unholy alchemy of his terror and her gifts.

Like her Pearl, like her Helegar, Faithful anticipated her next move. When he reared back just enough to dislodge the quarter inch of Hester's blade from his neck at the same time Hester pushed off his chest with her other arm, dropping into a crouch and using her weight to free her body from Roger's hook like a fat fish from the line, Roger was forced to adjust his stance to account for *two* strong people pitching into action. He failed to keep his feet firmly balanced.

Faithful's backward movement gave Hester less leverage than she'd wanted, and Roger's grip jerked into her hair, swinging Hester toward him at breast height with the knife still in her hand.

Calamity might have still been avoided, but Faithful took it upon himself to dive forward—dive with too little precision, as he had hardly gotten his balance back—and wrap his arms around Hester's waist, ostensibly to move her away from Roger. But since Roger still had hold of Hester's hair, Faithful's grip around Hester turned her body into a counterweight, and her upper body swung hard toward Roger's chest.

The knife sank into Roger's heart like teeth into cheese.

Roger collapsed to the floor, heavy as a sack of grain, and Hester on top of him, her scarlet letter soaking up the blood running from his chest as she found her breath, peeled her hand from the knife handle, and rolled away to stare at the rafters of Arthur's rectory house and, shortly after, at Helegar's pointed face as he licked away her tears.

Pearl crouched beneath the table by the door. She hadn't run, but she'd made herself ready to.

"We murdered him." Faithful fell to his knees beside Roger's body. "God have mercy on our souls."

"I'm glad you understand the events."

It was Arthur's rasping voice that spoke these words. Hester sat up, shocked. He stood in the doorway of his room, gripping the frame, his nightshirt cloaked with a woolen blanket. His breathing was so labored that his throat hollowed with every inhale, but his eyes, his beautiful eyes, were blazing. He directed all of the power of his countenance in Faithful's direction.

"Reverend?" Faithful, too, had tears running down his face.

"Papa!" Pearl got up from where she'd crouched under the table and ran to Arthur, nearly knocking him over as she embraced him. He steadied himself and wrapped his lovely hand around the back of her head, his touch unmistakably the soothing caress of a father.

"You," he said to Faithful. "You and Hester murdered him. Not only Hester. Not only you. However, given Roger Prynne's avarice, pride, envy, and wrath, I am called to believe that God intervened on these strange circumstances to take him home for judgment. As such, you have both been used as instruments of our Creator. I command you to contemplate this divine task silently in your hearts every day until you yourself are called home. This event is not the work of men and so cannot be judged by men. The manner of Roger Prynne's death is natural, as put into motion by God."

Faithful dropped his head. Tears ran from his eyes to mix with the blood slowly seeping from his neck. "Reverend, you cannot mean it."

"Do you call me false in my communion with our Lord? Here, in the hour of my death, when He is most close?" Arthur's voice had gained muscle as he stood, taking on the same authority and rapturous passion that touched the souls of his parishioners.

"No," Faithful whispered, his head still bowed. "But a man's life."

"Roger Prynne confessed to his sins. I do not believe he would have unless his life were truly held in the balance. We pray that he is met with mercy, and we give thanks he confessed. It is hubris to elevate your or his widow's role to anything more than mere witness, as we are all witness to the mysterious work of the Lord."

Faithful rose to his feet, staring at Roger's slack and lifeless face.

Hester did not feel the weight of guilt on her own heart. Her focus was on the blackened beard Roger had used to disguise himself, still dripping and diluted with her tisane. She doubted she would bother to prayerfully contemplate her role in what Arthur declared Roger's judgment by God. She doubted she would have prayed for mercy even if she'd stabbed him under her own power and cold decision.

She cared more about having her knife returned to her. It was a good knife, and it would be a waste if it were stuck in Roger's selfish breastbone for eternity.

"Another word." Arthur's lips were bluing, the cyanotic discoloration spreading over his chin. Hester longed to tuck him into bed with heated stones wrapped in flannel and feed him her broth, even if she had to feed it to him from her own mouth. Especially if. Her affection for him suffused every new beat of her heart. Her gorgeous, self-flagellating, loving, faithful, flawed, wounded, ridiculous Arthur. Hers, even before he was God's.

"Yes," Faithful said solemnly.

"It has gone on too long, my failure to declare my duty to both Hester and Pearl. I was misguided, both by my misinterpretation of God's word and by my overreliance on the word of men. Hester is bound to me as is a wife, and so on this day she is widowed first by her unfaithful husband—as he has been as unfaithful to the vows he took as any of us here—and, I suspect, soon to be widowed again by me this night. Pearl." Arthur looked down at Pearl's shining hair, and his daughter looked up at him, smiling beatifically. He brushed the last tears from her cheeks. "Pearl is mine. A future woman of God and the daughter He gifted to me, precious as pearls, worth far more than rubies, and welcome in this community to take vows and make her own life and family if she wishes. You are my witness to this declaration, as it is above, so it is below. Amen."

"Amen," Faithful choked.

Hester met Arthur's eyes and gave him her best smile. "Amen."

"Faithful, with love I ask you to bring Roger's body to the churchyard and commit him to God and to the earth. The community must know that he presented himself falsely and initiated an unwise attack on us, but they are to show him grace. Have your nephew Avenging help you with this. May your life be a testament to God's love. Christ be with you, my friend." Arthur reached out his hand, and Hester watched as Faithful came forward and reluctantly took it in his own, bowing briefly over it.

Faithful then turned to stand over Roger's corpse. He bent to wrench Hester's knife out of him, bringing dark blood gurgling from the wound. He tossed it to the table and took up Roger's body in his arms with a muffled groan.

Hester hurried to make sure the door stayed open for his exit. Before he disappeared on the path, he turned in the yard, holding Roger in his arms like a child. He spoke low, for only Hester to hear. "Once he has gone home and you've tended to the reverend's body, you will find me by the old oak past the wood's boundary near your cottage. We have our own bargain to make. I will honor what the reverend wants, but not your place on the golden chain, nor my own. We will pay. We will bind evil forevermore. We will continue to give good reason to the people to obey their God."

With that, he dragged his burden slowly down the path.

"Bury the stone in your arse when you lay that man to rest," Hester said, shaking her head. "Your hair shirt is growing tight."

And so she dismissed him from her thoughts and set her mind on her beloved instead. Embracing him and taking the weight of his body with thanksgiving, and settling him to bed, where Pearl and Helegar fell asleep beside him.

That was how Heaven found Arthur, surrounded by those who loved him, with a last kiss on his brow from the woman who knew him best and had welcomed him to know her these many years.

He knew no pain, and she knew no regret.

XVII.

BY THE OLD OAK TREE

Hester had often fancied that Providence had a design of justice and retribution . . . but never, until now, had she bethought herself to ask, whether, linked with that design, there might not likewise be a purpose of mercy and beneficence.

NATHANIEL HAWTHORNE, *THE SCARLET LETTER*

ASH WOKE UP deep under the covers and stretched, then stretched again. No part of her hurt. There was no pain.

She hadn't moved an inch all night—Lucy's nose tucked into her neck, their legs twined together, her hand over Lucy's heart, Lucy's arm around her waist—but nothing was stiff or burned, healing or inflamed.

She smiled at the gray morning light gathered against the ceiling, and the stretch in *those* muscles told her it had been a very long time since she had woken up in the morning happy.

Then she heard a noise she couldn't identify, a kind of hollow scraping she didn't associate with any of the noises her apartment building made. The sound wasn't coming from her stomach. Lucy's sleeping breaths were quiet. Her brain raced to remember if she'd locked the door last night.

She heard it again. Twice in a row.

"Fuck," she mouthed. She *couldn't* remember if she'd locked the door, but it occurred to her that the noise was just as likely to be coming from a supernatural intruder. She was not in the mood to reckon with pissed-off ancestors at the moment. All she wanted right now, before she had to stand in a cold field with Hector and Calliope and rehash the last three and a half centuries with a side of Hector's exile-inducing powers, was pancakes from a mix and to kiss Lucy again before she forgot how good it was.

She would never forget how good it was.

Ash eased her head up from the duvet, and then the smell hit her.

"Ugh." She slapped a hand over her mouth and nose as Helegar popped up his tattered head from where he had been curled at the foot of the bed and trained his round, filmy eyeballs on her, wagging his tail madly. His tail was the source of the scraping sound. The thin fur of his tail now exposed not only the bone tip but several more inches of dusty segments. "What are you doing here?" she whispered.

He uncurled from his spot, unwinding, and began to scoot toward Ash's head, wiggling and wagging, sensing her vulnerability to his love attack.

"Don't do it," she warned him. "The last time you got your tongue on me, I had to use Dawn to get the smell off my face. You know, the same stuff they use to wash crude oil off ducks?"

He wiggled closer, a low cry starting in his throat.

Ash held the duvet over her nose. "Fuck me, Helegar, it's worse than usual. Were you rolling in fish guts at Draven's?"

She could have sworn Helegar laughed at her, and then he

stuck his butt up in the air, tossed it from side to side, and *pounced.*

"Aaack!" Ash squealed as the little dog danced on her chest, licking every part of her he could reach, snuffling, sneezing, grunting, and farting.

"Sweet doggo!" Lucy disentangled from Ash's flailing arms and legs, and Helegar crashed into her face, elated to be reunited with his love. "Good morning!"

Lucy sat up and looked at Ash where she'd collapsed on the bed. She laughed. "You're a warrior in an ancient turf war, but it's always this teeny, tiny undead miniature dachshund that defeats you." Helegar hopped from Lucy's arms to the floor, ready to explore after leveraging maximum damage.

"You know what I have never understood?" Ash sat up, too, and wrapped her legs around Lucy's waist.

"So many things." Lucy started untangling Ash's hair from where it was stuck to her body and encircling her arms.

"Ha ha. Did colonial New England *have* miniature dachshunds? I feel like I looked this up at some point, and the answer is absolutely not. This creature should not exist."

"Helegar is singular. Which is hopeful, don't you think? Hopeful in the grand scheme of life's project, I mean. My best guess is that he's manifested as a miniature dachshund so that he can charm folks with his unlikely low-rider self. If Cal is an angel, Helegar is a . . . little god. Somewhere between gods and humans. Or maybe God themself. Made only to give and to receive love." Lucy kissed Ash on the forehead. "I like to think that he sticks around in opposition to the bargain, to bring a bit of balance back. He loves everyone, and he hasn't given up yet, and I don't think he's going anywhere until all of us are okay."

Ash brushed her hand down the side of Lucy's neck. "That's a nice perspective."

She leaned into Ash's hand. "I know Hester's angry, and I get it, but I can't stay mad. The continued existence and optimism of Helegar tells me that all the Prynnes and Steadfasts before us were doing their best with the information they had, which we have already determined is close to no information at all. This bargain keeps secrets."

Ash looked at Helegar rolling on a spot on her rug, sniffing it a little more, then rolling again, as if the poly-nylon rug that Ash vacuumed twice a week could be *more* odiferous than a walking dog cadaver. "In regard to those secrets and the two guys who kept them."

"Our dads, you mean." Lucy wrinkled her nose.

"Yes. I don't know what Hector has planned today, but I think they should be there."

"Really? Because I was feeling like it might be a good idea to keep my involuntary low-contact boundary with my dad in place."

Ash took Lucy's hands and squeezed them. "I get that. But Rye and Draven have been a part of this. They've experienced it. It even killed my dad. I have a hard time believing we can do anything to finally end this if they don't chip in."

Lucy's gaze was fixed over Ash's shoulder in the middle distance. This was what Lucy did when she was working out some particularly difficult problem. Usually math, but sometimes other dilemmas. "I think you're right," she said after a minute.

"Good. I like to be right, as you've pointed out a lot of times. Righteous, I think you've said."

"Sure. But what I was thinking circles more back to my thoughts about queerness."

Ash pulled Lucy closer to kiss her neck on the side where her hair had gotten huge in the night. "I'm such a fan of queerness."

"Yes. Me, too. But what I mean is what queer people need, which is family."

Ash's heart gave an achy thump. "That's been an elusive concept for this queer."

"I know, but we have a chance now. Hector is prepared to use the full power of his gift. I commune souls and mess with the elements. You can manifest second chances. My dad can rewind a moment infinitely. So far, he's only used this gift to erase memories and his own life, but I assume it has a better use. And Rye's gift for time travel is long overdue to serve someone other than himself."

The golden highlights in Lucy's brown eyes were starting to pick up the brightening light in the room. She looked beautiful, and it was difficult to stay on task, given that Lucy was also naked under the duvet, which was also slipping enough to leave her mostly topless.

Ash moved a little closer. "Lies, violence, and avoidance were never going to break this curse, but this time we've got miracles, angels, elements, second chances, time travel, and a way to rewind and replay and redo as needed."

"And Helegar."

Ash looked at him, lying on his back to catch the morning sun on his dusky belly. His threadbare fur didn't quite cover his ribs. She knew for a fact she couldn't have held on to a positive attitude for as long as this little god had.

“Why did we tell Hector to meet us at nine?” Ash wrapped her arms around Lucy’s head, nuzzling her. “Nine is too soon.”

“For?”

“Returning your favor from last night.” Ash kissed behind Lucy’s ear.

Lucy turned her head and kissed Ash’s top lip, then kissed it again, but slow. “Wasn’t a favor.”

“No?” Lucy’s lips were so soft, and her hands were bossy. The hot contrast made Ash push away the duvet from their bodies and get closer, needing skin on skin.

“No, it was what I’ve been thinking about doing whenever I’ve seen you for years and years. I’ll probably never not be thinking about it. If we’re together, imagine I’m envisioning your legs over my shoulders and my tongue inside you. You did me a favor.”

“Fuck, Luce.” Ash ran her hands over Lucy’s body, kissing her, edging herself with touches that came close to places she knew would make them both needy and demanding, but it was backfiring, because when Lucy sucked her earlobe into her mouth and bit it, Ash slid her own finger through herself before she could stop it.

“Do you want to do that? Watch each other?” Lucy kissed her before she could answer, and then they were sinking back down under the covers, their hands everywhere.

Helegar started barking.

“Ignore him.” Ash kissed Lucy’s chin, her ears ringing.

Laughing, Lucy pulled her up. “You know he’s keeping us on schedule.”

“Dogs can’t tell time.”

“Ninety percent of what a dog does is keep everyone else

around them on a schedule." Lucy reached down to the end of the bed and grabbed her sweatshirt, pulling it on over her head.

"Ouch." Ash untangled her hair from Lucy's elbow as it disappeared into its sleeve, pulling pulling her hair. "Hold up."

Once they were separated, Lucy looked at Ash and tipped her head.

"What?" Ash asked.

"How long do we have, for real?"

"Take off your shirt." Ash rose up on her knees to kiss her.

Lucy laughed. "No, I have something else in mind, and now that I've had the thought, it feels important. Vital to our mission, in fact."

"But it sounds like it requires our getting out of this bed."

"It does. Come with me to the bathroom, and I'll tell you."

Ash followed her, of course. She couldn't have guessed what Lucy wanted to do in the tiny black-and-white-tiled bathroom, but once they started, she agreed that it was exactly what she needed.

"How long has it been since you cut your hair?" Lucy had her chin on her knees on top of the toilet lid while Ash cleaned up what Lucy had roughed in, sharpening the line on her neck with clippers and smoothing out the buzz on the sides. When Ash had finished French braiding the thick stripe of long hair left in the middle, the person who looked back at her in the mirror was *her.*

"Since our fight by the tree. At first, I was too devastated to care about it one way or the other. Then I started getting sick, and I figured out if I shut myself down, if I wore black, if I didn't have any pride about my hair, if I didn't—"

"Express yourself?" Lucy picked up a long lock of Ash's hair from the floor and twirled it.

"Yeah. If I let all that go—music, too—I could almost survive an entire day without pain."

Lucy stood and raked her nails over Ash's freshly shorn scalp, giving her a million goose bumps. "We better go. I told Helegar to get Draven. Did Rye answer your text?"

"He's taking an Uber." Ash had been surprised at how quickly her dad agreed and how few questions he asked. He knew right where he needed to go, too, even though she hadn't been sure he'd ever visited Roger's Field before.

The cold bit into her newly exposed neck as they got out of the car in the small gravel turnaround at the field. The sensory reminder anchored her to the moment. It felt right. They crunched over the frozen, broken stalks of grass and weeds in the field under clouds whose dull pewter made the oak look enormous, its upper branches stabbing into the sky.

Her dad leaned on his cane nearest to Hector, who was bundled in multiple layers of winter gear in contrast to Rye's old wool short coat and the Velcro-closure tennis shoes that were the only ones he could tolerate with his gout. He didn't look cold, and neither did Draven, standing farthest from the others, one hand shoved in the pocket of his Carhartt, the other pinching a cigarette. Helegar danced around his feet, watching Lucy approach and awaiting confirmation that he was a good boy.

Cal gave them both a wave, jumping up and down in her ankle-length silver pleather trench. "Ashes Steadfast! Your hair! Yes! Yes, walk, you fresh lez!"

Ash almost covered her smile with her hand, but then took a deep breath and grinned so her angel could see her.

When they arrived at the tree, the others drew in closer, their dads standing behind Cal and Hector as though they'd walked into the wrong movie theater and felt weird about leaving. Ash walked up to the tree to put her hand on the carving. It still said HP + AD, the scarred initials linked to the heart with Ash and Lucy's.

"Come here." Cal brushed her palms over the short hair on the sides of Ash's head. "This is how you are in my dreams, but even more. More color, more shapes. More afterglow." She winked at Ash and Lucy in turn, and Ash discovered she had a lot more Puritan left in her than she might have guessed.

"Here you go." Hector handed her a bottle of water with no explanation.

She twisted off the cap and pressed her tongue against the roof of her mouth to counteract the brain freeze from chugging icy cold water on an icy cold January morning. "Is this a potion? Magically infused?"

"No. You should be hydrated." Hector took the bottle and slid it into his pocket. "Are you ready?"

"For what?"

But then he put a hand on her forearm and looked at her tenderly, his eyes filled with tears, and Ash quieted. She could feel her soul, pressing from the inside with a million warm needles holding it in. It struggled a little inside her, as if Hector's presence and touch were breaking away the golden thorns that it used to anchor itself, pushing into the floor of her emotions and dreams, every feeling part of her.

She was crying, suddenly overwhelmed with love for her uncanny, precious life. She was good. She was *good*. She was exactly who she should be.

"Hector." Her voice sounded like music.

"Remember this feeling." His voice sounded like music, too.

She wanted to get down the notes on staff paper, make sure she never forgot. "This is the feeling that's real."

Hector placed his other hand gently on Ash's throat and traced her scar with his thumb.

"Lucy!"

She tripped in the long grass where no path had trampled it down. She was too upset, too angry and scared to go out of her way to find the trail. She'd parked, rocketed out of her car, and started running toward the tree, her eyes fixed on its highest branches, focused on getting there as the crow flew.

"Lucy!"

It hurt to yell because of the crying she'd done at the hospital, looking down at her dad. She had seen his soul in their living room, a pewter wisp that rose first in the shape of his body and then compressed into a spiral, racing upward through the hands of the EMTs pushing on his chest.

Draven had done it. Broken her dad's heart with their endless arguing. The devil. The devil was the mascot of her high school, a smiling crimson face with a pointed beard and small, curving horns. It was on uniforms. Banners. T-shirts. But that wasn't what the devil looked like. The devil could look like anyone. The devil could be a friend of the family. A nice Wisconsin dad who wore ball caps and liked to go fishing.

The devil could be the girl you loved.

Ash had looked for Draven first, screaming his name into his empty house, then rushing into his daughter's room. Color. Clothes on the floor. A laptop on the bed, still open.

Ash could see souls, and she knew what it meant. It meant Lucy could take them. But it wasn't supposed to happen like this. This wasn't supposed to happen. They were supposed to stop it.

She didn't remember when she decided Lucy was at their tree, but she knew she was. Her knees were bleeding from where she'd fallen getting out of the car. She could still see the light from her headlights breaking through the grass, though it wasn't dark yet. Twilight.

At the base of the tree, where she and Lucy had carved their initials into a heart, she shouted for Lucy again. She looked around and saw her dad, Draven, Cal, Lucy, herself, and Hector standing in a circle around her, a few shades lighter than the color of the twilight, watching. She wanted them to help her, but they didn't move when she called to them.

"Ashes!" Lucy's voice was lower than it ever had been. "What did he do to him? Where did he go?"

She twisted her ankle running through the grass toward Lucy's voice, then nearly collided with her where she leaned against the far side of the tree, bent over and trying to catch her breath, sobbing. Her eyes were swollen and red. She looked furious. Even worse, right at the edges of her body, Ash caught a deep golden glimmer.

It was Lucy's soul, expanding from inside her, unable to sit in her body with the power of her anger. Ready to burst out.

"What are you talking about?" The mosquitoes were thick and biting, and the light was disorienting—twilight mixed with black shadows spiked through with weak yellow light from her headlights and a piercing over-white security floodlight on a barn hundreds of feet away. "My dad— He died, Luce, he died, he died. I saw his soul."

"Good," Lucy growled.

"What?" Ash swiped mosquitoes from her sweaty face, some of them crushing against her skin, wet, filled with her blood.

Lucy pushed off the rough bark of the tree and started toward Ash. Her face picked up the different lights and shadows, and for a moment she looked like Lucy. Then she didn't. "They must have finally fought. My dad's gone. Your dad's dead. It's over. You saw your dad's soul? I see everyone's, *all of them reaching toward me like tentacles. Even yours."*

Ash looked down at herself. The gritty, dense starlight of her soul hovered over the skin of her chest, and she pressed her hands to it, feeling pins and needles and heat wash over her fingers and arms. "Stop that!"

"Stop what, Ashes? Where is he? What did Rye do to him?"

"I don't know! They don't fight! Lucy, listen to me, they don't fight! Lucy!" She couldn't stand up anymore. Her legs stung like they were on fire, and her chest felt airless and heavy. She dropped to her knees and started to sob, thinking about her dad's gray face and his pewter soul and the dark, grim expression Lucy wore.

"Get up." Lucy was in front of her. "Where is he?"

"He killed my dad!" Ash looked up at Lucy. "My dad's gone, and now I have to do this, but we were supposed to stop it. Why *did Draven kill him?" Ash kept herself from grabbing Lucy's legs, but it was hard. She didn't have an anchor.*

Lucy took ahold of her elbow and pulled her to her feet. "Draven's gone. He disappeared and left me like this."

"Is he dead?" Ash looked past Lucy's shoulder at Lucy, Cal, Hector, Draven, her dad, and herself, transparent and still. Cal was crying. Ash wanted to tell them to stop this. It had to stop.

"I don't know *what Draven is," Lucy said, with tears spilling from her eyes. "I don't know what I am." She shook Ash's arm. "He never told me anything, Ashes! I thought he would tell me. I thought we would stop it. This isn't supposed to be happening, and I can't stand it!"*

"If my dad died and Draven's gone, that means your dad won. He did it. He won, and he ran, and now it's over and it's us."

Lucy shook her head so hard that her hair whipped across Ash's face. "No."

"You can't say no to it." Anger was beginning to swamp Ash's raw grief. "It's what happened. It's what happened.*" Frustration was clamping down on her throat with the understanding that everything she'd had so far was all there would ever be.*

She wasn't going to see New York.

She wasn't going to play music.

Lucy wasn't going to Boston. They weren't going to take the train to see each other and go for long walks in Central Park.

Lightning cracked above their heads. Ash was coming apart so hard and so fast, she screamed at the terrifying noise and flash of light. "Fuck!"

Lucy pressed her hands to her cheeks, and the wind got stronger.

"I'm telling the truth, Luce!"

The lightning cracked again, closer, so close. A flaming branch from the tree sailed toward them, caught in the wind.

Ash wanted it to hit the ground and set everything on fire—set the pasture on fire, the tree, their *tree. It would give them a reason to run away, to jump into her car before it started to rain. They could drive home. The lights would be on, and their dads would be irritated with them for being out in the storm and almost getting hurt, but none of this would be true. Lucy wouldn't scream at her or call down storms.*

Because that was what she was doing. Ash could see that. This was Lucy's storm, which meant it was over for them, really over. She looked up and caught the eye of the Ash who stood with the others, even more gossamer in the wind. Tell me what to do to make it stop, *she thought.*

But that Ash said nothing, uselessly said nothing, and now she *would pay for it, wouldn't she? She would be trapped fighting the devil until she died.*

Lucy was the devil.

The lightning flashed again, and she saw the people who she'd seen earlier when her dad was loaded into the ambulance. The dead people in black, surrounding her in a ring. They wanted her to fight. They were here to watch her fight. It was her duty now.

She didn't care who the next Steadfast was, the next Prynne. She just didn't want to fight Lucy. Her Lucy.

The flaming branch was rolling over the green grass toward them, pushed on a current of wind. Ash rushed toward it. She picked it up by the raw and ragged end where it had split off from the tree. It was bigger than it had looked when it was falling, and it was still burning.

"Ashes!"

As she watched, Lucy's soul reached toward her, and her own soul moved in response, ripping away from its anchors and stealing her breath.

Lucy's soul touched hers in the space between them, and sadness became a solid thing, fat and heavy inside her, immov-

able, unerodable. When she looked away from the light of their souls touching, she noticed a woman by the tree with dark hair and a long dress who held a knife in her hand.

Then there was a knife in Ash's hand.

The small, thin blade was so sharp, her blood wrapped around her fingers before she felt the cold sting of the cut. She drew the knife across her own throat. Her arm shook with the effort of preventing the blade from going any deeper.

Ash curled her fingers around the bone handle, sticky with blood, and her soul snapped back into her body with a cold, nauseating jerk that made her stumble. Lucy was coming toward her, saying something, screaming something, she wasn't sure.

Ash held the knife carefully away from herself. She glanced toward the woman again.

The woman was gone.

She dropped the knife and knelt down on the ground, where it would be quieter.

The light from the barn revealed a triangular patch of earth. Ash watched her blood sink into it.

Lucy skidded to a stop in front of her and dropped to her knees. She tore off her T-shirt and pressed it to Ash's throat, and where there had been numb shock, now there was searing, black pain.

Lucy picked up the knife from the ground with horror.

How could Ash have believed Lucy had cut her? Hester's knife was wrapped in Lucy's hands while she pressed her T-shirt against Ash's neck, weeping.

Had she seen Lucy with Hester's knife?

Hester's knife.

As Ash plunged to her feet, and as she cleaved herself away from the girl she loved, she wondered how many times this had happened. The unceremonious transfer of power, wrenching open a moment of bewildered violence, determined to proliferate itself and lie to the next generation to keep itself alive.

She looked for Hester.

There. A man stood beside her. Ash knew his name. He was Roger Prynne.

Roger's field.

Ashes flipped him off, and he disappeared.

Her arms around Lucy were maybe squeezing too tight, but Lucy squeezed just as hard back. The cold air was a relief after the heat of the summer night, and so was the release from the full memory of her younger self, her mangled heart and injured soul in flight.

"I'm sorry," she said into Lucy's neck. "I'm so sorry."

"No. I knew I hadn't hurt you, but I also knew that moment *wanted* to hurt both of us in any way it could. It wanted to eliminate us. It tried using me with the storm."

"Not *it*. Roger, I think." Ash didn't want to cry. Maybe she would, but she didn't want to. She was too tired to cry, heavy with the knowledge that had been returned to her by Hector's gift. "He didn't like that she had power. That she didn't need him. He wanted there to be a price for her freedom and how she changed the colony. He was a liar. He was everything that people say the devil is, but he's still not the devil. Hester isn't, either. There is no devil. Roger poisoned Faithful's belief over years, and his death convinced Faithful that this stupid curse was the only way to do penance and be free."

Lucy pulled Ash's face back in both of her hands. She had dark circles beneath her kind eyes. "Ashes. Who the fuck is Roger?"

"Your ancestor-in-law, I guess. But he's not our problem. Hector's miracle is to heal with the truth. I can see why he got run out of town for it."

The sound of Hector's sudden laugh grounded her in the moment. Calliope was watching with an arm around Rye's shoulders. Draven had drawn close beside him.

"Roger terrified Faithful," Ash said. "I don't know the whole story. I think I only know Hester's take. According to her, *Roger* was the catalyst for the bargain. That's why he's felt free to insert himself. When Rye died and Draven took himself out, it was Roger who came between us. He finds the biggest lie to tell each new Steadfast and Prynne in the hope it will destroy them."

"He lights the match." Lucy gave Ash a small nod. Then her eyes dropped and went wide. "Ashes."

"What?"

Lucy touched the base of her own neck. "Feel."

Ash put her fingertips to her throat. It was smooth. No scar.

She lifted her head to meet the eyes of her friend. "Hector. You did it."

"Healing isn't an easy thing," he said. "I will tell you that it's up to you to make it a miracle."

Her dad and Draven were standing close, Helegar under Draven's arm. She hadn't seen them in the same place at the same time for so long. She wondered if there would be any kind of healing there, and how far back they would have to go to find a point to heal from.

Where she and her dad went from here.

If Draven and Lucy would know each other again.

"So, my loves." Cal opened her arms, indicating everyone standing in the field. "When are we going to attempt a full Reverse Uno on this dusty bargain? Release every ancestor from this curse and Roger's lies?"

"Everyone rest up." Rye wiped his hand across his mouth and looked at Draven, who nodded. "We go tonight."

"I'll close the tavern." Hector removed his glasses and cleaned them on the hem of his shirt. "We'll start from there."

Helegar jumped out of Draven's arms and ran over the frozen snow. Ash knelt down and gathered him up. She let him kiss her face. It was disgusting, but there was something to be said for receiving the love she was offered.

The little dog moaned in delight and looked meltingly into her eyes.

Ash squeezed him. "You're a good boy," she said.

XVIII.

SHE HAD BEEN MADE AFRESH OUT OF NEW ELEMENTS

> It was as if she had been made afresh, out of new elements, and must perforce be permitted to live her own life, and be a law unto herself.
>
> NATHANIEL HAWTHORNE, *THE SCARLET LETTER*

"I CAN'T MOVE." Lucy leaned back on Ash's love seat and pulled up her sweatshirt, then unbuttoned her jeans and yanked down her zipper. "I will name this food baby Sammy, after Sammy's Restaurant, who made the lasagna, Caesar salad, tortellini soup, and tiramisu that conceived him."

Empty take-out boxes fanned out on the floor in front of the love seat, where Helegar was in the midst of the pleasurable project of methodically cleaning each one. Ash hadn't known where to go, what to do, or what to say after they got into her car at Roger's Field. Halfway back to her apartment, Lucy had asked if she was hungry, and Ash discovered she was ravenous. That led them to talking about the best meals they'd ever had, which led them back to junior prom, for which they'd eaten dinner at Sammy's, danced in the high school gym until they were kicked out, and had their first kiss after many, many almost first kisses.

“I should throw away these boxes.” Ash stretched her arms over her head. “But bending over seems ill-advised.”

“You ate half as much as I did. I didn’t even know they had a half-size portion of spaghetti. Who orders that? Spaghetti is leftovers of the gods.”

“Who orders that is recovering Puritans who don’t know the limits of their constitution after going secular.” Ash turned her head toward Lucy. “You’re talking to someone who has gotten sick reading the *descriptions* of fancy seasonal lattes, forget about ordering them.”

Lucy didn’t smile. She reached across the cushions and offered her hand, which Ash took. “The way your body was harmed on the front lines of this is especially wrong.”

Ash thought about this morning, in her bathroom, how it had felt when Lucy’s hands tipped her head one way, then the other as she cut and clippered. Dangerous—yes. But only a little. Mostly, it felt like letting go. Freedom.

The way it marked change. The way the wind felt against the skin of her scalp. How it had made the counter server at Sammy’s take a second look when she walked in to pick up their order.

“I think the pain made me pay attention,” she said. “Hives for sugar, overwhelming illness if I was caught wanting you. Needing you. Fluishness when I tried to listen to music or play it, but I would push through it when I could. Burning skin against colorful clothes and hair. I cataloged my symptoms. I kept track.”

“But you did avoid those things, too.”

“Sometimes. Just as often I tested them, and I definitely yearned for them. I’m not the sharpest stick, Lucy. I might have needed to actually see sores on my body to completely know what I wanted. What I wanted was you."

Lucy smiled. She wore Ovidia's jeans and old Packers sweatshirt for the second day in a row. Her hair was getting wilder by the hour.

Ash could hardly believe she had her back. "I missed you," she said.

"I missed you so much that this feels like a dream, but I'm going to be honest and say that it's not entirely a good dream."

"We don't know the ending yet."

Lucy turned her body back toward Ash. "I missed you, I'm with you, I'm fascinated by you. I can't stop looking at you, and I want to talk to you and fuck you and sleep next to you and hear every single thought you have about everything." She paused to breathe. "But I'm mad, too. I should have been doing all of that *and* getting my ass kicked in math classes and going to weird MIT parties I hated and—"

"Taking the train to New York."

"Yes! And not just taking the train to New York—seeing New York, having no money in New York, going to your music gigs in New York, telling everyone in Cambridge that I have a girlfriend in New York who is a musician, look at how hot she is. And you know what's worse?" Lucy's eyes filled.

"No."

"What's worse is that I never *really* believed that we would have that. I couldn't look at my dad and believe that the daughter of a blue-collar devil in Green Bay, Wisconsin, with a mom who took off because it was all too much, could math the math it would take to get out of here."

Ash felt a sadness so old, she'd failed to notice it before now. "Yeah."

"This is a beautiful dream, but there's grit all over everything, rubbing me raw. You know what, though?"

"What?"

"If I want you, I have to be ready to deal with the fear." Lucy sighed. "I could be wrong. I'm not a god like Helegar." He had collapsed on the rug to sleep, his mortal glamour melted away to leave nothing but a pile of snoring, knobby bones.

Ash moved closer to Lucy. "Do you want to try something?" She slid her arm around Lucy's shoulders.

"Fuck, yes, I want to try something. I was only waiting for Sammy to settle down. My food baby is a big boy."

Ash gathered up a handful of curls and pulled them gently. "Something else, and then whatever you were thinking."

"Yes."

"Come here, Luce. I'm going to take us to New York."

Ash leaned back into the almost-too-hot bed of Hector's pickup truck. "You know I'm in."

Lucy grinned and pulled out her phone. "Then we're doing it. We'll tell Rye and my dad there's a senior lock-in or something." Her thumbs started flying over her keyboard.

"What are you doing?" Hector grabbed the T-shirt he had left on the tailgate, pulling it on over his wet torso. He actually swam when they went to the beach in Algoma, but Ash and Lucy mostly napped in the sun in the back of his truck, got ice cream, shared a cigarette, and waded a little while talking endlessly about everything.

"We, my friend, are going to New York." Grinning, Lucy went back to her phone.

"I know that. It's all you guys talk about. Have you ever thought that if you did half the stuff right now, here in Wisconsin, that you are going to do someday in New York, you would get exactly what you wanted sooner at twenty percent of the cost?" He rubbed his hair with a towel.

"No," Lucy said. "I have literally never thought that."

"Not everyone wants to conquer Green Bay," Ash said. "That is particular to you and your very strange mindset."

"If you can make it here"—Hector pointed at Ash—"you can make it anywhere. And I don't want to conquer it. I want to create something that's a reason people really like it here."

Lucy looked up from her phone. "You know what? I think you will."

"I know I will. So what's this latest scheme?"

Lucy turned her phone around. "Not a scheme. Reservations for this weekend for a one-dollar-sign and, according to Yelp, 'very clean' hostel six blocks from Central Park in New York City for Lucy Prynne and Ashes Steadfast."

Ash circled her fist in the air and whooped.

"Tell me about your one-dollar-sign plane tickets." Hector hopped up on the tailgate and fished open his tackle box for a smoke.

"We don't need them," Ash said. "You're not the only one with wheels anymore. Behold, all my hard work in the file mines deep in the basement of City Hall on Mondays, Wednesdays, and Thursdays after school, plus Saturday mornings if the weekend security guard remembers to let me into the building,

has paid off! I am the proud owner of a 2003 Toyota Corolla, wherein the 2003 through 2008 era is considered by many to be the red-letter days of the model. I should anticipate this vehicle, purchased for a reasonable sum at Family Auto Discount Car and Truck, to roll over to three hundred thousand miles and last perhaps ten more years." Ash dug into her cargo shorts and pulled out a key ring. "I pick it up tonight. She rides to Manhattan bright and early tomorrow morning."

"I'm actually impressed." Hector stuck out his hand. "Congratulations. You're a woman now."

"Gross."

"We're really doing this." Lucy pulled her knees up and wrapped her arms around her legs. "Really, really, really."

"We're really doing this. It's a fifteen-hour drive. Tomorrow is an in-service day for the teachers, but our dads don't keep track of that kind of shit—"

"Wait, that's right," Hector interrupted. "Tomorrow's Friday. Aren't the three of us supposed to go see that movie where the bees come out of the guy's face?"

"We were, but consider this your official notice that we're canceling. I appreciate your understanding, and maybe next time. Instead, Luce and I are getting up at—"

"Three!" Lucy declared. "We get there in the evening. We push through and do everything we can before we have to crash at the hostel Friday night. Saturday, we have the whole glorious day in the city. Saturday night, we go to—"

"The Azure Cat. It's this amazing club, and there's a showcase. One of the groups playing is Sea Route, which everyone knows is the music in my head at all times. Then we get up earlyish on Sunday morning and drive back to Green Bay ten

times more sophisticated, three times more hungry for life, twice as experienced, and—"

"Broke." Hector snubbed out his cigarette on the bottom of his shoe. "New York is fucking expensive. Lucy, how are you paying for this? You don't have a job."

"I have birthday money. Not everyone is here to toil and spin."

"Both of you complain when we're in the car for more than an hour to go to Cave Point." Despite this litany of doubt, Hector was smiling.

"We have been to Cave Point ten million times." Ash reached over and touched Lucy's knee. She could do that. Her girlfriend, Lucy. "But we've never been to New York. We'll have so many things about going to New York to talk about while we're going to New York."

Which was true. When Lucy tapped on Ash's window at two forty-five the next morning, she was already awake. At seven in the evening, almost a thousand miles from home, they emerged from the Holland Tunnel into Lower Manhattan and gridlock, their arms sunburned from driving without AC, ten times more in love.

That night, they walked around Central Park, ate hot dogs, put dollar bills into the instrument cases of buskers, and held hands. They found a tree in Central Park, in the middle of the North Woods, that was so much like their tree back home in Roger's Field that it seemed like a sign, so they took turns as each other's lookouts and carved their initials into the New York tree, too, before they found their hostel (very clean but also very loud) and crashed, pressing together in one bunk because they couldn't stand being separated.

Saturday was bagels, and the Met, and a random matinee of a Broadway show that a man gave them tickets for because his date didn't show up. They pretended to shop at the Central Park Tower Nordstrom so they could use makeup samples and perfume cards in Nordstrom's bathroom to get ready for the showcase, where the bassist of Sea Route listened to all of Ash's plans for her own ensemble and nodded along to recordings of her sound that she played him with her phone. He hugged her and gave her a T-shirt. He followed her back on socials.

There wasn't anyone in their room that night when they returned, elated and exhausted and high on New York City, so they squeezed into the bunk with their legs laced together and kissed until it hurt so badly they tried more than they ever had, breathing hard, ecstatic.

When they drove back into Green Bay wired on gas station coffee very, very late Sunday night, they were ready for anything, everywhere, forever. After parking her car in the garage next to her dad's green truck, Ash went to Lucy's and climbed through the window to sleep for a couple of hours before school in a world much bigger than it had been before, and Lucy's breath against her neck was perfect.

They'd never been more sure that the curse would miss them.

Why wouldn't it? Their lives were their own.

Ash kissed the top of Lucy's head. They were cuddled together on the love seat. "Are you asleep?"

"No." Lucy sniffed. "How could I be? We just went to New York via magical portfenestration. When we planned this ten years ago, we never got there. We freaked out. I came to your window, and you let me in early Friday morning, and we thought of a thousand ways it could go wrong."

"We decided we had plenty of time to go later. We didn't know it wasn't going to work out."

"That second chance was the most loving thing anyone has ever done for me." Lucy sat up and moved to Ash's lap, her legs around her waist, her forearms on her shoulders. "I'm so glad we did it. It means I'm not afraid of what will happen tonight."

"Were you?" Ash slid her hands beneath Lucy's sweatshirt. Her jeans were loose around her hips because she'd unfastened them.

"Of course. I don't trust our dads. Why should I? They've promised us they would fix this before, and instead they lied about trying. We may not beat this thing. No one ever has before. We may be fighting it for the rest of our lives, trying to figure it out, trying to figure out who it will be left to, what Prynne and what Steadfast somewhere is dreaming dreams they won't get to have. It means we'll have to fight for us, because it will be hard not to find the grooves of all those patterns. It will be so *hard*."

"We believed our love would break the curse," she said. "No matter what happens tonight, I think it did. Our big queer love broke the curse. Tonight is *not* about breaking the curse. It's about ending the world that made it."

"Ashes." Lucy arched into her arms, and Ash slid her palms over every part of her back, just to check the solid, warm *Lucy* of her before she brought their mouths together.

She was softer than she had been last night. She melted, and Ash felt more of her, more of the way she moved and got restless as their kissing went deeper, their tongues slow and explicit and suggestive.

Ash kissed her way down Lucy's neck and then slid to the floor.

"Where are you going?" Lucy lifted an eyebrow, leaning back against the love seat.

The moment Ash felt the floor against her knees, a shuddering, liquid throb meant she had to lay her head against Lucy's thigh and catch her breath. "Fuck. Give me a minute."

"Okay." Lucy wiggled her hips, pulling off her sweatshirt and lifting her hips to shuck off her jeans, which meant Ash had to lift her head and see Lucy naked, one foot up on the cushion and, devastatingly, two fingers in her mouth, staring back at her. "Now you."

She took off her T-shirt and sweater at the same time. Her hands were shaking when she went to unbuckle her belt. Her breasts ached where her nipples were ruched tight. It *felt* like there would be some relief if she took off her pants and shoved off her socks, but there wasn't. Not at all. It was much worse with the nap of the rug pressed into her knees, the soft upholstery of the love seat rubbing her ribs, the perfect obscenity when she licked the cove between Lucy's labia and her inner thigh while Lucy scratched her fingernails over the shaved sides of Ash's scalp.

"I want you inside me," Lucy whispered. She grabbed Ash's hand and then slid two of Ash's fingers into her mouth. Hardly keeping it together, Ash adjusted to touch herself, pressing the heel of her hand against where she wanted to rub but keeping her hand still to try to stave off the inevitable. Lucy bit the end of her fingers before releasing them. "*Ashes.*"

Her voice had gotten stern, so Ash circled her wet fingers over Lucy, making them wetter, and slid them inside her, feeling a quick clench already. "Luce."

"I love that, baby girl." Lucy leaned back more, one of her feet on Ash's shoulder, the perfect angle for Ash to taste her while fucking her and fucking herself. She could feel herself coming apart, letting go, light and heavy with collapse at the same time as Lucy moved against her mouth and bit her own wrist. When she felt Lucy coming, she was rough with herself so she could get there, too, and her orgasm was a profane, indecent freefall that made her yell Lucy's name, then say it again through her first shudder, coming down.

"Ashes." Lucy touched her softly over her face, her shoulders. "Let me kiss you."

Ash stood up and curled against her body, in her lap, and Lucy kissed her.

Of course Ash loved her.

She was afraid, but she loved her.

XIX.

FAITHFUL STEADFAST FIGHTS THE DEVIL

> "Let us not look back," answered Hester Prynne. "The past is gone! Wherefore should we linger upon it now? See! With this symbol, I undo it all, and make it as it had never been!"
>
> NATHANIEL HAWTHORNE, *THE SCARLET LETTER*

ASH BROUGHT HER dad his Bud Light, then sat across from him at the small table where he'd chosen to sit by himself at Hector's Tavern.

"Thanks." He didn't touch the glass. His color could have been better.

"How's your new sackcloth fitting? Cold and humiliating enough?"

Rye huffed a silent laugh but didn't smile. "You know the way I grew up wasn't what you'd call regular."

"Funny, me neither." Ash slid out of her jacket and put it on the back of the chair. She didn't know how much she would get out of another conversation with her father, but she needed to learn everything she could before they tried to break this curse.

"I made a lot of resolutions. No kids. That was the first one.

Didn't seem hard. The others were mainly the kinds of things boys think are important. Surveil the situation, because of course adults will tell you nothing." He looked at her with a self-recriminating shrug. "Plan."

"Can't really plan to run into the devil's son a thousand miles from home."

"Something like that's already been planned a dozen steps ahead of you, more like." Rye finally took a sip of his beer.

"So are you saying that because you've tried before, you don't think this is going to work?" Ash had been trying to lower her expectations without killing her hope.

He put his beer down and wiped his mouth. "Your mother was so much like you. I didn't know her well. I didn't know her at all, really. But I wasn't insensate to who she was. She was a singer. I never told you."

Ash tried to keep the gut punch from showing on her face. "She was a musician?"

"Still is." Rye looked down and tapped his finger on the table. "Always thought you'd figure out who she was on your own. She's famous. Aoife Ryan."

Ash's heart stopped. Literally stopped. It was still in her chest, but the electric signal that fired to make it beat had shorted out in a black wisp of smoke. Her blood rushed downward, pulled away from her brain by gravity, and her vision went gray.

"Ash." Rye's voice was far away. *He* was far away, tiny at the end of a long tunnel.

"Ashes," he said.

A hand squeezed, hard, at her shoulder, and she guessed her father must have manually pumped blood back to her heart, because she was able to take a choking breath, her vision clearing, the drumbeat so loud in her ears it made her head ache. "Aoife Ryan?" Ash coughed. She heard Aoife Ryan music at the grocery store. Working jobs. A few times she'd dared to pull it up on her phone. Listening to Aoife Ryan made her sick from the beauty and feelings and the woman's rough-soft voice. In the closet with Ash's bass were a stack of Aoife Ryan CDs, the liners with their printed lyrics worn soft from Ash studying them, trying to puzzle out how she wrote such complex feelings without confusion, but with all the weight.

Her *mother*? Ash wasn't sure what a mother was. There was a ragged nothingness in her where a mother should go, and she avoided its edges. She didn't want to learn that a mother was one more thing she needed and couldn't have. It wasn't even quite something she and Lucy had in common, since Lucy had known an early life with her mother, and then phone calls and letters and cards. By the last year of high school, Lucy had learned enough to know that the best way to understand her mom, to love her mom, was from a distance—this woman who hadn't wanted children and had barely conceded to do enough to make peace with the one she'd had.

Lucy talked about that experience growing up. Ash didn't talk about her not-mom. The one who hadn't kept her and didn't tell her dad she existed until she left her with him.

She'd let Rye tell her what to feel about it, which was nothing.

Ash put a hand to her chest. Her headache was *spectacular*. Maybe this was how she would feel from now on, knowing who her mother was. Aoife Ryan. Maybe her heart would stop every time she listened to her music or saw her on the internet. Aoife Ryan was always on the internet.

"She played smaller venues back then." Rye cleared his throat. "I went to a show. I don't know what she saw in me. Probably what's important for you to know is that I told her everything. Don't know why I thought I should weigh down a one-night stand like that, but I did. She believed me right away. She was quiet about her thoughts, but she did say she thought I should do everything I could to let it be buried. I didn't disagree."

He touched the rim of his glass, pausing a moment.

"When you came to me, she left a note."

Ash's heart stopped a second time.

"She'd planned to keep you. Never to tell me. She thought you'd be well clear of it if she did that. But even before you were born, she started having dreams. A woman screaming in childbirth. Herself in the stocks, folks throwing things at her. She took you home from the hospital. You didn't have a name yet. She was waiting for the right name to come to her. The dreams got worse. Demons following her, sinking their claws into her flesh. Crouched in the corner of her bedroom, hissing at her. She dreamed of two teenage girls. One of them was you. She watched you slit your own throat open with a knife."

Ash put her palms over her eyes.

"That was the dream that decided it. She knew she couldn't keep you from this thing, and if she tried, it might be worse. She knew I hadn't yet done my part to save myself or you. Once she'd weaned you, she brought you to me. She named you Ashes in the hope you would burn it down."

He waited for her to respond. What did he think she would say? That her mother could have stayed? That the three of them could have burned it down together? "I don't know how to . . ."

She looked at him. She felt her feelings and looked at him.

"I'm sure you don't." He sighed. "I want you to understand that I know how big this is. How much it means. What it's taken. I know what I threw on its pyre to feed it. I'm ready to admit my culpability and let it kill me."

He stopped. His words rang in her ears.

"I'm here today for you," he said, solemn. "I won't sacrifice you anymore, and I don't want you to sacrifice yourself. If things go down tonight that require anything like that, step back. I'm not afraid of what's next."

Rye finished his beer. He had tears on his face. Ash had never seen her father cry.

At least, not that she remembered.

He stood up and reached into his pocket. A heavily creased note card dropped onto the table. "Your mom. She said she'd make sure this info would always be good. She meant for me to give it to you as soon as you would be able to read it, I think, and I didn't. I never understood how it would help. But I see now that it wasn't supposed to matter if I understood. This was yours, and I took it from you. I took a great deal from you. I'll try not to take anything else."

Then he grabbed his cane and hobbled away to where Draven leaned in a corner by the bar.

Ash crept to the women's bathroom, which Hector and Ovidia kept so clean that she didn't think twice about sinking to the floor, curling into a ball, and crying. She sobbed between the pulses of her headache, with snatches of her favorite Aoife Ryan songs, her *mother's* music, playing like phantoms in her ears. She cried until crying scoured the headache from her head. The ceramic tiles cooled her face.

She sat up and the room spun, but Ash had been knocked on her ass often enough to know how to deal with that. She breathed until the dizzy feeling subsided.

The door opened. The room filled with the smell of Arquiste Peau and the sensation of fingernails gently sifting her hair, tender and maternal.

"Calliope." Ash had no idea what she needed, but whatever it was, she believed Cal had it.

Her friend sat beside her, warm-looking in burgundy joggers and a drapey sweater, with a cacophony of jewelry around her neck and arms and fingers and shining from her ears. "It's rare that I meet more than one person in a family as their angel," she said. "The first time I came to Aoife was a few years ago. There is a whole *entire* journey there. There's a connection that's for you if you want it, but only you determine the consequences of not seeking it. They don't have to be bad. I think Lucy has told you how she navigated this in the way that brought the most peace for her."

Ash put a finger on the note card her father had given her. "Yes."

"What you should know right now, however, is that I finally drew a different card for you." Cal unhooked her bag from her shoulder and started rifling through it.

"Finally?"

"I check in with the cards. Every time I've drawn for you, there's our Devil. But not today." She held the card up for Ash to see. It featured a lavender-and-silver illustration with shiny foil. The figure was on a chaise, looking out a window at a tree full of cherry blossoms that had a nest on its branch filled with baby birds with open mouths.

The figure was a skeleton.

"Death." Cal pressed her palms together under her chin and smiled as if she were delighted.

"Death." The skeleton was also smiling, because that was what skeletons did. "And how am I feeling about that?"

"Oh, I couldn't tell you. I remain humbled by the cards."

Ash sighed. "Cal."

"Right. I forget my little divine lightning rods may need a bit of grounding. Death is the ultimate transition, equal only to birth. In this world, then out of it. Dear Rye knows something about this. That man holds too much too close to the chest, but he's right not to be afraid of these transitions. He's been there and back, very rare, often reserved for the most dense among us. I'd just love for him to give a big hug to all that wisdom he's ignored from dying."

"So this card is about my dad?"

"Pardon me." Cal waved her hands in front of her face, laughing. "I'm sidetracked. You'll remember I told you the Devil is a card that signals change. What I ought to have mentioned is that the change is the kind the world finds threatening. Think of the Devil card from my deck, her lovely top-surgery scars, his look of knowledge. They're certain that love will neutralize the world's fear."

"Then they're free."

Cal raised her eyebrows. "Then the world is free. This is why a queer lens is ever so helpful."

It was. Lucy had said so.

"Which brings us to Death." Cal held up the card. "Here's a window, a portal from one state of being to the next. One place is spring. New life. Birth. The other place is rest, the most spectacular letting go of all time, peace with everything that will go on without you. But the window is open. Each communes with the other. Which one is the beginning? Which one is the end? Is there any difference? You know what another angel said to me once?"

"There are other angels that you talk to?"

"Of course!" Cal laughed. "Angels are everywhere. They do tend to sift up in numbers at the drag venues, animal shelters, and braiding salons, but, truly, everywhere. What this angel said was, 'Time invented Death so it could watch things grow.' I think there is that wisdom in this card. Your card."

Ash looked at the illustration. She could hear Hector and Lucy laughing with each other through the door in the main part of the bar.

"I'm ready to meet Faithful," she said. "And whatever part of him is in me. Like in your dream."

Cal leaned forward and kissed her on the forehead. Ash took her hand to stand up, and they exited the bathroom together. Cal clapped to get everyone's attention. "All right! We're ready to ride! I see we're all dressed in layers and wearing sturdy shoes. Rye?"

"Wait. One thing." Hector walked from behind the bar and approached her dad, who sat on a barstool. "You're going to need a mind clear of the pain." He knelt down and pulled the Velcro open on Rye's shoe and slid it off, which made Rye suck in a breath. He wrapped his hand around her dad's big toe over his sock. His hands glowed briefly red, as if he were pressing a flashlight to his palm.

Then Hector let go, slid her dad's shoe back on, and refastened the Velcro.

Rye used his cane to stand up.

Ash watched him let go of it. He *bounced up on his toes*. "Thank you, son."

Hector rose gracefully to his feet. "Calliope?"

"Where do you need us, Rye?" Cal picked up her bag. "And where are we going exactly?"

"We can walk together out the door," Rye said. "From there, to be honest, I'm not entirely sure."

"Perfect. Ashes? Lucy?" Cal held out her hands. Ash took one, and Lucy jogged over and took the other before kissing Ash right on the lips in front of everyone, which meant she had to ignore Hector's somewhat insulting gasp.

They all moved over to the door of Hector's Tavern. Rye put his hand on the push bar. He looked at Draven, who settled his hand on Rye's shoulder with a nod. Helegar, riding in the big pocket of Draven's Carhartt jacket, gave a short, determined bark.

Cal dropped Ash's hand and moved behind her. Then Ash was grabbing extra tight to Lucy's hand, because Lucy suddenly tripped and said, "Fuck, sorry. It's so dark."

It was. Unbelievably, inconceivably dark. But as soon as Ash noticed this, she began to be able to make things out. Lucy had tripped on the floor of a forest they were moving slowly through. The ground was matted with ferns and plants, dotted with stumps four feet across. There were trees Ash could only describe as primordial, with thick, spongy-looking bark. The sharp resin of their smell was familiar but wrapped in something vegetal, with layers of dank mint and mushroom gills.

A few hundred yards away, she made out the silhouette of a

pointed-top, spalted-wood fence grown over with moss. A faint amber glow from the other side of it barely reached the points of the fence, and a scatter of noise—goats bleating, a shout, heavy creaks—was muted by the soft and ubiquitous roar of the ocean.

With her face toward it, Ash could smell the marine and mineral damp of the sea mixing with woodsmoke. They came on a small clearing. Here, the light from the moon and the stars nearly blinded her. They were brighter than she'd ever known them to be, so bright that nothing looked real, even as she felt the cool, humid air seeping into her sweater and the juicy slide of crushed plants under the soles of her boots.

The closer they walked, the more obvious it became that the clearing was the far edge of a flat yard carpeted with shaggy pine needles and rimmed with rough gray stones. A goat screamed at them from a fenced-in pen whose fourth side was a shed. The house was only a black shadow, deeper than the shadows around it.

An owl hooted, making Ash jump. She hooked her arm through Lucy's to be closer, then heard Lucy whisper, "This is too much nature. The air's so fresh I could chew it, but I want to hide from it, bathed in the sweet light of a flat-screen."

Ash turned to kiss Lucy's cheek, smelling her own rosemary soap mixed with Ovidia's unfamiliar laundry detergent. Lucy was real, even if they had traveled someplace unimaginable.

Then they saw Hester.

She sat on a stump at the edge of the yard, a knitted brown cloak covering her dark dress. Her hair was up and covered with a gray cap. In the middle of her chest, there was a large red decoration. She turned her head in their direction, but she didn't seem to see them. Her face was drawn, her eyes swollen. She looked tired and unfathomably sad.

From behind them, they heard twigs breaking. Ash's heart raced when she turned and saw a figure approaching. Hester slid from the stump and stood, crossing her arms over the decoration.

It was the letter A.

"Faithful," Hester called.

He came right up behind Ash and Lucy, then walked around them as if they were there but he was ignoring them. She'd always imagined Faithful as a huge man. He wasn't. He was no taller than her dad, slight, his hair very short and covered by a black hat with a low, soft brim, like something a person would wear when they were gardening. He was entirely dressed in black except for shoes of heavily creased brown leather. His grim face was the face of a forgettable white man at the bank or in a law office.

"Is Roger interred?" Hester asked.

The sound of her voice made Ash feel how far they'd traveled in space and time. When Hester had spoken to Ash and Lucy before, her English had been smooth and unaccented. In situ Hester, by contrast, landed hard on her *R*s, and her *E*s spread out as long and flat as they did in Wisconsin.

"Not even a shroud, thanks to us." Faithful's speaking voice was even more shallow with its vowels than Hester's. He delivered his words like he was hitting something. There was something of England in the accent, but it was mostly foreign. "Bloodied and staring up at his God with no one to weep over him."

"Good." Hester lifted her chin, looking remarkably like Lucy. "There's no god for Roger Prynne's soul, as dirty as his blackened beard."

Whoa.

"We murdered the man!" Faithful shouted, his expression anguished in the moonlight. "He sits in God's judgment, not our own."

Hester barked out a laugh that was as terrible as Faithful's shout. "A man who abandoned his wife to spy on her, first from the woods and then falsely under a different name and appearance, a *man*"—Hester shouted "man" like it was a curse—"who did nothing for our dying reverend but hasten his death with bleeding bowls. Who gave *you* false counsel. Who lied daily to our people and was coarse."

She took a step closer to Faithful, her expression sour. "And yet you stand here, make me meet you after I wrapped my true husband, Arthur, in a shroud, so you can mourn *Roger*? Judge me *more*? Disregard the edict of your reverend who declared my knife in that man's breast a natural death? Have you given such grace to *me*, Faithful?" She took another step, closing the gap between them. "Will you when I'm in that churchyard? Or am I only animal enough to be judged by *man*, while man is judged by God?"

With a final step, she looked him dead in the eyes. "What is it that you wanted me for tonight when I should be grieving? Do you want to affix another letter to my breast? An M for Murderer to stand with my A for Adulterer, my A for the sin of love? I'll wear it if it means my penance will stake Roger Prynne's body to the ground forever, right through the hole my knife made."

"*Fuck*," Lucy whispered. "This is not going to be easy. I'm really feeling the justification of a curse here."

"Roger was the catalyst," Ash whispered back. "Her husband, who I guess took off, and she fell in love with this Arthur, who's a freaking man of the cloth. He must be the AD. Arthur somebody."

"Dimmesdale," Lucy said. "That is definitely a varsity letter A she's got there."

"Faithful and Hester. They killed Roger somehow. But he was such a bad man that Arthur, who was a reverend, declared that it was a natural death. Am I getting that right?" Ash watched Faithful tremble in anger.

"It was an accident." Cal didn't bother to whisper. "It happened in the midst of a fight between Hester and Faithful that Roger got in the middle of. Look at Faithful's neck."

Ash could just see a thin black line above Faithful's Adam's apple. "Hester did that?"

Cal nodded. "But what Hester says about Roger Prynne is true."

"Ugh. Disgusting." Lucy tossed her hair. "This is a mess. And Arthur's *dead*?"

Ash had to agree, the various elements here were a lot. A world on the outside that believed Hester's love was wrong. An ex stalking his wife, catfishing a whole fucking town. Adultery. A dead lover.

Hester's ruined, purpled eyes remained trained on the original Steadfast.

Faithful's shoulders squared. "We have a way of life, given to us by God, instructions for living, and you throw it to the ground like it's nothing. You are *proud*, Hester Prynne. You make women envy your penance and wipe the mark of sin from your daughter's forehead. And yet God provides for you, even as you spit at him. These are *my* people. The safety of their bodies and souls rests in *my* hands. I sit in special judgment at the throne of my Lord to shepherd every one of their hearts to Him. You are separating the people of our community off like a wolf breaking lambs from the herd. You do not appreciate the peril you introduce to a community on the edge of the wild, a brethren who must be steadfast to survive these elements with their souls intact. And now you have damned me as surely as you have damned yourself. You're a devil, truly."

Hester was blazing eyes and a glowing red A. Ash could feel the freezing bite of her rage through the veil that hid them from these two people. Worse, she could feel the split opening in her own heart—a split she could have predicted.

On one side was fear of abandonment. Faithful did not want to be abandoned by God. He did not want to abandon his people. Ashes didn't want to have been abandoned by her mom, and then by her dad, for their different reactions to the same reason. She didn't want to abandon Lucy or be abandoned by her. Those fears were as real as the blood inside her body, and she would do anything—*had* done a great many things and made a great many mistakes—to keep them from becoming reality.

But on the other side of her split heart was freedom. To love Lucy. To play music. To stride through her life alive and queer and wanted. It was the New York side of her heart.

Ash had divided her life into before and after. Before her fight with Lucy manifested her worst fears. After, when she fought endlessly and righteously against the woman she loved.

The binary. The black-and-white answer to the rainbow of the queer spectrum.

But if death wasn't a before and after, if what things looked like wasn't always what they were, if fear lied, if she had been given the gift of second chances—

It meant she could make her heart whole. And so could Faithful.

"The black sheep *sees* the wolf!" Faithful declared. Rye's shoulders stiffened. Ash smiled with perfect understanding.

Faithful was telling Hester that he was willing to break off from his community and everything good it could offer him—to break from the love he invested his God with—just so that he could keep an eye on an enemy he'd constructed himself from fear.

She snorted. As someone from Wisconsin would say, *Yeah, no.*

"What you've done in this community spreads like pestilence," Faithful said, "but pestilence can be contained. If I try to stop your influence, three more just like you will emerge in your place. Which is why you should have what you want."

"And what do I want?" Hester asked.

"You can be the flame a few moths burn in, attracted to your life free from God. You take those souls, and so the spread ends, just as a wet mud keeps a forest fire from burning down a wooden house. But I will be God's instrument on earth, and I will fight for those handful of souls. I will fight you. If it is not done in this generation, the fight will spawn in our descendants until it is finished. Until our community reflects God's Kingdom."

Hester shook her head. "Faithful. You are unwell."

He gripped her elbow suddenly, bringing his face inches from hers. He clawed aside the hand that covered her mouth and gripped the back of her neck, then put his mouth over hers in a sickening assault. In the bright moonlight where Hester stood, Ash could see that he was covered in dried blood.

He shoved Hester away and spat on the ground.

The earth rumbled under their feet.

Hester wiped at her mouth. Her hands opened, then closed into fists. At first, it seemed as if the roar of the ocean had gotten louder, but the vibration beneath them was what was intensifying. Before Ash could work out what it could possibly be, she was nearly knocked over by a foot of icy water pouring through the trunks of the forest, churning with mud, sticks, and leaves. The flood knocked Faithful off his feet.

"How dare you!" Hester screamed. "How dare you curse me! My daughter!"

The floodwater rose to their shins. Faithful stumbled to his feet. Hester waded, tripped in the water toward him, her cap gone and her hair coming down.

His soul was leaden. It rippled like the floodwaters. He bent double, vomiting, as Hester continued to charge toward him.

Ash pressed her fist to her heart, her body freezing from her feet upward in the cold water. She could hear Helegar's full-throated cry, mournful and hopeless.

How could they stop *this*? This was an anchor, dragging her own end of its timeline to the earth. The helplessness weighed her down. She thought of her dad, gray on the table. The blood from her throat seeping into the dirt.

"No!" Draven stepped forward, and the needle-filled wind blasting past made her close her eyes, lifted her feet from the water, and sat her down in the dark.

An owl hooted.

Draven and Rye turned away from the now-quiet yard.

There was no water. No Hester. No Faithful. Just moonlight and the empty stump that Hester had been sitting on to wait for Faithful.

"Be kind. Rewind," Calliope said. "Is everyone okay?"

Hector was pinching the bridge of his nose. Rye and Draven looked exhausted but unharmed. Ash searched for Lucy, expecting to find a mirror of her own horror, but instead she found an expression of pure determination. Like a general's. Or a very pissed-off descendant's.

"That was the most ridiculous and mawkish bit of theater I have ever seen in my life!" Lucy said. "This man, on the heels of an admittedly traumatic event, hauls a grieving woman to the edge of the woods to call down the immortals, the second balcony, the deities, whatever whatever, so he can feel capable of the classroom management of proto-Boston, which, by the way, never elected him to anything but regular colonial colonizing? Because he found out he had a temper and blamed the woman who drives him up a tree? There is fragile masculinity, and then there is what we just watched." She made a gesture over the scene. "I thought we would see something with a lot more gravitas, considering it's responsible for stealing half my youth."

That was what brought Ash to her senses. Lucy being Lucy. "How are we going to Judge Judy this?" She wiggled her toes, thankful they were dry again. "It doesn't seem like we're *truly* not here. I feel very real and capable of doing shit. Faithful walked *around* us. How does this work?" She looked at Draven and Rye.

"We never got this far," Rye said. "In my book, just knowing how this started in the first place is a win."

"But it's not," Lucy said.

"I brought us as far backward in time as I could," Draven said. "My guess is there's something here we can influence."

Hector studied the yard bathed in moonlight. "Lucy, you were seeing his soul, right? Is it supposed to look like that?"

"I've never seen one so murky. Dad, have you?"

"Once. That man told me he'd done a bad thing. His soul was heavy with shame."

"Those things that sit in the dark." Calliope nodded, tears in her eyes. "Two people died."

"Hester cut him," Draven said. "Faithful, I mean. My guess is he doesn't know why."

"*We* don't know why," Ash pointed out.

"Maybe there are some issues ol' Faithful could see the truth in and heal from." Hector crossed his arms and did one of his decisive tiny nods that meant he'd figured something out. "Hey, Cal, do you think you'd be able to guide our way to wherever Faithful is right now? Let's see if he could use healing and the comfort of an angel like you."

Calliope licked her finger and held it up in the air, tipping her head. "Absolutely, I can. Let's go for a walk in Colonial Williamsburg, Daddy."

They started down the path that Faithful had taken to Hester's yard, a transgender angel and a Latine immigrant tavern owner on their way to set a furious Puritan to rights.

"What are *we* supposed to do?" Ash asked. "I mean, after Hector heals him with the truth, are we sure that an enlightened Faithful is going to be open to freeing himself and Hester, or . . . ?"

"Takes two to tango," Draven said. "Hester brought a flood down. I can understand that she's grieving, but it worries me that even if Faithful comes back more enlightened, this curse might get done some other way."

"She's your ancestor," Ash said to Lucy. "What do you think?"

"I think I know what it's like to be abandoned and then try to make something of yourself, fall in love, and lose your person."

"Should we talk to her?" Ash peered at the obsidian shadow of the house. "I don't want to traumatize old-timey Hester. Or give her a disease. She's unvaccinated."

"I've never tried anything like this," her dad said. "But I have to assume if we've gotten this far, there's some kind of grace that will help you figure it out."

"To grandmother's house we go, I guess." Ash laced her fingers with Lucy's. "Ready?"

Helegar struggled in Draven's pocket until Draven helped him out. Once he was on the ground, he shook himself off, looked at Ash, and wagged his tail.

"You coming, little god?"

Helegar barked.

They crossed the yard carefully, following him past the animals in their pen. There was light behind the wooden door of Hester's cottage. Lucy lifted her arm to knock, but before her knuckles hit the wood, the door slowly creaked open and let out an aroma of mint with other sharp and astringent layers, along with baking bread and an open fireplace.

Ash stepped over the threshold with Lucy close behind her. They faced a stone hearth. From the low ceiling beams, dozens of bundles of herbs hung to dry. There were shelves lining the big room with short brown crocks. The fireplace had a lot of big hooks on it holding different pots, and a flat stone hearth traveled almost halfway into the room until it met the wide planks of the floor.

There was a small wooden bed, almost like a cradle, with a knitted blanket, and under it was a sleeping child. Hester sat in a chair facing the fire. Her knees were drawn up. She didn't turn when they came in.

Ash had grown accustomed to thinking of Hester as an exasperating apparition, but the woman looking at the fire was a regular woman. Younger than Ash.

Helegar trotted into the room and put his nose in the air, sniffing, then jumped into the bed with the child. He settled and turned, nosing at the blanket until the child beneath it lifted up an arm and wrapped it around him without waking up. Hester did move then, to look at the child, but didn't seem to notice the dog.

Ash felt a stiff, cold breeze behind her, and when she turned to shut the door, it was already closed.

And there was a man.

"*Fuck!*" She willed her heart to unfreeze from the shock. She was grateful they were invisible to the people here.

The man grinned. "Very sorry to startle you."

"What?" Lucy stepped next to Ash. "You can see us? Who are you?"

The man looked past them to Hester, his face soft. He was handsome, dressed in black with a bright white collar. "I'm Arthur."

"You're dead," Ash said, more than a little awestruck.

"Very recently, yes." He smiled again.

"That's why you—"

"That's why I'm here. With you." He looked, now, at the child in the cradle. "Death is so interesting. Both what I anticipated and not at all what I imagined. What I had right about it, I knew because I was born. What I didn't get right, well. That's still a mystery waiting for the two of you. I suppose even daring to make that observation reveals my hubris, but I can't help it. I'm a pastor."

Lucy huffed a surprised laugh.

"You look like her a bit, you know." He tipped his head at Lucy. "More like Pearl, my daughter. Especially around—"

"The mouth. I know. Hester told me."

"But we don't know what to do," Ash said. "She can't see us. We don't want to scare her. We don't know what to say to help her understand how to make a truce with Faithful."

By the fire, Hester began to shake with sobs she muffled against her knuckles. Arthur frowned. "I can help with that part. But Lucy." He stepped closer to her, and the chill Ash had felt sank deeper. "I'll need you and your way with the natural world to assist me."

"What do I do?"

"Take my hand." His soul, deeply golden and fiery, shimmered just beneath the translucent colors of his palm.

Lucy reached out, and Ash watched as Arthur's insubstantial hand pressed into, then *inside* Lucy's. She shivered.

"Don't be afraid," Arthur said. "We'll do this together. Bring up the fire, keep its light shining through me, and call its element to substantiate me. I need the energy to stay here and do this. Even as we speak, my soul is straining to go home." With that, he stepped closer, and before Ash could protest, he'd melded into Lucy's body and she disappeared, leaving him glowing, the fire suddenly sparking high.

Ash put her hands over her mouth to keep from screaming for Lucy. Helegar jumped from the bed and ran to her. She knelt down and gathered him to her chest, grateful for his warm body.

Hester jumped when the bright rush of the fire sent a shower of sparks up the chimney. She rose to go to it.

"Hester."

She gasped and turned. "Arthur!"

"Hello, my love."

"You're here." She reached for him, then stopped. She'd seen that he was half ghost, half firelight.

"Just for a moment. I'm so sorry, so very sorry, that you were occupied with violence when I know you only wanted to be with me."

"It wasn't your fault. I can't *believe* Roger. I knew he was cruel, but not that he was completely broken. It was Faithful holding the idol of religion over the love of God, like always."

"We all have idols, Hester. You never wanted me to punish myself for our love, but I was conflicted. One part of me believed you that you didn't belong to someone else, *couldn't* belong to someone who had treated you with cruelty. Another part had to believe that marriage was sacred. But what I can see now, and what I thankfully saw before I transitioned, was that I believed it was sacred because *I* loved you. Because of how much I loved you."

"Arthur." Hester's tears looked like tiny drops of fire as they fell and reflected it.

"What I want you to do—what I need you to do for me, for you, for our precious Pearl—is to see Faithful's damaged soul the same way you saw mine, and to believe that he is split in two as well. Yes, he is sanctimonious. He loves his God in a way God never asked him to, as a penitent made to receive God's sanctions. But he persists because he truly wants to feel God's love. He hasn't been able to receive it, even as it's offered. He's too afraid that he isn't worthy, and if he lets himself receive this love, he will lose it. You and Faithful are more alike than you know."

Hester glanced to the fire, then quickly back to Arthur as if afraid he would disappear. "I love you. But that sounds . . . difficult. Faithful's cruelty has made me hard." She put her hand on the red A.

Arthur smiled, a big, wide smile. "You are *not* hard. Exasperating, opinionated, driven, but not hard. No one hard could raise a daughter so unafraid." He turned and put his hand on Pearl's head, and she stirred a little.

"Perhaps."

Arthur laughed. His laugh made Hester laugh, though she was crying, too.

"I've come to know our descendants," Arthur said, stepping closer. "The rift in this place only gets bigger and more unnatural through time. Part of making Pearl safe is ensuring she is unworried about her own children. Her own life."

Hester reached out her hand as if to lay it over his heart. "I hear you. I'll heed Pearl." She gave him a sly smile. "But not you, a man."

He laughed. The fire burned higher, and his form solidified just enough that he could bring Hester's face to his. He kissed her cheeks and her forehead. He kissed her lips. He stepped back, touched Pearl on her head again, and then he went.

The fire sank lower and lower as he faded, until there were only embers in the hearth, and a fire-gold swirl raced through the rafters.

Lucy put her arms around Ash, squeezing Helegar's bones between them. Ash held them both tight. Her body was hot, shaking. She wanted to go home. She wanted to be next to this woman in bed.

Before Hester could fully wipe her tears away, a loud series of knocks started on the door, waking Pearl so that she sat straight up in bed. "Mama?"

Hester sighed. "Yes!"

"Open the door! It's Faithful."

They watched Hester draw a slow, deep breath as she looked up at her rafters. "You are lucky, Faithful Steadfast," she said under her breath, "that Arthur told me more than once to always pay attention to my dreams."

She opened the door, allowing cool air into the cottage. "I understood we were to meet outside. Are you escorting me to this rendezvous?" She stuck out her elbow as if he would take it.

"I only came to say one thing to you." He glanced at her elbow, then away.

Helegar stirred in Ash's arms with a low growl. Not at Faithful. At Helegar—*Hester's* Helegar, at Lucy's feet, with bright, shiny fur and beautiful amber-brown eyes. He was wagging his tail for the Helegar in Ash's arms, unbothered by his future self.

"It's all right, old man," Ash whispered. "You're just seeing the spring of your soul through this window." She set him down. He pointed his skull toward Hester's Helegar, sniffing delicately, and then consented to receive a puppyish kiss. His bony tail wagged.

"What is it that you wish to say to me?" Hester asked.

Faithful took off his hat and bowed his head. "I am sorry for your loss."

With this, Faithful Steadfast turned around and started walking away.

"Wait." Hester stepped over the threshold. "Have the mason make a stone for Roger," she said. "You decide what it should read. I will pay for it."

Faithful didn't turn around, but he nodded and held up his hand before disappearing into the shadowed yard.

That was all it took.

It was over.

Ash and Lucy slipped out the door before Hester could close it. They walked toward the spot where Rye, Draven, Cal, and Hector waited at the edge of Hester's yard, in the dark.

Then they were standing at the door of Hector's tavern, shivering in the cold, waiting for Hector to put in the security code. The lights were out.

When he finally pushed the door open, Ovidia was inside the bar, holding up a camping lantern. "The power shut off just a few minutes ago. I brought flashlights down when I heard the security pad."

Hector pulled off his coat and let it drop to the floor. He wrapped his arms around his wife, one hand on her belly. "It's so good to see you."

She hugged him back. The lantern that dangled from her wrist made a circle of light around them both.

"Rye?" Draven turned to Ash's dad. "Come out to the shack to fish tomorrow?"

Ash's dad grabbed Draven's shoulder and gave it an affectionate shake. "Sure thing. No smoking, though."

"Gotta watch your heart. I think I'll pick up some gum, anyway. Been meaning to." Draven looked at Ash and Lucy. "Can I borrow Luce outside for a minute?"

Lucy pulled a face but followed her dad to the door, giving Rye an opening to tell Ash, "Draven and I had a bit of a moment, waiting for everyone out by the woods."

"I bet."

"I was wondering." Rye looked at the ceiling. "Since Hector fixed up my toe and I can drive myself just fine, would you be interested if I picked up you and Lucy for dinner sometime? Or just you. Don't know where that sits."

"Give me a call, Dad."

Rye nodded with a small smile and headed out the door.

A moment later, Lucy rejoined her, and Cal threw an arm around each of their shoulders. "Things fall apart, then come back together again in a new way," the angel said. "I need to go home and integrate, but I will be in touch soon."

"Good night, Calliope." Ash watched her friend leave. No part of her felt like it was quite touching the rest, as if there were too much new room inside her to get used to. She was tearful, but the love that rushed up whenever she touched Lucy was absolute, a combination of tenderness and exhilaration that made it hard to think but easy to feel.

They had just stepped out of the bar, preparing to head back to Ash's apartment, when Lucy suddenly stopped. "Wait. Wait, wait, wait."

"What is it?"

"Helegar. Where is he?" Stricken, she looked around the parking lot, squinting in the dark. "I handed him to my dad after we left Hester's cabin. Didn't I?"

"Catch up with your dad and see if maybe he has him. I'll check inside."

Lucy ran across the lot, and Ash went back in. Hector and Ovidia had gone. She looked carefully in the dark by the bar, using her phone's flashlight, then in every cozy upholstered seat along the wall. She ran her flashlight over the floorboards until her beam of light stopped to the side of the door in an area by a coatrack that no one ever used. A small form reflected back the white of bones.

She ran to the spot. "Helegar! You scared Lucy!"

But when she put her hand on his tiny skull, despite the fact she had never known Helegar to look at all like something alive, she could feel at once that he wasn't there anymore. Their little god.

These were only his bones, small and perfect.

From the palm of her hand, a bright swirl of multicolored glitter rose, followed by a flash of rainbow light that tornadoed its way up from where she crouched, rising higher and higher until it was gone.

She kissed her fingers and pressed the kiss on the little flat place of his skull just as Lucy collapsed next to her and began to weep.

Ash rubbed her fingertips over Helegar's impossibly delicate bones one more time and eased away from Lucy so she could curl around them and grieve.

She looked into the dark bar, lit weakly by lights over the exits.

A crowd of figures dressed in black surrounded her.

It was the Dead and Righteous Brigade, but she was embarrassed to have given them such a flippant name. They weren't the mournful, judgmental, horrible shades she'd thought they were. They weren't indistinct, pale, with bluish hollows under their eyes and cheekbones. She could see now that she'd made fun of them because of the parts of herself she had grown to hate.

These were her people. Her Steadfasts. But they had never been righteous or judgmental. *Ash* had been.

And they weren't here because she'd let go of the rope in an endless spiritual tug-of-war. She could plainly see the relief on their faces, the happy tears shining in their eyes. They gazed at her with understanding and forgiveness. Rye's father, Gabriel, put his hand over his chest and looked out at the parking lot, where he watched his son get into his car. She saw him soundlessly tell her father that he was sorry.

"Faithful figured it out," Ash told them. "He just needed a little help."

She couldn't believe she'd ever thought their clothes were dark. The Steadfasts wore every kind of fashion. There was a woman in green taffeta, her waist impossibly small, with a literal fountain of lace from her neck to the rope of pearls she wore around it. One man's pants were sparkling, with a low waistband. His hair was long and the lenses of his sunglasses were shaped like stars. He took a hit of a red glass bong while a woman in a bonnet and a long flowered dress waved the smoke away and laughed. "But it looks like all of you got the memo on that one."

They weren't saviors, upright and pure. They weren't the devil, not in the form of temptation and Faustian bargains, not even in the sense of glorious, naked transformation. They were people.

Wonderfully, gloriously, just that.

Lucy's power came from who she was. Someone who listened. Someone who believed what people told her about themselves. When she listened to them, they could hear what they wanted and identify what made them feel good. If, after that, they succumbed to fear and worried themselves into a corner, it wasn't Lucy's fault. Sometimes it had been Ash's.

But Ash could see now that all these Steadfasts, her ancestors, had gathered to watch her because they hoped she would challenge generations of self-loathing, deprivation, and hate.

They wanted her to transform herself. Transform their legacies.

And she had.

She did her best to find their faces, missing no one, and to look carefully at where she'd come from. Not one of her ancestors failed to smile. She watched as each of them reached into their coats, pockets, and satchels and pulled out a different hand-tied posy. A daisy, a rose, a lily, flowers Ash didn't recognize. They laid them down beside Helegar's bones and then dissolved into colorful souls, swirling upward one by one.

Calliope had drawn her a new card. Death, the open window, the end and the beginning. Arthur had said that what he knew about death was only what he'd learned from being born.

Gazing at the ring of flowers surrounding Helegar, Ash knew that she and Lucy had everything they needed to figure this out.

Two girls in love had broken this curse.

It had taken a great deal more to begin healing the damage the curse carried with it. It had required their gifts, the gifts of their dearest friends, and their dads, who were by some miracle still here. A whole community.

Maybe it happened that way because of their love, too.

But Helegar was gone only because they'd done something right. Love was a cycle of death and rebirth. It was rest, and then a nest full of brand-new life. "He'll be back," she told Lucy.

"I know," Lucy sobbed. "He's a good dog."

Draven came in behind her, took off his ball cap, and bowed his head.

"You did it, Helegar. You loved us the whole way through." Ash put her arms around Lucy.

It took them a long time to say goodbye.

XX.

LP + AS

"WHEN DO YOU leave for New York?" Hector helped Ash position the heavy speaker on its stand.

"Tomorrow morning, bright and early." She sat down on the edge of the small dais-style stage that he had constructed in the corner of his tavern. Tonight was his second-ever open mic night, but the first one with the proper sound equipment that had finally been delivered. Ash had come by to help him set up.

Nathan was going to kick it off.

"But this time you're not driving for fifteen hours straight." Hector nudged her with his shoulder.

"I have a real-life plane ticket right here in my phone." She pulled it out of the pocket of her purple overalls. "First-class, even. Pretty good for someone who's only flown on an airplane once before."

The expensive ticket was because of her mom. When they met the first time, Aoife had flown in on a private plane and taken a suite of rooms at Lodge Kohler next to the stadium.

She'd left a message on Ash's phone to tell her she was there if Ash wanted to come. And even though Ash had been texting with her a little, talking on the phone a little less, it took her half a day to finally work up the courage, with Lucy's hand in hers, to go to the front desk and tell them her name.

It wasn't easy. There wasn't an immediate connection or a magic moment. Ash was still very much learning how to have feelings and admit it, and Aoife had been fired in the kiln of celebrity, so they were a disaster together on multiple levels. But they did learn, in the shiny-wood-and-marble suite, that what came easily between them was music. And because it was Ash, and because it was Aoife Ryan, if that was all they ever had with each other, it would probably be enough.

Music was why her mom was flying her to New York. She'd invited Ash to come to her studio and record the bass tracks for Aoife's album and help her *produce* it, whatever that meant.

"But you'll be here when the babies are born." Hector stood and held out his hand to pull her up.

"I'm only going for two weeks. The babies won't come before that."

Hector just looked at her.

"And if they do, I will get my ass on a plane and be here as soon as it lands. If I can't get a plane, I will drive fifteen hours so that I can hold them at the moment of their birth and they will know me, Ashes Steadfast, their spiritual guide through the ride of life."

"Good." He smiled. "Lucy needs you to pick her up. She said her calls keep going to your voicemail."

Ash looked at the phone she had just pulled out, its glass completely black. Bricked. "Fuck. Gotta go."

She ran out of the tavern and plopped into her car, rolling down all the windows because climate change liked to hurl an eighty-degree day at Wisconsin in March. By the time she pulled onto campus, which was as far as it could possibly be from Hector's Tavern and still be in Green Bay, she had a feeling she was later than late. Worse, she couldn't remember if Lucy's afternoon class was Quantitative Language or Comp. One was on one side of the campus, and the other was on the other side. She had just pulled into a small lot to try to figure it out when a woman ran by her car, bent over at the waist, shouting.

Ash leaned out the window and saw that she was chasing after something, a dog or a cat, so she got out to help and, she hoped, ask for the use of the woman's phone in return for the favor.

"Where did it go?" Ash asked the woman when she caught up.

"Under that truck?"

Ash jogged over to the truck and knelt down on the ground, where she came face-to-face with great big shiny eyeballs, huge ears, and the teeny, tiny desperate whines of a puppy.

"Well, come here." Ash held her hand out. The puppy ran into it. It was tiny, a wiggling blob, wagging its tail like mad. She slowly stood up. The woman was beside her, recovering from her sprint.

"Oh my god, thank you. I don't even know how he got away from me. I was putting his brothers and sisters in their carrier in the car—don't worry, I have the air on for them—and then he was out, running on his short little legs like a bat out of hell. He's usually the lazy one, too. I adopted from a dachshund rescue a couple months ago, and they must not be doing very careful checkups, because it wasn't long before we figured out she was pregnant. Now I have five of these guys that I'm trying to find homes for. I was just at a puppies-and-yoga class at the gym, hoping I'd get takers, but all five of these fuckers peed on someone, so no go."

Ash laughed. She lifted the puppy to eye level.

There was a flash—the smallest flash—of rainbow in the puppy's eyes. Probably a trick of the light?

But as she looked more carefully at the shiny ginger *dachshund* puppy, she noticed the white striped markings on his side, bright against the rest of his fur. Like ribs.

And his tail—madly wagging—was bright white at the tip, as if a little bone were sticking out of it.

Ash buried her face in the puppy's neck and started to laugh.

Every day, she walked one more step in what she was figuring out was life. She walked one more step into love with Lucy. She found one more way to talk to her dad and think of something to share with her mom. And, yes, her hair was pink and orange, and her overalls were purple over her lime-green bra.

But as beautiful as all those steps were, she would always carry inside her the Ash in a black leather jacket with virgin hair to her waist who couldn't remember the last time she'd told someone she loved them, or breathed in without pain, or trusted her feelings.

As *this* Ash left her behind, she increasingly understood that version of herself had been more impressive than she'd ever known. She'd survived. It was true that surviving wasn't the same as living, but it wasn't easy, either, and every day, right alongside the love and the color, she was figuring out what being *that* Ashes Steadfast had taught her.

She missed her. Missed her dusty-dry humor and kick-ass

boots. She missed how the soft feelings she did have had felt *so* soft. That Ash was a ridiculous goth, but she was *her* ridiculous goth. And she'd known that Ash was lovable in part because Helegar, the little god, had loved her even when she breathed through her mouth and complained every time he came near.

She felt the stranger's hand on her shoulder. "I think he's yours, hon. And I don't just say that because my whole house smells like puppy crap."

Ash laughed some more. Right before she could ask the woman if she could use her phone, she heard her name.

"Ashes!" Lucy was jogging toward them with her giant backpack, waving. "I thought I would start walking toward the entrance and look out for you because I knew you didn't have your phone! Oh, hey!" She stopped and kissed Ash on the temple, smelling like sunshine and rosemary soap. "Who's this?" Lucy reached out her hand to pet the puppy.

Ash felt it the moment Lucy knew. She got to see the very instant Helegar recognized his girl, and then puppy pee was running down her arm while Lucy was laughing a watery, tearful laugh and reaching for him, accepting his frantic kisses.

"He's had all his first shots, been dewormed, he's been seen at Bay East by Dr. Reidi, he eats Royal Canin dachshund puppy wet and dry mixed together, just read on the bag how much, and please get him neutered. Be well." The woman waved and walked away, very fast, and Lucy and Ash watched her leave the puppy to his destiny.

Ash leaned forward and kissed Lucy's nose, receiving a kiss from Helegar in return. Sweet puppy breath.

"How was class? And do you have something for the pee in your giant magical bag?"

Lucy handed Helegar back to Ash so she could dive into her bag for a package of wet wipes. "Funny you should ask. Today is the first day I felt like I was doing the right thing, for real."

"Yeah?"

"Yes."

"Because the whole 'be a math teacher' thing is supposed to be an experiment, not a final destination. Or a compromise. Whatever you want. We can move to Boston!" Ash said. "You want to see Hester's grave anyway. We could field trip there while we're in New York and talk to some people about school."

"Or you could trust what I am telling you, as a woman who is more than familiar with figuring out when something she wants is real." Lucy grabbed the puppy back and kissed Helegar's face over and over as he kissed her back. Ash began to herd them in the direction of her car.

"It's just that you want me to trust that you want to be a *high school math teacher*, and no one likes high school math teachers. You like to be liked. Or, at least, you like to make people feel good. I've been meaning to talk to you about that, actually, because you know that you flirt with everyone, right? I'm not jealous, so don't look at me like that. I just mean, you don't have to do this if you're thinking—"

"Be quiet." Lucy stopped by Ash's car. "Today's the day, as I was saying, that it clicked. I thought about what it was like for me in my high school classes, asking questions and hoping to be seen for how much I wanted to do it. I thought about field trips where everyone has to sell candy bars to take a bus to Johnson Space Center. And then, when I was thinking about all of that, I could see it. My soul. Just a little, around the edges, where I'd called it up by thinking about something I really wanted."

"*Luce.*"

"Right?" She kissed Helegar's neck. He was already falling asleep in her hands, snoring.

Ash touched his soft head with a finger. "Do you really think he's our Helegar?"

"His soul is perfect. It doesn't have anything to learn. He wants to be ours and to watch us love each other forever. This is Helegar. I know it."

Goose bumps broke out all over Ash's neck and arms. She knew, of course, that Lucy loved her. But after they'd returned from Hester's cottage, grieving for everything they'd lost, Lucy had needed time. She'd needed to get Draven to sort out her identification and money. She'd needed to have as many linear days in a row as she possibly could.

They hadn't spent a night apart, as raw in their devotion to each other as they'd been when they were girls, but Ash had waited nonetheless. Not to tell Lucy she loved her, but for Lucy to tell her. For Lucy to feel herself here, more every day.

"I love you." Lucy leaned in and kissed Ash's upper lip, soft. "I do. Like I said, everything clicked today, and I'm so happy its spring break and we're going to New York tomorrow morning, and now Helegar, and—"

"Oh! Helegar." Ash jerked her brain back on its track after it had fucked off with hearts swirling around it from Lucy's words. "Can we bring him? How does that work? We can't leave him here. Is he potty-trained? I don't know how to do that. Will we need papers? What *are* papers for a dog? Where did the lady say his doctor was? I can call Aoife, and we can reschedule."

"We're going to New York." Lucy opened her car door. "Stop."

Ash got into the driver's seat. "Okay, sure. But I don't know the first thing about how to take a puppy on an airplane and take care of him at whatever fancy random apartment my mom has figured out for us."

"I love you."

Ash bit the inside of her cheek, frothing over with love. "I love *you*, Lucy Prynne."

She got them home, going slow because she was worried about Helegar, so small and such a tiny baby, and wishing she had some kind of puppy car seat for him. They went into her cool studio apartment, with its new colors from art that Calliope and Hamish helped them hang up, and from pillows and blankets and her bass, set up all the time, its deep chestnut-and-auburn wood glowing and reflecting back the twinkle lights and lamps.

"Go get that basket with the library books in it and dump the books out and put a towel in," Lucy said.

Ash fussed over the makeshift bed, and Lucy lowered Helegar into it, still snoring, and tucked him against the sofa in a sunbeam.

"I might actually explode with all of the clicking into place." Lucy turned away from staring at the dog bed to put her arms around Ash. "But I'm not surprised. I knew we could get to here. I always knew."

"You never let go of anything good. What a gift."

Lucy smiled. "It's my spring break."

"It is."

Lucy slid her hands down Ash's arms and then pulled her toward the bed. "Spring break is when you get up to stuff."

"You would know, college girl." Ash didn't get the joke to

land exactly right because the Ash who could make jokes while her girlfriend made devastatingly horny eyes at her and dragged her toward a horizontal surface was not driving the bus.

Lucy unhooked Ash's overalls and let them drop, and Ash kicked off her sandals while Lucy pulled down the straps of her bra and bit Ash's shoulder. She replayed Lucy's *I love you* over and over, and it made her softer but also impatient, and when Lucy started kissing her, slow and open and deep, she went from impatient to pleading with her hands under Lucy's T-shirt and a desperate need to be naked.

They both sighed, Ash shaky, when they *were* both finally naked, their skin touching, hot and sensitive. Ash wanted Lucy's mouth everywhere.

She *wanted*.

This Ash, the one she was learning to be, wanted. Knew how to. Asked, was answered, and wasn't afraid when she got it, wrapped in her arms, breathing hard, kissing her sloppy, smiling at her, loving her with the windows open and every moment connected to the next without end.

Broken. Unfinished. Free.

ACKNOWLEDGMENTS

Overwhelmingly, I am grateful to readers. Their embrace of the lovefest that is *Cosmic Love at the Multiverse Hair Salon* has been so encouraging at a time in our world when it has been challenging to find courage. This love has been a reminder of how important queer stories are, how transformative queer love is, and how much healing is possible when I affirm myself and my community. Thank you, thank you, thank you.

A couple of years ago, I needed a non-book creative exercise to stretch my skills, and I was inspired by a billboard I saw in Green Bay (identical to the one in this book, minus the goat horns) and made a Hawthornian joke about. I decided to write a short story that I called "Ashes Steadfast Fights the Devil." My gorgeous wife read it, and her primary feedback was "feels cute, might be a novel later." At first, I was resistant, but then I started dreaming about Ashes and Lucy, and I knew Ruthie (my wife) was right. The books seem to find me no matter what. Ruthie held my hand while I wrote this book about generational trauma and what it steals and what the genuine miracle of love gives back. Ruthie, our own conversations and healing and laughter are all over *A Star-Cursed Heart*, and you give me the strength to keep fighting.

My daughter—insightful, wise, and hilarious—is who we can thank for Helegar. She workshopped him with me with so much glee as we used our own house demon, the miniature dachshund Cricket, for inspiration. She gave me permission to lean into the adorably stinky and disconcerting realities of a very old dog, and to acknowledge the immortality of their perfect souls and their love. Likewise, my stepson indulged the obsession with his own jokes and a pretty great 3D-printed wobbly Helegar. These kids are such good kids.

My agent, Tara Gelsomino, is literally the best one. She encourages the complexities of a client with a gazillion ideas, never balks at a chance to shoot our shot, demystifies publishing, has incisive insights near daily, and doesn't back down from the fight to make publishing more transparent, equitable, and survivable in the long term. I've never been more supported doing this work. Thank you, Tara.

My team at Ace is not unlike the team assembled at the end of this book—powered by extraordinary gifts suitable for any mission. Arianna, my publicist, is a cheerleader and general both. Her "Friday round-up" emails are legend, and her ability to celebrate every single win is an important lesson for anyone in the arts. I came to learn that whatever amazing news she gave me would be only the final bow following the significant work she was doing behind the scenes. Thank you so much. Likewise, Kim, my marketing lead, has arranged for me some of the most amazing opportunities of my career, all of which have had real impact getting my books into the hands of readers. Her responsiveness, knowledge, and insight are what have delivered the book that my readers find on a shelf or in their libraries.

Esi Sogah, my editor, transforms manuscripts with an eye that can see my vision, what readers want, and where to begin reshaping, rewriting, and reimagining to get to the book. I trust her expertise utterly, and I'm very grateful for the clarity with which she communicates how to apply her expertise. I look forward to giving her my work and to the revision process, and that says so much about her focus and talent as an editor. The English professor in her saw the *Scarlet Letter* stan in me, but just like a good professor, she made sure I understood my job wasn't to talk to *myself* about the themes I found compelling, but to show the reader what those themes meant to my story and their own imagination. Esi has made the process of this book so much fun, and there isn't an editor with more interest in stories—all kinds of stories—than her. Thank you from the bottom of my heart for really seeing the nerds with their hands in the air.

I want to thank the booksellers and bookish people who have made my journey so great with their enthusiasm, funny video reviews, events, and conversations with readers about my books. The support has been a *light,* it's been *music,* it's been *color,* it's been taking care of my little soul. You're on the front lines of what we're fighting for, and your work recruits love. I love you.

Nathaniel Hawthorne is a problematic grump, like so many of the American Romantics, but he created Hester Prynne and made sure that we could find no fault in a woman who loved passionately and took care of her community so well that everyone came to associate her mark of sin as a beacon of hope. Alok Vaid-Menon—trans writer, performer, poet—says that no mirror can capture our beauty when we come to love ourselves; only poetry can penetrate it. He believes in souls, in their breathtaking beauty, in how queerness comes the closest to describing that beauty. More than anything, I wanted this book to talk to anyone who would say otherwise. I wanted a counterpoint to the idea that sin could be branded on anyone who loved, or that our bodies, appearance, or gender could be regulated, governed, or controlled. We're souls full of hope and light of every color. Only poetry can describe us. Only poetry can describe you. I love you.

Author photograph by a. lentz photography

ANNIE MARE (she/they) writes in the queer contemporary romance genre. With Ruthie Knox, she also cowrites mystery (as Annie Mare) and romance (under the Mae Marvel pen name). Their novels have been critically recognized and bestselling. Annie Mare lives with her wife, two teenagers, two dogs, multiple fish, two cats, four hermit crabs, and a bazillion plants in a very old house with a garden.

VISIT ANNIE MARE ONLINE

AnnieMare.com